ALSO BY THISBE NISSEN

The Ex-Boyfriend Cookbook (with Erin Ergenbright)

Out of the Girls' Room and into the Night

The Good People of New York

Osprey ISLAND

Osprey ISLAND

THISBE NISSEN

ALFRED A. KNOPF

New York 2004

THIS IS A BORZOI BOOK
PUBLISHED BY ALFRED A. KNOPF

www.aaknopf.com

Knopf, Borzoi Books, and the colophon are registered
trademarks of Random House, Inc.

Grateful acknowledgment is made to National Geographic Society for
permission to reprint an excerpt from "The Endangered Osprey"
by Roger Tory Peterson (*National Geographic,* July 1969).
Reprinted by permission of the National Geographic Society.

Library of Congress Cataloging-in-Publication Data
Nissen, Thisbe, [date]
Osprey Island / by Thisbe Nissen. — 1st ed.
p.   cm.
ISBN 0-375-41146-1
1. Single mothers—Fiction.   2. Custody of children—Fiction.
3. Accident victims—Fiction.   4. Community life—Fiction.   5. Summer
resorts—Fiction.   6. Islands—Fiction.   I. Title.
PS3564.I79085 2004   813'.54—dc22   2004040843

Manufactured in the United States of America
First Edition

FOR MY MOM AND DAD,

AND FOR S.I.,

WITH GREAT AFFECTION AND RESPECT

It may be thought that I have not dwelt sufficiently on the generally assumed evil tendencies of certain birds. I have tried to be perfectly just, but there had been so much exaggeration and sensationalism in writing of birds, that I have been careful to investigate all accusations.

—OLIVE THORNE MILLER,
The Second Book of Birds

CONTENTS

CONTENTS

THE CHIZEKS
Bud, owner of The Lodge at Osprey Island, 60
Nancy, his wife, 61
Chas, their son, killed during the war in Vietnam
Suzy, their daughter, a teacher, 36
Mia, Suzy's daughter, 6

THE JACOBSES
Roddy, maintenance worker at the Lodge, 37
Eden, his mother, 56
Roderick, his father, recently deceased

THE SQUIRES AND THE VAUGHNS
Lance Squire, head of maintenance at the Lodge, 38
Lorna Marie Vaughn Squire, his wife, head of housekeeping, 36
Squee, their son, 8
Merle Squire, Lance's mother, 54
Art and Penny Vaughn, Lorna's parents, 69 and 66, respectively

THE LODGE STAFF
Brigid, a housekeeper, 19
Peg, a housekeeper, 18
Jeremy, a waiter, 18
Gavin, a waiter, 19
Reesa Delamico, a hairdresser, 36
Janna Winger, a hairdresser, 19

Osprey
ISLAND

THE ONES THEY CAME BACK FOR

"Örn!" cries the Swede; "Águila!" the Spaniard; and the North Ameri-can or Briton exclaims, "Look, there's an eagle!" Probably the most misidentified bird in the world, the osprey or "fish hawk," with white on its head and a wing span of more than five feet, much resembles its regal relative. Even its scientific name, Pandion haliaetus, *compounds the confusion, for* haliaetus *literally means "sea eagle."*

—ROGER TORY PETERSON,
"The Endangered Osprey"

OWN AT BAYSHORE DRUG, postcards of Osprey Island sell five for a dollar from a spindly display rack by the cash register. They're all island scenes—the beach at Scallopshell Cove, the clapboard shops lining Ferry Street, the cliffs at the end of Sand Beach Road—but those postcard photographers all seem to have a similar soft spot for the osprey itself, that majestic bird from whom the island took its name. A sunset beach shot—beautiful—but if they can frame the photograph around that great raptor perched high in its nest, a silhouette against the sherbet-colored sky, well, it does make for a dramatic scene. Add OSPREY ISLAND in scrawling script across the sand. Those are the postcards that sell. Also popular: cards with photos of the Osprey Island Ferry as it pulls in to dock, heaving its mighty bulk against those sea-worn mooring pylons, half rotted and suitably picturesque. And if there just so happens to be an osprey perched atop a decaying pylon, or on the steeple of the boat's whistle, or at the crest of the captain's tower, well, so much the better. Portraits of the Lodge at Osprey Island—an architecturally impressive structure in some, though not all, of its many incarnations—are also standard, and if you wait patiently for your shot you can sometimes catch an osprey as it lights upon a turret or gable. Sunsets, boats, hotels—ubiquitous images of vacation, leisure, the idylls of a certain class. But it's really the osprey that makes the picture. An osprey you don't find just anywhere.

There was in fact a time when you *couldn't* find an osprey, anywhere. Back in the days of DDT. But before there was DDT, and before there were nesting platforms built onto abandoned telephone poles, and before the creaking ferry docks, before hotels with gaping lawns just begging to be the site of your daughter's wedding reception—before everything else on this island was the osprey.

It was the osprey's cry—*kyew, kyew, kyew*—that heralded the island's first European settlers ashore. A blustery autumn day in 1655, and their boat ran aground rather unceremoniously on a promontory known forever after as Shipwreck Point. It was a fortuitous shipwreck: the journeying party managed to wash up on precisely the land for which they'd been aiming. The ship bore a British sugar baron, his young bride, and their entourage, all of whom survived the calamitous landing. They'd come for the island's fabled forests of white oak: the timber of the sugar barrel.

Within twenty years the baron, an enterprising but not particularly foresighted businessman, had chopped down every last white oak on the island and the local economy was forced to shift its focus sensibly, if obviously, to the surrounding bays of calm and eminently fishable waters. Men with nets began to haul up great catches of moss bunker—*menhaden*—and churning kettleworks sprang up on Osprey's shores. There, in massive iron drums over great fires, the fish were cooked down for use in oil and fertilizer, a grueling process so rank and foul that had a group of wealthy New York businessmen not come upon Osprey in the late 1860s and hatched an entrepreneurial plan along her shores the island might well have been known not for its endangered birds and its beaches and sunsets and quaint summer resort hotels but for its unrelenting fish stink. Those rich New York developers bought up the moss bunker business, razed the enterprise to the ground, and relocated every last barrel, net, and cauldron a safe distance downwind, to a rocky brown patch of undesirable New Jersey coast, eradicating every shred of evidence that a fish-processing plant had ever stood and smoked on the island shores. When the Lodge at Osprey Island held its grand opening in the summer of 1874, folks said that, honestly, you never would've known.

The Lodge at Osprey Island that stands on the site today is not quite so illustrious as the original. There have been fires, hurricanes, wars, a Great Depression, and the resort has been built and rebuilt, knocked down and made over again. The Lodge in its present incarnation opened in 1940 under the ownership of a man named Chizek, a wealthy Texan whose oil money the Depression seemed to have passed right by. It's more of a family place now, hardly as grand and photogenic as it once was, but it's a nice place to bring the kids on holiday—a couple of hours from New York City by train, then a short ferry ride across the bay. Really, a perfect place to bring the family.

Here's a popular postcard scene: a man and a boy standing on a dock—the Lodge's boat dock, which still has some of the old charm that the Lodge itself now lacks—with the water and the shoreline and the world washed in golden sunset glow. The man and boy might be father and son—they aren't, but they might be. For the sake of the postcard: a man and his son washed in gold and peachy light at the end of a jutting, dilapidated pier. A man and his son, nearly silhouetted against the horizon, gazing across the water toward an outcropping of land where a post rises from the shoreline scrub brush. The post is as tall as a telephone pole, and sturdy. Atop the post, a tremendous nest. Atop the nest, a tremendous bird. The bird—it's about to take off—spreads its wings, ready to rise like a phoenix. The boy lifts his hand—*An osprey!*—and the man's gaze follows. They are not hotel guests, these two; both were raised on this island. There were hardly any ospreys when the man was a child, but now things are different: DDT banned, the food chain back on track. See? There's the proof, up in that nest: an osprey, one of many returned to the island that bears their name. See the boy on the dock—it's for him that the osprey has come home.

One

THE LODGE AT OSPREY ISLAND

Vacation this summer at the Osprey Lodge—open Fourth of July Week-end through Labor Day—Boating—Tennis—Beachfront—Swimming pool—Full-service dining room with local reknowned [sic] *chef—Cocktail bar with outdoor patio seating—On the shore of beautiful Osprey Island—The Lodge at Osprey Island—A Family Place!*

—promotional brochure, 1988

IT WASN'T UNTIL LANCE AND LORNA SQUIRE showed up to the barbecue—forty-five minutes late, and drunk, hair combed back wet from the shower—that anyone got dessert. The Osprey Lodge's head cook, Jock, was chain-smoking beside a table full of watermelon he'd hacked into slices with such samurai ferocity that no one would venture near it for fear of losing a limb. But Lance Squire strolled up, surprised Jock with a clap on the back that made him drop his ciga-rette in the pooling watermelon juice, and took over. "Come on now, don't be shy!" Lance barked across the lawn. A few brave souls crept tentatively forth for watermelon. Jock glowered from the sidelines.

Jock's name was actually Jacques, but that didn't sound any dif-ferent from *Jock* to anyone around there. Jock looked less like a Frenchman than a truck-stop short-order fry cook, and he took great pleasure in presenting himself as such. He hardly spoke except to swear at his waitstaff in vulgar Franglais. The Lodge's kitchen help spoke mostly Spanish. Each summer Tito and Juan brought in a crew of their friends and relatives who worked for cash under the table and, for reasons that seemed not merely obvious, but enviable, talked only to one another. It was the waitstaff who caught the brunt and gist of Jock's rampages. The boys laughed—"Steady there, Jocko!"—and went about their business, filling water pitchers and folding permanent-press napkins while Jock hurled epithets around the kitchen. Waitresses always had a bit more trouble: it was hard to keep count of your dinner salads or remember how many steaks and how many filets when Jock was flinging them on the grill, hollering, "What you say? How many you say? How many fucking shit steak slabs you say, gorgeous? We go outside, I fuck you so hard you speak up then, yeah? Fucking how many you say?"

Lance Squire handed out watermelon slices with the artificial magnanimity of a Good Humor man. A mildew-stained plastic banner was tacked to the front of the table, its faded red lettering giving a conciliatory WELCOME STAFF TO THE LODGE AT OSPREY ISLAND. Lance himself hardly needed welcoming; he and his wife, Lorna, had been at the Lodge for more than two decades. They lived year-round in one of the cabins up the hill and served—mostly euphemistically—as caretakers. When she was sober enough to walk, Lorna was the chief housekeeper. Lance was head of maintenance and claimed, loudly and often, that he didn't touch a drop. He was officially in charge of everything from preseason repairs to upkeep of the Lodge's small stable of vehicles to, say, rolling the clay tennis courts every summer morning for the early-bird enthusiasts who got up to practice their backhands before breakfast. Most often, though, Lance was too drunk to lay a straight baseline, or dig a posthole, or pick his nose, for that matter, and the Lodge was known for its "rustic disarray," which, fortunately, guests seemed to find quaint.

Lance Squire Jr.—Squee—was Lance and Lorna's only child. Eight years old that summer, hyperactive as ever, Squee skipped around the watermelon table, hovering behind his dad, as high on sugar and people and occasion as his folks were on whiskey. Squee waited all year for this Friday in June when everybody—all the college-kid waiters and Irish housekeeping girls—arrived on the island again to prepare for the busy summer season ahead. The kid had a tendency to get himself underfoot, everywhere, always, except at home: Squee was in the kitchen at five a.m. with Jock and Tito and Juan; he trailed the housekeeping girls room to room, telling jokes and stories and bringing them sodas from the bar and peanut butter cookies from the pantry; he sat on a barstool during happy hour at the Dinghy and played cards with Morey until someone else needed the seat; and he hung out at night on the side porch with the waiters until the last beers had been drunk, the last cigarettes stubbed out, and the last staffers straggled up the hill to a lonely camp-cot sleep.

Lance lifted the watermelon knife. "Squid," he said to the boy, "go get your ma a chair to sit down in." He jerked his chin toward a tower of plastic lawn chairs stacked against a wall under the deck. The Lodge held a piece of prime Osprey Island real estate on Sand Beach and the hill that rose sharply from its shores, and the hundred-room hotel had been designed to maximize the view. The basement was cut into the slope, exposed in front and buried in back, and a large deck on the main level overhung a stone patio that extended from the basement and bled onto a great lawn, where such momentous annual events as the staff barbecue were held.

Squee darted toward the chairs, the stack of which teetered a good yard above his head. He stared at the tower, reached out and gave it a nudge, then swept his eyes over the crowd on the lawn. He saw no empty chairs.

There was one person in the crowd who was neither sitting, nor eating, nor interacting with anyone at all, and it was this person who noticed Squee's dilemma. He was one of the newly arrived waiters, a lanky, brooding boy named Gavin who'd just finished his freshman year at Stanford University far away in California, and he stood alone, smoking, as he leaned against a pillar under the deck of the Osprey Lodge.

Gavin ground out his cigarette, sauntered over, and stepped between the boy and the tower of chairs. With a shake he disentangled the top one from the others and set it down before Squee like Super-man plucking Lois Lane from the Empire State Building. Then Gavin gave Squee a polite and obliging nod, like a Japanese bow, turned and walked away without a word.

For a moment Squee just stared at the chair. Then he snapped to, turned, and sprinted back toward his parents, grabbing hold of the chair with one hand almost as an afterthought and letting it bump across the patio behind him as he ran.

Though Lance and Lorna were standing not five feet from each other, Squee delivered the chair straight to his father, who took it with little or no acknowledgment of the bearer, laid aside the watermelon knife, wiped his hands on his apron, and set the chair down for his wife as though he were a gentleman. Lorna giggled, demurred, and then sat with a plop, her face wrestling to stay composed, growing redder by the instant as it dissolved in mirth. She was higher than heaven.

For an elongated second Lorna looked truly gleeful, and then the joy on her face swerved into fear as the plastic legs of the chair began to bend and buckle beneath her. She went over awkwardly, slowly enough that the impact didn't hurt her, just elicited a short "Oh!" of surprise. Squee looked on, frozen: he'd set this terrible domino-train of events in motion and was powerless to stop it now. Lance, too, was halted for a moment by incomprehension. But as his wife tumbled over before him, his confusion turned to anger. He flashed his young son an accusing glare. Then he bent over to help Lorna up off the ground.

Bud Chizek wore a chef's hat to scoop the potato salad and coleslaw onto Styrofoam plates. Bud and his wife, Nancy, owned and ran the Lodge at Osprey Island and had been doing so since Bud inherited the place from his father almost forty years before. Bud had learned early that housekeeping girls could be imported very cheaply through an overseas Irish employment agency and that a dining room could be quite adequately staffed with college boys who were thrilled to settle for low wages in exchange for a summer at the beach with an in-house stable of attractive, young, and impressionable lasses eager to experience the American way.

Once upon a time the Lodge's season had run Memorial Day to Labor Day; now there weren't enough guests to make it worth Bud's while to open earlier than Fourth of July weekend. The staff arrived on Osprey mid-June and spent the rest of the month getting the lay of the land, getting the Lodge ready for guests, and getting good and drunk most every night. At the barbecue to welcome them to Osprey the Irish girls held their hot dogs awkwardly, as though unfamiliar with the concept of the frankfurter. They sipped generic colas and orangeades and sat tentatively on the grass as if afraid to muss their shorts. The boys—the waiters—clustered by a large trash can like hobos around an oil-drum fire, as though it gave them a greater sense of purpose to guard the garbage, keep tabs on the rate of paper plate discard, see who might fail to heed Nancy Chizek's infamous sign: DON'T HAVE EYES BIGGER THAN YOUR STOMACH—TAKE ONLY WHAT YOU WILL EAT.

"Is the food this brutal as a rule, do you think?" said one of the seated Irish girls, a buxom, redheaded Dubliner called Brigid. She poked suspiciously at a stewy splotch of potato salad, yellow with unidentifiable flecks of red and green. The other girls shrugged blandly, unwilling to pass judgment just yet on this strange new place and its American accoutrements. They were jet-lagged and knew they'd do better to hold their condemnation until they'd had a good night's sleep, or at least a pint of beer.

Brigid's new roommate—with whom she could look forward to sharing, for the duration of the summer, a shoddily wallpapered heat trap on the first floor of the staff house—was a girl from County Cork named Peg who was neat and mousy with smooth skin and thin lips that she pursed as though in great distress. Brigid's sister, Fiona, had worked at the Lodge the previous summer, and Peg reminded Brigid of her, which was both comforting and repellent. Had they been back at home in Ireland, Brigid and Peg would have loathed each other on sight—an arrogant Jackeen from the city! a bloody mulchie!—but as it was, in this new place, the girls would likely cling to the familiarity of their own until they'd gotten steady enough to detach from the clan.

As paper plates mounted in the trash can, Bud Chizek climbed atop a picnic table, tapping a plastic spoon against the side of a Styrofoam cup. "Hello," he said. He raised his voice: "Hello and welcome!" He swept a hand out at the panorama of sea and sky before him, a gesture at the crescent that was Sand Beach. "I couldn't have ordered a better sunset for you tonight," he said, and his wife, Nancy, applauded softly, proud as a grandmother of that pink-plumped sky. The evening was indeed exemplary, the western horizon streaked like a tropical drink. Seagulls flew in from the beach and lit upon the Lodge lawn to poke their beaks at fallen hot dog buns and discarded melon rinds. And in its nest atop a utility pole near the shoreline, a lone osprey stood displaying its profile to the crowd as if aware of the dramatic silhouette it cut against the horizon.

"So, welcome," Bud said again, "to the Lodge at Osprey Island. We're glad you're all here, ready for another busy season. And I know all of you who just arrived this afternoon have your unpacking to do and settling in, so I'll let you get to that just as soon as I introduce some important folks who keep this place running." Affability was something Bud Chizek could manage to muster only through great and diligent effort, but he'd found over the years that if he could display something that approached graciousness during these first few interactions with his summer staff, then he could pretty much drop the charade for the rest of the season and keep them all on their toes, afraid they'd disappointed him somehow and scrambling to regain his favor. "I'm Bud Chizek," he boomed. "I own this beautiful place here"—he gestured to the Lodge and its grounds and up the hill toward the guest cottages scattered around the tennis courts and swimming pool—"been in my family . . . oh, what is it now, Nance? What did we say?"

"Nearly fifty years," his wife chimed in from the sidelines.

"My wife, Nancy Chizek," Bud said proudly, and Nancy gave a wave, turning side to side like the Queen Mother on motorcade, and with as little sense of irony.

Bud continued: "And, with us for the past twenty-six of those summers, our chef, Jock. Let's give a hand to Jock for this delicious barbecue!" There was a wave of polite applause. Jock continued to glower from behind the serving table.

Bud Chizek looked around at the picnic guests. "OK, on with the family: Where are you, Mia?" he asked into the crowd.

"Here!" A voice came from beneath the deck where Squee was frantically pointing at the little girl seated beside him on top of the Ping-Pong table, paddle and ball in her hands, waiting diligently for her grandfather's speech to be over so they could continue their game.

"Thank you, Squee," said Bud. "That's Lance Squire Jr., there—his folks are our heads of maintenance and housekeeping . . . Lance? Lorna?" Bud looked for them, but they had already retreated up the hill. "Anyway . . . my granddaughter, Mia. And somewhere out there . . . is her mother . . . my daughter, Suzy . . . out from New York City for another summer at the family hotel . . ."

He panned the crowd. His introduction was intended as a jab, and both he and his daughter knew it. Suzy was hardly a part of the family business—hardly a part of her family's life on Osprey Island but for these summers when she accepted her parents' offer of three rent-free months of vacation with built-in babysitters and maid service. She and her parents had been on speaking terms again only since Mia's birth. It appeared that *granddaughter* trumped *grudge*. Or at least the *idea* of granddaughter. Mia and her grandparents never seemed to know what to do with one another once they were in the same place, but the Chizeks liked the sound of the phrase *We'll have our granddaughter with us for the summer*. Suzy was never entirely sure why she ever agreed to the arrangement, and usually spent much of the summer trying to figure out what in god's name she'd been thinking. Suzy Chizek thought her parents ungenerous, judgmental, and phony, and she was quite certain they'd have traded Suzy's life in a fraction of a second to have her older brother back. *Chas,* she was sure, would have merited a nice room at the Lodge. A room with a view, say. Suzy Chizek was not a daughter who deserved a view. Bud never gave Suzy and Mia a particularly nice room. Those were for the paying guests, not for the wayward daughter and her (for all intents and purposes) fatherless child, the daughter who'd sworn her distance from Osprey Island's oppressive confines as soon as the Island High diploma was in her itchy hand. *That* daughter took what she got: a room that looked out over the parking lot, on the kitchen and delivery entrances.

When Bud's eyes lit on Suzy, seated at a nearby picnic table, he stuck out a hand in his daughter's direction. Suzy lifted an arm slightly, the gesture of a gesture, and half smiled, her eyebrows raised to the crowd as she tried to share with them, silently, a mutual understanding of her father's absurdity. She was thirty-six years old and had put up with introductions like this for more of her life than she could bear to think about.

"And let's see . . ." Bud Chizek looked around again. "Who am I forgetting?" He paused, searching faces, different each summer yet so much the same: the college boys, the Irish girls, the Island hangers-on.

One person Bud *had* neglected to introduce was both a new and an old face to Osprey Island, but he was standing in the shadow of the deck's overhang against the stone wall of the basement, hoping that Bud wouldn't notice him there. Roddy Jacobs would have preferred to hide in that shadow until the sun had set and he could slip away in darkness than be forced to wave jubilantly at the crowd and endure some patronizingly tactful speech about how glad they all were to have Roddy Jacobs back on the island after so long—*God, Roddy, what's it been? Twenty years?*—while old-timers and people who knew enough back then whispered to their neighbors about *just what had* Roddy Jacobs been doing with himself for the last twenty years? And wasn't it *charitable* of Bud Chizek to hire him on to work grounds and maintenance at the Lodge with his old high school buddy Lance Squire during the busy summer season ahead? *Didn't even come back in time for the funeral,* they said. *That boy waited till his father's body was cold in the ground before he was going to set foot on this island again.*

Roderick Jacobs Sr. had passed on toward the end of the winter. Heart attack. Boom. Gone. Wherever in the world Roddy had been keeping himself, he'd apparently been keeping up with obits in the *Island Times,* waiting for the one death that conditioned his return. A few weeks later he'd shown up on his mother's doorstep. Eden still lived in the same house, a clapboard box on the scrubby side of the island up by Lovetsky's Auto. She had offered Roddy the guest room, his old bedroom, but he preferred the cottage out back. If you could even call it that: forty square feet, maybe, more like a small shed. Roddy outfitted it with a bed, a sink, and a woodstove, and split enough firewood to last the next winter and beyond. And when Bud Chizek hired Roddy on at the Lodge, people figured he was back for good.

There were people who said it was a recipe for disaster—after all, Roddy'd left under such a pall of indiscretion. Most Islanders had found it in their hearts after twenty years to pardon him—they blamed his youth, his mother—but some still felt that having Roddy Jacobs back on-island was just asking for trouble.

It was a tremendous relief to Roddy when Bud adjourned the barbecue and sent people dispersing in all directions—the girls scuttling up the hill toward the staff barracks, waiters scraggling up the beach toward Morey's Dinghy, where they could get started on the drunks they'd work diligently to maintain until Labor Day. Squee and Mia eagerly resumed their Ping-Pong, so excited to be reunited after another school year apart that they couldn't keep the ball on the table. Roddy watched as Suzy Chizek made her way across the lawn and ducked under the deck to ruffle her daughter's hair and kiss her forehead. "I'll be in the room, Miss Mia-Mi," she said. "Squee, you look after her, OK?"

Squee grinned—he was two years older than Mia and relished the notion of watching over her—and Suzy crossed to give him a fluff and a kiss as well. He stood for it, if not happily then at least with patience. "It's good to see you, kid," Suzy told him.

Squee nodded vigorously.

Suzy gave the Ping-Pong table an affectionate smack as she passed, and as she disappeared up the stairs and into the Lodge above them, Roddy breathed another sigh of relief at being granted a little more time to figure out how the hell to say hello to Suzy Chizek for the first time in twenty years.

Two

WHERE THE OSPREY MAKES ITS NEST

The first Europeans on Osprey Island were a British sugar baron and his family who "purchased" the lovely (and profitably wooded) island from the Manhanset Indians who had, until then, called it home. The baron christened the place "Osprey Island," and dubbed himself the first "civilized" settler of the five-mile dollop of dense forest, downy marsh and pebbled beach. The Manhansets were summarily evicted and an exciting era in the entrepreneurial exploitation of Osprey Island had begun.

—CHERYL OLINKEWITZ, "The Rape and Exploitation
of Indigenous New England Populations: Osprey Island,
A Case Study," an unpublished undergraduate thesis

IT SHOULD HAVE BEEN LORNA—and if not Lorna, then Lance—who took the housekeepers on a tour of the Lodge and grounds the following morning, showed them the supply closets, oriented them to the vacuum cleaners and the stubborn faucets and the tricks it took to try and make a down-at-the-heels resort appear rustic and not ratty. But as mornings had it, the Squires were "indisposed," a state of being more commonly associated with aging screen idols than hired hands.

Mia had woken up early, as six-year-olds are wont, and had gone knocking her way down the hall in her nightgown to introduce herself to other guests and make friends. Half asleep, Suzy tried to explain that there were no guests yet. Mia didn't get it. A hotel was supposed to be a big place with people in every room, the way the sky was a big place with lots of stars, there even when you can't see them. Mia put on clothes and went out scouting. Suzy rolled over and went back to sleep.

An hour later, Suzy got up and put on a bathrobe. She stepped into the hall to see where Mia might have gotten to and was greeted by a throng of peaches-and-creamy, brogue-throated girls, all dolled up for housekeeping, leaning awkwardly against the walls like stood-up prom dates.

"Good morning," they seemed to sing in unison.

"Hi," Suzy said, peering past them down the hall for Mia.

"Hi, Ma!" Mia squawked. She was seated in the cross-legged lap of an Irish girl, her hair done up in a chambermaid's babushka with Suzy's blue bandanna.

"Hi, Suzy!" Squee was perched on a wicker loveseat, gnawing his way through a Snickers bar.

"*There's* a nutritious breakfast." Suzy tightened her terrycloth belt.

Squee grinned. Covered in caramel-peanut goo, his two new front teeth were about the size of his ears.

"So"—Suzy leaned on the door frame—"just . . . hangin' out in the hallway?"

Brigid spoke up. The lavender top she had on made her skin glow orange as a jack-o'-lantern. "Mr. . . ." she began, "Mr. Ciz . . . Mr. . . ."

"Bud," Suzy told her.

The girl sighed her relief. "Bud," she said. "He . . . We'd been told to gather for an orientation at half-seven, though we've seen no one but the children." She looked entreatingly to Suzy, taking little pains to conceal her annoyance with the situation.

It was nearly eight-fifteen. Suzy looked to Squee. "Where're your folks?"

Squee shrugged, pouted out his lower lip—*search me*—and continued his breakfast.

Suzy wandered out to the lobby and onto the deck. She found Roddy up on a ladder, cleaning rotted leaves and muck out of the dining porch rain gutter. "Excuse me," she called from the sliding door, "do you know anything about the housekeeping orientation this morning? We've a slew of maids and no matron to be found." One exchange and she was sounding like the Irish already. Suzy was convinced that she went back to New York with a brogue every August.

Roddy did not look at her. "You don't remember me, do you?" he said, eyes trained on the gutter.

"Excuse me?"

"You're Suzy, right?"

"I'm sorry," she said. "Did you work here at the Lodge last summer? I've got a terrible memory for faces, for people at all, really, actually, about everything . . ."

"I'm Roddy Jacobs." He tossed down a clot of slimy twigs. "I was friends with your brother. I High. Class of 'sixty-eight."

"Oh," Suzy said. Chas. Chas as he was at I High: cocky, young, crossing the football field with his friends, heading out to the woods beyond school grounds to get high. Chas's friends: Lance Squire, Jimmy Waters—decent guys, not the brightest, but neither was Chas. "Roddy *Jacobs*?" Suzy repeated.

He nodded.

"Sure," Suzy said, "sure. You were friends with Chas."

Roddy nodded solemnly. Chas had died in Vietnam not long after graduation.

Suzy said, "So, you know anything about this housekeeping thing the girls are waiting on?"

Roddy climbed down from his ladder.

"Oh, I didn't mean to interrupt you. I just wondered if . . ."

Roddy nodded. "I'll take care of it," he said, and passed her, pulling the glass door shut behind him. Suzy remembered Roddy somewhat. A quiet friend of Chas's. With Chas and Lance, it would have been hard to exist as anything else. Roddy had hovered in the background of high school, and of Chas and his gang. It was a long time ago. Almost twenty years since Chas's death, and Suzy tried to think about that time as little as she could. She'd managed to hardly remember Roddy at all.

⌒

"HE WAS ALWAYS a nice child," Nancy said, her tone circumspect. She and Suzy were drinking coffee on the porch of Bud and Nancy's house, up the hill from the Lodge, overlooking Sand Bay. The house Suzy'd grown up in. Nancy nibbled disinterestedly on a muffin Suzy'd brought from the city, pinching up cranberries with her fingertips, divesting them of crumbs, and then dropping the fruit back to the plate like nits picked from a stray cat. "He was the one who always went around cleaning up after Chas and Lance," she said. "Not that he wasn't into their mischief too, but he was the one with the conscience about it. They'd break someone's lawn ornament or a driveway lantern playing ball, and it was Roddy who'd wind up apologizing . . ."

"He get drafted right out of high school too?" Suzy asked.

Nancy swallowed a sip of coffee, shook her head. "Well, sure, but . . ."

Suzy waited for more.

"You *honestly* don't remember, Suzy?"

"Kind of . . ." She didn't, really. Suzy had inherited her mother's selective memory. Pieces of history came back when they were useful to her but otherwise remained in a hazy wash of "the past." It drove Suzy's friends and boyfriends nuts, but she thought it a fortuitous affliction, herself; the inability to recall things you didn't want to recall seemed a pleasant way to live one's life. "There was a big something, wasn't there? Something . . . ?" Suzy tried.

Nancy's voice when she spoke was prim and snippish. "He didn't go." She stiffened dramatically. "Just didn't go. Said no. Burned his draft card, or whatever those people did."

"Hmm." Suzy knew this sort of conversation led to nothing productive.

"All *Eden's* doing," Nancy went on. "*Roderick* told the boy if he wasn't going to fight for his country then he certainly wasn't welcome in *his* house."

Suzy smiled facetiously. "Well, I'm surprised you and Dad conceded to hire such a lowlife—I mean, it's only been, what? Twenty years? Shouldn't he be banished a little longer?"

Nancy shot her a look. The conversation was over. "You *know* I don't like talking about this, Suzy. *Please.*" Nancy took a gulp of coffee, washing away the topic like an unpleasant taste. There were certain things you didn't talk about, pretended not to notice, learned tactically to ignore. It was what had kept Nancy Chizek from losing her mind completely when her son came home from Vietnam in a casket. She'd fallen apart at the news, then patched herself together into a rigid, near-catatonic state of mourning for the funeral. Once he was in the ground, Nancy spoke of Chas only with great honor. Her boy had died for his country. In pride she had found some sort of comfort.

RODDY LED THE TROOP of housekeepers on a rudimentary if not particularly scenic tour of the Lodge—showed them a few different rooms in the main building, the kitchen, and dining room, and the lobby that opened out to the large deck overlooking Sand Beach Bay. He took them through the office and reception areas and pointed through a set of glass doors to Reesa Delamico's Osprey Lodge Beauty Salon and Gift Shop. Out the back kitchen door and up the hill, Roddy showed them the guest cottages, the weedy clay tennis courts, and the swimming pool that looked more like a swamp. "We're going to have to dump a hell of a lot of chlorine in that thing to get it swimmable by July Fourth," Roddy said. The girls nodded skeptically, following behind Roddy in a tight huddle like cold and wary immigrants. At the laundry shack, which sat between the staff barracks and Lance and Lorna Squire's cabin, Roddy held open the door and let the girls file past and peek their heads in one by one. They squinted into the darkness, just able to discern the outlines of looming washing machines and dryers. Drying racks and plywood shelving blocked the few small windows. There was a ratty couch and an old minifridge, and the place just seemed to be crammed crevice to crevice, floor to ceiling, with piles of mildewed newspapers, rusted aerosol cans, water-stained and disintegrating cardboard boxes spilling soda cans and carpentry tools and sewing kits and paper napkins and crusted shampoo bottles. The air was cigarette-stale and uncomfortably close. Brigid took a step inside the shack. On the splintery wooden floor, in the shaft of light from the open door lay an old sponge the color of spoiled meat. She made a gagging noise in her throat and ducked back outside. "I'll for one be spending as little time in *that* place as I can manage, I'd say," she announced.

Her roommate, Peg, passed all of three seconds in the doorway and turned away, disgusted. "It's like a fire trap, eh?" she said to Roddy. He let the door swing closed, shoved his hands back into his pockets, and shrugged at the girl, nodding slowly, his mouth an unreadable line.

They stood outside the laundry shack, scuffing their shoes in the dirt amid patches of sad, dead grass. "Um," Roddy began, and the girls looked at him eagerly. "If you all wanted I could take you around, show you the island some, if you want . . . ?"

The girls conferred wordlessly, shrugging, nodding. Like their spokeswoman, Peg turned back to Roddy. "That'd be grand, Mister . . ."

"Just Roddy's good."

"Thank you, yes, that's grand, if it's not like a bother to you?"

He drove them in a Lodge van down Sand Beach, that mile of crescent moon that never waxed or waned. Near the Lodge a few large homes sat on the bluffs overlooking the water, salt-stained old mansions whose grand lawns sprawled above the bay. They took the long route around the island, through town, and he showed them Ferry Street, Bayshore Drug, the Luncheonette, Tubby's Fishhouse, all of which had been there when Roddy left Osprey twenty years before and were still there now, the prices higher, but otherwise pretty much the same.

At the ferry dock Roddy parked the van and climbed out. He slid open the side door and watched as the bevy of redheads and brunettes tumbled out onto the asphalt, chirping and twittering among themselves like a clutch of nestlings.

"This is just where we arrived yesterday, isn't it?" said a tall, pigeon-toed girl with lank brown hair.

"Only way on-island," Roddy said.

"Ever read that novel—Agatha Christie, was it? Where they're stuck on the island, being murdered one by one?" the girl said, taunting a shorter, plumper girl beside her.

"For fuck's sake—as if I needed reminding of it!" the girl cried.

"And Then There Were None . . ." warbled the instigator.

"Shut your hole," scolded the other.

Roddy turned away, out toward the water. It was hardly more than a mile across the bay to Menhadenport on the mainland. Still, it was an important mile. It spanned more than distance.

At the edge of the beach stood an improbably tall pole with a platform affixed to its top on which an osprey had built its ramshackle nest, streamers of dried seaweed hanging down like decayed party decorations. It was a quirky twist of things that had an entire island of people standing in awe and reverence to a bird who built a nest like something out of Dr. Seuss. To judge from its nest, you'd imagine the osprey would be a motley-looking bird, tattered and discombobulated, with maybe a few absurdly placed, unnaturally colored bouffant feathers froofing it up like a show poodle. In reality, the bird's elegance more than made up for its slovenly home. The osprey was a gorgeous creature—the majestic stretch of its wings, partly skeletal, like something prehistoric, but then plumed in contrasting black and white, alternating patterns like the ruffling skirts of a flamenco dancer. The white head with its black bandit's mask seemed to make perfect sense when you looked at the osprey's talons: four hooked claws on each foot, deadly as a dragon's. With such weapons permanently affixed to its body, the osprey seemed smart to wear a mask. It was unquestionably a fearsome and magnificent creature, but perhaps even more so to the people of Osprey Island, who could not help but feel a sense of eminence as the chosen ones, the ones the osprey watched over, the ones who had named their home in the bird's honor.

Three

THE RAPTOR IS A BIRD OF PREY

The literal translation of the osprey's genus name, "Pandion haliae-tus" is "Pandion's sea eagle," but it seems that the scientist who named it thus—one Marie Jules-Cesar Lelorgne de Savigny—was somewhat confused. You see, Pandion was the king of Athens in Greek mythology. Pandion had two daughters, Philomela and Procne. Procne married Tereus. Theirs is a lengthy and bloody story, but suffice it to say that in the end Philomela, Procne and Tereus are changed—as was the convention of Greek mythology—into, respectively, a nightingale, a swallow, and a hawk. If anything, the osprey should have been named after Tereus, as he was the only raptor among them.

—DR. EDGAR HAMILTON, PH.D.,
"How Our Island Was (Mis)Named"

I T WAS PAST NOON WHEN Roddy returned the girls to the Lodge, traded the van for his own truck, and drove up the hill toward the Squires' cabin. It was like the guest cottages, but with a real kitchen, and someone had thought to plant flowers. A neat row edged the shore side of the house, but on the inland side, though the bed had been cleared, it was left as a plot of churned-up soil, a few flats of dying pink impatiens stacked precariously by the hose spigot. In the large tree that shaded the cabin someone had begun to build a tree fort and had raised a solid, well-made platform before abandoning the project and leaving the rest of the lumber to rot in the grass.

Though afternoon, it appeared to be morning at the Squires'. Lorna sat on the edge of the unfinished porch, her long hair down and middle-parted, which made her look younger than her thirty-six years. Roddy gave the horn a toot and waved. Lorna lifted an arm, cigarette in hand, and waved distractedly, a slow smile crossing her sleep-swollen face. The rings under Lorna's eyes were dark and sunken. From around the corner of the house, Squee shot out on his two-wheeler and careened past his mother in a display clearly for her benefit. Lorna gave a hoot of encouragement that sounded as if it took more energy than she had.

Roddy climbed from his truck, forcing a smile. "Hey, pretty lady," he called.

Lorna arched an eyebrow and took a sip of coffee as though it were something far stronger. Then, with effort, she smiled. "We're so glad to have you home, Roddy Jacobs." Lorna was sixteen when Roddy left Osprey, and though they'd never been close friends, Roddy's homecoming seemed somehow important to Lorna. He got the feeling she felt he'd done something right, for once, in coming back.

The screen door edged open and Lance appeared, thin and leathery-tan, his head grazing the top of the door frame. At thirty-eight, Lance was nearly as good-looking as he'd been in high school, save the taut potbelly he'd developed and the broken red capillaries that zigzagged his nose. He took a long drag on the stub of cigarette he held between two fingers like a joint, then crushed it out against the screen and tossed the butt into the yard.

"Pig," Lorna said.

"Goat," Lance said back.

Lorna took a drag of her cigarette, the ashy tip growing longer and more precarious. She did not tamp it off. Squee came circling around the house again. When he saw Lance in the doorway he swerved and skidded to a stop, but then, at a loss for what to say, he simply stood there on the grass, the front wheel of his bike raised off the ground like a horse rearing its head. He rolled the rear wheel back and forth beneath him, digging a rut and matting the summer grass.

"Hey, bucko," Lance scolded, "watch whose yard you're wrecking."

Squee looked down at the bike as if it had sprung from the earth beneath him, and let the front wheel drop to the ground.

"Gonna help Roddy today, Squirto?" Lance asked, his voice suddenly distant as his gaze. "Keep out of trouble?"

"He's no trouble," Lorna said to Roddy. It came out like a question.

"He's my partner," Roddy said. His enthusiasm sounded false and hollow.

"Yeah. Your partner." Squee's voice was sure, though he did not look at Roddy, his stare fixed on his father. Lance was looking off to the water.

"We got lots to do," Roddy added.

Suddenly from the porch Lance let out a whoop. "Got 'im!" he cried, raising an arm toward the bay. Just offshore an osprey rose slowly from the surface of the water, a wriggling fish snared in his curled talons. The bird paused, adjusting its grip, then shook its feathers, sending off a hearty spray of sea-salt water. It flew toward a nest perched atop an old telephone pole by the beach. The bird hovered a moment over the nest before he released the twitching fish to the bird family below and took wing toward the water for another hunt.

"Poor fucking fish," Lance said, and then he turned and went back inside without another word to anyone. From the nest by the water they could hear the osprey's high whistle, *kyew, kyew, kyew.*

Lorna was putting everything she had into mustering her expression for Squee. "C'mere, kid-of-mine, and give your mom a kiss!" She held open her arms to him, then remembered her cigarette and ground it out on the step.

Squee dropped the bike and galloped across the yard. Lorna mussed his hair, then grabbed a fistful of it on either side of his head and held him that way so she could look in his face. "When'd you get so goddamn handsome?" she said. "God, you turned out so good, Squee. You're turning out so good, every day, you know." She let Squee go and he tripped away. "Don't get sunburnt," she said to Squee. "Be good, mind Roddy, don't get in folks' way, all right?" She racked her thoughts for more essential motherly advice. "Don't do anything I wouldn't do . . . ," she said, then laughed, picked her coffee back up, and looked into it hopefully. "You just be good," she said to the mug.

They stepped away from the porch, and Squee waved to his mother as Roddy clapped a hand on the boy's shoulder, guiding him to the passenger door of the truck.

Roddy parked down in the lot by the beach, near one of the tall osprey nesting platforms that dotted the Sand Bay shoreline. There'd been a time in the early seventies when the osprey population was in such danger of extinction that if a bird made its nest where there were electric or telephone wires the Island Utility and Power guys got out there as quick as they could to remove the lines, put up a new post, and divert the route to make the nest safe for the birds. All this at the instigation of Eden Jacobs, Roddy's mother. She'd spearheaded the movement to save the osprey from imminent extinction—the only time Osprey's residents had ever followed Eden Jacobs's lead. The osprey platforms strung the length of Sand Beach—amid the scrub grass by the dunes, and set back from the shore in the marshy reeds just past Morey's bar—were known as "Eden's nests."

The afternoon sun was strong, and Roddy dug an old Tree Farm hat from behind the truck seat and adjusted the band as tight as it would go for Squee's head. They spent the afternoon repairing winter damage to the boat dock that stuck out into Sand Bay from the shore-front of the Lodge. Squee and Roddy worked companionably, testing and replacing rotten planks. Eden Jacobs was pleased to have Roddy back home on Osprey after all those years, but she was extraordinarily pleased at the way Roddy and Squee had taken to each other. Eden felt Squee was in desperate need of a father figure, on account of the actual father he'd gotten saddled with.

Eden said, "You don't know what that boy lives with."

Now Roddy did know, and it made him happy that Squee seemed perfectly content just to trail Roddy around doing whatever he did and didn't seem to mind that Roddy spoke little, gave little away. It was hard to come back to a place where everyone he saw seemed to have a head full of questions for him, and Roddy spent much of his time trying not to go anyplace where he'd have to talk to anyone. Squee didn't have questions for Roddy—or if he did they were about how to pin a line into the tennis court clay or how to refuel the Weed Whacker. Questions like that, Roddy was more than glad to answer.

WHEN LANCE FINALLY DELIVERED his housekeeping lecture to the Irish girls, it was late that night and they were on the side porch, downing beers with the equally underage waiters. How could you ask an Irish girl not to drink? For the most part no one bothered them about it, except Lance, a raging alcoholic incapable of letting so much as a vial of vanilla extract pass under his nose without delivering a speech on the evils of alcohol. "Wouldn't touch that shit with a ten-foot pole," Lance declared. "Not a *twenty*-foot pole! That juice is poison. *Poison.*" The girls sipped at their cans, wiped their lips afterward. They listened politely to Lance, although Roddy had pretty much already told them everything they needed to know about the Lodge, and far more coherently.

"He's married, isn't he?" Peg asked Brigid once Lance was safely out of earshot. Brigid shrugged. One of the waiters standing nearby overheard and shushed them with a wag of his head toward Squee, who sat cross-legged on the edge of the porch. It was the dark-haired waiter, Gavin, the one with the sleepy, hooded eyes. He leaned his long frame against the porch rail and smoked a cigarette, squinting, and casting—Brigid was almost sure—a few furtive glances in her direction. Brigid had been watching him; she watched people in a way that they could see they were being watched. About this Gavin fellow the rumors were already circulating: he'd followed a girl here, an Islander he'd met at college in California, had followed her home for the summer only to get dumped on arrival when the girl had gotten back with her Island High beau. It was said that Gavin was not a happy boy these days.

Another waiter, Jeremy, a skinny boy with pimples in his neck stubble, slid into the chair beside Brigid and set his beer down with an emphatic thud. His voice was conspiratorially low. "Lance is Squee's dad. His mom's Lorna. She's pretty much a drunk." Jeremy took a sip of his beer.

"Is she here?" Peg asked, waving a hand toward the cabins.

"Yeah, you'll see her around every so often. She's in bad shape. It's really sad." Jeremy's display of sensitivity was embarrassingly over-earnest.

"So she's just about the place, and drunk, and no one cares a thing about it?" Peg asked.

"What're you going to do?" Jeremy had worked summers at the Lodge before, as a busboy. He knew what things went unquestioned.

"And Lance?" Brigid pressed him. "What about him?"

Peg said, "He's a bit of dosser, eh?"

"A what?" said Jeremy.

Brigid cut in: "A doss—a fellow who just lays about, like a bit of a waste, you know?"

"Yeah," Jeremy concurred. "He's a dick. The whole teetotaler thing's a total sham. Mostly he's totally rocked too."

"Doesn't anyone care at all?" Peg asked.

"Yeah, but you know . . ." Jeremy stammered. "I mean, what can you do, you know?" They were all quiet then for a moment, sipping their Pabsts, thinking, *God, yeah, what could you do, really?* The air smelled of sea salt and smoke, the breeze from the shore delicious.

Peg leaned in closer to Jeremy. "And the boy?" she whispered. Little Squee was swinging his legs back and forth off the side of the deck.

"It's messed up," Jeremy said, "but, you know, he seems OK. He's a pretty well adjusted kid, you know, in spite of everything."

"It's wrong, isn't it . . . ?" Peg said.

Brigid looked again to Squee, his skinny legs still waggling off the edge of the deck. She turned back to her beer and drained it.

Half an hour later, Brigid excused herself—*jet lag*—from the porch party. Gavin, the dark, smoking waiter, had disappeared, and with him had gone Brigid's motivation to stay awake any longer. She cut through the Lodge, the fastest route to the staff quarters, but as she crossed the lobby she heard something—an animal, she thought at first—hiss from the far side of the room. She stopped where she was and spun around. The lights were all off for the night, and the moon glared in at Brigid like a spotlight. It shone through the sliding glass doors and obscured the far half of the large room in darkness.

The hiss came again, this time decidedly human. Brigid wasn't a scared sort of a girl, and it was her romantic imagination that kicked in first: the sultry-eyed waiter was calling from the shadows! She peered off in the direction of the noise, smelled cigarette, and watched as a tiny dot of orange glowed bright for a moment, then subsided. As her eyes began to distinguish shapes, she could make out the old grand piano in the corner and the figure seated nearby in a low-slung armchair. There was something eerily exciting about it. Brigid wanted that—some strange and overwhelming indiscretion in this new place. "In the habit of hissing at girls across dark rooms, are you?" she said coyly.

From the corner came a snort, a hack thick with phlegm. "Only the ones with tits like yours," he said.

Brigid thought at first that she must have misunderstood, but her eyes were adjusting to the dark and the man's features began to come together and coalesce. She turned without another word and walked away, leaving Lance to finish out his cigarette alone in the empty Lodge lobby. And as she passed through the kitchen exit, Brigid thought for the first time that perhaps she wasn't quite as ready as she'd thought. Or maybe she was ready, but for something a bit less strange and overwhelming than she'd previously considered. A brooding waiter was one thing; the crude, married, alcoholic handyman another entirely. He was rather attractive, she thought—quite attractive, really, in a sad, brutish sort of a way. But no. No, she told herself firmly. It was an altogether stupid idea to fuck the father of anyone at all.

Four

TO WHAT DIRECTION
WILL YOUR CHICKS TAKE WING?

Ah! mother bird, you'll have weary days.
— MARGARET E. SANGSTER, "The Building of the Nest"

IN THE BACK OF THE nonfunctional minifridge in the laundry shack Lorna kept a bottle of vodka (Lance would likely have killed her if he knew) and a purple spiral notebook she'd bought at the drugstore when she was pregnant with Squee and Eden Jacobs had told her to write down her thoughts and feelings. Lorna and Eden had gone for walks together in the mornings back then, Eden pointing out every downy woodpecker and Carolina wren, pushing her binoculars at Lorna, telling her, *Look.* Eden tried to get Lorna involved in the henhouse too, but that wasn't really Lorna's thing, raising chickens and worrying who was eating whose eggs and who was sitting on whose nest and picking whose feathers. It was enough building the osprey platforms. It was actually enough just taking care of herself, let alone every winged thing that managed to land itself on Osprey.

Lorna knew she'd let Eden down in ways that had nothing to do with birds. It was hard for Lorna to see Eden now, the disappointment on her face. On her own mother's, Lorna had gotten used to that pinched look of dread and hopefulness. But from Eden, who'd had so much faith in Lorna . . . from Eden it was pure judgment. Eden called her on it, plain and simple. *You're drunk, Lorna. Don't you think of*

Lance Jr., Lorna? How can you do that to yourself and think of him at the same time?

Sometimes Lorna really did want to live a different life. The thing was, she knew better. Unfortunately, knowing better didn't in any way mean she was going to *do* better, just that she knew more clearly how wrong she was. Lorna had, she knew, done a lot of bad things. For her, the choice to do good or bad was the same sort of dilemma as when there was a platter of finger foods out in front of you and you knew you should eat the carrot stick but you also knew that it was the sausage roll that was going to hop right into your mouth. Soothe the biggest greasy hankering and leave you feeling nasty the rest of the night. When a choice like that presented itself to Lorna, she'd start to deliberate: *Which path should I follow?* And then it was like her body would just lurch forward. Lorna and Lance had laughed when they'd heard about a guy—a fisherman who lived just across the bay—who had a disease that made him all of a sudden, all the time, unexpectedly and uncontrollably yell things out. And though they'd laughed, Lorna couldn't help but wonder what her own life would be like if all the terrible thoughts inside her rose to the surface like dead bodies and made themselves known. Lorna thought that if all people like that fisherman did was yell out "cunt" in the supermarket or "mother-fucker" from the church pew, then those people weren't even the tiniest bit as bad a person as she was.

On that late June Sunday, while the rest of the staff got to work readying the Lodge for the season, Lorna hid in the laundry shack. A few minutes after the blare of the five o'clock whistle at the ferry dock, she heard a truck pull up outside. She stood from the couch and stowed her notebook and vodka bottle in the minifridge. Lance never came into the laundry shack—literally gagged at the smell of the place—so her secrets were relatively safe inside. Lorna pushed bravely out into the sunshine, her hand shielding her eyes from the light. She didn't see Roddy, but Squee sat in the passenger seat of the truck, patiently running a Matchbox car along the dashboard.

Lorna hung her hands on the open truck window and leaned there the way she once had in the window of Lance's car, when he'd stop in the high school parking lot to talk to her. "Hey, sweet son," she said.

Squee's smile opened slowly and fully. "Mom!"

Lorna held on to the window of the truck. Sometimes, with her son, love felt to Lorna like barbecue coals with too much lighter fluid and the flick of a match: love for Squee knocked her like a flare of heat so powerful she had to wait for the blow to pass before she was good for anything again.

From around the back of the staff barracks, Roddy appeared, toting a few long pieces of lumber. He slid them into the bed of the pickup. Lorna lifted a hand in greeting, and Roddy nodded, but his brow was furrowed. He went to the driver's side and fumbled behind the seat.

"You getting hungry?" Lorna asked Squee. Her voice was tired.

Squee was nodding as Roddy reemerged with some orange plastic ribbon, which he tied to the boards that stuck off the end of the truck bed.

Lorna sighed. "Guess I better think about some dinner for you then, huh?"

Roddy looked up at her again, the way she was leaning on the truck. Her skin looked too pale, and the hollows of her face too dark. "I'm heading to Morey's," he told Lorna, though he'd had no such plans until that moment.

Lorna looked relieved. "You want to go with Roddy?"

Squee shrugged his acquiescence.

"You come too, Lorna," Roddy suggested.

"Oh, I've got work left . . ." she lied, gesturing vaguely toward the laundry shack. "You men go. Let me give you some money, Roddy." She began to reach into her jeans pocket but Roddy held up a hand to stop her. "I got him," he said. Lorna paused. She let her hands drop back to her sides. "Thank you." She nudged Squee: *"Thank you, Roddy."*

"Thank you, Roddy," Squee repeated.

"Welcome." And when he'd secured the lumber in the truck with some twine and a bungee cord, Roddy climbed in beside Squee, who blew his mother a last kiss.

Morey's Dinghy was an old fisherman's shanty fifty yards up the beach from the Lodge and across a small footbridge. It perched on a curved lip of land where the beach cut back on one side into a swampy inlet of reeds where lurking heron were often spotted in the twilight hours. Old fishing nets threaded with colored Christmas lights and cast-off buoys hung from the rafters. The kitchen consisted of a freezer and a deep fryer; Morey served only food that cooked in a vat of boiling oil. Everything came on a grease-soaked slip of wax paper nestled at the bottom of a red plastic basket, all without so much as a sheaf of iceberg lettuce to soften the blow.

Morey presided over the bar daily from noon, when he opened, until about seven, when Merle Squire, Lance's mother, showed up for her shift. The Lodge staff were traditionally renowned for copious drinking, often starting out the night at Morey's, then returning to the porch of the Lodge when the bar closed, by legal decree, at one a.m. The bar had four taps—Bud, Bud Light, Miller, Miller Lite—but when the Irish girls arrived in June Morey switched one tap over to Guinness. His local crowd was steady and loyal, more family than clientele, since his was one of only three island bars, not including restaurants that served bottled beer and wine, and his was the only one that stayed open through the off-season, which was everything but the summer. For three months a year, renters from New York City and its moneyed environs invaded Osprey with their private-schooled children and their au pairs and their Volvo wagons, and pumped enough cash into the island economy to keep it nominally running for the nine intervening months until they came crashing back for another season.

When Roddy and Squee walked in that evening, Suzy and Mia

were seated at the bar. Squee swung himself up beside Mia, who was rationing sips of a tall Shirley Temple, climbing up onto her knees to drink from the straw and then ducking down to check the level of pink in the glass. Roddy hovered awkwardly, then finally took the stool next to Suzy.

"What do you want?" Roddy called to Squee. Morey stood behind the bar twitching his mustache.

"Chicken fingers." Squee didn't take his eyes from Mia and her glass. "And a Coke."

Suzy looked to Squee. "How 'bout Seven-Up?"

Squee shrugged, nodded disinterestedly. Suzy nodded to Morey. Roddy looked confused.

"You don't want that kid hopped up on caffeine all night," she said. "Trust me."

Roddy conceded. "You have those clam strips?" Morey nodded. "And a Bud." Roddy glanced to Suzy, gestured vaguely toward her drink.

"Sure," she said, after a moment's pause. "Maker's and soda." She drained her glass and set it solidly on the bar.

Roddy and Morey met each other's eyes, impressed.

Though the sun was still shining outside and wouldn't set for another few hours, Morey's was dark and cavernous, the Christmas lights twinkling in a sort of sordid merriment. Squee and Mia twittered together, and Roddy tapped his foot on the bar rail, feigning interest in the muted news on a TV mounted high in a corner.

Morey set drinks in front of them, and Suzy began to lift hers in a toast, then thought better and paused, the glass half raised before her. "Ever considered matricide?" She looked at him. "Murdering your mom?"

Roddy shook his head. "My dad." He nodded now. "Yeah. Never my mom."

"I should take out *both* of mine, maybe—two birds, one stone . . . God, why do I *do* this to myself?" Suzy whined.

"Do what?"

"Come here." She drank. "Agree to live with their bullshit. I don't know what possesses me to think it's going to be OK. It's never OK. I never should have let them know I'd had a kid in the first place. I was gone; I was free. We were on perfectly lovely nonspeaking terms . . . and then I had to go and ruin it all!"

"Hmm," Roddy said.

"You're not much of a talker, huh?"

"Sometimes," he said.

"Sometimes you are, or sometimes you aren't?"

"Isn't that the same thing?"

Suzy laughed. "Are you always this difficult?"

"Probably," he said.

"So I shouldn't take it personally?" Her eyes were still laughing, though her face had stopped.

"No," he said. "I mean, yes, you should take it personally." He looked at his beer. Down the bar, the kids were in their own world.

"I *should*?"

Roddy smiled now, took a sip of his beer, watching it steadily, as if it might morph into something else if he lifted his eyes. "It's personal."

"It's *personal*?"

"Yeah," he said, and smiled a little. "It's very personal." He looked right at her.

"You," she said, and she drank again. "You're going to have to forgive me for saying so again, but you are a very difficult man to have a conversation with." She smiled this time, peering up at him from her glass, suddenly shy to face him straight on.

"Yeah, I know."

"You *know*? So you're trying to be difficult?"

"No," he tried to explain: "I mean, do you try to make me nervous?"

"What? You? No. Why would I do that?"

"That's my point," Roddy said. "I don't think you do. I don't think you *try* and make me nervous, but you do anyway—"

She cut him off: "Why do I make you nervous? What do I do that makes you nervous?"

"I don't know," he said. "It's not such a bad nervous. It's an OK nervous." He paused. "It's a nervous I'm willing to live with."

He took a deep breath, let it go, and then changed his mind about what to say just as the words were coming: "You . . . would you like another drink?"

She lost her composure, lapsed into nervous laughter. "You just did it again. That's not normal conversational practice."

There was too long a pause. Then he said, "What exactly do you want from me?"

"Nothing." She was surprised. "I'm sorry, I don't want anything from you. I didn't . . ."

"*That's* the thing," he said.

She waited, but he offered nothing more. "What's *the thing*? I don't understand anything you say!"

"Yes, you do. Of course you do." He paused, drank, stared straight ahead, and lowered his voice. "I wish you'd stop making fun of me."

She put her hand out across the bar toward him—didn't touch him, but made the gesture, the movement toward the touch. "I am *not* making fun of you."

Morey appeared then with food, and Suzy drew back her hand as though she'd been caught at something illicit. Morey deposited Squee's dinner before him, then passed the other basket to Roddy. He reached under the counter, withdrew a handful of plastic packets, and slid them across the bar: tartar sauce and lemon juice.

Suzy looked down toward Mia, who still had an inch of grenadine fizz in the bottom of her glass.

"You know?" Roddy said, his composure returned, a clam strip dangling between his thumb and forefinger, "I had a crush on you in high school."

"You *did*?"

"Big one." He nodded at his clams.

Suzy sat there, dumb.

"Yup," Roddy said, still nodding.

"I have to say," Suzy managed finally, "*that* was sort of a surprise there . . ."

"Yeah?" Roddy stuck a clam in his mouth and chewed.

"Yeah." She laughed.

"Sorry."

"That's OK." She laughed again, nervous. "Well, you have definitely succeeded in making *me* feel *very* uncomfortable now, so maybe, while we're even, I'll just take my leave." She drained the last of her Maker's, called to Mia—"Hey, kid, let's hit the road"—slapped a few dollars on the bar for Morey, and stood to go. Mia slid reluctantly from her stool.

Roddy chewed his lip, then said, "It wouldn't be too hard to have a big crush on you now."

She stared at him for a second, as long as it took him to blanch and turn back to his food. Then she let out another laugh—a laugh of bafflement—and clapped a hand on Roddy's back like a football buddy or a frat brother. "We'll be seeing you, Roddy," she said. "See you, Squee. Morey. Let's beat it, kid." And Suzy opened the door and followed Mia out into the disconcerting sunshine.

The kids arrived early that night, so it was Morey who got them started on their drinks and made quarter change for the pool table. By the time Merle Squire showed up for her shift the air was thick with smoke and the din was as dense. Merle wasn't particularly in the mood for summer to begin. Summer folk didn't tip worth shit, and though some customers were better than none, she wasn't sure she even cared. She didn't mind tending bar when it was just George Quincy ordering his same old Jack and Coke for hours every night before he stumbled back up the hill, or the girls from the IGA who came in after work. But the summer folk set her on edge. They didn't even try to fit in. The summer folk treated the year-rounders like mosquitoes: summer pests, inevitable but tolerable if you slathered on enough repellent and didn't wander out of your screened-in gazebo. One summer Merle had gotten to talking with a chatty and particularly stupid housekeeper—and in Merle's opinion those Irish girls were as bad as the New York lawyers and their skinny wives. The girl had asked where Merle lived.

"Here," Merle told her.

"No, but during the year," said the girl.

"*Here,*" Merle said again, her patience rapidly waning.

"People *live* here?" The girl seemed genuinely surprised.

"What do you think?" Merle asked. "You think it's like Disney World? You think we shut down after Labor Day, pull the docks in out of the water, put a big tarp over everything and pack up and go home?" The girl listened, drunk and bleary-eyed. "Like this is some summer camp for assholes? And what am I? An actress? They pay me to dress like a waitress and pour beer!" Merle laughed loudly, and clearly to herself.

The first person Merle spotted when she arrived at Morey's that night was her own son, sitting by the bar, drinking a Coca-Cola as though no one knew why he carried his drink with him out to his truck or what he added to it there.

"Hi, Ma."

"Lance." Merle nodded. She poured herself a shot of tequila, drank it down, and chewed a lime. Lance glared disapprovingly. "Save it," Merle told him. He turned back to the Irish girls who swirled around the pool table, carrying their cues like scepters. Merle didn't know the redhead approaching the bar, but Lance practically jumped out of his skin offering drinks, offering anything. Brigid accepted a beer—Guinness, two of them, actually, both of which Lance paid for—thanked him, and then stepped away.

"You can't let them know," Merle told her son.

"Huh?"

"They don't want to know—ones like that—how bad you want them."

"Shut up," Lance said. He was watching Brigid, who handed one of the beers to a college boy skulking in the corner.

"Don't tell your mother to shut up."

"Well, shut up, then."

They were quiet a minute, until Merle said, "So how's Lorna these days?"

Lance looked at his mother, then pushed his drink away. He shook his head, pulled the glass back, and took a big swallow. "Drunk," he said.

"Lorna," Merle said, "or you?"

But Lance didn't answer, just stared into his drink, shaking his head no.

Brigid had run into Gavin, the waiter she had her eye on, that afternoon behind the staff barracks where he'd sat, smoking, on the fire escape steps. "A gang of us are planning to head over this evening to Morey's Dinghy, that pub, there . . ."—she pointed—"at the end of the beach, you see?" Gavin had nodded, holding smoke in his lungs, never saying a word. But he'd come, and though he didn't look particularly thrilled to be there, he seemed the sort who never looked particularly thrilled about anything at all. He didn't speak much either, which only fueled Brigid's intrigue. He looked like someone who needed someone to talk to, and though he gave no outward indication that Brigid might be that person, his presence at the Dinghy had her feeling buoyed and hopeful.

She lost the game she was playing and retrieved her beer. Gavin hadn't moved from his corner, where a corona of brightly colored Christmas lights clustered in the fishing net above his head. Brigid went to him. "Come outside and have a smoke, won't you?" she asked.

Gavin exhaled a cloud of smoke through the side of his mouth.

"Come for a smoke *with me*?" she revised.

He smiled slightly, awkwardly, as though his face were unaccustomed to such contortions. Then he shrugged and followed her out the back door.

The deck, too, was lit by Christmas lights: pink, blue, red, yellow, green, strung along the wooden railing, reflected in the water below. Brigid sat and swung her legs over the edge of the dock. Gavin eased himself down beside her and offered a cigarette. She made a show of surprise at his gallantry, and he continued to oblige, making sure hers was lit before his own. Wind ruffled the swamp reeds, and they both looked quickly toward the disturbance as though it might offer a possible conversation topic. A gull flew up toward the moon, half full and ringed with haze. Neither of them thought of anything to say. They sipped their beers. They smoked their cigarettes. You had to be grateful for props at times like this.

Brigid downed her last sip of beer. "Did you love her, then?" she asked. They'd all heard—through a very short and swift grapevine—of Gavin's decimated relationship with the island girl he'd followed from California. She'd dumped him on arrival.

"I thought so," he said. The topic ran constantly through his head and needed no intro or segue.

"And now?" she prodded.

"I don't know."

He offered nothing more.

"So how long were you two a couple, then?" she tried.

"Since September."

She nodded, as though she knew what that was like. In truth, Brigid hadn't had a boyfriend in her life who'd lasted longer than three weeks. Most didn't last twenty-four hours. She'd slept with three boys and had shared only so much as a postcoital meal with just one of those.

"Yeah," Gavin said. "Yeah, well, it sucks. Pretty much end of story." He shrugged again, slapped his palms against his thighs, pulled his legs in and stood. He hovered above her a moment as she gazed up at him.

"Would you be interested at all in getting involved with someone else, then?" she asked. She cocked her head. "Insofar as it might take your mind off things a bit?"

He laughed, a muffled snort, which was dampening but not unkind. When he spoke, it was gratefully. "Thanks, but I don't think so."

"You're sure, are you?"

He laughed again. "No."

"Well, I suppose that's something, isn't it?"

"No," he said. "I don't think it's something. I don't know what it is."

"Hmm," she said.

"Yeah well . . ."

"Yeah . . ."

"I'm going to head out, I guess," he said. "Hey, thanks for the beer."

"No bother at all."

"G'night" he told her.

" 'Night, then," she repeated, her voice forced and bright.

He turned away, walked down the steps and around the outside of the bar toward the Lodge.

Brigid sat a moment, looking at the water. And then all there was to do was go back inside and order another beer and shoot another game of pool, and so she did.

Five

HOW BLACK THE NIGHT
THAT BLINDS OUR HUMAN HEARTS

Within the chalky prison-walls the infantile screams of the little hawks could be heard as they pounded feebly on the shell.
—WILLIAM I. FINLEY, "Photographing a Hawk's Nest"

LORNA SAT ON THE CABIN PORCH, awkward and misplaced in the morning sun. She wished the light were like the stiffness of a new pair of shoes, and she closed her eyes and tried to imagine breaking it in. The sun eddied orange beneath her eyelids. If it were always sunny, maybe she could stay. If the darkness never set in to her again, holding her sure and tight, if she never turned away from the sun, just stayed outside with Squee forever and never went back inside, where blankets were hung over the windows to keep the light from bringing into relief all that was wrong with the way they lived. Squee belonged in the light, an angel child—that blond head of his, that devil's grin on an angel's face, her boy. But she could already see how worry wore him down, worry over his mama, shut tight in the dark like her life depended on it. To stay with Squee in the sun she'd have to vow never to take another drink. Never look at Lance again, because Lance *was* darkness, and Lorna's dream of light ended right with him.

Lorna pushed inside through the screen door, let it close behind her, and then shut the wooden door as well. It was hard to see inside the cabin. Sunlight edged the window curtains like it might burst through, blow the drapery to smithereens the way hurricanes shattered windows from the outside or fires burst them open from within. It seemed wrong to Lorna that a day could be both dark and light. If it was dark and stormy you could stay inside with all the drapes drawn and lie in bed and drink and play cards and watch a movie with your kid curled up on your lap, and the world wouldn't seem like it wanted something from you. It was so much easier to be a person when it rained.

Lance was on the couch, and he called to her, "Baby . . ." and she went to him, drawn back to the safest, warmest place there ever was. No fight, no struggle. Falling into Lance took no effort at all. It was like being conceived again, going back to the place before you were born, before there was work to bring you into the world. Sometimes Lorna wished she'd been allowed to stay in the first womb she'd known. No birth, no adoption, just a quiet death there in the darkness, before all the trouble of life had begun.

"C'mere," Lance said, and held his glass to her lips, and held her head while she swallowed. The whiskey was warm and burned through her, so it wasn't that she'd won the fight or lost the fight, there just was no more fight. And, yes, there were chores to be done, but what did it really matter if she did them or not? What did the world really matter? Squee was OK, off with Roddy, and what did anyone in the whole fucking world want, really, except to be left alone, and no one could accuse her of not leaving everyone the fuck alone. This. This was all she really wanted, just this.

She curled in Lance's lap, and he pushed his hand down into her pants, warm into warm, like everything was meant to be, Lance warm in her, his fingers reaching all the way up inside to the darkest place they could find, because that's all Lance wanted too: more darkness than he could get on the earth. He wanted to crawl inside her, as she crawled inside him. She opened around him and he pushed into her, like he could travel forever until he was gone. She felt herself contract around him, reached up with her arms to encircle him, realized her cheek was resting in his lap. Sometimes she wondered how he still got hard, because she'd heard that drinking made you lose that, but he'd never lost the ability to push himself inside her, everything concentrated deep in the pit of her pelvis. The darkness was immense, and she could swim in it, feel it open up inside of her and around her, and when she came it bloomed bigger and her consciousness fell away.

When she woke Lance was standing with one hand against the wall, the other probing painfully at his bare foot, which he was holding off the ground. There was a pilled yellow blanket nailed over the window beside him, and he yanked it down so he could see better, Lorna wincing as the blanket crumpled to the floor and sunshine poured in through the window. Dust glowed in the air like evidence of infection.

"Put it back," Lorna pleaded, hand shielding her eyes.

"There's a fucking piece of glass in my foot." Lance tested his weight on the floor, grimacing.

Lorna levered herself up to sitting. Her head hurt, as though she'd missed her coffee. She leaned on the arm of the couch and tried to push herself up, but she didn't have the strength, so she rolled onto her stomach and slid her knees to the floor, then climbed from a kneel to standing. She went to the window, bent slowly to pick up the blanket, and tried to jab it over the nails in the window frame, but it hurt her arms and she sank back to the floor and pulled the dusty blanket over her head. The light shone through—false, hopeful yellow—and she shut her eyes against it.

Lance was gone when she woke again, later, to a couple of waiters shooting the shit on the staff barracks' back stoop.

"You go to Morey's last night?" one boy said.

"Dude, I didn't get this hangover in my room."

"Yeah, so who was out?"

"I don't know—you know, everybody, the usual."

"How 'bout that girl?"

"Which girl?"

"The Irish one—Brigid."

"Yeah, *that* Irish girl, yeah, she was there. With Lance fucking pissing himself over her."

"She was with *Lance*?"

"He wished!"

"He was hitting on her?"

"It was pretty sick." The boy paused. "Pathetic, you know? I totally feel for his wife, you know? I mean, that's fucked up."

"She's been here before?" asked the boy who'd stayed in.

"Who, Lorna?"

"No, no. Brigid."

"Nah. Her sister was here last summer. Fiona."

"She as hot as Brigid?"

"Nah. I mean, she was good-looking enough, but not the same way, you know?"

"Yeah . . ."

The boys were silent a moment, lost in their own private reveries on the hotness of Brigid.

"What do you think of her?" the new boy said finally.

"Who, Brigid?"

"Yeah."

"Dude, she's hot."

"Like I'm blind!"

"I don't know. She's totally hot. But kind of prickly too, you know? Like she's super smart or something. Kind of sneaky, sort of."

"Yeah," said the new boy, "you get the feeling, kind of, when you talk to her, like she's listening kind of too carefully or something. Like she's memorizing things or something."

The other boy let out a long negative sigh, shaking his head and considering his reply as it slowly escaped. "Naaah," he said, "I don't think she's *that* smart . . ."

They were quiet.

"Dude, you got another smoke?"

"Upstairs." A moment later the door slammed.

Lorna lay in her house under the old dirty yellow blanket. It wasn't anything she didn't know, really, and nothing she hadn't heard before. Nothing worse than she'd done herself. And still, it hurt. Because there was nothing in the world—even joy—that didn't hurt.

ON THE LODGE PORCH THAT NIGHT, Peg and Jeremy sat off to themselves, away from the rest of the staff on the edge of the deck, their feet dangling. Squee and Mia were playing Ping-Pong at the table underneath the deck, and their squawks and cries of victory and defeat rushed up through the planking. Gavin was playing Spit with a waiter named Joe who didn't talk much and seemed even less happy with where he was than Gavin. Brigid sat around a table with three guy waiters who were playing I Never and seemed thrilled to have a girl, especially Brigid, join their ranks.

"I never had sex with someone I worked with," said one of the waiters, who looked fifteen and had probably never had sex with any-one at all. The group paused, collectively considering their own checkered pasts. Brigid was the only one to drink. Never mind that she hadn't actually shagged the boy, only messed about with him once at a party somewhere. But *these* boys didn't need to know that. Brigid liked how impressed they looked, all agog at a girl who'd freely tell them whom she'd fucked and how. She liked that she could look down on them now: so immature to be impressed the way they were.

The next boy took his turn and upped the ante. "I never had sex with my boss." He had on a pink Lacoste shirt and looked to be feel-ing mischievous.

Again, Brigid drank alone. The boy whom she hadn't actually shagged hadn't actually been the boss, only a coworker, but Brigid felt a sense of obligation to give these boys something to fuel their little dreams.

The third boy said, "I never watched someone else having sex."

Brigid turned to him, coy. "Does that include the person you were having the sex with then? Like: *I never kept my eyes open?*"

The guy laughed. "I never watched two *other* people, who were not me, having sex," he said.

"Live?" Brigid asked. "Or pornography as well?"

"Live," said Lacoste boy.

No one drank.

"All right, then," Brigid said, "so I've got to think up something I *haven't* done, is that right?" She pretended to be racking her brain.

"Don't tax yourself," said the boy in the pink shirt.

"I've got it: I never rented pornography," Brigid said. All the boys drank, and she laughed at them and they laughed back.

By the time the game broke up there were at least ten of them playing and Brigid was plastered—there were actually *plenty* of things she hadn't done, involving all manner of relatives and root vegetables, that she was all too happy to admit to never having done. Jeremy and Peg, who were clearly about to become the new staff lovebirds, had gone for "a walk on the beach," and there was much speculation among the rest of the group as to what that meant. Gavin had made his way over from the card game and sat in a chair just behind Brigid, close enough that she could feel him shift and sigh, not close enough that she was sure he'd done it deliberately. She liked the feel of him close to her. He was driving her a bit insane. She liked that some. Not too much. But some.

"YOU THINK I DON'T KNOW, LANCE? You make an ass of yourself— you think I sit here with no fucking clue?"

"You talked to my mother?"

"I never talked to your mother. I don't talk to your damn *mother.*"

"So what the fuck are you talking about?"

"You come in blasted out of your fucking mind, three in the morning . . . You think Squee doesn't hear? You think I don't know what you're doing?"

"What am I doing? You tell me what I'm doing. Waking up your goddamn *baby*? *Oh! Oh!*" Lance threw his hands in the air, his voice high and squeaky. *"Oh, don't hurt my baby!"*

Lorna looked as if she might strike him, but then she sank down to the table and buried her head in her hands.

Lance's body released. He went to kneel by her chair, pushed his face into her lap, his cheek against her leg. "Baby," he said, "Lorna."

She let one hand fall to his head, ran her fingers through his hair, soft, greasy at the scalp, but so soft for a man, softer than anyone would think. "Go," Lorna said quietly, "just go. Fuck whoever you want. Just go."

"I didn't fuck anybody."

"Sure you did," she whispered to the table.

"No I didn't." He opened his mouth on her thigh below the seam of her shorts. "I didn't."

"Why?" Lorna was crying now. "Why not?"

"I love you, Lorna Vaughn."

"It doesn't matter."

"It matters," he said.

She shook her head.

"Don't talk stupid, Lorna."

"What do I care anyway? Fuck them . . . all those girls . . ."

Lance lifted his head abruptly, his demeanor changed again, his face accusing and hurt, a shield of defense shot through beneath his skin. "Why?" he demanded. "You guilty about something, Lorna? Maybe it's you we should be talking about now? Who's the one who goes and fucks whoever she goddamn pleases? You tell me that, Lorna. Who'd you go and fuck this time? Find yourself a waiter? What were *you* doing last night? Want to tell me that?" He stood and backed away haltingly, as if suddenly repulsed.

Lorna didn't move, didn't lift her head. She just stayed there face-down at the kitchen table in their shack by the Osprey Lodge, her arm wet with tears, her nose dripping on her arm, her head stuffed so full she couldn't breathe, just let the snot and tears run down her, too afraid to lift her eyes. It was dark outside, but the overhead light above the table was on, and she heard Lance turn from her in disgust, stride away, across the room toward the door. She wanted to call out, to ask him to please put out the light, but she couldn't. She tried, her head down, eyes shielded—"Please . . ."—but the slam of the screen door cut her short, his feet heavy on the porch steps as if damning each one as he went. Then she was alone under the glare of the kitchen light. All she could think was that she would stay there with her head down until it burned out on its own.

JEREMY AND PEG HAD RETURNED from their walk on the beach and were wending their way slowly back toward the staff barracks. They climbed the stone steps on the path between the laundry shack and the Squires' cabin and had stopped to kiss awhile on the cobbled path when, from inside the Squires' cabin, they heard the shouting. Peg broke away first, startled. Jeremy turned his head toward the cabin and in the same motion pulled Peg to him—away from the noise of a husband and wife, a mother and a father, yelling *fuck you* for everyone to hear—as though spending the better part of the evening with their tongues in each other's mouths had served to designate him as her protector. Peg strained against his grip and craned toward the cabin, then ducked back when, a minute later, the front door flew open and Lance charged out, swearing to himself. Peg hid there under Jeremy's wing and stayed very quiet until Lance had passed, tearing off toward the Lodge. Peg and Jeremy stood, stunned. Then Peg looked up to Jeremy, his face a good foot above her own.

"Where was the boy?" she asked, breathless and rushed.

Jeremy seized the imperative. "Under the deck, playing Ping-Pong before . . ." And without another word the two took off toward the Lodge to find Squee, his self-appointed guardians, teenage social workers certain they had only the best intentions: to look after the child.

Peg and Jeremy rushed out the sliding door and onto the porch, hand in hand, stopping just beyond the threshold, the sea breeze blowing in their faces as they scanned the crowd like young cops closing in on their man. Squee was scrunched into a wicker lounger with Mia, playing cat's cradle with a piece of old string. Peg and Jeremy came at them. Jeremy stopped and suddenly checked his watch. It was just past ten.

"You two want to go into town and get some ice cream?" he said brightly, a camp counselor at heart.

The children struggled excitedly out of their chair.

"Go on and ask your mum," Peg said to Mia, who dashed upstairs.

When she returned, nodding vehemently, she took Peg's hand, and the group made their way down the steps to the parking lot and Jeremy's car. The porch sitters heard the grumpy car engine turn over, die again, then turn over at last. When the car rolled around the bend in Sand Beach Road, conversation on the porch resumed as though nothing had happened. A few people made excuses and started up the hill toward the barracks. Brigid and Gavin sat and had another glass of whiskey. The last of the drinking boys headed off to bed. Brigid and Gavin smoked a cigarette. The night was warm, the air saturated with mist.

"What's between our respective roommates, do you think?" Brigid asked.

Gavin gestured toward the stairs down which they'd disappeared with the kids. "What you see, I guess." He shrugged and took a long, pensive drag on his cigarette, as if to imply that he had other things on his mind.

"You don't get on, then?" Brigid asked.

Gavin shrugged again. "Don't think we'll be best friends."

Brigid laughed, too eagerly.

"I think I'm going to head up." He motioned to the hill. "You going to hang here?"

Brigid yawned conveniently. "Nah, I'm knackered."

He gave a laugh, then pushed back his chair, gestured—*after you.*
She let herself lead.

They walked single file up the trail, not quickly, but with purpose.
Brigid let her heart beat faster. The back door was propped open with
a cinderblock, and Brigid pivoted on the stoop of the barrack so that
she stood facing him in the threshold. The look on his face conveyed
an acknowledgment of the inevitable. He took another step to her as
if to plow her down in the doorway, but then he stopped abruptly. A
breath escaped him, high and short, and he leaned in. His hands went
to her shoulders, pushing her inside the building, against the dark
wall of the downstairs hallway. He kissed hard, allowing her no
opportunity to kiss back, only to take, as if this kiss was something he
needed to give to her, like a present she might refuse if he equivocated
in the slightest. She wanted to say, *I wouldn't turn you away,* wanted
to say it in her kiss, but couldn't find the voice, the right intonation of
movement, so she just let herself be kissed by Gavin and let herself
think about how Peg and Jeremy were out with Squee and Mia, and
how both their rooms were empty, and how, maybe, with this same
kissing fervor, he might push her down onto that pathetic creaking
cot bed and do whatever he wanted. She was quite sure she knew precisely what *she* wanted.

Gavin pulled away, took a step back in the hall as if to see what he
was doing. "Good night, Brigid," he said, and he turned and started
up the stairs.

For a second Brigid thought he meant for her to follow, but then it
seemed clear that wasn't the case at all. She'd been kissed good night,
nothing more. She leaned against the wall for a minute, her lips feeling large on her face. Then she collected herself and stepped back
onto the stoop. Sleep seemed impossible now. She thought about
going down to the pub; she wished everyone hadn't already gone to
bed. She even half wished she'd run into Peg and Jeremy, persuade
them to come along. She could go alone. And maybe would, she
thought.

She started back down the hill she'd just climbed and entered the Lodge through the back kitchen entrance, headed toward the dining room. She'd cross the porch, down the steps to the beach, which she'd follow to Morey's, have a pint, sit on the back deck by herself if it came to that. She wanted that moment back, to do it again and prolong it, extend it, change it somehow so it would come out different. She felt cheated, and sore, as if she had reached for her wallet and realized it was missing, unsure whether she had lost it or someone had fleeced it from her. Just as she reached to slide open one of the glass dining room doors, her eye caught a tiny orange glow, which for a split second relieved her. *There's a bonfire down on the beach,* she thought. *Someplace to go!* Then the image rearranged itself and she stopped and turned quickly. In the armchair in the dark back corner of the room, Lance was smoking a cigarette.

"Hey, gorgeous," she heard him say. His tone was predatory but not menacing.

"Mr. Squire?" Brigid said to the dark corner.

Lance laughed, his head thrown back for a second in exaggeration. *"Mr. Squire,"* he repeated, mocking.

"Sorry," Brigid said.

Lance shook his head. He waved her toward him, but she stood where she was. "No, no, honey," he said. "That's all right." And they both stayed there, not saying anything for a minute.

"I was just on my way . . ." Brigid began.

"Rough night?" he asked.

"Yeah," she said.

"Yeah, me too, baby," he said.

"I'm about gumming for another drink . . ." she said, her voice drifting as she spoke.

"Go-min?" he mocked.

"Oh bleedin' "—she took on a dreadful American accent—"I want a drink," she drawled.

"Yeah?" he said. "Yeah, I almost think I could use a drink myself," he said softly, so sadly she almost felt sorry for him.

"I've some whiskey," she offered.

"Oh . . ." he said, as though relishing the thought, knowing its power, knowing he shouldn't, feeling how much he wanted it. "Oh . . ." he said again.

"Come, have a whiskey with me on the porch, won't you?" she said.

"Oh, honey," he said. "Could I do that?" His voice was different, the harsh tones gone, sadness overtaking.

"Come on," she said. "I'll fetch it. Find us some jars—glasses— find us some glasses, why don't you? And meet me on the porch." She felt compelled to give him some direction, as if he were sitting there asking her, *Please, tell me what to do.*

He seemed grateful, and he struggled to his feet to make his way toward the bar at the far end of the dining room. "A hot redheaded angel," he said, more to himself than to her. "A hot little angel." Brigid went to the office, to Gavin's staff cubby, where they'd stashed the whiskey.

On the deck, Lance took over Gavin's chair from earlier that evening; Brigid reclaimed her own. She tipped whiskey into their glasses. He lifted his gingerly. "Cheers," she suggested. "To better evenings."

"Shit," he said, and clinked her glass. He was a practiced drinker— downed his shot and lifted the bottle, his eyes on her: *OK if I take another?* She gestured: *Be my guest.* He poured and drank again.

"I thought you didn't drink," she said.

"Fuck you." His tone mocked hers. Then he said, "It's been a bad night."

"Cheers," she agreed.

"So what fucked you up tonight, pretty girl?" he asked.

"Whiskey," she said, "and men." She drank.

The night was quiet. Across the sound, pier lights from the mainland wharves and docks reflected on the water. A radio tower blinked. In the water, red and white lighted buoys bounced as the tide lapped and strummed against Sand Beach. A seagull flew in, landed on the porch railing nearby, and pecked at a fallen corn chip.

"And what's it been that fucked with *you* this evening, Mr. Squire?" Brigid said.

Lance laughed again. "*Mrs.* Squire." He took another long drink.

"I expect that's as it's meant to be," Brigid said.

"Hmm." Lance snorted. "Yeah, guess so."

The seagull knocked the chip to the porch, hopped down behind it. *Peck peck peck.*

"Ever been married, beautiful?" he asked suddenly.

She laughed at that. "I'm just nineteen."

Unfazed, he said, "So was I."

"Nineteen? When you were married?"

He nodded. "Lorna was *seven*teen . . . prettiest girl you ever saw."

"Is she still, then?" Brigid asked.

"Sure," he said. "Lorna," he said, as if introducing them.

"I haven't had the pleasure," she told him.

He wrinkled his brow. "You're kind of a bitchy little thing, aren't you?"

"What?" she said. "Why? What've I done?"

"*What, me? Who, me?*"

"And I'd begun to think you weren't such a bollix as they've made you out to be."

"What the fuck's that?"

"*Bollix?* An arsehole," she said.

"Well, you'd be wrong about that," he told her.

"I suppose I would, wouldn't I?" She drank the rest of her whiskey down and reached for the bottle.

"Should I fuck him up a little for you? Your college boy? He's the one you're pissed at? Should I fuck him around some for you?" Lance offered.

"No," she said. "Grand of you to offer, all the same."

"No problem." There was another pause. "You like it when they treat you wrong?" he asked.

Brigid let out a soft snort. "I bloody must, mustn't I?"

Some quiet, sipping.

"What's happened between you and your wife?" she asked.

"Oh, married woes," he said, as though she wouldn't understand.

"I see: you'll *ask* the questions, but you won't stoop to answer them then, will you?"

Lance was flustered, suddenly afraid she might get up and leave. "No no no no no," he said. "No, you got me wrong."

"Oh I do, do I?"

"What do you want to know? I'll tell you. You tell me what you want to know." He waited. "Come on, you ask me. Anything you want to know."

Brigid considered. "Do you cheat on your wife, Mr. Squire?"

Lance paused before answering. "I do not," he told her.

"Hmm," she said.

"What's that mean?"

"That's the truth, is it?"

"Do I look like I'm lying?"

She fixed her stare on him. "You always rather look as though you're lying."

"Nothing new," he said, dejected. "You're nothing new, sweetheart. That's nothing, nothing, nothing new to me in the world."

"Hmm," Brigid said again. "Why's that?"

"Why's what?"

"Why's it you always look as though you're lying?"

"Couldn't tell you." He pouted out his lower lip and shook his head slowly.

"Couldn't or wouldn't?" she asked, but all he did was laugh.

"You wouldn't believe I was telling the truth anyway, would you?"

Now she laughed. "You claim you'll not cheat on your wife," she repeated, a detective taking inventory of the facts. "Yet you look on me as though you surely would . . ." It was not something she'd have said sober, and she knew it. Her ego was talking, nursing bruises.

Lance laughed uncomfortably. "Just wishing . . ."

"Wishing, are you?"

"Wishing," he said, "wishing things were different . . . that everything was different . . ." he trailed off, then snapped back to attention. "You're a nice girl," he told her. "You're a real nice girl."

"I'm not *all* that nice of a girl," she corrected him.

"Oh, you're a nice girl . . . You don't even know how nice of a girl you are."

"If you'd be so kind as to tell that to the fucking college boy . . ."

He raised his glass. "To the fucking college boy."

"To fucking the college boy, cheers," she said, and he laughed, and they clinked and drank.

A car came up the beach road, its headlights cutting the night between water and Lodge. It slowed and turned into the Lodge's driveway. Headlights disappeared, doors slammed. Brigid and Lance looked to the stairs. Peg was herding the kids, who stumbled before her as if they'd been awoken from sleep. When Peg looked up and saw Brigid, she started. Then her gaze fell to Lance and she froze, disapproval washing across her face. "Hel—hello."

Lance's eyes went to Squee, nearly asleep on his feet, and everything about Lance changed. The fuddled man drinking with Brigid on the porch receded, his confusion replaced by anger. He addressed his son. "Where the hell do you think you've been?"

Peg's jaw set firmly. "We've taken the children for an ice cream," she said, a thousand curses held under her tongue, which she'd never speak aloud. Even to Lance Squire.

"Your mother's probably worried sick," Lance accused Squee. He didn't so much as acknowledge Peg's presence. Jeremy stood by ineffectually. Lance said to Squee: "You didn't even think about telling your mother where you were at, now, did you?"

"My mom said it was OK," said Mia, who was standing beside Squee looking spooked, as if she'd had a bad dream and couldn't shake the fear.

Lance fixed his stare on the little girl. "Did I *ask* what your mother said?"

No tears came to Mia's eyes just then, though they were surely only delayed by shock.

"You get home," Lance told Squee. *"Now."*

No one moved. Then Peg spoke, finding her voice before the rest of them. It seemed likely that Jeremy might never speak again. Peg looked to her dumbstruck beau, her tone leveled by fury. "Take Mia to her mother, won't you?" she said. "I'll walk Squee up the hill." And she turned without waiting for Jeremy's response, touched Mia's shoulder by way of good night, pivoted Squee around with her other hand, and led him away from the porch without another word.

There was no one in the cabin when Squee got there. He looked out the window and watched Peg walk away toward the staff house. Then he went to his room, prying off his sneakers and stepping out of them as he walked. They made a little trail to his bedroom door, which he closed firmly and locked. In his clothes, which were dirty and sweaty from a day of work outside, his hands and chin sticky with Chocolate Chocolate Chip, Squee climbed into his unmade bed, pulled the covers over him, and shut his eyes so hard against tears that he succeeded in stopping them from coming at all.

Six

AS FODDER BLAZES
STORED ABOVE THE BYRE

On November 18, 1926, a fire swept through the massive Osprey Lodge and burned the three-hundred-room hotel to the ground. No one was injured, as the Lodge was closed for the season. Reconstruction began optimistically in 1928, but was halted by the stock market crash of 1929. A skeleton of the new hotel stood in half-erected ruin until the great hurricane of '38 wiped it off the map entirely.
—FRANK PERCIVAL, *A History of Osprey Island*

IN 1939, WHEN BUDDY CHIZEK was eleven years old, his father, a tightfisted yet entrepreneurial Texan, happened upon Osprey in the course of some business dealings and saw right away the opportunity to be had. He bought up the site of the old Lodge, the waterfront, beach, and hillside, and built a hundred-room hotel, more modest than its predecessors. Just up the hill, by the tennis courts and swimming pool, Charles Chizek commissioned the construction of a fleet of family cabins, nestled among the oaks and pines. The Depression was over, and he foresaw an America of renewed hope, familial dedication, and newfound appreciation for the simpler things in life: badminton with the children, five o'clock cocktails on the terrace, morning coffee percolating in your very own kitchenette.

Charles's wife, Dolly, was a fussy, irritable, and perniciously charming southern belle who placed herself in command of all matters pertaining to decor, cuisine, and social life, and ruled the Lodge at

Osprey Island like a dictatorial cruise director. As a parent, she was no warmer than Charles, who was himself about as genial as a prawn. The couple's three sons were neither nice nor interesting, nor pleased by their parents' decision to uproot them from sunny Texas and plunk them down on this mildewed penitentiary of an island. They'd have preferred Alcatraz. The two elder boys were put out enough to make sure they were among the first volunteers to head for Europe when the next war broke out. When it came to pass that they were also among the first to die, it was as if they'd done so purely out of spite.

Bud, the youngest son, was somewhat less spiteful than his dead brothers, and he remained alive to help his grieving (yet prospering!) parents run the hotel. Bud was not a man of great energy or ambition and seemed generally to accept the island and the Lodge as his lot in life. Young and healthy, he may have wanted for more intimate companionship than the occasional romp with the capitulating daughter of a hotel guest, or even a seductive chambermaid, but it was not in his nature to seek anything other than that which was set in front of him.

In 1948, when Bud was twenty, the Bright family came to Osprey Island from Indianapolis to open—with common and foolish optimism—a women's apparel shop, and by the time the store, like so many others, failed two years later (there were three months of business a year on Osprey, and when the summer folk left each Labor Day they took the economy with them) Bud had already managed to impregnate and marry the Brights' daughter, Nancy. Her parents folded up their ruined business and moved back to Indiana. By the next year, Bud's father was dead from cancer and Bud and Nancy Chizek took over proprietorship of the Lodge at Osprey Island.

They feared the worst two years later when Hurricane Carol raged up the eastern seaboard and swooped down on Osprey Island as if she'd set her mind to stripping it entirely. The Lodge faced west, somewhat protected by the hill, and fared far better than the rest of the island. Bud lost his dock, half the hotel's front deck, most of the shore-view windows in the Lodge, an aluminum swing set that was lifted and dropped thirty feet downwind, where it lay splayed like an unfurled paper clip until it was removed, and one of the cabins, which was irreparably damaged when a two-hundred-year-old oak uprooted beside it and jacked the structure up as if to catapult it into the bay.

In 1970, a candle left burning in the staff barracks incinerated it to ashes within hours, thankfully without casualties. Nine years later a grease fire in the kitchen closed the restaurant for the last month of the season: unfortunate, and mildly financially crippling, but the fire hadn't spread and the Lodge recovered quickly enough. Though the cabins on the hill had been constructed with every fire-retardant material invented in 1939, Bud feared some stupid renter leaving a clothes iron plugged in and sending the place up in flames, but after fifty years and countless renovations, such a calamity had not yet come to pass.

When Hurricane Gloria threatened the island in 1985 they braced for the worst and were rewarded with clemency: a number of trees lost, but no major damages.

Still, the island had surely known its share of tragedy. Most summers saw a drowning, a boating accident, some careless kid diving into the shallow end of a pool and snapping his neck. There had been the car crash on Ferry Hill that took George Quincy's wife and baby, and a few fishing boat accidents over the years. Your occasional electrocution or fatal tumble down a flight of steep cellar stairs. There were house fires—more in the days of woodstoves and kitchen cooking hearths, though even in modern times houses still went up in flames— with babies and old folks, the pre- and postambulatory, trapped inside, succumbing to smoke. But on that June night in 1988, when Lorna Squire died inside the laundry shack as it burned to the ground around her, it was the first documented human death by fire in the Osprey Lodge's 114-year history.

Later, when the men from the volunteer fire department said that it had just been a matter of time, it took people a minute to realize they meant the laundry shack, not Lorna. "A fire trap," Chief McIntire called it: a rotting wooden structure stuffed crevice to crevice with dry cotton sheets and towels, piles of old newspapers, bottles of highly flammable cleaning chemicals, and aerosol cans just ready to blow. No windows to open, no trapdoor through which to escape. All exits but one closed off and sealed. (They might have fined Bud for keeping a structure so far below the fire codes, but it never came to that. He'd suffered enough.) "Probably a cigarette," said the chief. Bob McIntire also taught third grade at the school and was the track coach and the Boy Scout troop leader and sometimes refereed the varsity and junior varsity football games. "Looks like the origin of the fire was right there on the couch," he said. The couch on which Lorna had fallen asleep. Drunk, they said. The smoke would have gotten her first, they said. She wouldn't have felt anything. There was that, at least. She'd have felt no pain.

Gavin and Jeremy saw the fire first. Jeremy had awakened in the middle of the night to pee, smelled smoke, and thought Gavin must have fallen asleep and dropped his cigarette, probably smoldering in his sheets somewhere, ready to flare. "Gavin," he called, then louder, "Gavin!" as he approached his roommate's bed. Gavin jolted awake, and it was at almost the same moment that they both looked out the window beside Gavin's bed and saw that across the path the laundry shack was quite clearly on fire.

Jeremy began banging on doors the length of the hall, shouting, "Fire! Fire! Everybody wake up! There's a fire!" He moved downstairs, banging and hollering: "Everybody get out! There's a fire!"

Gavin ran outside. The night was oddly still, and it was warm, no breeze at all rising from the shore below. Under the glare of the safety lights he looked at the laundry shack and then to the Squires' cottage next door. It was the only other building nearby. Dashing up the steps, he reached the door in seconds and banged on the screen—the real door wasn't even shut—then went inside, hollering, his voice high and panicky. He ran to an inner door, shouting, pounding. He tried the knob. It gave. "Fire!" he shouted. "There's a fire!" In the room, clothing and crap were piled everywhere—dishes, cups, cracker boxes, Styrofoam to-go containers, lotions and nail polish and all sorts of women's things, towels, packing bubbles, a double bed, empty. Gavin whirled around to the other door and took up pounding. "Fire!" He hammered the flimsy door. "Fire!" Gavin paused, listened, heard nothing, and tried the knob and found it locked. He shouted louder, kicking at the door now to rest his fists. He leveled his kick at the doorknob and let go. There was a splintering sound, but the latch held. Gavin glanced around him. Lying there on its side on the floor was, of all things, a fire extinguisher. He hefted the red cylinder, got his grip, and swung it at the knob, which folded into itself as if made of tinfoil. The door, light as cardboard, swung inward. In the twin bed, still fully dressed, Squee's body was just beginning to twitch awake. His head was tucked under a pillow, which he held around his ears with a grip so insistent it seemed incongruous to sleep. Gavin grabbed the kid by the middle and hoisted Squee over his shoulder— the boy still clasping the pillow to his ears—and carried him through the cabin and down the steps outside to safety.

A few lights had gone on in the Lodge, and Suzy was dashing up the hill barefoot, in a tank top and underwear, clutching Mia as if rushing her to an emergency room in the middle of the night, the girl's skinny legs dangling limply from beneath her oversize T-shirt.

One of the waiters had raced up the hill to get Bud, who came tearing down moments later in a pair of thin pajama trousers and a white V-neck. He held a broad-beam flashlight and was struggling into a bathrobe as he ran.

Bud's wife, Nancy, called the fire department from their house up the hill, then came tripping down toward the motley crowd assembled by the staff barracks. The fire was hot, but contained—it looked as though it was going to take out the laundry shack and leave it at that. Still, the waiters and housekeepers stood before the barracks as if they might somehow shield their new home from danger. Squee was just like the rest of them, staring at the fire, glowing in the firelight.

Nancy clutched her robe about her, scanning the crowd. She saw Squee and stopped. "Where are Lance and Lorna?" she shouted. Then something in her tripped over to the hysterical. Her voice screeched and broke: *"Where are Lance and Lorna?!"*

Bud wheeled around, scolding his wife for her noise. "For god's sake, no one's in the laundry at two a.m.!"

Gavin, who was standing beside Squee, spoke: "I checked their room, their house." He gestured toward the Squires' cabin with his chin. "They weren't there. Just Squee."

Nancy stared at Gavin. "Squee!" she cried. "Where are your parents?!"

Squee shrugged absently, unconcerned. That his mom and dad might be inside hadn't crossed his mind.

"No one's in the laundry in the goddamn middle of the night!" Bud hollered again, and what Squee was realizing was how sad his mom was going to be when she saw what had happened to her laundry shack.

It was the scream of the fire engines that woke Lance from his whiskey sleep on the porch of the Lodge, jolted him awake and sent him running up the hill toward the lights, the people, the scene, his own scream rising as he ran, as though he knew—already knew—that his life was over.

RODDY JACOBS LEFT HIS PLACE behind Eden's house and jumped into his truck at two in the morning to follow the sirens down Sand Beach Road to find out what the hell was going on. Firefighters were stretching hose lines toward the shack when Roddy drove up. A primary search into the laundry shack had been attempted and aborted soon thereafter. It was such a close space, engulfed in flames—impossible to get in, let alone see anything.

Squee saw Roddy's truck and dashed for him as he stepped to the ground, yelling as he ran: "Have you seen my mom? My mom! Do you know where she is?" The initial resolve that there was certainly no one inside the laundry shack had given way to fearful speculation when Lorna Squire could not be found. The one hope they all held but did not say was that maybe Lorna was just drunk somewhere, passed out and too blitzed for even the sirens to wake her. They may have hoped it would turn out that Lorna was off fucking someone's brains out, or curled asleep against some man's tattooed chest on the other side of the island. They hoped the thing they'd be dealing with the next day would be scandal. They hoped they'd be keeping Lance from tearing the guy's throat out, keeping Squee entertained while Lance and Lorna fought and screamed and cried until they hurt each other so badly that they had to make up and make love and forgive each other everything, again.

It was nearly three when Roddy went back to his truck to set out to find Lorna. It seemed a bad idea for Squee to go with him—where would they find her? what would her son have to witness?—but it was beginning to seem a bad idea for Squee to stay at the fire scene, where Lance was being physically restrained by two guys from the volunteer squad after he'd tried to rush the burning shack, scream-ing for Lorna, who he now feared might truly be trapped inside. In the end it was Squee who made the decision when he grabbed on to Roddy's hand and wouldn't let go, which was when Suzy—still clutching Mia to her, though the girl was really just too big to be carried—allied herself with the search party and climbed into Roddy's truck as well.

They drove through the darkness, Mia slumped asleep on Suzy, Squee awake throughout, his eyes wide but trained ahead, as though he could see nothing beyond the windshield. Roddy and Suzy panned the road, their eyes open as if propped. Air blew into the rolled-down truck windows as they drove. All across the island lights were on, people seated at kitchen tables, framed in their picture windows, talk-ing on the phone, peering out as though the laundry shack fire might spread, as though Lorna might come stumbling out of *their* woods, past *their* woodsheds, like some stricken heroine, and they'd give her hot coffee and wrap her in an afghan before getting on the phone to pass along the word that she was fine.

It was almost light when Roddy drove the truck back to the Lodge. The fire was mostly out. The ambulance was there, but its sirens were quiet, flashers off. People no longer stood on the periphery of the scene, but sat on porches or in tight circles on the ground. Some girls hugged each other, crying softly. Most sat stoic, stunned. Lance had been taken away, sedated. He was at Merle's now, his mother tending to him. Doc Zobeck had given something to Nancy Chizek too, for her nerves, and she was sleeping it off at the Chizek house up the hill.

Sheriff Harty approached Roddy's truck. Roddy and Squee climbed out slowly, as if to forestall what was about to happen. Mia was still asleep against Suzy. Squee had Roddy's hand, was pressed as close to the side of Roddy's leg as he could get, eyes big and glassy and cold. Sheriff Harty nodded solemnly to Roddy, then squatted down to Squee's level.

"Squee," the sheriff said, and then he paused, not knowing how to proceed. He took a breath, tried again.

Squee spoke first, his voice controlled. "My mom was in there," he said.

Sheriff Harty let out his breath, nodding slowly. He kept looking right at Squee, right in the eye, as if he needed to see if the boy really understood. Squee said nothing more, but his throat and jaw jerked as if he was biting down on the inside of his cheek. Sheriff Harty looked up from Squee to Roddy, planted his hands on his thighs to push himself up. "You OK?" he said to Roddy as he straightened himself, glancing at Squee—*Can you stay with him? Take care of the boy for right now?*—and Roddy nodded.

"She's gone," the sheriff said, and then his voice caught, as if he was gagging but knew he had to say it. It was his job to say it. "She wouldn't of felt any pain . . ."

Squee kept nodding, his fingernails digging so hard into the flesh of Roddy's palm he'd find cuts later, like tooth marks.

The sheriff turned to go, left Roddy and Squee there, and Suzy leaned from the truck window behind him and spoke his name. "We should go tell your mother," she said.

Roddy lifted Squee from the ground onto his hip. The boy's body was so rigid and light it was like lifting the hollow skeleton of a bird. He put Squee into the cab, then climbed in himself and started the engine.

Eden Jacobs was a stolid, elusive woman who had taken her own husband's death and her son's homecoming the way she took her morning herbs: pennyroyal, sip, swallow; dong quai, sip, swallow; valerian, licorice, skullcap, black cohosh, toss back the head and wash it all down. And, sure, the other Islanders thought it odd that such human dramas should evoke so little response in their own subject, but everyone had known that Eden Jacobs was an odd woman the minute she stepped off the ferry thirty-eight years before, one hand holding a small suitcase, the other enveloped by Roderick Jacobs's massive paw.

Roddy put the truck in park in Eden's driveway but left it running as he went and knocked on the front door like a traveling solicitor. He stood and spoke to his mother from the stoop, turning back to gesture to Squee, Suzy, and Mia in the truck. Eden took the news stoically. Pesticide use on the roadsides, and she mounted an immediate offensive. Death of a woman she'd known since that woman was a baby, and Eden said, "Well, why don't you all come in? I'll make some breakfast. The children must be hungry." Roddy nodded, though he wouldn't likely eat inside himself, and went back to the truck to get Suzy and the kids, who filed across the yard and up the front steps like zombies. Roddy held the door for them. When the others were inside, Eden stood in the doorway. She faced her son. "So this is how it happens in the end."

He pursed his lips, nodding, and followed his mother reluctantly inside.

Eden Jacobs's living room was a tidy clutter of doilied end tables and framed photographs. On the coffee table were a covered glass dish of raw sunflower seeds and a floral saucer filled with cellophane-wrapped sesame candies. There was an old electric organ in one corner that Roderick Senior had inherited from his own mother, which hadn't been played in thirty years. On the far wall, near the bedroom hallway, stood Roderick's gun case, his old hunting rifles racked inside like good china stored away for special occasions against a lining of bronze-colored velveteen. Neither the window curtains nor the baseboards were dusty. Eden Jacobs had been keeping house here for almost forty years.

"Come, I'll put up some coffee," Eden said, and she led Suzy to the kitchen. Suzy glanced back to the kids, who had climbed onto the couch, too stunned and dazed to do anything but sit quietly.

Roddy hovered awkwardly, reluctant to sit down. Eden poured apple juice into two small glasses and carried them to the living room.

"Thank you," said Mia, her voice small.

"Thank you," Squee echoed. His voice was strange as well, unnatural, as though grief had made him, both of them, polite and quiet and scared. Mia held her juice without drinking it. Squee gulped his down in four swallows, without breathing, handed the cup back to Eden, and then turned and vomited into the leaves of the potted spider plant beside the couch. "I'm sorry," he choked out.

"Nothing to be sorry for, sweetheart," Eden said. She handed the boy a color-printed cocktail napkin—a squirrel nibbling acorns—and Squee wiped his mouth. Mia watched, terrified.

"Do you feel better?" Eden asked Squee.

Squee said, "I don't know," and Eden asked if he'd like to use the bathroom. The boy nodded.

"Through the bedroom there, on the left," she directed. "Just do your best to ignore all the old lady stuff. The basic appliances are the same as you'll find anywhere."

Squee nodded again and walked toward Eden's bedroom door.

Eden set the empty glass on the coffee table, bent down, and hefted up the plastic-potted spider plant. "We'll just put you out for some sunshine, huh?" she said into the spindly green leaves. She opened the front door and set the plant down on the stoop as if it were a cat put out for the night. "There you go."

Eden made the coffee and whisked up eggs with milk and cinnamon and vanilla extract and set it to soaking with a few slices of a bread she'd baked the week before, which was going stale. Suzy had gone to use the restroom and came back reporting that Squee was asleep on Eden's bed, his sneakers dangling off the end as if he'd known well enough not to dirty up the bedsheets. Roddy excused himself now that Squee was asleep, retreating from the house that so clearly discomforted him and fleeing for his shed out back. Mia then promptly fell asleep on the couch, the apple juice glass still clutched in her hands, a splotch of it spilled across the belly of her T-shirt. Suzy extracted the glass from her daughter's grip and set it in the sink. She managed to remove the shirt from Mia's body and rinse it out in the bathroom without rousing the girl, who slept beneath a quilt Suzy drew over her.

Suzy choked down a few bites of French toast before Eden said, "Baby, if your stomach doesn't want it, don't force." Suzy sighed gratefully. She sipped at her coffee and pushed the plate of food away. "Should I bring something out to Roddy?" she asked.

"Why don't you." Eden was already preparing a plate. "I do wish he'd talk more," she said, as though she were picking up a conversational thread that had been dangling between the two of them for years. "I worry he keeps it all bottled too close." Eden handed the plate to Suzy. She said, "I'm going to buzz down the hill, see if Art and Penny need anything." They were both quiet a minute, Roddy's French toast steaming the air between them. Eden closed her eyes. "God, to lose a child . . ." She shook her head, then snapped back to. "I don't know how your mother lived through it, Suzanne." She looked at Suzy with disarming frankness. "I never liked your mother particularly, but my heart went out to her. To lose a child, I can think of no more terrible a thing. Art and Penny . . . not that they've been much as parents for the last twenty-odd years, but still . . ." She left off. "I'll just go see if there's something they need."

Suzy took the plate of French toast and went out back toward Roddy's cabin. It was a good fifty yards behind the house, tucked into some oaks perched just before the hill dipped down into a ravine. She passed the picnic table where she'd done shots of something awful on a night twenty years before, which she didn't much like to think about. Three cement blocks served as a stoop to Roddy's shack, and Suzy stood atop them, knocking tentatively, as though she might catch him at something she'd rather not see.

He came to the door, opened it, and stood waiting for her to say something.

She thrust the plate toward him. "Here," she said, "your mom . . ."

"Thanks." He took the toast. "Do you want some coffee?" He gestured to the pot warming on a hot plate on an overturned crate beside the bed.

"I think I want some *whiskey*," she said.

He reached for a bottle on the shelf above the hot plate.

"No, no, no, I think I'm . . . shit, maybe I do." She ran a hand through her hair. "Jesus." She was standing in his one-room house, holding her hair back out of her eyes, slumped like she wanted to crumble to the floor.

Roddy pointed to a chair beside the door. "Why don't you sit down?" he said. "Why don't you have some coffee?"

She sat, as directed. She held her head in her hands, eyes closed tightly behind her palms.

Roddy poured coffee from its tin kettle into a small blue plastic mug and held it out to Suzy, but her head was still down and she didn't see. He stood there, arm outstretched, unnoticed.

"I don't have milk," he apologized.

"I couldn't care less," she said. She was about to cry for the first time since she'd been awakened by the hollering and commotion outside the laundry shack.

"You should get some sleep," Roddy said.

Suzy laughed with resignation and resentment. "I feel insane," she said. "I feel like I am losing my mind. I feel like I want to take Mia and walk down to the ferry and take the first one across and get on a bus and go home and pretend I was never here."

"Yeah," Roddy said. "I know."

"I feel insane," she repeated, as if maybe he hadn't believed her the first time.

"I know," he said again. His desperation was quiet. He looked around the room, his eyes searching frantically, his body moving barely at all. "Do you want to lie down?" He made a gesture toward the camp cot. "Maybe you'd feel better . . ."

"I don't think I *want* to feel better," she cut him off. "I think I want to feel *worse*, like I want to make it so bad that it breaks . . . that it breaks *me* or something and then I don't have to be responsible for what I do or say or don't. Or taking care of Mia or anyone else. Doc Zobeck could just shoot me full of something that'd make all the decisions for me. Jesus. I just want someone to knock me out." Suzy stood suddenly. She looked as if she wanted to pace, but there was no room for it in the little cabin and her momentum stalled once she was upright. It seemed briefly that she might topple. She glanced around, looked to Roddy, flapped her arms awkwardly, then wrapped them around herself as if to contain something, to hold herself back from some downward tumble. Roddy watched her, afraid for what she might do. She hugged herself tightly, her tears finally breaking. "What are we supposed to *do*?"

It wasn't a choice Roddy made then, not something he could say he decided to do and then did. He just moved. Here was Suzy, breaking, and there he was, feet away, moving to her. She held herself tight and small, and he enveloped her, the way his father used to envelop his mother, by his sheer size. He held her, his chin nearly level with the top of her head, and when she looked up at him he kissed her tears, and her eyes, and her cheeks, and everywhere the tears touched, because it was the only thing he could possibly do.

Seven

IN THE SHADOW OF THY WINGS
WILL I MAKE MY REFUGE

*Lorna Marie Vaughn Squire died early Tuesday morning in a tragic
fire at the Osprey Lodge laundry. She was thirty-six years old. The
daughter of Arthur and Penelope Vaughn of Island Drive, Lorna was
a 1970 graduate of Island High. She had been the head housekeeper at
the Osprey Lodge since 1969 and was beloved by all. Lorna is survived by her husband, Lance Squire, 38, and a son, Lance Jr., 8. May
she rest in peace.*

—Island Times

ART VAUGHN WAS INCONSOLABLE. He'd been holding off
mourning the loss of his daughter for more than twenty years,
keeping alive the hope that she'd return to him someday. Now there
was nothing more to put between himself and the pain, between the
fact of the world with Lorna and the fact of the world without her.
There were no maybes, no more possibilities, no more roads that led
his daughter back to him. She was just gone, and Art Vaughn sat on
his living room sofa and cried as he should have cried on Lorna's wedding day.

Art and Penny Vaughn had been unable to conceive. But they had
adopted Lorna in infancy, and Osprey Island was the only home she
ever knew. The Vaughns were cut and dried: they acted according to
the dictates of the Church, ate ground beef, Kraft Singles, and Rice-a-

Roni, and lived in an aluminum-sided ranch house, blue ducks and pink cows stenciled on the walls, wicker baskets of syrupy potpourri and stitched quilt samplers festooning every cranny. Lorna's parents loved her as a streak down the center of their otherwise eventless lives. They distrusted Lance even before they knew him, had always looked down on Merle Squire and the disgraces that defined her. When Lorna met Lance she was not yet thirteen years old—a child!— and Lance's mere existence seemed to grant Lorna all the permission she needed to break into the lawless limbo of adolescence.

On an autumn evening in 1965, Lance had arrived at the Vaughns' nest of faux-country charm to pick up Lorna for their first official date. It was his first and last encounter with Lorna's father.

Lance was formal and officious, standing militarily at ease beside a framed cross-stitch of the Lord's Prayer and answering to the third degree that passed for small talk when it came to some chump from the high school wanting to get into the panties of Art Vaughn's only daughter. Art knew you could never trust a boy. His only hope, as he saw it, was to instill enough fear in the young man's heart so that even if Lorna was ready to put out (as he feared she would), the boy might develop a case of temporary impotence. Art didn't know if he had that kind of power to frighten, but for the sake of his little girl's virginity, he gave it all he had.

"You're Merle's boy," Art said. It was not a question.

"Yes sir." Lance nodded once.

"Your mother's doing well." The pause that followed Art's statements were his only indication of inquisition.

"Hasn't done herself in yet," Lance said.

"Say what?"

Lance shook his head in self-effacement.

"No word from your sister," Art said. But if there'd been news from Kiki, everyone on Osprey would have heard it within hours. Art knew that. He'd heard talk about the Squires. Rumors about Merle finding the girl in Lance's bed. Others said it was Lance in hers. And maybe all those were exaggerations. Maybe nothing like that had ever happened at all. But rumors started somewhere, suggested something of the truth that spawned them.

"No one's heard from Kiki since summer," Lance said, his eyes narrow as paper cuts.

Art lifted his wrist and looked at his watch as if it could tell him just how long she'd been gone and when she might be expected to turn up. "She'll come 'round," Art told Lance.

"She might," Lance said.

"What kind of prayer is that, son?"

"Not a prayer, Mr. Vaughn." Lance paused. His tone shifted darkly. "And I'm nobody's son except my mother's, sir."

Art Vaughn blanched.

"Unless," Lance went on, his voice slow and controlled, "unless you *are* my father. Which would make you a real sonofabitch."

Art drew in his breath. "I beg your pardon," he hissed.

Lance laughed, low and mean. He still held his hands behind his back. His feet were spread in a stance so vulnerable it was menacing, a stance that said, *You threaten me so little I'd roll over on my back and bare my belly, you prick.* "You don't beg a thing from me, Mr. Vaughn. And I know you don't give two shits for pardon, mine or anyone else's."

Art sucked in his gut. He reached for the front doorknob. "You better pray you've got the *Lord's* pardon, boy. For *that* you better pray." He opened the door, and Lance never set foot in the Vaughns' house again.

Lorna, as a matter of course, was forbidden to see Lance Squire under penalty of every penalty that her parents (who were not creative people) could dream up. Perhaps equally predictable was how little these threats affected Lorna. She disobeyed every order laid upon her, and in the end it was more than clear who held the trump card in that family. What Lorna had on her parents was that they loved her a lot more—or at least in a qualitatively different way—than she loved them, and they forgave her every time, pulled her back into the fold, because they wanted her with them more than they wanted her justly punished. Lorna learned this lesson early: the less you cared, the more power you possessed. And it was maybe just that which kept her with Lance for so long. For everything you could say about Lance and Lorna—and there was certainly plenty to say—one true thing was that their love existed in a balance few people ever know. For everything they did wrong—and that was almost everything—there was something fundamentally right about the fact of them together.

In 1968 most of Lance's high school buddies were breathlessly awaiting their eighteenth birthdays and the chance to go fight in Vietnam, but Lance, who'd had a childhood bout of measles that stole a good fraction of his hearing, didn't go anywhere after graduation. He kept his job at Lovetsky's car shop, rotating tires and patching flats, and Lorna stayed in school. She was no honors student, but she stuck it out, even after she got pregnant in the spring of her junior year and married that June in a big Island to-do held at the Lodge. The party was an uncharacteristically generous wedding present from Bud Chizek, although anyone would tell you he'd been acting strange—if understandably so—ever since Chas (his only son) had gotten killed in Vietnam six months before. But Bud didn't only host Lance and Lorna's wedding celebration—he invited the newlyweds to come live at the Lodge as heads of maintenance and housekeeping. Lance didn't know why the tragedy of Chas's death would prompt Bud to do such a thing, but he didn't question a gift horse, at least not until he'd accepted the gift.

Art and Penny Vaughn were invited to the wedding out of cordiality, but they stayed home. That Lorna was pregnant surprised no one, least of all the Vaughns, who could have predicted it, despite higher hopes. And when Lorna lost the baby later that summer, it was no longer *necessary* that such a pretty seventeen-year-old girl be married to the island ne'er-do-well, but it was too late to take it all back. It was 1969, and Lance and Lorna were already well along on the path they'd follow to the end.

. . .

In the immediate aftermath of their daughter's death, Penny was coping far better than her husband. She was eerily composed and ministering to Art when Eden knocked on their door that morning.

"Eden. Come in." Penny stepped aside to let her pass.

"Oh, Penny," Eden sighed, her tone meant to impart a world of sympathy. "Oh dear, no. I won't bother you now. I only came to see if there's anything you needed, anything I can do . . . Have you eaten? Can I bring you something? Something for Art?"

"Eden, you're a dear. So thoughtful. I think we're OK. Trying to stay busy, you know. Making up the guest room for Squee . . . Lord knows Lance can't be caring for the boy now on his own."

Eden nodded. "I have him at the house—Squee. He's asleep—they were up all night. I guess we all were . . ."

Penny absently lifted her hand to her ear in the gesture of a telephone. "You just give a call when he wakes up and I'll swing by for him . . ."

"Oh, I'll run him down to you," Eden cut in. She waved off toward her car. "Goodness, of course I'll bring him down to you." For the degree of emotion in their exchange, Penny and Eden might have been discussing carpooling to Wednesday-night bingo at the VFW. This was hardly unusual for Eden, well known for her disturbingly placid reactions to events that sent others careening. Penny Vaughn, on the other hand, was a woman who regularly wept during her weekday television "stories" and was known to carry a purse-pack of Kleenex for when she teared up during a particularly moving Sunday service. But there she was, at the dawn of the most dreaded tragedy of her life, puttering about like a chickadee. Penny Vaughn was perched at a very precarious place; whenever she finally fell, it seemed clear she would fall hard.

"You sure there's nothing I can do . . . get . . . for you?" Eden asked again.

Penny shook her head primly. "Just my sweet grandson," she

clucked. This was odder still, in that Art and Penny had never spent much time with Squee at all, had never been particularly interested in Lance Squire's progeny. Lorna and Lance had certainly spoken poorly enough of Lorna's folks to color Squee's opinion of his grandparents. Some Sundays Art and Penny asked to bring Squee with them to church, to which the Squires occasionally conceded, reluctantly. Art and Penny seemed less concerned for the actual *person* who was Squee than for the *soul* they believed to be housed therein, which they felt obliged to look out for. If they could have taken *that* to church with them and left the ragamuffin back at the Lodge, playing in the dirt outside his parents' ill-kept home, they would quite surely have packed the Squee-specter into Penny's pocketbook alongside the tissues and smuggled it into the service for some necessary deep-cleansing.

Eden took a detour by the Lodge on her way back home to stop in at the Squires' cabin and pick up some things for Squee. She parked as close as she could get to the cottage and walked past the firemen and police still on the scene, past the charred remains of what had been the laundry shack.

"Hey, Eden," the sheriff called out as she passed. As if it were any ordinary day.

She waved. "Just picking up some clothes for the boy," she said. The sheriff waved her along.

Inside, in the room that had to be Squee's, there was a chest of drawers, but everything seemed to have exploded out of it onto the floor. Eden would have collected some clothes in a pillowcase, but there didn't even appear to be a pillow. The bed was covered in a stained mattress pad but nothing else. A Star Wars sleeping bag lay in a slump on the floor. She found a trash bag in the kitchen and threw in an assortment of T-shirts, shorts, underwear, and socks, all of which she'd have to wash when she got home.

On her way back up the hill, Eden passed Roddy in his truck. They paused, idling in the road, leaning out their windows to talk.

"I'm going to see what I can do down there," Roddy said. "Find Bud . . . see . . ."

Eden nodded. "You're a good boy, Roddy."

Roddy closed his eyes and shook his head. "Oh, Ma," he said, as though it pained him. "Oh, Ma."

Back at Eden's, Suzy and the children were half awake on the living room couch, blindly watching a television screen they could hardly see in the glaring midday sun. Mia was now wearing a T-shirt of Roddy's that came down past her knees. Eden loaded Squee's clothing into the washer, then busied herself baking a lentil loaf and an apple brown Betty for Penny and Art. She prepared peanut butter sandwiches for lunch and got Squee to eat a few bites, though he did so mechanically and seemingly without hunger. Squee was operating robotically, but his lack of animation almost seemed a blessing. He seemed dampened, his reactions to the world dulled. Against everything Eden believed, she allowed the kids to sit dumbly in front of the television all afternoon. Even Eden understood the necessity of mindlessness on some occasions.

When Suzy began to ready herself and Mia to return to the Lodge that evening, Squee wanted to go back with them. "Is Roddy there?" he asked. "I need to go help Roddy." It was more vitality than he'd exhibited all day.

Suzy knelt down beside him. "Squee, babe," she said, "you're going to keep helping Roddy just like you have been, but what'll help him the most right now is if you go and stay for a little bit with your Grandpa Art and Grandma Penny. They've got a room all ready for you, and they're really going to need you with them now." Suzy's voice was teacherly and terrible.

Squee's face was, for the first time that Suzy had seen, set in a child's angry stubbornness. "I have to go to Grandma and Grandpa *Vaughn's?*" he whined.

"Yeah, babe, for a little bit, you do . . ."

Squee looked weary and drained. He said, "Grandma and Grandpa Vaughn suck."

It was all Suzy could do to keep from bursting into laughter. Her struggle seemed to please Squee, who brightened some. Suzy said, "That's exactly what I used to say when I had to go visit my Grandma Dolly."

Squee didn't speak, just looked to Suzy as if he wanted more.

"It's just for a little bit, Squee. Just until your dad's back from Grandma Merle's . . ." she trailed off. It was a prospect that didn't make anyone feel any better at all.

THE LODGE WAS OVERLY QUIET. You might have suspected hubbub, but there was none. It was quiet as a funeral, small groups of people huddled in corners, processing the events. Everyone had a version to tell: how they'd heard, where they'd been, what they'd thought at first, how that had changed. Sheriff Harty and Deputy Davey Mitchell spoke to the employees a few at a time. As some of the last people to hear, if not see, Lorna Squire alive the previous night, Peg and Jeremy were questioned together, their responses taken and recorded with great enthusiasm on the part of the deputy who didn't often get to do much but look stern and holler at kids he caught climbing the yacht club fence for late-night swims.

No foul play was suspected—what was foul about it? A very sad, very, very drunk woman who's just had a fight with her husband passes out on the couch, a lit cigarette in her fingers . . . What more was there to say? She left no note. No intimation of suicide. But whose mind didn't it cross? It wasn't hard at all for anyone to picture Lorna Squire doing herself in. They'd watched her take her own life, day by day, for years. They wondered what would happen to Squee, what would happen to Lance, but people had wondered all of those things when Lorna was alive. She'd always been dying; now she was dead.

. . .

In the wake of the fire Gavin found himself overcome by a sense of protectiveness that made him envy his roommate, Jeremy. He wanted someone in his arms the way gawky, pimpled Jeremy cradled Peg in his, and though Brigid wasn't exactly what he wanted, she was also clearly not unwilling to have him nearby.

None of this was what Gavin had expected. He'd been prepared for a summer of long walks with Heather, his Stanford girlfriend, on the beaches of her childhood, which she'd so languorously described to Gavin as they lay pinned to each other in his dorm bed back at school. It was meant to be a dream summer. She'd told him about the hotel, straight out of *Dirty Dancing,* she'd said. And he'd pictured the two of them, like Patrick Swayze and Jennifer Grey, only reversed, kind of, since he was the one from the upper-middle-class family in LA, she the island girl he loved. Gavin liked that about himself, that of all people to fall in love with, he'd tumbled not for a Palo Alto sorority girl or a politician's daughter from D.C., but for a girl from the other side of the proverbial tracks. His parents had liked Heather, thought her, as he had, smart and sensible, someone who valued a good education but also held onto dreams of a family and a quiet life, dreams Gavin had felt himself latch on to, perhaps for lack of real, tangible dreams of his own. But his parents had certainly not understood their son's desire to go off and serve prime rib dinners to the East Coast vacation set rather than lead wilderness trips in the Sierras or scramble for some prestigious summer internship in San Francisco. Gavin had been proud of his decision. Also, he liked the notion of following a woman, not a career, liked thinking of himself not as a doer but as a lover.

When Heather had announced her intention to return home to Osprey Island for the summer, Gavin had felt gallant in offering to accompany her. She'd protested, albeit meekly, saying no, that was crazy, what was he going to do, wait tables at the Lodge? *For real?* And he liked the picture he'd painted himself into: he was the boy who loved her and wanted to get to know her family. There was even a part of him that wanted to fall in love with that island, to step off the clanking old ferry Heather'd described and into a place that would feel more like home than home had ever felt. Heather was to be his entrance into another world. They'd finish their degrees and move back to Osprey, have an island wedding at the old golf house on the hill. Maybe secretly Heather'd already be pregnant, and they'd move into an A-frame overlooking the sound and start their own family. They'd make their living restoring old houses and selling them to wealthy New Yorkers looking for vacation homes. Or they'd open a restaurant, work like hell from Memorial Day to Labor Day and have the rest of the year to themselves. Gavin had allowed himself these dreams.

He felt now—given the circumstances which had arisen since his arrival—that Heather hadn't protested his coming to Osprey quite as much as she should have. It was possible, he conceded, that she *had* protested vehemently and he'd merely taken it as her thoughtfulness for his other prospects, his welfare. Now all that thrummed through his mind were imagined conversations he invented between Heather and her high school boyfriend, Chandler—late-night phone calls in April and May between Heather's dorm room and Chandler's parents' home on Osprey. Heather complaining about the boy from LA who wouldn't take no for an answer, Chandler saying, *You got to tell him no.* And Heather whining, *I tried.* And Chandler saying, *Not hard enough.*

From the Lodge deck Gavin could see a redhead sitting down on the beach. Beyond her, just offshore, the seagulls swooped and rose from the water like lazy yo-yos. To the right was Morey's Dinghy, tucked where the sandy beach gave way to reedy swamp. To the left Sand Beach Road extended a good mile along the shore. Gavin crossed and made his way along the narrow, splintering boardwalk that ran between the asphalt and the sand. The whitewashed railing left a chalky residue on his hand, and he wiped it on his jeans as he tromped over the sand toward Brigid. She had on gym shorts and a striped bikini top. She was reading a fashion magazine.

"Looking to catch a little skin cancer?" he called, approaching.

She turned, shielded her eyes from the sun, and leveled her gaze at him soberly. "I think they've determined it's not contagious."

He hovered. "Still, you're pretty pale to be lounging out, aren't you?"

"Ah!" She clasped her hands at her heart. "Look at him! He cares!"

Gavin sat down in the sand beside her towel, legs bent out in front of him, hands on his knees. He looked over the bay. "How you doing?"

"Such attention! Hardly know what to do with myself."

"You want me to go?" Gavin offered.

Brigid fixed him in her stare. "Now, what do you think?"

Gavin gave her a conciliatory smile but said nothing. They looked out at the water. After a minute Brigid said, "Not so bad, considering." Then she said, "How are you, then?"

"OK," he said. A pause. "You going out tonight?"

Brigid shrugged noncommittally: *Make me an offer.*

"You think it's wrong to go out?" Gavin asked.

"Fuck if I know."

"Yeah . . ."

"I never so much as laid eyes on the woman," Brigid said.

"Yeah," Gavin said, "but everyone who's from here knew her." He thought for a moment. "I wonder if they'll even open the bar. I mean, it's a pretty damn small town."

"Pub or not," Brigid said, "I'll be fucking gumming for a pint by evening."

"That worry you ever?" Gavin said, half-teasing. "That nationalistic need for beer?"

"About as much as your nationalistic need for cheeseburgers worries you, I'd say."

"Touché." Gavin smiled.

Brigid faced him then and nodded once. She was taking note of his challenge, registering it; he'd set out the ante and she'd met it. She didn't raise him. She was waiting. Exercising some caution, for once.

"How are we on whiskey?" he asked.

She looked startled for a moment. "Out entirely," she said, regaining composure. "Polished it off last night, Mr. Squire and myself, in fact."

"Oh?" he said. "Oh, *really?*"

"He's not such a bleedin' maggot as everyone thinks . . ."

Gavin looked surprised. And skeptical.

"I mean, he's desperate sad . . ."

"And losing your wife doesn't make that any easier." Gavin shook his head, as if he had a clue what Lance was going through.

"He's just full of wind and—"

"Maybe . . ."

"I just think he's maybe not so up entirely brutal as all that." It was hard to condemn a thirty-eight-year-old widower, especially one who, it seemed, had garnered nothing but condemnation for much of his life. It was even harder when considering Squee, because you wanted to think that somehow Lance might be able to be a good father to the kid. You wanted to hope, however far-fetched that hope might be.

"Getting sweet on old Lance, now?" Gavin teased.

"Course I am," Brigid growled. "I just love a man in mourning."

"Jesus!" he said.

Brigid sighed. "I've not rapid endeared myself to you now, have I?"

Gavin laughed a little. "You're not exactly *delicate,*" he allowed. "I think you take some getting used to." He thought for a second. "You're not so easy to figure out."

"*I'm* not bloody easy!" she balked. "It's not been *me* shoving people up against the wall and kissing them and then tearing off like a bleedin'—"

"I'm sorry . . ."

"Oh, you are, are you? Sorry for kissing me, or sorry for tearing off—"

"Wait a second," he said, his voice silencing hers. "Wait. Look: I'm sorry. I just . . . Look, I'm just really confused these days. I'm not really sure what I want, OK? I'm just—"

Brigid cut him off defiantly. "Well, put some manners on yourself then, but don't be—"

"I'm sorry," he said again.

"Shut your gob with 'sorry' already!"

"Jesus—why are you *so* antagonistic with me? What did I ever do to you?"

"You haven't done a thing, aside from shoving your tongue down my throat, which I quite enjoyed, so I won't go on about it . . . Only you've pissed me off—"

"Look," he interrupted her. "Look, can we just start over? Please? OK? Can we just start over from the beginning? Wipe the slate clean? Try this again?" His eyes entreated her; his hands were open in offering.

She let out a breath, an ironic laugh. She shook her head and, rolling her eyes, brushed the sand from her hand and held it out to him. "Brigid," she said.

"Hi, Brigid, I'm Gavin," he said, shaking her hand. "Really nice to meet you . . . So where're you from, Brigid?"

"Bloody Americans." Brigid snorted. "So bleedin' friendly, the lot of you!"

⁓

WHEN IT WAS TIME to leave for Penny and Art's, Squee ran and hid down in the ravine behind Eden's house. Eden hollered his name into the twilight for half an hour, pleading, cajoling, begging, before she threatened to go get Roddy, who she was sure would be none too pleased with Squee for acting so irresponsibly at a time like this.

Squee emerged, somber and reluctant, from the woods. "Don't tell Roddy, OK?" he asked, and that was the last thing he said as Eden handed him a small old suitcase of Roderick's packed with his washed and neatly folded clothes, and they drove down the hill to his grandparents' house. Art had already gone to bed, but Penny greeted them at the door with a grandmotherly flourish and welcomed Squee inside like some sort of delicious prey. Eden stroked the boy's hair as he stood beside her and paused a moment, her hand upon his head as though she were saying a prayer, before she bade them good night and made her way back to the car alone.

Eight

THE MECHANICS OF FLIGHT

To fly
Is to come toward
And
To go away from

—WILLIAM MOSLEY LANDIS,
self-appointed poet laureate of
Osprey Island, "The Osprey"

THERE WAS A KNOCK AT THE DOOR of Suzy and Mia's room after dinner that evening, and Suzy leapt to answer it. If she was disappointed to discover that it was not Roddy, her surprise at seeing her father in the doorway certainly masked any other emotion. Suzy started, then regained herself and put up a hand to shush Bud as she slipped into the hall with him and took pains to close the door quietly behind her. "Mia's finally asleep," she explained.

Bud nodded. His eyes were trained down. He looked almost humble, and humility was not something to which Suzy was even remotely accustomed in her father. "I've got to ask you . . ." he began, then fixed his eyes on her and spoke quickly, with urgent purpose. "I need you to take over for Lorna. I'll try to find someone, but until then . . ." He stared, waiting for a one-word answer he might snatch from her like a relay baton.

"You want—?" Suzy screwed up her face. This was something she sensed she didn't want to hear.

"You're the only one who knows the Lodge. How things work. I'll pay you, of course."

Suzy's lips pursed defiantly. "This is your way of *asking*?"

Bud regarded his daughter blankly.

"Would *please* be *so* difficult?"

She exhausted him. Bud made a gesture as if to say, *I concede to you, take anything you want from me, take everything, take it all! If "please" is what you require, then I give you "please."* He never said the word aloud.

"Fine," Suzy said. "Fine. Whatever. Until you find someone."

Bud sighed, eyes closed, shaking his head. "It's going to be a hell of a time."

"Yeah, well, for all of us."

Bud nodded. He turned to go.

"You're welcome," Suzy called after him, the way she did with her first-graders.

He turned back around mid-stride, gave a cursory half nod, and continued down the hall.

Bud called a staff meeting in the dining room that evening. Nancy was back up at the house, still sleeping off the tranquilizers Doc Zobeck had pumped her full of that morning. The Lodge felt as it had the day they'd gotten word of Chas's death in Vietnam. It had been Doc Zobeck back then too who'd given Nancy her fill of Valium, just to get her past the screaming, past the part when they were afraid she'd truly lose her mind. Bud hadn't known what to do with himself that terrible day. He was the owner of a large hotel, always a thousand things to do. Except that day, when he couldn't think of one. He was of no comfort to his wife, who howled like a dully stabbed beast; he could not even conceive of going to his daughter, who was sixteen and terrified him for that reason alone. Bud's memory had blurred and distorted that time just after Chas's death. Nothing had felt real. And it was dangerous, Bud knew, what a person might do if what was real didn't feel real. Some time down the road, what was real would come back, and when it did the chances were good that it'd slam him so hard he wouldn't have a choice but to feel the pain.

What Bud felt now wasn't pain; it was more gnawing ache. There was fear, and along with it an uncomfortable lurking sense of being swindled. All these years finally culminating in Lorna's greatest revenge. But revenge for what? Hadn't he been good to Lorna and Lance? Hadn't he kept them on at the hotel years after any normal person would have fired them for being drunks and freeloaders and not one ounce of help at all? Hadn't he spent years defending that charity to his wife? Bud had long felt a certain responsibility for Lorna, and he'd taken care of them all those years, and what was her final thank-you? To load herself up and pass out and nearly burn the whole place down? It was a move that would surely hurt him, if not close the whole goddamn place down before the end of the season if he wasn't careful. Bud had no choice but to be extraordinarily careful.

The staff was gathering in the dining room, in chairs and on the floor. Already the alliances were forming, the summer romances, hands grazing the backs of necks, the ever-insistent touch: *I am here.* Bud had seen it so many times before, those summer loves, so few of which would last, so few of which would make it as far as Labor Day, most of which were nothing more than summer sex. But it kept the staff happy, their furtive trysting in the bushes, and that's what Bud was about, wasn't it? Keeping everybody happy? His life, his livelihood—ironic as it may have been—was about keeping people happy. And keeping people happy, Bud had learned, was about keeping them from seeing what they didn't want to see. They came for a vacation: a dream, a refuge, an escape. And if it didn't turn out quite exactly as edenic and impervious as they'd dreamed, they didn't want to know. *Death is everywhere,* they might concede, *but for god's sake, don't point it out on the sightseeing tour!*

Bud addressed his staff: "Thank you all for coming down this evening." Bloodshot eyes fixed him with spongy stares. "It's been a difficult day," he said, "a very, very difficult day for us all.

"This hotel—this *island*—will not be the same without Lorna Squire, and we need to support each other and Lorna's family during this time. We have a big season coming up, and it'll probably do us more good than we know to put a face on and face the guests. Help us get through our own grief . . ." He looked around at his audience. The Irish girls all looked the same to him, every summer. In the far corner stood Roddy Jacobs. Leaning in an archway near Roddy, Suzy was staring Bud down, her face critical, waiting to hear what he would say, waiting, as usual, to hear what he would say wrong. And in her view, Bud knew, that would be everything.

"I know," Bud went on, "that no one here's much in a holiday spirit right now. Lots of sadness." He fumbled for a lead-in. "But our guests are going to be here on vacation, they're coming to enjoy themselves. Fourth of July weekend we're booked full. It's important for our guests to enjoy themselves, and it's also important that we set a tone for the rest of the season to come. Show our guests what kind of an establishment we run here, and send them home with great memories to tell their friends about the Lodge at Osprey Island." This part of Bud's speech was canned. He'd given it so many times. "Fourth of July weekend is important for us: we do well on opening weekend, we do well for the season." Bud paused. He looked around. "Already . . ." He didn't know how to go on. "Already this . . . accident . . . is going to make things difficult for us here, as a business. We've got a lot to overcome." He spoke quickly now. He spoke to the floor. "In proper honor, of Mrs. Squire, we'll cancel our Fourth of July celebration— bus the guests over to Wickham Beach for the fireworks there. For those of us who knew Lorna, this will not be a time for celebration. But our guests, they didn't know Mrs. Squire. This is their vacation, and they don't want our worries laid on top of what they already got. Not while they're on vacation."

Bud was in business mode: The maintenance shop off the rear parking lot would become the new home of the laundry facilities—

equipment would be arriving the next day; he'd made the necessary arrangements with great speed and efficiency—and a new maintenance building would go up on the site of the old laundry shed. A demolition crew would begin in the morning, construction immediately following, and everything would be finished—*We'll cross our fingers,* Bud said—in the next week and a half before the guests started showing up.

One of the Irish girls raised her palm in the air like a schoolchild. Bud looked at her uncertainly. She took his stare as a sign to speak.

"What should we do when people—guests—when they ask about it?" Her voice was riding as though she might quake and dissolve into tears. "What should we tell them?" She was whining now. "What exactly should we say?" She slumped back then, deflated.

"Well," Bud began, "I think we say as little as possible. I think if anyone asks, you send them to me so I can tell them what's going on and we don't have to get into a game of telephone, with wrong stories, exaggerating . . ."

"What do you mean?" someone asked.

"I mean," Bud said sternly, "anything other than the plain truth: there was a fire in the laundry room late last night, a fire started by a cigarette when Lorna Squire, our head housekeeper, was smoking and fell asleep. The laundry burned down. Lorna died in the fire. That's the real story. That's the story I will tell our guests if they ask." He was almost pleased by it, pleased at how a story like that could work like a campaign: Don't Smoke in Bed. "And please," he added, "please just don't be discussing all this—these events—around the Lodge, around the guests. Of course, they'll find out. I'm sure we couldn't keep that from happening. But we can keep it simple. Keep things clean. Keep it from bothering them the way it'll be bothering us."

From the archway, Suzy piped up, acting as though Bud himself had finally succeeded in doing Lorna in after all these years. "Don't you think it might be a little more honest, Dad, a little more up-front, if we just came out and told them? Made up a letter, one for each room, just letting people know what happened. Explaining how sad we are, explaining there won't be fireworks here at the Lodge, just to let them know . . ."

"No," Bud said, "no, I *don't* think that's best. The more we play this thing down, the—"

"Someone is dead! You think we should play that down?"

"I do not think we need to point our fingers at it," he said briskly.

Suzy was gearing up for a fight. Bud looked as if he might try to send her to her room.

"I think that's a serious mistake on your part, Dad. I think you're making a grave error in judgment."

Bud was in no mood. "Well, when *you* own a hotel"—and he did not say "*this* hotel," did not concede even that much—"when you own your own hotel, you can do things however the hell you want . . . But seeing as I've got just a few years' more experience, this is my decision to make."

In the dining room the staff squirmed. Bud and Suzy glared, each daring the other to speak. Suzy broke off first—turned in the doorway and strode from the room as though in undisputed possession of the upper hand. She never failed to leave her father boiling.

When the meeting adjourned, the staff retreated to the porch, and Morey's, and the barracks. Bud was talking to Roddy Jacobs when Suzy reentered the dining room. She came at Bud like she meant to strangle him. Roddy stepped clear for her to do just that, if she so intended. He had his own hands behind his back to keep himself from reaching out and strangling Bud of his own accord. Bud stepped back, cornered.

"I think you're wrong, Dad. I think you're making a really bad call here," Suzy said.

"Oh, really?" Bud countered. "You sure didn't make that clear."

"I shouldn't have . . ." Suzy conceded: if there was anything she had learned in childhood it was that conflicts took place out of the public eye—or, preferably, not at all. Bud did not like to be questioned; when Suzy learned to ask *why,* she had ceased to be someone he could relate to, or even tolerate.

Suzy plowed on. "I really think you *absolutely* need to let the guests know ahead of time what's gone on here. I can't even believe Mom isn't insisting on that already—"

He cut her off: "Your mother and I made this decision together."

"Oh, now that's just bullshit! Don't even try to . . . Mom's been knocked out all day. Don't treat me . . . Jesus!" She stuck one hand on her hip, pushed the other through her hair and held it back from her eyes as she peered at him, lifting that final curtain of illusion about just what sort of man her father might be. She let the hair fall. The hand went to her other hip. "You have to tell them. You'd be an idiot not to tell them. If you tell them—a simple, discreet note in each of the rooms—then you present it to them exactly the way you want, exactly the way you want them to hear it. You have control over the information then." It was like explaining combat theory to a wary recruit. "If you leave it ambiguous"—she said this as though her father might not know the word: *am-big-u-ous*—"then you're chancing what they find out, how they find out—you're risking all the rumor that might find its way in along the way. I can't even *fathom* why you'd take a chance like that."

It was entirely the wrong tactic. "I think, Suzy, there are a lot of things about this situation that you don't *fathom* at all."

"Oh, don't give me that shit when—"

"That's it, right now. I don't want to hear any more. This conversation is over."

Bud stood for a moment, staring down his daughter, then turned to Roddy, a few feet off, as though it were Roddy he'd just been chatting with all the while, and said, "I'll be up at the house with my wife if anyone needs me," and then he turned and walked away.

Roddy and Suzy just stood there in Bud's wake, waiting for him to clear the threshold, for the slam of the kitchen door marking his exit. They stood a moment longer as the room settled, and looked around as though remembering the shape of the place, the smell of sea air and furniture polish.

Suzy let out a breath. "I need a drink."

Roddy laughed before he could catch himself, before he thought to wonder if it was OK to laugh. Suzy stared, disbelieving, her mouth open slightly. "Should I make you one too, or are you just going to stand there mocking me?"

"Oh," said Roddy. "I got it." He went toward the bar as if to beat her to it. "What do you want? What can I make you?"

She flung up her hands.

"OK," he said slowly. "Anything you're particularly in the mood for?"

"Jesus!" She laughed. "Just hand me a bottle."

And he was able to laugh too. He grabbed a bottle. Lorna was dead. Bud was an asshole. And Roddy Jacobs and Suzy Chizek were about to share a bottle of Maker's Mark in the dining room of the Lodge at Osprey Island.

"Did you want some peanuts or anything?" he asked.

She gaped. "You are really one of the oddest people I think I have ever met." His expression sank. "I'm sorry," she said. "I'm sorry." A pause. "I'm sorry."

"That's OK. Not like I haven't heard that before." He came toward the table she'd chosen, the bottle of Maker's under his arm and a glass in either hand. He went to pour, and his grip was visibly shaky. Suzy laughed again. "You need a drink more than I do."

"You're right."

She took the bottle, poured both glasses, passed one to him, and they drank. The large room was strangely still: a fleet of empty tables, a few sconces glowing dimly along the far wall. Outside, through the panoramic sliding glass doors, the lights across the bay in Menhadenport were beginning to go on as the sky pitched from blue to black. Suzy took a sip from her glass, then set the drink down decisively. "You *kissed* me this morning."

Roddy sucked his lips. He was nodding continuously, almost rocking. "I guess I did."

She waited for more. They drank.

"Is that . . ."—she pawed for words—"is it something I should be on the lookout for . . . something I should be warned you might do again?"

He rocked. He didn't answer.

She sent a quick push of air through her nostrils. A minute passed. "What exactly are we doing here?" she said.

"Having a drink."

"Why?"

He waited. "Because you said you wanted one . . . ?"

"Why'd you stay away so long?" she asked him suddenly.

He bristled. "I don't really want to talk about that, OK?"

She felt a little cowed and covered it with brassiness. "Why'd you come back, then?"

He looked at her. "It's home . . ."

"Not *my* home," Suzy said.

"You can *say* that."

"You don't know me," she said, her tone meaner than she'd intended.

"You're right." He stood up. "I don't." He pushed in his chair. "Sorry to bother you." He turned away.

"Wait," Suzy said. "Wait!" Her voice got louder. "Please . . ."

Roddy stopped and faced her again. "What?" It came out sounding like, *What more do you want from me?*

"Come back." Her voice was gentle, but awkward. "Stay. It's not the kind of night to be alone."

Roddy snorted a laugh. "You mean, *you* don't want to be alone."

"I *don't*," she agreed.

He nodded once. "Yeah. I'm not some guy to fill in the time for you. Sorry." He turned again and went out the sliding door.

Suzy stared for a minute. Then she got up and went after him.

Suzy found Roddy sitting in his truck in the north parking lot. The keys were in the ignition, but he hadn't turned the engine over, was just sitting there, hand at the starter, one leg bouncing like crazy, his body hunched forward as if he were driving in a snowstorm, struggling to see the road ahead. The windows were open. Suzy knocked on the passenger door, then opened it and climbed in. "What the hell is going on?"

His leg stopped for a few seconds as he paused to look at her, then resumed as he spoke. "OK, let's not even do this." He tried to hurry the words out of himself and will them far away. "No one kissed anyone, OK? I can't be thinking about that, all right? Lorna's dead. We've got to build the new laundry. Guests might as well start arriving in ten minutes for how ready we'll be. I don't know what the fuck's going to happen to Squee. To fucking Lance. The poor pathetic bastard. What the fuck is going to happen to Lance?" Roddy's voice was breaking.

Suzy stared down at her hands in her lap. She said, "I don't know." Then she lifted her head, unclasped her hands, and turned on the seat to face Roddy, who was still staring straight ahead, navigating that imaginary dark and winding road.

She slid over, took his head in both her hands, turned his face to hers and kissed his mouth. She pulled back, looked in his eyes, then did it again.

He pulled away. "We're in the *parking* lot . . ."

Suzy's hands slumped to her lap. "I'm sorry." She reached for the door. "Good night."

Roddy sat alone in the truck for a long minute before he turned the keys in the ignition and drove home.

On the porch of the Lodge, the staff members were drinking as usual. Suzy nodded as she passed, a sad, acknowledging smile. Jeremy raised a hand. He was sitting on the deck, close with Peg, their backs propped against a pillar. Suzy lifted her hand to return the greeting, but it was Peg who spoke. "It's true, is it, that you're taking over for Lorna, then, Miss Chizek? As the head of housekeeping?"

"*Suzy*, please. Please: *Suzy*," she said. Then, "Looks like it. At least until we find someone else." She shifted her weight. "I feel bad for *you* guys," she said. "I'm no housekeeper . . ."

Peg laughed a little. They were all self-conscious: Was it ruthlessly inappropriate to smile when someone was dead? Peg glanced around, noticing Suzy was alone. "Mia?" Peg said. "How's she been holding up, then?"

"She's OK, I think. She seems OK. I'm not sure how she's supposed to be dealing, really. She's sleeping upstairs." Suzy gestured in the direction of the Lodge above them.

Peg was extraordinarily poised and efficient. Even lounging on her boyfriend, she held herself in good posture, straightening even taller as she spoke. "Please," she said to Suzy, "if you're ever in need of someone to mind her, I'd be pleased to. She's a lovely girl."

"That's very sweet of you." Suzy was used to such offers at the Lodge. She pushed it aside in her mind. Babysitters weren't particularly necessary when you had your mother living up the hill. Except perhaps if that mother was temporarily, incapacitatingly drugged up and knocked out. Or when you didn't much feel like explaining to your mother, as was often required, where it was you thought you were going at such an hour and when exactly you expected to be home. "Actually," Suzy said, taking a step closer to Peg and Jeremy. "Actually, were you planning on hanging out here awhile tonight?"

Peg looked to Jeremy, who met her glance. They turned back to Suzy simultaneously, faces wide and blank, heads wagging, *yeah, no, no plans, why?*

"Mia's asleep," Suzy said. "Chances are she'll stay that way. I could really stand to get out for a few hours. Just to clear my head a little."

Peg was already waving her off. "Yeah, grand, go on. We'll look in on her."

"That'd be great," Suzy said. "Thanks." She was already moving back toward the parking lot.

Peg settled back into the crook of Jeremy's arm. She watched Suzy go. "I'd be unable to do that myself, I imagine."

"Do what?" Jeremy nuzzled her hair.

"Go off and leave my child at such a . . . time, you know? I imagine I'd be unwilling to separate altogether." Peg's voice held a certain disdain.

"I guess," Jeremy said. He cuddled her closer.

Suzy took a Lodge truck. She parked in Eden Jacobs's driveway, then took the path out back and knocked on the door of Roddy's shed.

Roddy's voice said, "It's not locked," as though he knew who it was. She pulled open the door but didn't enter. He sat on the edge of the bed, still wearing his work pants and boots, the dirty pale blue T-shirt he'd been wearing since the night before. She stood in the doorway: "Can I come in?"

He said nothing immediately, but sat surveying her in a way that might have been insulting—this moment at which he seemed to be deciding something, thoughts flying through his head like numbers across a stock ticker as he tried to sort them, each idea in its place somewhere inside his flashing cortex. He was plotting the route they'd take once she stepped across that threshold, and Suzy could almost tell when he'd mapped it, because his face cleared and edged over into resolve. He took a breath, a swimmer ready to plunge, and said, "OK."

Suzy stepped in and pulled the door behind her, then hovered above him in the close confines, the bare walls of unfinished wood, the smoky air.

"It's not a very comfortable bed," he told her.

"That's OK," she said. "I didn't really come to sleep."

He smiled, slightly, then pushed himself up. "Why don't you sit down?"

She took his place on the cot, which was firmer than it looked; he'd laid a board between the mattress and the springs. He stood above her a moment, then knelt before her and parted her knees, edging himself between them. He watched her, his eyes over her clothes as if

he was planning the order of their removal. His fingers were s[...]
his breath infrequent, as if he had to remind himself: *Brea[...]
grabbed on to her T-shirt with both hands and pulled it stra[...]
inside-out, over her head, then brought the shirt to his face and
inhaled before dropping it to the floor. He reached around her then to
unhook her bra. It took a minute, but he got it, let the straps fall forward and slide from her arms. She watched his face while he held her
breasts, closing his eyes again, memorizing the feel of them. She
reached out and pulled his T-shirt off him then and dropped it to the
bed beside her. The tan on his arms and neck stopped at the edges of
where the shirt had been; his torso was pale and oddly hairless. Suzy
reached out a hand, let her fingers graze his skin. He jumped. "I'm
sorry," she said. "No," he said. "No." He drew his breath. She lifted
her hand slowly. When her skin touched his he shuddered again but
held his ground, eyes closed. She kept her hand on him, flattened her
palm to his stomach.

She traced her finger over a broad scar that spread across his side
and disappeared beneath the waistband of his pants. "Where's this
from?"

"War wound," he said, then stood abruptly, slipped out of his
jeans, and rounded the bed. He raised the cover like a wing and beck-
oned her beneath it. She pulled off her shorts and slid in, and he
curled her body into his. He held her too tightly, but that seemed right
somehow.

THE GUEST ROOM AT Art and Penny Vaughn's was Lorna's old bedroom, which Penny had never been able to bring herself to redo. It
hadn't actually seemed all that ludicrous a notion that Lorna might
return to it one day, that she might need a place to run to. But she'd
never run.

The day after Lorna's death, while Art sobbed to himself in the
other room, Penny took a box of Hefty bags and a stack of cardboard

boxes from the IGA into her daughter's bedroom and did what she should have done twenty years before. She went through, removing photographs from the vanity mirror, stuffed animals from the bed and shelves. She folded and packed up the clothes of a seventeen-year-old girl to bring to the secondhand shop off-island, moth holes notwithstanding. Books she boxed for the library. The curtains Squee would have to live with, but she stripped the bed and remade it with plain white sheets and Art's old army blankets for a more masculine feel. It was as though, for that day, Penny Vaughn had decided to adopt a different life as her own. She was preparing for a visit from her beloved grandson—not eradicating Lorna, just welcoming Squee.

If Penny thought it strange that Squee uttered not a single word as she ushered him through the house and the rituals of bedtime, both of which were somewhat alien to him, she said nothing of it. She tucked him to bed without much flutter, as she'd tucked Lorna in for the better part of seventeen years, closed the door, and went across the hall to join poor Art in his heartbroken slumber.

Ten minutes later, Squee had his shorts and sneakers back on and was out the window and on his way back up the hill toward Eden's.

GIVEN AN OPTION, it's not likely that either Suzy or Roddy would have chosen sex on a camp cot. But sometimes such constraints render certain couplings more urgent. Roddy and Suzy were restricted by space, by time, and by circumstance, and driven by a desire that felt like necessity. It made such sense, and felt, for both of them, so good that they found themselves surprised, laughing afterward at how their bodies were like dogs, that they were the owners watching their puppies gallop and play. *They sure seem to like each other, don't they? Yeah, they sure do.*

And then the world came back to them, and they remembered in earnest the things that had led them to the place they were in.

"What's going to happen tomorrow?" Roddy asked.

"What do you mean?" Suzy balked.

"I guess I start clearing . . . debris . . ." He said it as if it were an unfamiliar word, difficult to speak. "Make way for that new-and-improved laundry!"

Suzy said, "Please don't hate me because my father's such a . . ."

Roddy propped himself on an elbow, touched her hair. "That hasn't ever been much of a problem," he said, laughing a little.

She craned up and kissed him, ran her hand across his chest, down his side. "Really, how'd you get this scar?" She traced her fingertips over its surface again. "It's a nasty one, huh?"

"Yup," Roddy said. He pulled the sheet up to cover himself, bent in to kiss her.

She pulled away. "Not your favorite thing in the world to discuss, huh?"

"No." He paused, then relented. "I was working out West at a sawmill for a while . . . You don't really want the details."

"OK," she said, though it was clearly not.

The air outside was awhirl with early-summer crickets. "What's your tomorrow like?" he asked.

"I could check my appointment book."

"That was a joke, right?"

"Yeah." She lay back down, ran both hands through her hair and held it by the ends away from her head as if to yank it from the scalp. "Jesus, I guess depending on Mia, how she is, I guess I take on my new and illustrious position as head housekeeper! I guess I might get called on to help plan a funeral."

Roddy closed his eyes, shook his head back and forth.

"I should get back," she admitted.

"Yeah."

"I'd rather stay . . ."

Roddy nodded. "Your bed back at the Lodge'll give you a hell of a better night's sleep than here."

"A little lonely, though . . ."

Roddy went back to shaking his head. "Oh boy," he said. "Oh boy, am I in for it now . . ."

Suzy grinned mischievously. "And why's that?"

Roddy's head just wagged back and forth.

"I'll see you tomorrow?" Suzy asked.

"I'm sure you will," he answered.

Suzy quietly shut the door to Roddy's cabin and started up the path toward her truck. She was just passing Eden's house when something moved on the porch. Suzy yelped. She backed away, peering into the shaded darkness. In seconds, the shed door slammed and Roddy was rushing toward her, the bedsheet clutched around his waist.

"What happened? Are you OK?"

She nodded, gestured to the porch. "There's something on the porch. It's probably just a raccoon."

A light went on inside the house. Roddy grabbed a log from Eden's woodpile. There was shuffling from the house, a series of lights flicking on inside as Eden made her way to the back door. She pushed open the screen and flipped on the porch light to reveal Squee crouched beside the rocker like a criminal caught in the searchlight, head darting, trying to decide which way to flee.

The porch light also brought to Eden's attention her son, a log raised over his head, his other hand gripping a sheet around his otherwise naked body. And Suzy Chizek, standing on the path between the house and the driveway, looking as if she didn't know which way to run.

"Jesus Christ, Squee!" Roddy dropped his log to the ground. "What the hell?" He clutched the sheet tightly.

"I'm not staying at Grandma and Grandpa Vaughn's. I don't care what you do to me, I'm not staying there." Squee remained squatting in the shadows by the outdoor sofa's armrest.

"For goodness sakes," said Eden. She opened the screen door again and held it ajar. "Come on inside. We'll give Penny a call, let her know where you are." Squee scuttled up, his eyes on Roddy the whole time, lest he pick up the log again and lunge.

Roddy and Suzy turned to each other and began to speak at the same time.

"You OK?" he asked.

"I'm sorry," she was saying.

"Go on. Go back to Mia."

"OK."

"Get some sleep," he said.

"Yeah, OK." She backed away a few steps, then turned and walked briskly toward the truck.

Roddy watched her drive away, then went down to his shack to put on some clothes.

"Toga party's over?" Eden said, smirking, as Roddy came to the back door. Squee was at the kitchen table eating graham crackers with milk, and Roddy shot Eden a look through the screen.

"You get ahold of Penny?" Roddy asked. Eden nodded. Then, with a mustering of will that perhaps only Eden could have perceived, Roddy pulled open the door and stepped into Eden's home. He went and stood behind Squee, put his hands on the boy's shoulders and gave him a playful and affectionate shake. Squee's body went slack under Roddy's hands. Roddy dropped to his knees at the boy's side. "What happened?" He searched Squee's face for signs of distress. "You OK? Are you OK?"

Squee had straightened up quickly.

"Something happen at your grandma and grandpa's?" Roddy asked. "How come you ran off like that? What'd you do, go out a damn window? Jeez. Squee . . . you'd've scared your grandma half to death. What'd you go and do that for?"

Squee could be as evasive as Eden. "I like it *here*," he said.

"And we're very glad to have you," Eden jumped in. "But that doesn't make it OK to go running out on your grandparents like some sort of . . . runaway."

Squee stood up suddenly and stepped away from the table as if he might make a dash for it. Eden pretended to notice nothing. "You finished with these?" she asked him, her hands near his glass and plate.

Squee nodded, disarmed. "Are you going to make me go back?"

"Of course not," Eden said. "You've disrupted everyone's rest enough tonight already. You'll stay here and we'll handle all this in the morning."

Squee looked to Roddy. "Can I stay with you?"

Practically before the question was out of Squee's mouth, the "No" was out of Roddy's.

Eden laughed. "You'll stay up here in Roddy's *old* room. In Roddy's bed from when he was your age."

Squee was clearly disappointed.

"Yeah," Roddy agreed. "There's more room for you up here." And with that he seemed to take full stock of the fact that he was inside Eden's house, which really wasn't someplace he liked to be. He turned to his mother: "You got everything under control up here?"

Eden tried not to crack a smile. "I think we're fine," she managed to say.

"Where are you going?" Squee blurted, then looked embarrassed.

"Just back down to my place."

"Can I come?" Squee asked.

Roddy winced inwardly, struck dumb for a moment until Eden jumped in: "Oh, so you don't want to stay with me either?" She sniffed dramatically.

"I'll see you in the morning, OK partner?" Roddy said.

Squee nodded but did not meet Roddy's eyes. Roddy reached out and tousled the kid's hair. He made a quick exit through the back door.

"Let's get you to sleep, OK?" Eden said to Squee. He followed her obediently down the hall.

MOREY OPENED HIS BAR to the mourners that night, gave them a place to gather and grieve, locked off the pool table, unplugged the juke, though the muted TV was on as always. Morey tended bar himself since Merle Squire was at home with Lance. There wasn't a big crowd, just a few tables of people talking more quietly than usual, drinking harder alcohol, drinking it more slowly. They all went home early. Last to depart, at half past twelve, were Brigid and Gavin, who purchased a fifth of whiskey from Morey, under the table, before they left.

They crossed the footbridge over Fisherman's Cove, then stepped off into the sand and made their way slowly along the beach, feet dragging, circling back and around each other. They were just passing the Lodge dock when Gavin looked up the hill then turned back to Brigid and said, "Would you want to camp, maybe, on the beach tonight?"

"Would I want to . . . if what?" Brigid asked.

"Um . . . if I asked you if you wanted to?"

Brigid mulled this over. "Fucking in the sand . . . it's terribly gritty, don't you think?"

Gavin stopped. "Could you preserve just an ounce of mystery here? Just like one little element of the romance of it or something? Would that be *so* hard?"

"Oh, for fuck's sake." Brigid laughed. She was in a position with him now that she liked—at least, one she felt she understood. He was not half as menacing when she could see where he stood, anticipate where he was heading. He was a romantic after all, not so rakish as she'd imagined.

Gavin raised his hands as if addressing gods in heaven. "I can't win," he said. "What have I done to deserve this woman? What have I done *wrong*?"

"Oh, you poor thing," Brigid cooed.

"I ask the lady to camp out on the beach with me—such a nice gesture!—something I think she's wanting me to do, and what does she do? She makes fun of me! Incredible!" Gavin's drunkenness was becoming apparent. "What's a man to *do*, I ask?"

"Such melodrama!" Brigid goaded.

"I can't *win!*" he cried again, and with that he sank to his knees in the sand, then rolled so he was lying down, looking up into the sky.

Brigid came over and towered above him. "Think you'll recover, then?" she asked, peering down.

Suddenly, Gavin grabbed her by the knees and toppled her into the sand. She yelped, laughing, squealing like a girl, wrestling him in a kicked-up flurry of sand. He pinned her easily, sat straddled atop her, poised. Then he leaned down, still pinning her shoulders to the sand, and kissed her, much as he had the previous evening, only this time he let her kiss back. The sand beneath them was cool, and cooler still as they wriggled down into it, damp and prickly and forgiving, and they rolled around for quite a while until they were forced to pull their clothes back onto their bodies and trudge up the hill to find a damn condom. Except that when they got up to the barracks they found Jeremy and Peg each asleep in their separate rooms, and while they tried to figure out someplace else to go, Gavin managed to sober up enough in the eerie hallway bug light to say, "You know, maybe we should chill out a little, slow down, get some sleep." And before Brigid could catch her balance enough to protest, he was hugging her limply good night and heading back to his own room, which left Brigid feeling more frustrated then ever.

Nine

AN OSPREY BUILDS ITS NEST OF STICKS AND ALL THE RUBBISH IT CAN COLLECT

An osprey nest is a stupendous affair of branches, sticks, driftwood, cornstalks, seaweed and what have you. The same pair will return to it year after year, adding more and more junk in their repairing operations until the whole thing ultimately weighs several hundred pounds and can be seen against the skyline for a mile or more. There are instances of small birds of several kinds nesting in the crevices of osprey castles, quite unmolested, which speaks well for the big fellows' tolerance.

—ROBERT S. LEMMON, *Our Amazing Birds:*
The Little-Known Facts About Their Private Lives

WHEN RODDY AWOKE IN HIS SHED the next morning he sat up, swung his feet from the bed, and nearly fell over Squee who—until Roddy kicked him in the leg—was asleep on the floor. To avoid crashing down on top of the kid, Roddy managed to catch himself against the stovepipe, which only provided a moment of resistance until it gave and sent him bashing into the woodstove. Squee recoiled by instinct, without a word or a cry of surprise, and was curled upright but fetal against the far wall when Roddy regained his balance. He straightened his boxer shorts, made sure he was decent, inspected himself for damage. "Did I *say* there wasn't enough room for two in here?" he said, shaking his head, half laughing and incredulous. "You been there all night?"

Squee shrugged. He was wearing the same dirty clothes he'd been in since Gavin had pulled him from his bed at the Lodge two days before; he looked like even more of an urchin than usual. Roddy jerked his head up toward Eden's house. "I'll put on some clothes, you go up see Eden about taking a shower or something—you're looking like hell—and I'll run the truck down to the Vaughns' and pick up your stuff there. Give you something clean to put on. 'K?"

Squee nodded, lingering by the doorway.

"Go, get on," Roddy waved at him.

Squee looked as if he was preparing some sort of challenge. Finally he said, "You let *Suzy* come down here . . ."

"A *visit's* one thing," Roddy managed to say. "You don't see Suzy sleeping on the floor with her sneakers on, now do you?" He paused. "Unless . . ." he leaned over and peered beneath the bed. Squee laughed. Which—Roddy was starting to think—was maybe the only thing that actually really mattered anymore at all. "Get on," Roddy told him. "Eden won't let you near her kitchen table as filthy as you are. You want breakfast, you better get up there and get clean."

Squee moved closer to the door. "I'm sorry." He stuck his pointy chin toward the spot of floor where he'd lain.

"You're the one who slept on the floor," Roddy said.

"Yeah!" Squee's spirits were lifting his whole body, as if someone had pumped some more air into him. He edged out the door, then turned back at the last second, as if to surprise Roddy. His face washed in a smile. "What kind of a hotel is this, anyway!" he cried, and dashed outside and up the incline toward Eden's house.

Squee was in the shower, and Eden out collecting the morning eggs from the chicken coop when the phone rang. Eden hurried back to the house as quickly as she could without jostling the basket. She gathered eggs a couple times a day—had a sign out on Island Drive, FRESH ORGANIC EGGS FOR SALE since she had more than she could use herself. If you didn't gather the eggs often enough the hens'd start laying them on top of the old ones, and it was crowding like that that led to eggs' breaking, and broken eggs led to egg-eating, and Eden had learned the hard way what happened when one hen started eating eggs. You didn't cull an egg-eater from the flock immediately and the rest of them just followed, and pretty soon your hens weren't good for much more than soup.

She got to the phone mid-ring and snatched it up, setting her eggs on the counter. It was Suzy, calling to say she was bringing Mia over to Reesa Delamico's place out at Scallopshell Cove for the day and did Eden think it sounded like a good idea to get Squee over there too? Reesa Delamico cut and styled hair at her home, but in the summers she relocated her operations to a small salon and gift shop in the lobby of the Osprey Lodge, where she could more conveniently cater to the summer-vacation crowd. Reesa and Suzy and Lorna had all grown up together, same grade in school. Reesa had four kids—one grown, one a baby, but the other two were near Squee's and Mia's ages, and they'd been summer playmates in the past.

On the phone with Eden, Suzy was talking quickly, her tone overly businesslike. She was trying not to let Eden get a word in one way or another, lest it be a word about what Suzy might have been doing out behind the house in the middle of the night, with Roddy wearing only a bedsheet. Suzy prattled on: Reesa wasn't going in to the Lodge Salon, she'd be with the kids all day . . . Might be good to distract Squee from everything, play with Mia, and Stacey and Mark. Reesa was thinking of setting up the Slip 'n Slide . . ."

Eden said, "Well, I've got him here now in the shower—"

"Oh, good!" Suzy said. "I was thinking we'd have to have Reesa toss a bar of soap on there with them!"

"He *was* getting a little ripe."

Suzy faltered: "I told Reesa about last night . . . about Squee, I mean, that he ran away from Penny and Art's . . . anyway, she said she'll keep a close watch." Her pace picked up again. "I was thinking if he ran from Reesa's, that if he runs, it'd just be back to your place probably . . ."

"Maybe," said Eden. "That may be."

A terribly awkward pause followed.

"Suzanne," Eden said, "we've got history, you and me, but I've got no problem in the world with you, dear—you should know that—and no troubles with whatever's going on between you and my son. So please, sweetheart, calm down."

Suzy laughed. "This island is too small!"

"Well, that may be true," Eden agreed reluctantly. She was ready to let the whole conversation go. "Why don't you come by here and pick up Mister Squee on your way to Reesa's, OK? How'd that be?"

"Think I can manage that," Suzy said, relieved. "That'd be fine."

If it weren't for Squee climbing into the passenger seat of Roddy's truck and insisting on coming with him to help at the Lodge, Roddy would almost certainly have been gone before Suzy made it over to Eden's that morning. As it was, Suzy pulled up to find Roddy's truck blocking the driveway, Roddy standing outside the passenger window, talking to Squee in the seat.

"You just can't," Roddy was saying. "I don't want you around there. It's dangerous, besides. You can come back in a few days—when your dad comes back. You want to help with the construction then, we'll see about that. But not when it's . . ."

"Morning!" Suzy called. Roddy had lifted his head when her truck pulled in, then turned back to Squee, no acknowledgment. Now he lifted a hand in greeting before he faced the boy again.

Suzy came and stood beside Roddy at the open window. "What's happening here?" She was rested and showered, her hair still wet, pulled back into a ponytail that was leaving a damp splotch on her back. Roddy hadn't yet bathed, and his beard was getting beyond shadowed to scraggly. He'd at least put on a clean T-shirt.

"Come on, partner," Roddy tried again. "Look, Suzy and Mia are here, all set to take you over to Reesa's. Come on, Squee, OK?"

Suzy leaned in closer, put her hand on the small of Roddy's back as she spoke: "You got your swimsuit, kid?" she said. Roddy tensed beneath her touch. "Reesa's setting up the Slip 'n Slide as we speak . . . Mark and Stacey are psyched you guys are coming over to play . . ."

And then, suddenly, there in Roddy's truck in the middle of the driveway, more than a full day after the news of Lorna's death had been made known to him, Squee began to cry. What broke him right then was anyone's guess. Most likely he was too tired to hold it in anymore. His face did not contort and twist. He did not look like a child crying. He looked as though his tear ducts had been pierced and left to run themselves dry.

"Oh, baby," Suzy said, and she reached past Roddy to open the door, step close, and take Squee in her arms. She cupped a hand around the back of his head and held him to her, stroking, soothing. Instinct drove her movements, and Roddy backed away.

Squee did not sob, or choke, or cough as crying children do. Suzy held him to her like a slump of towels. Every so often he gave a gasp on the intake of breath, but otherwise he wept silently, too exhausted to do anything but let the tears drain from his body. Then, somewhere in the midst of that outpouring, his body gave a sudden jerk. He seemed surprised. He pulled himself away from Suzy for a second and waited, then spasmed again. Hiccups. It took about three rounds for his brain to catch up and figure out what was going on, and then he began to cry harder, more ardently, as though his own desperation had been fully revealed. And maybe it was that he lost his resolve in the momentary chaos of emotion, but he didn't put up any struggle at all when Suzy lifted him—a limby, dragging bundle—out of the truck and carried him toward her own idling vehicle. She kept a hand on Squee's head and craned around to Roddy, mouthing words he couldn't make out.

"SHERIFF, GOOD MORNING." Eden opened the door as though Sheriff Harty paid her a visit every day.

The sheriff tugged off his hat and clutched it to him as he shifted in Eden's doorway. "Eden, how are you?" He replaced his hat.

"Oh," Eden said, "under the circumstances . . ."

"You busy this morning? I wonder if I could talk with you. Is it a bad time, Eden?"

"Coffee, Sheriff?" she said by way of invitation, and held the door as he entered.

"Oh," he said, "sure, thanks, if it's not too much trouble. Haven't got much sleep . . ."

Eden went to the kitchen. The sheriff stood awkwardly, then strolled around the living room, inspected Roderick's gun collection, and finally took a seat in the least comfortable-looking chair in the room.

"Eden," he began when they were settled, "I'm not meaning to be like some detective about this, but I'm no good at the sensitive stuff and I've got sensitive stuff I got to talk about and I know you're not one to stand on ceremony or beat around the bush so I'm just going to tell you what I've got to tell you and say what I've got to say and ask you what I got to ask you, and then we'll just take it from there, OK?"

"You go right ahead, Duane."

The large envelope he was carrying opened with a crack of Velcro. "There's something we found at the scene of the fire . . ."—he looked up to make sure Eden was following him—"and it's probably not exactly one hundred percent police protocol for me to be here like this . . ." He paused. "Well, no, actually it probably is—it's just, I'm not asking anything in a real official-type way. But here: there was a small refrigerator in the laundry shack—not in operation, but used as a kind of a storage cabinet—totally against the law, and thank god we didn't have some kid get themselves trapped in there in a game of hide-and-seek—I can only imagine . . . So, but, well, the contents of that fridge survived the fire real well—mostly just junk, but also something else we found, and it's only been seen now by Deputy Mitchell and myself and we're both of us tied in knots about what to do and so we decided I'd come and talk to you, on account it seems by the contents of the thing that you're perhaps familiar with the contents—some, at least, already, and so I guess . . ." From the envelope he removed the thin lavender spiral notebook that had served as Lorna Squire's diary. "We've got this thing," said the sheriff, "and we don't know what the hell to do with it." He passed the book to Eden.

The sheriff, wiped out by this delivery, sank against his stiff-backed chair, then remembered his coffee and seized the cup as if it held the key to his survival.

Eden held the notebook, the warped metal curls of its binding like the spine of a small animal. On the cover, the ballpoint letters traced over so many times they were nearly engraved, it read: THE DIARY OF LORNA MARIE VAUGHN SQUIRE.

"Duane"—Eden looked the sheriff in the eye—"why're you showing this to me?"

The sheriff set down his cup. "Like I said, Eden, or tried to . . . There's mention of you all over in there—says right on the first page you're the one suggested she write down her thoughts in the first place. Back when it starts at first she writes the date in—late 'seventy-nine is it?—then it just kind of drops off. It's right there on the first page . . ."

Eden opened the cover. *Nov. 23, 1979.* Right when Lorna was pregnant with Squee. Eden flipped the page. The initial entries were dated, then devolved into *July . . . ?* Until they disappeared altogether. The notebook was maybe three quarters full, and most of it seemed to be letters of a sort. *Dear Diary* had given way to *Dear Squee,* and then later in the notebook the pages began with just *My Sweet Baby Boy.* "Duane," Eden said again, "what are you here for? What are you asking me?"

The sheriff looked as though he'd have liked to climb into his coffee cup and hide. "Roderick was my friend," he said. "I've known you nearly all my life, Eden. Eaten dinner at your table. You know I've got nothing but respect for you, Eden—you know that."

Whether it was true, and whether Eden believed him, were questions for another time. She nodded.

"There's stuff in there that Lorna wrote that concerns a lot of people on this island. It says some things that're not easy to believe, and even if you do believe them it's nothing easy to swallow. There's lots about you in there, Eden, and I won't pretend to understand all what it says, but I have a real good feeling that it's not things you're wanting too many folks knowing about . . ."

Eden screwed up her face in sudden and nearly comical surprise: "Are you *blackmailing* me, Duane?"

Duane Harty's eyes popped. "Christ lord, no!" he cried. "I just don't know what in god's name to *do* with the damn thing!" His face was pleading. "Police procedure'd be to register that diary and then send it along with any other personal belongings we salvaged, hand it over to her next of kin, and if that's Lance or that's Art and Penny I don't even care who, because I for one don't want to be around when any of them lay their eyes on what it says in that book. I am at a loss here, Eden. I don't know what in god's name to do. I am asking for your help here, is what I'm asking."

Eden nodded.

"There's part of me thinks I should just burn the damn thing," the sheriff continued. "Let it be one more thing lost in the fire. But I *read* it, Eden. I read it all. And there's things in there—I mean, I don't fully understand all she's saying, but I've got half a mind to go down to the Lodge and haul Bud Chizek into jail and toss away the goddamn key! That book there"—he pointed to it accusingly—"that book makes me feel like I'm going to lose my mind. What it says, I can't even keep the half of it straight. I don't even want to know half of what's in there. But the other part—most of it, really—it's all those letters, like, addressed to Squee . . . That boy's going to grow up without his mother. She left him something there, and there's a part of me feels like if I did one good thing in my life—forget police protocol—if I did one good thing I'd make sure that boy gets that book. Not now, but someday. You know—someday that boy might need to understand that there was someone on this earth once that loved him more than anything there ever was." Sheriff Harty was fighting back tears. "I don't know what to do with the rest of all of what's in there. Part of me should be taking you in for friggin' questioning, Eden," he cried. "I don't know what in hell you were running out here—I don't *want* to know—I don't want to know *any* of this . . ."

"I suppose," Eden began, "I suppose the way one ought to handle something like this'd be to arrange some sort of way to get the book put away until Squee's of an age to see such a thing—"

"But then you're talking lawyers," the sheriff interrupted. "You're talking more people seeing this thing. You're talking about the possibility of what's in there getting spread here to Menhadenport—"

"What do you want me to say, Duane? You want me to take this thing and hide it away in my closet until the boy's eighteen?"

Sheriff Harty froze, his mouth set in a grim purse. "No," he said. "I want you to go get a safe-deposit box or some such down at the bank and keep it *there* until the boy's eighteen." And he just kept looking at Eden then, right at her, letting her know that he didn't get any more serious than that. Eden looked down at the notebook, then back to Sheriff Harty. She drew in a long breath and let it out slowly. She said, "OK."

⁓

COUNTY SANITATION HAD already brought a dumpster to the Lodge, set down—at Bud's direction, no doubt—so that it blocked the view from Sand Beach Road to the laundry shack's blackened husk. It was a terrible-looking thing: monolithic charred and melted washers and dryers rising above the rubble, like a miniature city, incinerated. Fire Chief McIntire was there, inspecting the wreckage, collecting data for the reports he would have to file. There were a few construction guys from the island milling around, hired for the demolition. Bud had dressed himself in a pair of old, stained Bermuda shorts and a striped polo shirt splotched with bleach, as if he planned to help with the demolition work, though it was hard to imagine Bud doing anything but bark orders from the sidelines and go inside to make "important" phone calls just when large items needed lifting. Bud was waving Roddy over. "Good morning, good morning."

Bud started rattling off instructions when Roddy was still a good distance away. "There's nothing we can do right here till the insurance boys make it out to have a look. They promised me they'd hustle through—we'll start tearing it down the minute they're done." Roddy stopped about ten feet from Bud and listened to him orate. The construction crew guys listened too, though it seemed they'd already heard the speech. "For now, this morning, we're waiting for the new equipment—they promised before noon—and we'll need to get the maintenance shop cleared out. We'll use this as an opportunity to get rid of whatever crap's in there we don't need—toss it all in the dumpster, but check with me first, you hear? Then I've got dimensions for the exhaust holes we're gonna . . ." Bud dropped off. "Ach," he said. "Screw it, save that for later. Let's get the damn thing cleared out first. Load it into the pickups. We'll store everything in the meantime off the staff quarters . . ." He turned and pointed. "That storage shed, there." And thus a tedious and labor-intensive process began.

AT THE EAST END of the first floor in the Lodge there was a door without a room number. An index card was thumbtacked over the peephole. On it, in ballpoint pen that had faded to nearly nothing, someone had written "MAID." Hunting down a key to the door was Suzy's first order of business, and she walked up the hill to her folks' house to see if Nancy had any ideas. Her mother was up and dressed and wanted to come down to the Lodge and find the key for

Suzy. Making herself useful was an effective form of martyrdom for Nancy. Suzy was too tired to fight. They walked down the hill in silence, watching the men haul tools and equipment. Suzy slowed her pace to her mother's. Nancy's face looked thinner; she seemed perpetually near tears.

The insurance guys had shown up, and they circled the periphery of the burn site, one speaking into a handheld tape recorder, the other making marks on a company clipboard with a company pen. Bud could be heard nearly from the road, directing traffic down inside the maintenance shop.

In the Lodge office, Nancy mustered a bit of her usual fussiness to search for the maid's key. She bustled about with an air of downtrodden frailty, like a consumptive on a mission. Suzy found something in a file cabinet labeled "Housekeeping" and sat down to pore over a sheaf of duty rosters circa 1967, which she supposed was probably the last time anyone had kept track of what got done and what went slack.

"Oh! Suzy . . ."

Suzy spun toward her mother, whose hand was clutched at her chest.

Nancy spoke as if the breath might be her last. "I think I found it!"

"Well," Suzy said, attempting brightness, "let's give it a try, shall we?" And she went toward the maid's room again with the key in hand. Nancy followed, pausing for breath by the main staircase before she continued behind Suzy. Suzy tried to steel herself, not so much for what lay behind the locked door as for her mother's reaction to it, which, she was certain, would most likely make her want to strangle the woman on the spot. She gritted her teeth.

The lock took some fiddling, and Nancy tried to edge Suzy out of the way to try it herself, as though Suzy might not know how to use such a fancy contraption as a door key. Suzy held her ground. Too much fight on Nancy's part would have betrayed health or vigor.

The room was, of course, a wreck. As bad as the laundry shack had been, only tighter and more cramped. Nancy peered in over Suzy's shoulder and clucked at the shame of it. "That poor girl." Nancy shook her head sadly. "She really had control of nothing in her life, did she?"

That was that—Suzy lost it. "She was a fucking slob, Mom. Your head housekeeper was a total fucking slob! Period. It doesn't mean she needed *saving;* it means she was a lousy housekeeper, OK? Can you drop the saint act, please? I just really can't take it today, all right? I just can't . . ." Suzy looked pleadingly at her mother. She'd have given a lot at that moment for Nancy to fire something back at her. Anything but continue the martyr act. Which is exactly what Nancy did: her face dropped and her body seemed to contract in a wince of psychic pain. Suzy would not have put a fainting spell past her mother at that moment. But Nancy just turned on wobbly legs and walked back down the hall, leaving Suzy alone in that filthy maid's supply room.

When the five o'clock whistle sounded down at the docks, whatever headway Suzy had made in the room was not yet visible to the naked eye. It was highly unrewarding work as such. She relocked the door behind her, tucked the key into her pocket, and started back toward the maintenance shop–cum-laundry. The appliance truck had finally arrived while Suzy had been sequestered in the Lodge, and now a gaggle of burly men in incongruous lavender baseball caps were unloading some less-than-state-of-the-art industrial washers and dryers down the truck ramp and into the shop. Roddy was already coming toward her, pulling off his work gloves as he walked.

"I don't know why I'd been imagining *new* equipment. This *is* my father we're talking about . . ." Roddy and Suzy were unclear on how they should greet each other, so they simply did not greet at all, just stopped at a few paces and hovered uncomfortably.

"How you doing?" Roddy asked, feeling out her mood.

"Let's get out of here," she said.

"Get the kids from Reesa's and go to Morey's?" Roddy asked. "Squee likes it there."

Merle Squire treated Squee like a secretary might treat the boss's child: fine, but not as her own. That evening she entered Morey's through the back door, came up behind Roddy and Suzy and the kids at the bar and silently placed her hand on Squee's head by way of hello. He was nearly asleep on his stool, his dinner uneaten, and he didn't even start at the surprise of Merle's touch.

"How's everyone holding up?" Merle asked them quietly. She looked at Squee, smoothed his hair tenderly. "Your dad's missing you something awful."

Squee was not the only one confused by this assertion.

Roddy said, "How is he?"

Merle shook her head. "He's OK, I guess. Honestly, I think he needs to get back to the Lodge. I think he needs something to do."

"You think he's ready, already?" Suzy asked.

"Eh, I don't know," said Merle. "When are you ever ready for something like that?"

Roddy nodded at his plate of clam strips. "So when's he going to come back?"

Merle touched the hair at the back of her neck, patting it in place. "Tomorrow, I think. It's not doing either of us much good having him with me. Bickering . . ." She looked to Squee then, to see if he was listening, but he was zoned out completely.

"And that means Squee goes home too?" Suzy said quietly. "With that fire pit right outside his front door?"

"Lance really wants to . . . so soon?" Roddy asked Merle.

"Well, he doesn't want to stay with me!" she said certainly.

Later, Roddy and Suzy waited in the truck while they sent the kids into Shakes for ice cream.

"We just can't guarantee that he'll stay up at my mom's," Roddy was saying. "We can't exactly lock him in. I could lock the door to the shack, but still, it's weird, if he comes down . . ."

"You're right." Suzy was nodding as Roddy spoke. "You're right . . . I know, I just wish we could find, like, an hour, just that . . ."

Roddy was nodding too. "I just don't know how . . ."

"This is so stupid. The kid's mother is dead and I'm trying to stash him somewhere."

"He'll be back with Lance tomorrow night for better or worse. And then you can ditch your own daughter all you want and come share my shack with me." He smiled.

"I'm not such a terrible mother as I sound," she said.

"I didn't say you were a terrible mother."

"I sound like one, though."

"How come you had her?" Roddy asked, too quickly to check himself.

"I was pregnant . . . ?"

"Yeah, got that," Roddy stammered, self-conscious now. "I just wondered, I mean, did you mean to be . . . or . . . ?"

"I didn't mean to get pregnant, but . . ."

"Happens sometimes," he said.

"I was on the pill too, even. Different kind than now," she assured him. "I'm well protected now . . ."

He smiled. "And you decided to keep it . . . her . . . I guess, obviously . . ."

Suzy laughed. "Obviously."

"Did you . . . Were you . . . *with* her dad then? Did he . . . ?"

Suzy chose her words carefully. "I *was* with someone then. I mean, I was *with* someone. And I was also . . ."—she spoke slowly, as if testing his reaction to each word, waiting to see how it landed before she spoke the next—"having an . . . well, sleeping with . . . someone . . . else . . . also . . ." Roddy was staring at her intently, waiting for each word as apprehensively as she issued them. "It wound up being kind of messy and yucky."

Roddy was shaking his head. "And you didn't wind up staying with either of them?"

"I wasn't exactly anyone's favorite person at that point."

"And so did you ever . . . I mean, do you . . . ?"

"Know who her father is?" Suzy finished for him. "Yes," she said definitively, "*I* do."

Roddy just kept looking at her, unsure what she meant.

"They both left thinking it was the other, and it seemed like that was best for all of us. And I was going to abort anyway, but then I decided I didn't want to. I have a good job; I could afford it. I knew she'd have good genes. It just seemed like: OK, I could do this."

"Wow," Roddy said.

"I guess."

The door to Shakes swung open and Squee and Mia pushed through, cones in hand, Squee's already beginning to melt down his arm.

"Make you not want to sleep with me anymore?" Suzy asked, her face scrunched up in exaggerated worry.

Roddy snorted. He reached down to conceal his erection before the kids climbed back into the truck.

He dropped Suzy and Mia at the Lodge, then drove with Squee beside him back up to Eden's. She wasn't in the house when they arrived, so Roddy deposited Squee in front of the television and went out to the chicken coop to find her.

There'd been no henhouse out back while Roddy was growing up. All that had happened in his absence. Eden had a custom-built cement-floor coop with divided nest areas for each of her birds and a separate "coop for one," as she called it—a darkened, screened-off place for a broody hen to sit on her eggs and ready them for hatching. That spring Eden had mated one of her hens—Lorraine—with a cock from George Quincy's farm. Now Lorraine got off her eggs only once a day—not more than twenty minutes—to step outside, eat, drink, and do her business. It was Eden's only chance to get in there and check on things, tidy up. As Roddy approached he could see Lorraine at the food. The gate was made of chicken-wire fencing stapled to a scrap-wood frame. He opened the latch, slipped inside, and secured it closed behind him. It stank of chicken shit.

"Hey, Ma," Roddy called.

Eden's head poked out the splintering door frame. Lorraine stalked back to her nest, feathers puffed, defensive and proud, and Eden stepped out of her way and into the light. As Lorraine settled on the eggs inside they could hear her *buk buk buk,* low and constant and somehow contented-sounding.

Eden was smiling broadly. "I tell you they're due to hatch 'round the Fourth of July?"

Roddy let out a sad snort of a laugh. "Yeah, Ma, you told me."

Eden beamed like a grandmother would over brand-new Sears photo studio portraits.

Roddy's tone when he spoke was anything but light. "What'd Sheriff Harty want with you, Ma?" Roddy and the Sheriff had passed each other in the driveway that morning.

Eden wasn't prepared for such a change of gears, and she stalled a moment.

"*Ma?*"

"Oh, that . . ." She waved a hand away from her body to demonstrate the utter inconsequence of the sheriff's visit, as though she'd all but forgotten he'd come by.

"Yeah," Roddy said, determined, "*that.*"

A wash of panic swept Eden's face suddenly. "Where's Squee?" She looked toward the house. "You had him . . . ?"

"He's watching TV. He's fine. Don't change the subject."

"Oh ho," Eden laughed bitterly, shaking her head, a finger pointed at Roddy in reprimand. "Oh, that is the subject, son. That *is* the subject."

"Don't," Roddy said. He was growing impatient and frustrated. "Don't get cryptical—"

"Well isn't *that* the pot calling the kettle—"

"*Ma*—"

"Look, son. I know you're not going to argue against there being some things best left untold, and I am not going to tell you what I talked about to Sheriff Harty this morning any more than you're about to sit down and tell me where you've been since nineteen sixty-eight. So don't tell me you don't know that some things are best kept. There's no reason to say them, and there's too many other folks who'd get hurt if you did. OK? So, I am done talking about this, son. Done."

Ten

HOW THE OSPREY TENDS ITS NESTLINGS

From my canoe on the Connecticut River I have often watched the male enter the eyrie with his catch. After he eats the head, his mate takes the remainder from him and feeds the young the choice center part, bit by bit, saving the tail for herself.

But in Florida, Fred Truslow, who photographed ospreys so beautifully for this article, saw a male depart from etiquette.

"He brought back a pound-and-a-half weakfish and sat there nibbling," Fred said. "When he ate beyond the head, the female clucked impatiently. When he reached the halfway mark on the body, she grew strident. And when he ate the tail section, she flew off with an angry scream. A few moments later she was back with a fish of her own. This she divided—center part for the youngsters, head and tail for herself."

—ROGER TORY PETERSON, "The Endangered Osprey"

S UZY'S FIRST OFFICIAL ACT as head housekeeper was to clean the Squires' cottage. Lance would be coming back from Merle's, and word from Merle was he wanted his son with him, which worried everyone, since Lance had never particularly wanted Squee around when Lorna was alive. Still, they tried to understand. Squee was all Lance had left of his wife. It made sense he'd want to cling to him. *Wouldn't you?* they murmured, pausing to chat in the aisles of the IGA, at the bar, as they shuffled out of the Episcopal Church.

Suzy gathered the housekeeping girls that morning. "Let's just get in there and do it. A whole crew of us, it shouldn't take that long."

She was wrong. It took six of them all day. "Remember," Suzy kept saying as they uncovered another den of mouse corpses—trapped on sticky-tape, bloody and desiccated—inside a kitchen drawer, "the rest of your work this summer is going to feel like a piece of cake after this." By afternoon the girls were rolling their eyes, and Suzy shut up about it. When she and Brigid started going through the bedroom, collecting Lorna's things, folding her clothes into discarded produce-packing boxes from the IGA, they were on their last legs.

"How well did you know her, then?" Brigid asked, standing at the closet door, surveying the contents, unsure where and how to delve in.

"In high school, I guess I knew her pretty well . . . better than I wound up knowing her, I guess." Suzy sighed heavily. "It was hard, with Lance . . . she just kind of cut off other people."

Brigid reached for an empty box. "He couldn't be so altogether dreadful as everyone imagines, could he?" She sat down in the open mouth of the closet and dug in. They had designated a "Lance" mound on the bed, to be dealt with later, and Brigid began riffling through the closet, sorting "Lance" and "Lorna," bed or box.

"Yeah, he probably is . . ." Suzy chuckled bitterly a moment, then sobered up. "No," she revised herself, "he's probably not . . ."

"Do you know *him* well, then?"

Suzy let out another spurt of hard laughter. She didn't think very far ahead when she said, "Well, I *knew* him."

Brigid turned around to see Suzy's face, and grinned. "Oh, *did* you . . . ?"

"It's a *really* small island," Suzy said. "You grow up here and it can get a little incestuous."

"So, you and Mr. Squire . . . you were a couple, then?"

"Me and Lance? Oh, god no." Suzy tried to laugh, but her discomfort was growing.

Brigid stopped what she was doing. "But you . . . ?" she prompted.

Suzy shook her head regretfully, swallowing hard. She was an idiot to have said anything. "Unfortunately," Suzy managed to get out, "very unfortunately, yes."

Brigid let her jaw drop as she attempted to picture the scene of it. She wasn't just going to let the subject go.

Suzy reached for the packing tape. "It was such a huge mess . . ." She had to dig herself back out of this somehow. "I mean, Lance and Lorna, they'd been together for a couple years at that point. And not that Lance didn't fuck . . . Not that Lance didn't mess around, back then at least . . ."

Brigid was about to speak, but then didn't.

"Oh, it was such a big mess," Suzy said. She wanted the conversation to be over. She wanted it never to have begun. "I was friends with Lorna. It never should have happened. And then my brother—my brother was like Lance's best friend. He found out and got furious . . . And then *he* went off and *died* . . ." Suzy peered at a plastic bag she'd discovered under the bed; she held it up to the light to discern what might be inside.

"Your brother?" Brigid said.

"Yeah. Vietnam. That glorious war." Suzy opened the bag, sniffed at it tentatively, and pitched it into the industrial garbage bag in the far corner. "It's just one goddamned drama after another around here."

"I'm sorry," Brigid said softly.

They were quiet then, for a time, sorting clothes. Brigid thought about the ethics of going through someone's closets—*Lorna* might have been dead, but Lance wasn't, and the closets were half his. Did being married to a dead person suddenly mean that the whole world could go riffling through your underthings? Brigid thought in some ways that living on this island seemed to simply *imply* that the guy pumping your gas had probably changed your diaper, and the woman serving your burger was likely sleeping with your dad. Dirty laundry was public domain. Which was either a terribly healthy, out-in-the-open, no-secrets-here sort of a thing, or it wasn't. And what seemed most likely was that no matter how soiled the laundry hanging out on the clothesline, you could be altogether sure there was something far dirtier balled up and festering in a plastic bag in a corner of the basement where even the snoopiest didn't think, or dare, to go.

If Brigid had wanted to ask more of Suzy—about Lance, about Chas, about the island dramas Suzy had known—she either refrained or was too caught up thinking about how she might find her own way into Osprey lore: as the girl who took up with the fellow who almost came between Heather Beekin and Chandler Crane. So now Heather Beekin and Chandler Crane could go on and pump out their nineteen children who'd all grow up hearing the stories of how their ma had nearly gone off with a college boy from California, but didn't, and, well, so now here they all were. Brigid was entirely pleased with the role she might play: the Irish chambermaid whom Gavin had taken up with, with whom he had a torrid and passionate affair, while Heather and Chandler got soft and fat and ever more local.

Brigid wasn't stupid. She could see quite well—in herself, for fuck's sake—why a place like Osprey Island could be addictive, why it might be dead hard to break away from it entirely. Your life mattered enough here that people would be talking about you long after you'd gone. And there was something lovely about that. Yes, all right, Brigid conceded, big fish, small pond and all. Yet she was altogether gratified to be making her way into island history as she was. You didn't hear anyone on Osprey Island talking about her sister Fiona, now did you?

LANCE RETURNED TO THE LODGE, with Merle, in time for dinner that night, but he didn't eat with the rest of the staff in the dining room or on the porch. Merle made up an invalid's sick tray and brought it to him at the cabin. He sat in that newly sanitized home, barely noticing the work that had been done. It struck him as somehow logical, or at least right, that his world should be suddenly swept clean, all evidence of Lorna stacked along the wall in boxes marked CREAMED CORN and MALT-O-MEAL. The cottage looked as empty as Lance felt, yet just because everything had gotten picked up and wiped down and vacuumed away didn't mean that nothing had ever been there. You could erase mess, but not history. Lance just sat in the armchair, poured himself a stiff glass of bourbon, and demanded his son. "Where is he?" Lance asked Merle. "Where's my boy?"

"I'm sure they'll bring him over in a bit," Merle said, calming him. She'd never talked to Lance a whole lot, hadn't known intimately what went on in his and Lorna's life; nonetheless, she felt strangely hopeful. Maybe that was something you never lost as a parent: the hope that your kid might do something right someday. She'd certainly had more than enough discouragement on that front, but you wanted to believe that people always had the capacity to change. Especially your children.

"He wants Squee back at the Lodge *tonight*?" Eden's incredulity was matched only by the ferocity of her anger at Lance's sheer, arrogant, ignorant, selfish gall.

"That's what I was told," Roddy repeated. "Bring him back after dinner."

"No!" Eden cried. She stamped her foot into the ground between garden rows. She held a bushel basket to her chest defensively. She'd been harvesting snap peas.

"Ma, you can't keep the man's son against his will. He's got rights. A man wants his son with him, you can't deny him that . . ."

"*His son!*"

"Look, he's no model parent, I'll give you that, but the man's grieving, you know? He just wants what he's got left of family . . ."

"Oh for the love of god!" Eden cried. "His *family*? He wants his *son*? Lance Squire's been denying his paternity since the day Lorna told him she was pregnant! Goddamn it, Lorna!" Eden swore as though it was Lorna, not Roddy, standing in the garden beside her. "Goddamn it!"

Roddy stood by, helpless.

"Let me tell you something, son," Eden said, and her voice was low, as if she was afraid that Squee might hear them from the house, over the babble of the television. "Let me tell you that that man would have *no* claims on that child if Lorna'd done what she ought to have done and put *Father Unknown* on Squee's birth certificate and made a goddamn will and put someone else as legal guardian in case something ever happened to her—Art and Penny, me, Reesa Delamico and Abel, anyone, anyone'd have done it. But no, that was too much for Lorna to manage. She didn't want to hurt Lance. Swore up and down it was Lance's baby—" Eden paused, her face twisted with emotion. "Do you see how hard it was to be any part of that girl's life? Can you see what it was like to sit by and watch her ruin every chance she ever got to right herself? She was a smart girl—I don't even know if you know how smart of a girl she was. But so *stupid*! So goddamn stupid about things. Goddamn it, Lorna!" she swore again, gripping her green pea basket to her body as if it were the child she'd protect at any cost.

Roddy's own anger at that point was growing less focused on Lance and more on Eden. "You planning on telling me what in hell you're talking about?"

Eden ignored the question. "Go talk to him, Roddy. Go over there and talk to Lance—maybe he'll listen to you . . ."

"Not if I don't know why I'm talking to him or what I'm talking about! No."

"Roddy," she begged. "I tell you: it's too complicated to open up that sack of worms without letting out every other question that comes along with it. Too many things you don't need—and you don't want to know. Could you trust your mother, please? Just take my word and talk to Lance . . . ?"

Roddy stood his ground.

"For Squee's sake, Roddy," she pleaded. "Please, for the sake of that child . . ."

"How about for the sake of that child you tell me what the hell is going on."

Eden saw her defeat, her mind already calculating how much he'd need to know. She would reveal the bare minimum of what there was. "You," she accused her son, "have turned out to be a very stubborn and unforgiving man, Roddy Jacobs."

Roddy almost smiled. "Just like you raised me to be."

Eden narrowed her eyes. She spoke quickly, as though she'd agreed to say it once and only once, and he could catch what he caught and forever after hold his peace.

"I'm no doctor," Eden said, her voice so low it was nearly lost. "And I've surely never examined the man, but as far as I can tell you, I'm pretty damn sure that it's a medical impossibility for Lance Squire to have children. I'm pretty sure he's infertile, or some such, and never has been anything but. He's well aware of that fact. And whatever Lorna said, I know Lance doesn't believe for a second that any part of him went into making Squee. He's certainly held that over her head in every way he could. So now he's gung ho about being the boy's father all of a sudden. But *I* know what that man's capable of. He's been rough with Lorna and he's been rough with others. Lorna and I broke not too long after Squee was born, you know, so I don't know if Lance ever lays his fist into that boy, but I don't want to find out now. Please go talk to him, Roddy, and stop wasting time asking me questions, please . . ." She waited, breathing hard.

Roddy's face betrayed nothing. He spoke evenly. "Who's Squee's father?"

"I don't think Lorna even knew herself."

Roddy thought on that a minute. "But she was pregnant before, wasn't she? Isn't that . . . ? When they got married?"

"Wasn't his either," Eden said. "And he knew it then too." She stopped. She wasn't giving away any more than he demanded.

"But why do you know?" he said. "Why do *you* know all that? And why's the sheriff know you know?"

"It's got nothing to do with the sheriff," she lied. "Lorna and I, we were close for a time . . . When you were gone . . . When she was pregnant with Squee I helped her—staying healthy and not drinking and whatnot. She told me things, OK? She told me things. So would you go get down there and talk to Lance, please?"

Roddy paused, confused and unsatisfied, then finally turned without a word and started up the hill toward his truck.

It was nearly seven o'clock when Roddy showed up on the porch of the Squires' cottage. Merle was watching the television, Lance seated in a chair near her, his eyes closed, head held back as if he were willing away a nosebleed. Roddy knocked and Merle waved him in.

"Stay for Pat and Vanna . . ." Merle gestured toward an empty chair.

Lance squinted open one eye and half raised a hand in greeting.

Roddy hovered a few yards away from them, the way he hung on the periphery of his mother's house, not wanting to get too close, become too involved. "I'm only going to stay a minute," he said. "I just had something I wanted to talk to you all about."

Merle glanced to the TV.

Lance opened his eyes and lifted his head from the back cushion of the chair. "You bring Squee?" he asked.

Roddy stuck his hands deep into his pockets. "That's what I wanted to come ask you about . . . is Squee. I'm . . . I know you're ready to have him home with you here, which I respect, and understand. But he's been having a hard time, like you might expect, and I'm worrying about bringing him back here so soon, what with the . . . the fire . . . the site still all . . . well, before we've been able to get everything cleared away, you know? I'm wondering if you think maybe he should stay back at my mom's a little longer, till things get cleaned up here?"

Lance swept a hand around the room. "Pretty fucking clean in *here*," he said.

Roddy nodded. "Suzy and the girls did a real nice job."

"You know," Lance said, looking to his mother now, "Suzy, in high school . . . Roddy here was just about creaming in his pants about every five minutes for that girl." He laughed, mocking.

"Lance!" Merle shushed him playfully, disapproving the way a woman her age might flirt with her own husband: *You filthy old goat, you!*

Roddy tried to ignore Lance. It was just like high school again, really. "Look," he said, directing his plea to Merle now, "I wanted to know if it would be OK with you if we kept Squee at my mom's place a couple more days, just until . . ."

"My son belongs here," Lance declared.

Roddy looked at him a second, then turned back to Merle. "I'm not saying . . . just, maybe it's too soon for him to be here at the Lodge . . ."

Merle opened her mouth to speak, but Lance got there first. "He'll have to get used to it at some point. Might as well be now." Everything he said had the weight of a decree, as though with Lorna's death he had ascended to royalty.

"Look"—Roddy spun toward him—"could you please try to think about the boy for one damn second . . ."

"Well, now you fucking sound like *Lorna*!" Lance jeered.

"Dammit, Lance," Roddy swore. "The kid won't even stay at his own grandparents' place." He looked to Merle, remembering who she was. "He went out the window in the middle of the night and ran to my mom's."

"Well, I don't blame the kid," Lance said smugly. "Who the fuck wants to stay with *Art and Penny*?" He warbled their names in sing-song mockery. "I'd run too."

"Lance," Merle cautioned.

"Jesus Christ! It's my fucking house, Ma!"

Merle stood decisively. "I've had about all I can take of you, Lance Squire." She looked to the television to once again register the con-testants' scores, then flicked off the set, grabbed her car keys from the table, and went toward the door. Passing, she clapped Roddy on the back. "Good luck with this one." She jutted her chin at her son. "Lance, could you try not to be such a goddamn bastard for once, OK?" And with that Merle turned and went out of the cabin and down the steps.

Lance had closed his eyes again and leaned his head back. He raised one hand and flipped the bird to his mother's back as she walked away.

"Look, Lance . . ." Roddy prepared to try again.

"*Look, Rodless,*" Lance mimicked. *Rodless* was from junior high. *Rodless, Dickless,* stupid adolescent-boy humor. "I said no. Which part of that didn't you understand?"

"Oh, Jesus, Lance, would you look at—" Roddy's anger was barely contained. "Could you just look at what you're . . ."

Lance was about to blow. "You know what I see when I look at myself, Rodless? You know what I fucking see? I see a man whose wife just died! A man whose wife just fucking died . . ." He started to break apart then, his voice cracking into words that came out with no sound. "She just fucking . . ." He dissolved.

Roddy took his cap off his head, ran a hand through his hair. He gave a nod, one. "I'll go get Squee."

Back at Eden's, Squee was also watching *Wheel of Fortune* on a TV that hadn't been tuned to anything but PBS since Roderick Senior had died. Roddy rapped on the back door and summoned Eden to the porch. She came out of the kitchen drying her hands on a dish towel, passed Squee on the couch, and glared at the TV. "Do you know how much television that child is accustomed to watching?" Eden said to her son.

"No, I don't. Look, Ma . . . I tried. I don't what else there is to do . . . Lance is *losing* it."

"All the more reason that child should be nowhere near him," Eden hissed.

"Fine, but what am I supposed to say? *My mother says he's not your kid anyway and you know it, so go shove it, Lance?* What exactly—"

"I'm calling him," Eden declared.

"Oh, Ma, come on." But Eden had already turned away, into the house. She went to her bedroom and closed the door behind her.

It had been long enough since she'd called the Squires that she didn't even remember the number. She looked it up, dialed, readied herself for Lance, and then let the phone ring and ring and ring. She hung up and tried again. This time he answered.

"What?" he said. "What now?"

"Lance, this is Eden Jacobs calling . . ."

"Oh, yeah, Eden. Sorry, thought you were my mom."

Eden was nothing if not straightforward. "Firstly, Lance," she said, "I'd like to express my greatest condolences to you. Lorna meant a great deal to me, and though we weren't on much of terms these last years, I think of her daily and will continue to do so. She's always in my prayers, along with you and Squee."

"Oh," Lance said. "That's nice. Thanks."

"Which brings me to the other reason for my call, which is to talk with you about Squee. I understand from what Roddy's told me that you're looking forward to having him home with you at the Lodge."

"Yes, I am," Lance said decisively.

Eden plowed on. "And while I understand your wishes at this time," she said, "I can't help but feel that you'd think differently about bringing him home if you were to really *only* think about him for just a moment, about *his* well-being . . ."

"Look, Eden," Lance said, more forcefully now, "Roddy already tried, and the answer's still no. I want my son home—what's the big fucking deal? I come home, he comes home too. Done, OK?"

"No," Eden said, "no, it's *not* OK! Suddenly you *decide* he's your son . . ."

"Jesus Christ!"

"I am terribly sorry that Lorna is dead, mister. Maybe mostly because of what is going to happen to that little boy"—Eden remembered Squee again, out in her living room, and she lowered her voice—"without her around to be some sort of a parent to him . . ."

Lance spoke loudly, and bitterly slow. He said, "I am coming to get my son now." And he hung up the phone.

Eden sped by Squee on the couch and went out the back door. Roddy was sitting at the picnic table, cleaning his fingernails with a pocketknife. "I made it worse," Eden said, coming down the stairs.

"Shit." Roddy sighed. He closed up the knife. "What happened?"

Eden shook her head. "He's coming over to get Squee himself."

"Aw, Christ." Roddy stood, then sat back down, then stood again. "Christ!"

Eden had her hand on her hip and was nodding, as though running a conversation through her head. Then she straightened pointedly, her jaw set in fury, and made a noise like a growl of frustration through her teeth. She went up the steps. "Squee!" she called out as she went through the screen door. Her voice was changed entirely. "Hey, Squee, time to get packed up, mister. Dad's on his way over to get you, bring you home." She was trying to sound cheerful, and the effect was almost ghoulish.

Five minutes later Lance pulled into Eden's driveway, left his truck running, and climbed the front steps. He rapped good and hard on the door, then opened it without waiting for anyone to answer. He looked around.

Squee came out of the guest room. He looked at his dad, looming large in the doorway of Eden's little home. It was the first they'd seen each other since the fire.

"Hurry up," Lance said, and Squee went back into the room to finish gathering his things into Eden's old suitcase. From the kitchen doorway Eden stood and watched Lance without a word.

Squee came out of the bedroom a minute later, suitcase in hand. He didn't speak either, not to his father, not to Eden. Didn't even run out back to say good-bye to Roddy before he got into Lance's truck and was driven away.

THEY PUT THE MATTRESS ON THE FLOOR. That worked better. Or used the chair; the chair worked too. It was a good, sturdy chair. But honestly, it didn't much matter what they did it on, just so long as they did it. Because that's what it was like: urgent and necessary and inappropriate and clandestine. They couldn't get past it, neither of them, couldn't get past just how incredibly *good* it felt. *Jesus,* it just felt so incredibly good: the kind of sex that took over everything, so that whatever else you were doing, you were never really doing that thing, you were just *not* having sex. It divided the world for them: there was the sex, and there was everything else. And everything else felt—oh, well, who the hell even *knew* what everything else felt like? They knew what the sex felt like, and beyond that, well, there was death and drinking and runaway children and fires and washing machines and rooms to be cleaned and parents to be placated and hotels to be run and what-the-fuck-ever else, because how could you possibly care about anything else when there was sex that felt like that sex felt?

The thing was, they *did* care. And it wasn't that sex didn't feel good, but about three seconds after it stopped feeling like the most amazing thing you ever felt in your life, about three seconds later they *did* care about the children and the laundry and the dead people and the live people and everything-the-fuck-else there was to worry about. So they got up. They went back to the world. And then they scrambled back to Roddy's shack as soon as they possibly could, because that was the only way they were getting through any of it.

It was past twelve that night when Suzy left Roddy and drove back to the Lodge, not much more than a five-minute drive on the dirt road that cut between the back of the hill into which the Jacobses' place was wedged and the beach below. The night was warm, the air alive with crickets and fireflies. You felt it outside of you, inside of you, everywhere, that kind of summer night.

Suzy took the Lodge truck down that rutted, pitted road, bouncing in the seat, stressed about getting back to Mia, about having to get up at the crack of dawn when Mia inevitably got up, stressed about whatever else she might have done wrong, since that's what being on Osprey made her feel: as if she had done something wrong but didn't know what it was yet. Whether or not her father and mother were actually watching her, her father and mother were *always* watching her, and she had *always* done something wrong.

To the right of the road were woods—if you bushwhacked through you'd hit the ravine down beyond Eden's place. On Suzy's left, the old golf course stretched out, overgrown, unused, except as a sledding hill in the winter. They'd built a new eighteen-hole course out by Wickham Beach, let this one go to seed. The dirt road had begun its life as a golf cart path, then became trafficked by locals when they realized what a shortcut it was. It pounded the shit out of the underside of a car, but the locals drove trucks mostly, and it kept the summerers in their Saabs out of the way and on the pavement, since they didn't know how to drive dirt anyway and were more nuisance than the raccoons who got plowed down nightly as they went scampering across from the golf course to the woods. *Bam.* There were always a few good raccoon carcasses sprawled across the dirt road, their insides baking into the sand.

Coming over the first rise and around the sharp bend by what was once the seventh hole, Suzy spotted in the headlights, on the side of the road, what looked to be a raccoon. She slowed. They always waited, then dashed out in front of your car at the last second, like the kamikaze squirrels in autumn who got drunk on fallen fermented fruit from crab apple trees and started racing zigzags across Route 11. Suzy peered out, straining to see farther than her headlights' range. She prepared to brake, anticipating the raccoon's mad dash. And then as she got closer, she realized it wasn't a raccoon. And as she got closer still, she realized it was Squee.

She swerved to a stop, yanked the emergency brake, leaving the engine running, and jumped down from the truck. Squee stood, frozen, off to the side of the headlights' beam as though he couldn't decide whether to run toward Suzy or away from her. Suzy managed to quell her alarm and slowed as she approached him.

"Just out for a stroll?" she said, her voice modulated.

Squee didn't say anything.

"You . . . um . . . need a ride or something?" she asked nonchalantly.

Squee shrugged, suspicious.

She got close and squatted down to his level. "Pretty late to be out alone, huh?"

Squee shrugged again, but there was concession to it. He knew she was right.

"You going anywhere in particular, or just walking?"

In the half-lit, overgrown field, Squee scratched at his shin. His fingers came away touched with blood, a mosquito-bite scab. He wiped them on his T-shirt.

"Come on," Suzy said, beginning to stand again, "let me give you a ride. I'd hate to leave you walking up that hill in the dark. Come on. Hop in. Where to?" She started toward the truck, as if to assume he'd follow. He did.

"Seat belt, please," she instructed. Squee complied. "So, where can I drop you off?"

Squee gestured with one limp hand up the hill, reluctantly, as though he hadn't had a destination in mind, but since Suzy was asking, well, he guessed he might as well go to Roddy's. She pulled a U-turn on the old golf course and drove back the way she'd come.

Pulling into Eden's driveway, Suzy shut the truck's lights. "You wait here a sec?" she asked Squee. "I'll see who's up?"

Roddy was already at the door when she got there. He looked puzzled.

"I've got Squee in the truck . . ." She lifted her chin toward the driveway.

Roddy interrupted, stepped out onto the stoop, as if he didn't believe her. "What?" It was too far for him to see.

"He was coming up the golf course road."

"Jesus *Christ*."

"This is clearly where he was headed."

"Good thing he didn't make it about half an hour earlier!"

Suzy laughed helplessly, a picture in each of their minds of whatever position they'd been in a half hour before. Roddy stepped back inside and started to pull on a pair of pants.

"What do you . . . ?" Suzy started.

"He slept on the floor here last night," Roddy said. "He can do it again. I didn't know he was there till morning then, I don't have to know now. Lance can fucking deal with it, then. The kid doesn't want to be there." Roddy shoved his bare feet into his work boots and sat down to lace them enough so he could walk.

"You want him down here?" Suzy looked around, checking the shack for evidence of herself. "Or up at Eden's?"

Roddy did the same once-over of the room. "I think he'll probably want to be . . ."

And then they were interrupted by the lights and the sound of another vehicle pulling into Eden Jacobs's driveway.

"Fucking shit." Roddy bolted up. In seconds they were both out the door and running up the hill.

Lance had gotten out of his truck and was walking quickly and angrily toward Suzy's.

"Lance," Roddy called as they approached, the name curt and damming, warning Lance away from whatever he was going toward.

Lance had just reached to open the passenger door of Suzy's truck, and he stopped to peer out into the darkness for Roddy. He stood, poised there, while Squee scrunched down in the seat, curled into himself, silent.

As the scene became clear to Lance, his expression shifted. He made out Roddy coming up the hill, and then Suzy behind him. He seemed to forget entirely about Squee in the truck and let go of the handle, put his hands on his hips, and said, "Well." He started again: "Well, what do we have here, now?"

Neither Suzy nor Roddy said anything. They kept moving toward Squee.

"Well, after all these years! Did Rodless finally get what he wanted? After all those years . . . Hey, Suze, isn't that just about the place where you and . . . You reliving old times with Rodless, here? You give him the mercy fuck he always wanted from you, Suzy?"

"Shut your mouth, Lance! Just shut . . ." Suzy flung her hand toward Squee, hunched there in the seat, which only served to remind Lance of the mission he was actually on. He turned again to the boy in the truck, confused for a second, and looked back to Suzy running at him with Roddy beside her. "What the fuck's he doing in your . . . ?" He flung open the door. "What are you doing in there?" he demanded of Squee. "You kidnapping my son, Suzy? You fucking bitch, are you kidnapping my son from me?"

Suzy and Roddy reached the truck and hovered there on the driver's side. "He was on the golf course road, Lance," Suzy said calmly. "He was out on the road in the middle of the night. I picked him up."

This news only refueled Lance's anger at Squee. "What the fuck did you think you were doing?" Lance slammed his fist down on the hood, and Roddy lunged at the sudden movement, the desire to protect Squee overtaking all else.

"Oh, what? Rodless gonna fight me? You're gonna fight me, you dickless motherfucker?"

Roddy fell back immediately, hands raised in surrender. "I don't want to fight you, Lance. The *only* thing I want is for Squee to get a good night's sleep. That's all, Lance. I just want your son to get some rest."

"Oh, now you're a fucking saint, you dickless piece of . . ."

"Lance!" Suzy screamed, just as a light in Eden's bedroom came on. Suzy lowered her pitch. "His mother is . . . He wants to stay here. What is the problem with that?" Suzy's voice was a low wail, one step from tears.

"Because I said he's coming home with me!" Lance bellowed. And then he reached into Suzy's truck, grabbed Squee around the waist, and hoisted him out of the seat.

Squee let out one cry of fear, that first, irrepressible wail of panic. It was obvious that he was crying from the way he held his hands over his eyes, but otherwise he let his body go slack, and Lance held him at his side with one arm, like a bag of topsoil. Lance opened the driver's side door and shrugged Squee inside, then pushed in behind him, slammed the door, and backed down the driveway.

Eleven

THE BLESSINGS OF HYPOTHERMIA

Here be my loves among the feathered things
The angels lend their tunes to, and their wings.
—JOHN VANCE CHENEY, "Here Be My Loves"

SQUEE SAW THE REMAINS of the laundry shack for the first time the next morning from the window of his father's truck as they drove to his mother's funeral. It was nine a.m., and the sun was shining through the ruins. He glimpsed it for only a moment, passing, craning back over the seat to see as Lance pealed out onto the blacktop. In his mind it had looked different. He'd last seen it ablaze, in the night, and the fire had seemed so whole and so consuming that it was hard to imagine anything surviving. Over the days, thinking about it, he still couldn't help thinking of the fire specifically as something that his mom would be so sad about, and then it would click in that she had gone with it. Squee had somehow been imagining the burnt site of the laundry room fire that killed his mother as a beautiful place. Or even just like the fire pit left over from when the waiters and housekeepers made a bonfire on the beach at night and sang and danced and held hands and kissed each other in the glow of the flames. If you went down the next morning, kicked at the embers and remains of log with your foot, underneath, sometimes, the coals were still warm, and the black of the pit was so black and so complete, you could look at it and remember what it had been like the night before, how beautiful it—everyone—had been.

This fire pit wasn't beautiful. It was awful, a trash heap. Squee realized how much it smelled, the burn. Once, his mom had fallen asleep on the couch in their house, and her cigarette had fallen to the carpet, which melted out around it in a spreading circle. The house had smelled for days like smoking rubber. That's what it was like. Squee's stomach twisted on itself, made a rock rise under his diaphragm. When Lance stopped at a red light on Route 11, Squee rolled down his window, leaned out, and vomited quickly onto the pavement below. Lance looked over at him, ready to yell, then saw how Squee was taking such care to lean out far, not to hit the outside of the truck door, and he reached out and patted Squee's shoulder.

Attendance at Lorna Squire's funeral was not mandatory for Lodge employees, but it was "encouraged." Gavin, Brigid, and Peg rode in Jeremy's car to Our Lady of the Island Chapel, a few blocks from town center. The church lot was full, so they parked on the street in front of Bayshore Drug and hoped island police would turn a blind eye to the half-hour parking limit, on account of the occasion. The day was warm, the sky clear, the sun bright. It was the wrong weather for a funeral. Right for a sailing regatta, a pool party.

Brigid hadn't wanted to come. The idea of seeing Lance at his wife's funeral felt creepily wrong to her somehow. But Peg had convinced her that *not* going would be a lot weirder in the end. And Gavin was going, and she didn't want to seem callous.

None of them had anything by way of funeral attire. The closest the boys could get was to wear their work clothes: black pants, white shirts. The girls had come to Osprey with backpacks of beach clothes and bar clothes, and not much of either. They went to Lorna's funeral in black stretch miniskirts and sandals.

Lance had in fact barricaded Squee in the night before, in the only windowless room in their cabin, lest he attempt another escape. Squee had slept on the bathroom floor and looked it. Lance let him out five minutes before they left for the chapel to "put on some good clothes." Squee unearthed a pair of dress pants, hand-me-downs from Reesa's boy that were already too short in the leg, and a Ralph Lauren polo shirt of a sickly shade of mauve that someone had left behind in a room one summer. Suzy cursed herself later for not having thought to lay something out for him when they'd cleaned the cabin.

Lance wasn't showered—what with Squee shut in the bathroom—and he was unshaven. That he'd combed his hair back with water from the kitchen sink and put on a cheap suit (that Lorna'd bought for him to wear to Squee's graduation from kindergarten a few years back, which he'd bailed on anyway) only made him look more disreputable.

Understanding had caught up with Penny Vaughn, precipitated by Squee's midnight flight from her home, and she now looked precisely like the mother of a dead woman. Art had been a wreck for days, and his dark suit wasn't doing anything to compensate. Merle Squire looked worn—but, then, Merle always looked worn, and she had just spent three days with Lance, which would break anyone down. Nancy Chizek had packed so much makeup onto her face she looked twenty years older than she was, and Suzy and Roddy were doing everything they could just to keep their eyes open. The only one who looked composed in the least was Bud Chizek, who, despite his suit, looked ready to grab a club and tee off.

Lance kept Squee by his side throughout the ceremony. Neither of them cried. Squee stood baffled, dazed-looking, like he didn't understand what was happening. Lance, too, looked slightly deranged. He had never been to a funeral before, and was affecting a posture he'd probably seen over Lorna's shoulder on *Dynasty*. His gestures and mannerisms were not his own. He was dramatic, which might have been appropriate for the funeral of his young wife, but he was dramatic about all the wrong things: insisting on being the first one to approach Lorna's casket, spending ten minutes scraping his shoe violently against the roots of a tree outside the chapel to dislodge a clump of mud from the treads.

The crowd was thick and dutiful, the minister obliging and uninspired. His service was mercifully short. What was there to say anyway? *She was sad. Now we are sad. Actually, we were already sad. She made everyone sad. Now she's not sad anymore, since she's dead. So maybe we shouldn't be sad either?* Really: what the hell was there to say?

After, while parties assembled and the funeral home folks got Lorna packed into the hearse, everyone just milled around, trying to figure out what to do next.

Lance seemed overwhelmed by the attention being paid him, and at the same time jealous if it was paid to anyone else. When Peg, in her minidress, bent down to talk to Squee after the service, Lance made a joking move as if he was trying to see up her skirt and said loudly, "She was my *wife,* you know?"

Peg stood quickly, her hand on Squee as if to shield him. "Of that I'm well aware, Mr. Squire. I'm terribly sorry for your loss."

"Yeah, I bet you are," Lance said. "I bet you're really broken up about it." And he spun off and walked away.

Peg turned her face to Squee's, peered intently into his eyes. "There's a lot of us at the Lodge who care about you a great deal—you ought to know," she said. "You can wake me up at any hour should you need—just come to our room and rouse me up, if you need anything at all, all right? It's room D, in the staff house . . . OK?" Squee nodded blankly, as though he couldn't quite remember who Peg was.

At the graveside Lance began to weep. There were fewer people around, fewer people in front of whom to act like a show dog, and he began to break. Nancy Chizek passed him tissues, which he grabbed up blindly and then gradually dropped to the ground, so that by the end he stood inside a little ring of white flowers all his own. Every time Lance looked at someone in the crowd at the cemetery, he seemed to realize his loss anew. He looked up, caught someone's eye, and gasped as the sobs came heaving from his chest. By the time Lorna's remains were actually lowered into the ground, Lance was leaning against his mother for support in standing. Squee stayed by his side, right between Lance and Penny Vaughn, who had grabbed Squee's hand in a clammy, powdery grip and would not let go. The angle was wrenched, and partway through Squee's arm started tingling, then lost feeling altogether. He hung beside her, looking more like a drooping stuffed animal than a boy. His eyes were glazed as a sleepwalker's. It was days since he'd spent a full night in one bed, and the delirium of sleeplessness was blunting his pain. In the wake of his mother's death, Squee was like a hypothermic: a person freezing to death actually stops feeling the cold; the body and mind protect themselves like that.

Suzy and Roddy kept their eyes on Squee, and as they left the graveside and Lance seemed to lose all interest in the boy, Suzy and Roddy nabbed Squee and brought him with them to Penny and Art's for a visitation that Lance would clearly not attend. In the course of one night in Lance's custody, Squee had gone from seeming to cope pretty admirably for a kid in his situation to looking as if he'd been hypnotized and made to witness unspeakable things. His skin was greenish, and they had him sit all the way on the passenger side against the window in case he had to throw up, which didn't seem unlikely.

⌒

A GROUP OF YOUNGER PEOPLE—locals and Lodge staff—caravanned over to the Luncheonette after the funeral. The sun cut in the windows, bleaching out their faces, illuminating acne scars, chin hairs, the sallow remains of purple bruises on pale skin. Gavin thought it was depressing how bad everyone looked, sweaty and bulging and pinched, as if all their clothes were too small. They wolfed omelet platters, not knowing what else to do. Brigid sat near one end of the tables they'd pushed together, no longer looking voluptuous, but stocky, her skin pasty and mottled with freckles, like rust-stained linen. Peg looked bluish, and Jeremy pimply.

Gavin felt a discomfort he knew from childhood: Thanksgiving dinner, too hot, overdressed, trapped at an overcrowded table. To make things worse, Brigid kept stroking his leg under the table, and Gavin thought he might run for his life from that luncheonette were it not for a girl sitting diagonally across the table among some other locals. He'd seen this girl at the funeral. He'd seen her because she'd stopped to talk to Heather Beekin, who was there with her parents, and Chandler, and his parents, and everyone. What had surprised Gavin, as he watched, was how it wasn't Heather he was fixating on, but the other girl, who was thin and a little vampiry-looking, hair dyed black, skin pale. Somehow, even in this terrible diner-window light, she looked almost regal, sort of untouchable and interesting. She had bony arms with a tendency to flail, and hips Gavin could think to describe only as womanly, and he kept finding himself picturing her with a little kid hitched to her side, one deceptively strong, skinny arm wrapped around the chubby baby.

The story coalesced in Gavin's mind as not merely logical, but inevitable: He'd come to Osprey for one girl, but really it was another he was meant to meet. Heather became a sort of inadvertent Cupid in the story, Gavin's anger melting to nothing. In the years to come, they'd all be friends—Heather and Chandler and Gavin and this girl—and their children would all be playmates! There'd be no hard feelings, no grudges, just the sheer good fortune of their good, loving lives. The girl kept catching him staring across the table, kept giving him a look, a profile, a demurred eye that said, *You looking at me? Yes*—he smiled bashfully—*yes, you!* And she came back at him confidently, pleased, seeming to say, *Well, let's introduce ourselves once this is all over, how about?* And Gavin signed back *yes* with his eyes. If the girl was aware of Brigid's fingers picking at the inner seam of Gavin's pant leg as if searching for a secret way inside them, she did not let on. Gavin would have to squeeze himself out of this Brigid thing somehow. He sensed it wasn't going to be pretty. He was tired of dealing with messes. He just wanted to go and do what he wanted to do. He wanted to know: Was that *so* unreasonable?

Brigid didn't want to go to the Vaughns' after brunch. Neither did Peg or Jeremy. And what was Gavin supposed to say? *No, I really feel like I should pay my respects and eat coffee cake with the parents of a dead woman I never met?* He had no choice but to return with the others to the Lodge.

Jeremy parked in the staff lot, and they climbed from the car, sleepy and hot and cranky as children. The asphalt under their feet was pitted and cracked with sand-filled fissures. All pavement on Osprey looked like it was made of tar mixed with pebbles and sand and shells, and it split and crumbled apart like the top of an overcooked sheet cake. They stood around and against the car, stretching, stalling. No one knew what to do next. "A swim'd be grand," Peg suggested, and Brigid said, "I wish the baths were open, you know . . ."

"The pool, you mean?" Jeremy asked. "Should we go down to the water?" he suggested, as if it were his idea to begin with.

The girls shrugged their assent.

Gavin scratched his head, then rubbed at his eyes with his thumb and middle finger as though he had a headache coming on. "I think maybe I need to go take a walk, just clear my head . . ." He tried to make himself say *alone, I need to go take a walk, alone,* but it seemed too cruel. He knew Brigid was waiting for an invitation. He tried to make himself look as beat as possible, tried to show her that what he really needed was solitude. There were a few strained moments when they all seemed to be waiting for him to ask her along. When he didn't, Brigid turned to Peg, lifted her head toward the barracks, and said, "I'll fetch my swimming costume." She reached out a hand and rubbed Gavin's sternum—an intimate gesture, something to show she was *cool.* Not clingy, not resentful. Cool. "Enjoy your walk," she said, and started up the hill. Jeremy wrapped an arm around Peg, and they followed Brigid, nodding to Gavin as they passed.

Gavin leaned against Jeremy's car, the sun bearing down on him, heat from the car pressing up through his clothes. He waited until he heard the barracks door slam on its hinges. Then he stood decisively, looked around him, and walked toward the Lodge. In the dark basement, Gavin closed himself up inside the old-fashioned telephone booth and pulled the Osprey phone book from its resting place. *Vaughn, Mr. and Mrs. Arthur.* And there was a foldout island map on the inside cover. He found the street, studied it a moment, and then tore out the map and shoved it in his pocket.

Sand Beach Road curved away from the shore past Morey's Dinghy and became Island Drive as it looped up behind the Chizeks' house. As Island Drive climbed, the road wound, serpentine, up the hill, the canopy of trees growing thick, densely netted with leafy vines as insidious as kudzu. Down on the beach, the island felt hot, bare, and exposed, but just a few minutes inland and the woods were lush and green, the air damp and rich with the smell of rotting leaves and dark soil. Every so often a long, snaking dirt drive led away from the main road toward an old weather-beaten farmhouse.

Gavin imagined himself living up here, tucked away in one of those houses. He'd always be working on the place, painting and repairing, and his wife would say to him over breakfast, *You think you'll get to that rain gutter today?* He'd take the kids outside with him when they were big enough to help hold the rusty coffee can full of nails and hand him the hammer when he needed it. Heather had always talked about the gingerbread Victorians closer to town, and they were beautiful, with their curlicues and porticoes and screened-in hammock porches surrounded by blooming hydrangea bushes. But Gavin liked it better up here, hidden away from the summer people, not packed in clusters like sleepover-camp cabins, where you could look over and see what the neighbors were barbecuing for supper. He liked the notion of living up here, out of sight of the world.

The eastern side of the hill was scrubbier, sparser, as though it were at a higher altitude or got more wind or sun or something. The road narrowed to one cratered lane, forcing cars to pull practically into the woods if another car came from the opposite direction. There were more visible houses over here too, lower-slung ranch houses set incongruously in tall meadows of cattails. Coming round a bend, Gavin caught an incredible view of the water below, a patch of cliff-bound rocky shore, a decrepit stone pier crumbling out into the bay, an abandoned bridge to nowhere. He walked in the middle of the road, ready to leap to the side at the sound of car wheels approaching from either direction. A rumbling behind him sent Gavin nearly diving into a honeysuckle bush as a dirty white truck passed him, then slowed, slowed further, and pulled right. The driver leaned out his window and craned back around toward Gavin. It was Roddy.

"You work at the Lodge, right?" Roddy called. "You going to the Vaughns'? Want a lift?"

Gavin jogged up to the truck. "Hey," he said. He peered around Roddy and smiled tentatively into the cab at Suzy, Squee, and Mia. He couldn't think of an appropriate greeting. He said, "Hello."

"Welcome to hop in the back," Roddy said, gesturing to the bed. An empty gas can lolled on its side amid a tangle of bailer's twine and seaweed.

"Is it a lot farther?" Gavin asked. "I'm kind of . . . I like the walk, you know?"

Suzy leaned over Mia. "Another mile or so, but it's all downhill."

"Thanks," Gavin said. "I guess I'll just see you there. Thanks again anyway."

"No problem," Roddy was saying. He was already shifting out of park.

"Enjoy the walk," Suzy called. The truck kicked up a cloud of dust that followed them down the road.

. . .

The Vaughns' kitchen looked like the site of a suburban Tupperware party circa 1957, platters and containers overflowing with three-bean salad and fluffy green ambrosia. Mourners spilled out the open front and back doors and onto the lawns, so Gavin was able to approach and slip in without making a distinct entrance. He was glad to have run into Suzy and Roddy, as he knew people to look for now, and he was palpably relieved to spot the kids out back in the shade of a willow tree. Standing by them was a really pretty dark-haired woman holding a heavy-looking baby in her arms, and a older woman in a rose-colored dress, squatting down to talk to Squee and Mia at eye level, which was something Gavin sort of remembered his prof talking about in Psych 100, about putting yourself on the same level as being important for communication. He and Heather had crammed for that final together, up all night in the lounge of her dorm, drinking coffee from the vending machine in the basement. That world seemed a lot more than three thousand miles and a few months away.

Gavin approached the party coolly and squatted down like the rose-dressed woman. "Hi again," he said to the kids. He smiled shyly at the women.

Squee said, "Hi," then just stood there, looking at Gavin. No mention had been made at all of the fact that it was Gavin who'd pulled Squee from the Squires' cabin the night of the fire. Not that mention *should* have been made; it wasn't a big deal, really, and it wasn't that Gavin wanted a spotlight. He just wasn't sure if Squee remembered or recognized him or not, and it seemed weird to have that hanging out there somehow, to know, *I was there when your mother died.*

Mia said, "What's your name?"

"Gavin," said Gavin, but then couldn't think of anything else, so he said, "What's yours?" though he already knew.

"That's Mia," Squee said, protective as an older brother, as if to feel out Gavin's intentions before he'd allow Mia to talk with him.

The squatting woman pushed herself creakily back to standing, unfurling a hand as she rose and extending it to Gavin. He stood as well.

"Hi, Gavin," she said. "I'm Eden Jacobs, and this is Reesa Delamico, and *that* big boy is Ryan Delamico. Can you say hello, Ryan?"

"Huh-lo," said Ryan dutifully.

"Nice to meet you," said Reesa. She smiled broadly. And though she'd just done Heather Beekin's mother's hair the afternoon before and therefore probably knew more about Gavin's romance and breakup with Heather than Gavin knew himself, she didn't say a word, just acted like anyone making a new acquaintance.

Gavin wasn't very good with people, and he stood dumbly, as if he didn't know how he'd managed to get where he was without pausing for a panic attack, during which he'd have clearly realized he was heading for a place full of people he didn't know, and ditched the whole plan entirely.

And then, as if in response to his thoughts, suddenly there was the girl from the Luncheonette, sidling over to join their cluster, saying, "Hey, Reese, you got a light?" as she breezed in, cigarette poised at her lips. Reesa's arms were full of Ryan, and she shrugged her apologies, but Gavin was already whipping a pack of matches out of his pocket and fumbling to light one for her. She paused as he got it lit, and then leaned in toward him like an old-time movie star. The cigarette caught, and Gavin fanned out the match while she inhaled deeply, blew the smoke out over her shoulder, and grinned. Eden, who heartily disapproved of all forms of smoking, gave a cough of distress and bowed out of the circle, saying, "Gavin, lovely to meet you," and scuttled off toward the house.

Reesa stood watching the cigarette lighting with distinct amusement, and as Janna took another drag and let the smoke escape slowly from the corner of her mouth, Reesa's face broke in her famous smile, and she said, with the graciousness of a southern debutante, "Gavin, have you met Janna Winger? Janna works for me down at the salon."

Gavin shrank into himself defensively as he extended his hand, as though Janna might not shake it but grab hold and slap him to the ground in some exotic karate flip.

"Janna," Reesa said, her smirk only growing, "Gavin."

"We had breakfast together this morning," Janna said.

"Oh!" exclaimed Reesa. "Well, I guess you know each other a lot better than I thought!"

Janna turned to Reesa and rolled her eyes dramatically. "Oh, please . . ."

"We were both at the Luncheonette," Gavin explained, "not together, just both there . . ."

"So you working over at the Lodge this summer?" Janna asked.

Gavin sucked his lower lip and nodded rocking on his heels. "Outfit give me away?" he said. "Did you have a chance to take a look at our specials this evening . . . ?" He was ridiculously nervous, trying desperately for the joke.

Janna acted as if he hadn't said anything at all. She spoke in a hush, as if imparting a piece of vital and delicate information. "If you ask me, Heather was really a bitch about the whole thing."

Gavin blanched. Reesa scolded, "Janna!"

Gavin was looking back and forth between them, the truth of his situation dawning on him fully. "Oh, Jesus" was all he could say.

"We graduated together," Janna was saying. "In a class of thirteen kids," she added. "Doesn't take too long for word to spread."

"Oh, Jesus," Gavin said again. He buried his head in his hands.

Twelve

ON THE INTERACTION OF SPECIES

[A]t present the place is a grubby fishing port of dirt lanes strewn with sun-baked fish heads, eatery floors tramped with mud and blood and salt. A moss bunker refinery destroys the western shoreline—great smelting kettles and massive iron drums, the smell that emanates therefrom is enough to raise the dead. But where others less visionary will come away with only a visceral memory of the unrelenting stink, I see here a great hotel, stately, luxurious suites overlooking the majestic sunset shore. There will be tennis courts, a bathing pavilion, a restaurant and theater, and on a Sunday afternoon the ladies from Fishersburg and Menhadenport will stroll the whitewashed docks, parasols cocked overhead as they watch the schooners set sail into the bay.

—SYLVESTER DANIEL, investor,
from an 1869 letter to his wife, Amelia

D EMOLITION FIRST. Then, construction. Bud, needing all the manpower he had, even cycled his waiters into the crew. Besides, it was pretty much free labor: the arrangement for June had always been *beachfront lodging and meals in exchange for help in readying the Lodge for the season.* And fine, true, that "readying" usually involved work of a highly undemanding, nontaxing variety. That it had turned into full-time hard manual labor was not something to which Bud was planning to draw anyone's attention.

The police lines were down, and some progress had been made in the demolition. Off-island boys had worked the day of the funeral, guys who knew Lorna only as the someone who'd died in the fire. The grunt-work guys were there early, drinking coffee from Thermoses or Styrofoam cups, getting ready for another day. Roddy and the unlucky waiters joined the crew, pulled on heavy work gloves, and got down to it. A matter of throwing shit into the dumpster. Why they weren't doing it with a bulldozer, no one had stopped to inquire. Probably because it was cheaper to pay a bunch of stupid thugs than it would have been to rent the necessary machinery. And Bud Chizek was nothing if not thrifty.

They'd busted down the remaining walls and posts with sledge-hammers—the fun work, no doubt, for a few guys with more muscle and spare energy than they had any constructive use for—so there was wet, charred timber splintered over everything. They started gathering and tossing, collecting and discarding. It was rhythmic, methodical, awful work. Roddy hefted awkward shovelfuls of soaked and blackened linens into a wheelbarrow, and a guy with the remains of a black eye and tattoo lines snaking out from the sleeves of his T-shirt wheeled the loads away, got help from another guy—who'd already removed his shirt in preparation for the morning emergence of the Irish girls from their dorm—in hefting the load to the dumpster's mouth. How Bud planned to lift the monolithic old sheet presses was anyone's guess. The sun shone down with macabre earnestness. A lone yellow butterfly flirted at the periphery of the wreckage, as though it knew not to come any closer.

Suzy brought Mia over to Eden's for the day to keep Squee company there, away from the Lodge. Then she got half the Irish girls out inspecting rooms—noting anything torn, broken, grotesquely or obscenely stained—and took the others with her to the maid's room. Upon entrance, they looked crestfallen.

"Look . . ." Suzy was already defensive. Did they think she wanted to be there any more than they did? They'd all signed on for this god-forsaken summer job! Did they think this was the way Suzy had *planned* to spend her vacation? "I know it's bad," she conceded, "but the rest of the summer'll be a fuck of a lot easier if we can turn this place into an organized base of operations." The girls' expressions seemed to lighten at the utterance of "fuck." Suzy made a mental note: swear. Often. She took a box of Hefty bags off a shelf and began dispensing them, one per girl, like uniforms. "Let's take advantage of the dumpster out there." She flicked the garbage bag in her hand in the direction of the old laundry. "The more of this shit we can get rid of"—she swept the bag around the room—"the happier I'll be. And right now, I'm not very fucking happy." The girls cracked smiles. It was like teaching, Suzy thought. You just had to get down there in the dirt with them and hash through it.

Brigid was probably no older than the other girls, but she comported herself with an air of some disdain, as though they were younger siblings she'd been forced to babysit. She gravitated toward Suzy, who seemed more of an equal. The other girls needed direction— *Here:* you *take this closet, and why don't* you *check the vacuum cleaners, see what works, what doesn't, what just needs a new bag . . .* Brigid had initiative, which was a relief to Suzy. She was able to assess a situation, see what needed doing, and get on it. She took over an old housekeeping cart that probably hadn't been used as anything but a junk repository in more than a decade, checked the cleaning products to see if anything was still usable, chucked the rest, and pretty soon had flipped the cart over, found a screwdriver and some WD-40 in a toolbox, and was working on the wheels. She looked confident enough in what she was doing that Suzy went to work clearing another similar cart of debris so Brigid might have a go at its wheels as well.

"So," Suzy began, with an animation so contrived that she didn't even want to finish the sentence, but there was nothing any better, nothing particularly less ironic to say. "So how are things going for you here at the Osprey Lodge?"

Brigid snorted. "I'd rather be scrubbing shitters for the IRA at this juncture, I'd say." She bugged her eyes, her mouth pursed in a psychotic grin.

"Oh, that sounds fabulous," Suzy cried. "You think they'd take on an American? Really, I could be packed, ready to go, in"—she looked at her watch—"five minutes."

They laughed halfheartedly.

Awhile later Suzy said, "I feel really awful for all of you guys, coming all this way . . . it's usually a *little* better around here than *this*."

"My sister was here a year ago."

"That's right," Suzy said. "I forgot. So you know . . ."

"To be honest with you," Brigid said, "I'm rather sure I'd still be something of a miserable article if Mrs. Squire . . . if there'd been no fire at all. I'd've managed to get myself messed with quite regardless, I expect."

Suzy looked at her in confusion.

"Oh, it's a damn boy," Brigid said.

Suzy winced in empathy. "Someone back home?"

"Oh, no luck of the sort, no. Right here." Brigid nodded resentfully.

"On-island?" Suzy was surprised.

"Oh, right here at the Lodge, if you'd believe."

"A waiter?" Suzy's face was still pinched, as if expecting a blow.

Brigid brightened then. "You wouldn't happen to know him, would you?" Her eyes were expectant. "Gavin? He's from California?"

"Yeah," Suzy said. "No, I mean, I know who he is, but . . . the one who came from Stanford, with Heather Beekin, right?"

"Is *that* her name?" Brigid hardly concealed her disdain.

"Did you meet her?" Suzy was confused again.

"No, not me. Not exactly . . ." Brigid paused, as though figuring out how to explain. "After the funeral yesterday, a gang of us went for a bite at the Luncheonette."

"Heather went out to lunch with you?" Suzy was more confused than before.

Brigid slowed, explaining as though Suzy were not very bright. "There were quite a lot of them I hadn't met. From the town. Introductions weren't properly made, you know. Then, last night, quite late—Gavin—he was out here on the deck with her, he was. Not that I know him well, you know," she confessed. "I'd only just met him, but he's acted . . . oh, bloody, I don't know—"

Suzy cut in. "I'd have a hard time . . . What'd she look like? The girl?"

Brigid made a face to imply she wasn't much to look at. "A bit tall," she said, "fair skin, dark hair, a bit heavy in the hip . . ."

Suzy was shaking her head.

"Rather a gothic look . . ."

"Janna," Suzy said. "That's not Heather Beekin. That's Janna Winger."

Brigid's face went blank. The name meant nothing to her.

"Janna works for Reesa? At the salon?"

Brigid was shaking her head. "I'd entirely assumed it was the girl-friend, the . . . *Heather.*"

"Janna," Suzy said again. "They were talking at the Vaughns' yesterday, actually . . ." She caught herself. "The Vau . . . Lorna's parents, they had a little gathering after the funeral at their—"

"And *Gavin* was there, you say?"

"Actually, we passed him on the way there—he walked over the hill." Suzy was nodding.

"He *did* head for a walk . . ."

"No," Suzy said, "no, but, he knew where he was heading. We stopped. We offered him a ride. That's where he was going."

"What a *shit.*" Brigid's tone was bitter; she cared a good deal more than she wanted to reveal.

"I'm so sorry."

Brigid slammed down her screwdriver. "The fucker," she said.

"Were you . . . ?" Suzy tried.

"Oh, I don't even *know*. We'd had a . . . We'd just begun to . . . Oh, bloody—how bloody stupid."

"Maybe they're not . . . ?" Suzy began again.

"Right." Brigid snorted. She'd passed the fucker in the hall of the barracks that morning, and again at breakfast in the dining room, and he'd given her an absurd, sheepish, apologetic, nodding hello, then tucked his head down and barreled off as if he had savagely important business ahead. Brigid was so blindsided that she had yet to so much as acknowledge his greetings. She thought she might soon be able to muster a response of acutely conveyed distaste: nose wrinkled and lip curled as though repulsed by a horrid smell, hand slightly open, a breathy snort to say, *What the fuck?* It seemed as if it might be the only look she had left. As they worked in the maid's room that afternoon, Brigid developed a private theory to explain Gavin. She told Suzy about how he sounded when he'd spoken a bit about Heather, and about his fantasies about moving to the island and living happily ever after. Brigid's theory was that he had it in his head to take up with another island girl—it was the only way to make Heather adequately jealous, to make it really sting.

When Brigid left the lodge that afternoon, her skin felt itchy and raw from the cleaning chemicals. She was walking up the hill, desperate for a shower, when she saw Gavin come out the north door of the barracks, freshly showered himself, and start down the path.

"Hey, pretty girl . . ."

But it wasn't Gavin calling. The Squires' cottage sat just south of the staff building, and from where she stood Brigid could see Lance sitting on his porch, beer in hand, waving her over. To her left, she shot Gavin her well-rehearsed *What the fuck?* look, though he was probably too far off—or too clueless—to appreciate it, and she veered right, to Lance Squire.

"Hey-ay," Lance called as she approached.

"Hi." Brigid felt awkward, unsure of what to say to this man. She knew what was only appropriate: "I'm so dreadfully sorry—"

He cut her off. "You know," he said, "that's all I heard today from anyone. Can't take much more sorry."

"I'm sor—" she began, then dropped it with an involuntary laugh.

"*That's* what I need," Lance said. "I need to see a pretty girl smile."

Brigid obliged.

"Would you like a beer?" Lance asked. "We can shoot the shit here, just talk, just talk, not talk about sorry, about how sorry we all are, just not talking about anything, just shoot the shit . . . Would you do that, gorgeous? Can I get you a beer? Please? Sit and have one beer with an old man?"

Brigid took the bait. She swiveled her head from side to side. "What *old* man's that? Where?"

Lance veritably leapt from his chair, pulling it back and offering it to her. "You sit. Sit. I'll get you a beer."

Brigid did as she was told.

When the door slammed again, Lance was placing an icy can of Schlitz in her hand and plunking down a chair for himself beside her. The beer felt exactly like what she wanted. She cracked it open, took a long sip, then rolled the can along her stinging forearms.

"It's that cleanser stuff," Lance said. "Right? It itches?" His eyes were already welling with tears. "Lorna'd rub ice on it." He flicked at his eyes with the back of his hand, then fumbled to light a cigarette. "God, I'm a fucking mess." He got the smoke lighted and inhaled deeply.

"Could I bum one?" Brigid asked.

"My pleasure, baby." He handed her the pack and the lighter. As she extracted one and got it lit he was saying, "Tell me something— anything. Tell me some dumb normal thing. Like you'd of told me last week. Some stupid thing about noth—hey," he remembered, "how's that boy? That college boy—how's things with the fucking college boy?" He was extraordinarily pleased with himself for the retention of that small memory outside his own circumstance and pounced on it. "How the fuck goes it with the college boy?" He smiled so wide, it was ghoulish.

"To tell you the truth," Brigid said on an exhale of smoke, "he's a shitty bastard and I should have known it from the outset."

"Oh, no," Lance cooed, enjoying himself now. "What'd he do to hurt you, baby?"

Brigid brushed hair from her face with calculated nonchalance. "Just found himself another girl to take up with entirely."

Lance let his mouth drop open. Then his face contorted in disbelief. "Who?" he said, so vehemently it sounded like a dare: *You just try and name someone hotter than you on this island.*

"The one from the beauty salon . . . ?"

Lance nearly tipped over in his chair. His eyes bulged with laughter. *"Reesa?!"* he cried incredulously.

"No, not her," Brigid said, "the younger one . . . Janna, is it?" Brigid now knew precisely what her name was, but the fact that she gave a fuck was no one's business but her own.

Lance's disbelief abated only slightly. "That fuckhead's going to take *Janna Winger* over *you?* He's out of his fucking mind, baby! Baby, anyone who's going slumming with Janna Winger instead of the hottest little girl to hit this shithole in a hell of a time—he's not in his right mind, baby. That boy's fucking nuts!"

Brigid drank her beer eagerly. She didn't know what to say.

Lance drank too, marveling at the insanity of the world. "Fucking nutcase. What a dumb stupid fuck."

When Brigid had finished her beer, she set it down on the railing and stood to go. "I've got to have a shower . . . these chemicals . . ."

Lance's eyes lit up. "Oooohhh-ooh! Can *I* come?"

And if the look she wanted to give him was the look she'd practiced for Gavin—the *What the fuck is your problem, asshole?* look—she managed somehow not to. Somehow she managed just to laugh—a hearty, heady, *Ha ha ha ha, we're all so bloody funny, aren't we?* laugh that at least got her down the porch steps and headed toward home.

⁓

SUZY STOPPED INTO the beauty salon when she'd finished in the maid's room for the day. Reesa, too, was about to close up and head home, and Suzy helped her and Janna tidy the place a bit as they chatted. Reesa had trained a few of the local girls herself—Janna, and Cybelle Schwartz too. They were just past eighteen, and Reesa had invested a great deal of time and energy in trying to persuade both of them to get off Osprey Island and go live in the world before they wound up married or pregnant.

When she was younger, everyone thought Reesa would be the kid discovered by some movie director spending a weekend on Osprey, plucked out and whisked away to turn her all-American good looks into someone's pretty penny. No one thought she'd be on Osprey past her sixteenth birthday. But sixteen, eighteen, twenty, all came and went, and there was Reesa, lovely as ever, waiting tables at the Island Grill or Tubby's Fishhouse. She'd gone with Abel Delamico since before anyone could remember, and they'd married just after high school. Abel's fishing business did well, and they had a nice house out near the point at Scallopshell Cove. Four beautiful kids. There was nothing in Reesa Delamico's life to indicate that she was anything but content. She was the pride of Osprey: she could've flown away at any time, but never had.

Instead, she made sure that others took the sort of opportunities she hadn't. Jasper, Reesa's oldest, was eighteen and gone already, off to college a year early. She missed the hell out of him, and that was exactly the way she wanted it. Reesa wanted Jasper to have choices. She wanted him to do whatever he did because he'd chosen it, not because he'd never known enough to see a choice. If, after college, Jasper chose to come back home to Osprey, it'd be because Osprey was where he wanted to be, not because he didn't know how to get to anywhere else.

It was just past five o'clock when Gavin appeared outside the salon's glass door. Janna took off her smock, checked her face in the styling station mirror, checked it again in the next styling station mirror, said " 'Bye," and dashed out to meet him. They paused self-consciously on the deck to kiss, and Reesa and Suzy just watched, too interested to feign otherwise. If you'd looked in through the glass door at those two old friends inside the beauty shop, you'd have thought they were watching two entirely different scenes. Reesa beamed with pride— pride mixed with nostalgia. Janna was something of a second daughter to her, and she feared the girl might never muster the incentive to leave Osprey. But now—a boy from California! Even if it didn't work out in the long run, he might at least induce Janna to see something of the world.

Suzy, on the other hand, might as well have been watching some graphic nature documentary, staring in horror as though a cannibalistic mating ritual were being enacted on the deck of the Osprey Lodge.

And then, in a flurry of twenty-four-hour-old love, Gavin and Janna were down the stairs and disappearing up the beach. It was Reesa who spoke first, wagging her head in marvel. "How about *that*?" she said. "I introduced them at Art and Penny's yesterday . . . who'd've thought? I've never seen her like this—she's usually harder, you know? Harder to crack. What?" Reesa noticed the look on Suzy's face. "What? Suze? What's the . . . ?"

Suzy shuddered off the feeling that had overcome her. "I just . . . I was just hearing . . . I mean, do you *know* him?"

"He's the one . . . Gavin, the Stanford one . . . Heather's . . ."

"No, I know *that*," Suzy said. "I was just hearing about him, from Brigid."

Reesa shook her head; the name meant nothing to her.

Suzy's dislike of this Gavin kid surged. "The girl *after* Heather and *before* Miss Janna. Brigid. She's one of the Irish."

Reesa's face registered amusement and confusion. "There was a girl *between* Heather and Janna? For how long—three days?"

"Not even, I don't think," Suzy said.

Reesa's good humor soured. Her hands went to her hips and her smile puckered in. She was awfully protective of Janna. "So, he's a player."

Suzy nodded ruefully. "Apparently he just disappeared on Brigid yesterday . . . One night he's inviting her to sleep with him on the beach—" Both women shook their heads, rolled their eyes. People came from off-island and thought it romantic to camp on the beach, while Islanders knew far too well that it was neither romantic nor comfortable, and between the sand crabs and the mosquitoes it ranked up there as one of the more regrettable experiences to be had on Osprey. "—And the next night he's nowhere to be found. Not a word of anything, Brigid says—no explanation, no apology, nothing . . . She's sort of crushed," Suzy said. "I feel for her."

Reesa frowned. "And here I was getting all psyched for Janna. I'm plotting the wedding, packing her up, shipping her off to California." She'd spent the day envisioning it all: the dress (strapless, with a full skirt, in something darker, not white, something to set off Janna's paleness—maybe red, deep red), the reception (here, at the Lodge, in fall, when the summer folk were gone, as the leaves began to change— maybe the dress would be a burnt orange, or an autumn red, like Japanese maple), the sweet farewells, the infrequent visits home, just for the weekend, a baby or two in tow . . .

Suzy said, "I don't think he's looking to take someone away with him."

Reesa didn't get it.

"I think he's looking for a way *onto* Osprey."

"What is he, insane?" Now Reesa was worried. Understanding lit her face. "He's just looking for a way back to Heather! I'm such an idiot!" She smacked her own forehead in emphasis. "Here I am, just thinking, *La la la, a love story for Janna* . . . He's just trying to stay close to Heather! Oh Jesus . . . poor Janna! What a little shit."

Suzy, coming quickly to regret the leaps of logic being made from her nuggets of gossip, began to hedge. "I don't know, Reese. For all we know it could all be in earnest. They're kids. He's probably not *scheming* to—"

"Scheming or not," Reesa said, firm conviction in her voice, "I don't need some stupid college boy messing with Janna. That'd be just enough to scare her off the outside world. And I wonder why will no one leave this place?"

Suzy softened. "They leave," she said quietly. "Some do, some leave . . ."

But Suzy was really talking about herself, and now Reesa was thinking of Jasper. Suzy *had* made it off, but so many of them— always the ones who were *dying* to get off—they'd last six months, maybe a year, and then they were back. Most of them. Suzy joked that it was like prison: you spent too long in that once you got out you were so scared you started making trouble just to land yourself back. But that was *Suzy*. Most people, if you asked them seriously, would say that if you grew up on Osprey you had ideas about how it would be to live out in the world across the bay. Osprey was your childhood; it was your troubled teen years. It was what you knew to want to escape. Then you got out and saw how things were out there, and then you understood how good you had it on that idyllic little island, where people knew who you were and what you came from, where it was safe to walk at night, where people took care. On Osprey you had credit at every store in town, and someone would always find you a job in construction, or helping out at the church, the school, the dump. You didn't spend so much time deciding things on Osprey Island: You wanted coffee, you went to the Luncheonette. Prescriptions were filled at Bayshore Drug. You needed cigarettes, you stopped at Lovetsky's. A haircut, Reesa's. Life on Osprey was easier. Sure, there were things you missed out on, but if you'd grown up on Osprey you'd never had them, so you couldn't really miss them much. And all those things out there in the world didn't help if what you really missed was home.

Reesa folded a smock under her arm. "Thank fucking god Jasper didn't have a girl here!" she said.

Suzy let out a laugh and held up both her hands, fingers crossed. "He's going to make it, Reese. He'll make it."

Reesa closed her eyes, shook her head, and held up her hands in a short prayer for her son.

Thirteen

THE NATURE OF THE STRUCTURE OF A LIE

If the osprey passes from the American scene, we will lose a majestic and unique bird. Alone in a family between the hawks and the falcons, the osprey, unlike those numerous tribes, has but one genus, one species.

— ROGER TORY PETERSON, "The Endangered Osprey"

T HEY LAY ON THE MATTRESS on the floor of Roddy's shed. An old upright aluminum fan buzzed and whirred and blew out the sound of the crickets. Roddy lay on his back, stretched long, longer than the mattress, hands crossed behind his head. Suzy curled in toward his body, head in the crook of his underarm, knees at his hip, finger tracing the length of his torso, collarbone to pelvis, shoulder to hip bone. She ran her fingers along the scar on his side, her eyes closed.

"I never worked at a sawmill," he said.

"Huh?" She opened her eyes.

"I didn't get it working at a sawmill."

"I guess I figured." She closed her eyes again. She lay very still, just the fingers, tracing.

He was quiet a long while.

He hadn't intended to tell her. He'd intended to tell no one. But none of this was foreseeable, and circumstances dictated their own imperatives. He had sense enough to have learned *that* much. He had sense enough to be afraid. Afraid that to give up a secret to one person on Osprey Island was to lose that secret to the world. And it wasn't that the walls had ears or the trees had eyes, or that the birds overhead overheard your confessions and whispered them into the wind. It was that people just couldn't help themselves.

He felt it in himself, that desire to talk. Perhaps it was his vigilant check of that desire that kept him so unnaturally quiet much of the time. He wanted to tell her, though. He wanted to give her something he'd never given anyone: a truth, of sorts.

He had trouble understanding what truth meant. He had lived with secrets, and secrets were just lies of omission and as hard to live with as any other lie. For there was no such thing as a solitary lie. It wasn't that lies begot more lies; the casting of one lie merely brought into focus and relief a sprawling net of other lies. Roddy had been living those lies—a whole world of them—for twenty years, which was long enough for the world of lies to become its own truth. Or reality, at least. Maybe there'd been a time when he could have acknowledged the lie and stepped away from it, stepped back into the truth, but that time was long gone. That lie was now part of a foundation upon which other things had grown, and truth and fiction were entwined, which meant that there was no such thing as truth anymore. Nor had there ever been. What Roddy had once seen as truth—the truth of his childhood, for instance, before his lie—had only *seemed* like truth, when, really, it was as much of a lie as everything else. It was only in lying himself that he'd learned of the nature of the structure of a lie. And now that he could see it, he could see how everything was built of lies and how the world was a city of pick-up sticks raised on quicksand.

To acknowledge his lie to Suzy may have meant a good many things, but it meant one thing very clearly to Roddy: He knew he couldn't undo the reality spawned from the lie, couldn't ever return to the truth he'd left behind. But he could, at least, make sure that Suzy knew the lie for what it was. He could tell her. And he started to.

He told her what it was like to turn eighteen on August 8, 1968. He told her some things she already knew: like what it was like to live in a place where certain things didn't get questioned—if you were a man and your country went to war, then you, as a man, went to fight in that war. End of story. Unless you happened to have a mother unlike every other mother you'd ever known. A mother who swore she'd burn your draft card herself if you didn't do it first. A woman who begged you, whatever you did, not to fight that filthy, wrong, horrible war.

Suzy listened. She understood.

Roddy's father had been a weak man who lived by a rigid set of codes, not smart enough to face the world without them. A man who told his son: *You burn that draft card, you'll be on the next ferry off of Osprey and never coming back, you hear?* A man who said: *You don't fight in that war, you're no son of mine,* while his wife screamed and cried: *No son of mine is fighting in that war.* You had until you turned eighteen, and that had bought Roddy time—a few months past graduation—but not peace. What they'd done was effectively demand that he choose: *Your country or your mother? Your mother or your father?* Roddy'd had a war waged through himself.

"I couldn't register. I couldn't *not* register. I couldn't talk to anyone." Who would he have talked to? There were no draft counselors on Osprey Island. There were no hippies. Aside from Eden's, there was only one point of view to be had.

"I left," he said. "I had to. Whatever I did, it had to be my decision. It didn't matter. I didn't have a home anymore." Eden and Roderick had managed to both lose their son and erode their marriage to a civil arrangement of household tasks and finances. That lasted a year, until *National Geographic* and the plight of the osprey served to render their relationship nothing more than legal. But until then, Eden cooked dinner, dusted, hung the laundry up to dry. Roderick cut the lawn and put out the trash.

Roddy hadn't cared what people thought. They thought he'd fled. Never imagined that once he left their world he'd have gone anywhere but north, all the way. "Canada?" he said. "What the fuck was I going to do in *Canada*?" He'd never been anywhere in his entire life. "It wasn't about right and wrong," he told Suzy. "I didn't know what was right and what was wrong. Or even if I knew . . . it was about what I could live with. It's impossible to say, to talk about now, know-ing . . . you know? Understanding. Then? I wasn't like Eden . . ."

Suzy's hand left Roddy's scar for the first time since he'd begun. She pushed herself up on an elbow and looked at him in a way that Roddy would never be able to forget as long as he lived. She said, "Oh my god, you fought."

He didn't answer.

What Roddy saw on Suzy Chizek's face in that moment of revela-tion was, he thought, pride. And as quickly as that new "truth" was born in her, his truth and his confession—*the* truth—slipped away. He fought back tears, which she read as the pain of a veteran of that ter-rible, wrong, awful war, the pain of having to deceive his mother, pain that made so much about Roddy Jacobs suddenly make so much sense.

Really, he fought back tears because he knew that in the truth *she* saw, his actions were valiant. In her eyes, he was suddenly brave. He could see the life she saw: unable to live with the idea of himself as a deserter, he'd enlisted, fought, seen unimaginable things, been injured, come home. In Suzy's eyes, Roddy had known firsthand the horrors and survived to share his stories, to feed the strength of the antiwar movement and crusade for an end to the brutality. This story painted Roddy as so much more a man than the peace-love hippies who danced away to Canada while Suzy Chizek's brother got his body blown apart in a flaming rice paddy. Roddy now joined ranks with the bravest of the brave—he'd fought and *then* renounced—and it was the only story of Roddy's past that Suzy would ever be able to imagine now. She had too much Osprey in her to see otherwise. Too much Roderick Senior and Chas Chizek and Bud. Too much football and fireworks. Too much red, white, and blue. When Suzy Chizek left Osprey Island and went to college and joined the long-haired, braless, barefoot protests, she'd believed with a passion born of anger not at the U.S. government but at the fact that her brother Chas was dead. Hers was a passionate adolescent rebellion against everything her parents believed, everything she'd been raised to believe, and everything that had conspired to produce a world in which her brother didn't get to be alive.

When he couldn't hold back the tears any longer, Roddy let them come, and he let Suzy Chizek rock him and hold him as he cried.

Because the actual truth was this: On August 8, 1968, Roddy Jacobs turned eighteen and mailed the goddamned draft registration, because it was easier to mail it than not to mail it. And then he waited. It was the waiting he couldn't take. Waiting and not knowing.

He lasted one month—the longest month of his life—and then he marched into the draft board and said, "I volunteer, I'll fight. Send me anywhere. I don't care." At that point he was surprised to pass the psych exam. Because someone should have seen that he was far from all right.

It was *after* he volunteered that he ran, which was like signing himself up for the Most Wanted list. So then there was fleeing, and getting caught, and doing time. Then getting out, and then President Ford coming along, offering pardon, but by then there were enough people who thought the whole thing had been bullshit from the start, so he didn't have trouble finding work, getting by.

The scar—the scar Suzy'd held under her hand as if to hold his body together in one piece—the scar was from fighting, yes. He'd gotten the injury in a bar in Tucson shortly after he'd fled, in a fight with a vet who'd called him a traitor and a coward and pushed him down. Roddy stumbled, beer in hand, and fell hard against the pool table, his beer bottle breaking on impact between the table and his body. The felt surface was ruined, and Roddy suffered wounds that required emergency surgery in a hospital where the cops had no trouble catching up with him, leveling charges of draft evasion. And that, as his mother would say, was that.

Fourteen

THE BROODINESS OF HENS

A Brief Lesson in Avian Reproduction

The chicken, like the Mormon of old, is a polygamous creature. At any given moment, and with little pomp or circumstance, the male selects the female whose vent is closest to his own. He drops one wing to the ground, grabs his intended under the other wing, and mounts. Flapping his wings, the male balances, his vent flush against the hen's. Transfer of sperm from his cloaca to her oviduct is swift; the male dismounts. An avian sex act lasts roughly fifteen seconds. It is only afterward, in fluffing her feathers, that the female appears to experience any satisfaction whatsoever.

—WALKER WINSTON, *A Gentleman's Guide to Raising Chooks*

IN JULY OF 1969, a year after Roddy had left Osprey Island in the skirmish of his parents' tug-of-war, Eden Jacobs was reading the latest issue of *National Geographic,* when, between a tribute to Ike Eisenhower and a photo travelogue of Switzerland ("Europe's High-Rise Republic"), she discovered an article of considerably greater personal interest. The opening photograph was arresting: a screaming bird, its wings spanned across a double-page spread. "THE OSPREY: Endangered World Citizen." It had been quite some time since Eden had spotted an osprey on her daily beach walk. Mornings, Eden laced on her sturdiest shoes and patrolled a stretch of Scallopshell Beach, Roderick's heavy WWII-issue spyglasses trained to the sky. She did not waver in her morning rituals, and over the years could boast having spotted any number of owls and red-tailed hawks and what have you. But the sighting of an osprey, its eagle-wings stretched majestically across the sky, that was rare—even on an island named for the creature—and, by 1969, getting rarer. The *National Geographic* article confirmed it: the osprey, as a species, was nearing extinction.

"It's because of chemicals," Eden told her husband that evening at dinner. She helped him to another serving of potatoes. "Dee—Dee—Tee," she enunciated. "It's one of the ones they use for pesticide. That's what's killing off the ospreys."

"Maybe they're pests," Roderick suggested. He pushed a forkful of meat into his mouth. Relations in their home had been strained in the turmoil and wake of their son's departure, but it was Roderick who'd been broken by it, not Eden. She had won—the boy was off in Canada with the rest of the cowards—and Roderick had taken his defeat badly, if quietly, in the end. It had taken the fight out of him.

"You hush," Eden scolded. "This is serious."

Roderick succumbed. He was a large man, physically imposing, but really no match for his wife in most things. Too heavy a drinker, he had never overcome the sense of his own intellectual inadequacy— that he was, ironically, just intelligent enough to recognize.

"Listen," Eden instructed. She lifted the magazine from the table beside her. *"If taken from an insecticide-polluted area, fish may introduce poisons into the birds' bodies. The author"*—and here Eden's voice rose with importance—*"world-famed ornithologist Roger Tory Peterson"*—she spoke his name as if he were her own flesh and blood, repeating it as if to congratulate herself on such a prestigious relation—*"Roger Tory Peterson believes that this may be the reason for egg failures in Connecticut River eyries."* Eden looked up at her husband. "We're just across the sound from there," she said, "and they mention us in the article." She flipped a few pages forward and began reading again: *"Ospreys are more than just birds to be enjoyed. They are an alarm system of things gone haywire in the river, the estuary, and the sound. They are sensitive indicators of the environment."*

"Probably true," Roderick conceded.

"More than probably," Eden added. Then she said, "I'm going to do something about it."

Roderick's body tightened. "What are you, one woman, going to do about it?"

"I'm going to build nesting platforms," she said, "first of all. To help them know they have a safe place to lay their eggs. But it's the *eggs themselves* that are the problem," she told him, "and they're worst in *this area*. The eggs are breaking before they hatch. They weigh *twenty-five percent* less than they used to. The eggshells. *Twenty-five percent less.*"

"How are you . . . ?" But she didn't let him finish.

"We have to stop them from using those pesticides," she said. "I'm talking to Mayor Worth tomorrow."

"There's no farms on Osprey anymore," Roderick said.

"And I probably can't stop farmers from using them on the mainland," she agreed, "but we can ban them from here for good so no one can start. And we can try to get to people so they know."

"Whoa! There's no *we* here, Eden. Stop that with *we*. This is *you*, Eden. This is you alone." This was Roderick, putting his large foot down wherever he could, just to feel the stamp. Roderick was born on Osprey, met Eden on a summer trip to Maine, and had her knocked up and home with him on the island before Halloween, and though she'd succumbed to the facts of her life early on—wife, mother, Islander—she'd never acquiesced to Osprey's ways. This embarrassed Roderick; it marked him as a man who couldn't control his wife.

"Our garden." Eden gestured toward the back of the house, where tomato vines grew in neat, staked rows, and beans climbed their tripod poles like trained ivy. "It'll need to be twice the size next summer." Her plans were long range. "Enjoy that roast"—she pointed to Roderick's dinner plate—"because once the freezer's emptied you're not getting any more of it unless I can find a farmer who raises them without all that poison. Because that's where it *is*," she insisted, "in the food. And I won't have it anymore. Not in my house. Unless you want to raise the pigs out back yourself. Otherwise, you need a chop or a steak, you get it down at Tubby's or the Grill. Not here." She paused. "We'll turn the shed out back into a henhouse, so we'll have eggs. The library's ordering me a book about milk cows, but I just don't know if we'll have the room. They have to graze, you know."

"A cow!" Roderick exploded. "I'm a carpenter! Not a farmer! I am not raising goddamn cows!" And though the rage was bubbling deep inside him, the words that came out were nothing more than steam.

"Then we just won't have milk," Eden said, and the case seemed to close in her mind.

Eden and Roderick's had never been a marriage of love, but a product of their time and circumstance: not companionable, but suitable. He paid the bills; she cooked the meals. Arguments, she won, which only sent him to the bar, or hunting, which was fine. In the end he did as he was told, and in turn she took care of him, which he couldn't have done on his own. Like a governess and her ward, they were mutually dependent. They got on sufficiently to make it through the days together, and they did in fact make it through a good many days.

Eden Jacobs had never kept a rooster. No need. Not if you just raised hens for laying, that is. Those girls each put out a good eating egg every couple of days, no matter what—as long as you fed and kept them well and gave them a few hours under an electric light in winter when the days got short and temperatures brought production down. It was a lot easier to keep things under control without a rooster in the henhouse.

Eden liked the chicken shed full to about ten hens. She believed—firmly—in population control for humans, and she believed in it for birds. Naturally, in the late spring, early summer, a hen might start going broody: that biological imperative to amass a clutch of eggs and sit on them until they hatched. And sure, there were plenty of hybrid hens with the instinct for broodiness bred right out of them, but those, Eden thought, were birds for the egg-laying corporate empires. She didn't believe in some kind of superchicken bred for human convenience. If she was going to raise her own, they were going to be honest-to-goodness, nonengineered, unsaccharine hens.

Mostly she raised them for eggs, but Eden liked a nice roast chicken or a broiler as much as the next person, and *her* chickens were safe and healthy to eat, not like the poisoned garbage they sold down at the IGA. So Eden raised dual-purpose birds—good for eggs and good for meat—and every so often she'd cull one from the flock and slaughter it. *No business raising them if you're not willing to do the work,* she'd say. The killing and cleaning wasn't her favorite job, but it was a necessary part of it all. To keep up with the ones she ate and the ones she inevitably lost to predators or the random undetected disease, about once a year Eden took a drive over to George Quincy's place and borrowed a rooster for a week or so to mate with one of her girls and raise up another brood of baby chicks.

George Quincy had a sizable piece of land on the north end by Osprey Cove, and he'd been raising all sorts of critters out there for years, and those animals had kind of become his pastime and his family. George was happy enough to have Eden take one of his birds over to her place for a roll in the proverbial hay (hay actually made a very poor nesting litter for chickens, all those hollows to trap moisture—much better to use wood shavings, but that was a whole other issue . . .) with one of her hens.

In late May, soon after Roddy's return to Osprey, Eden had driven over to George's with a large cage in the back of her car to pick up Franklin, a remarkably good-natured Cherry Egger who'd already fathered a few of Eden's broods in the past. George had been having some trouble mating his own birds that season, but he said he was nearly one hundred percent sure that Franklin wasn't the problem.

"I think I got it figured out," he'd said, as Eden climbed from her car. She went around back to collect the cage. "It's the *roost!*" he declared, and he'd looked at that moment as happy as Eden had ever seen George Quincy. "Talked to a guy on the mainland—poultry guy—told me: check the roost. Sure enough, the thing's getting wobbly. Poultry fellow said sometimes that'll do it—eggs won't fertilize right if you got a shaky roost." George took the cage from Eden and stood by, beaming.

"If only it worked like that for people," Eden had mused. "You got an unstable home and the kids'll flat out refuse to get conceived. Oh, if only . . ."

George just stood there shaking his head, smiling thoughtfully, not quite following Eden's train of thought but nonetheless appreciative.

After a moment he lifted the cage, recalling what Eden had come for. "Who's going to be Franklin's little lady this year?" he asked.

"Lorraine's getting broody, I'm pretty sure," Eden said. "The New Hampshire Red?"

George nodded his recollection. "She's been through this before."

"With Franklin, even, if memory serves . . . three, four years back?"

George was still nodding, scuffling his feet in the dirt, eyes down. "Think so," he said. "I think so, yeah."

Lorraine was about seven, had been born right out back at Eden's. She was quiet, motherly, a little neurotic, but she handled well and wasn't fussy. Some chickens were just plain stupid creatures—peckish, nervous, brainless beasts. You didn't lose sleep over slaughtering one of them. Some of them practically sprawled themselves across the chopping block, as if they knew that's where they'd been headed all along. Those were the ones to eat: the idiots. And the boys.

And then there were chickens like Lorraine, or like Paulette, or Margery. Eden'd had Margery since she'd started the whole coop—from the very first shed that Roderick had built, under grudging and grumbling duress. Margery was about as old as a chicken could get, had spent probably six, seven summers total in the coop for one, broody, sitting on her eggs. She was a good mother, but Eden had put her into retirement, let her rest in her dotage. Margery'd been with her through it all. For Eden, on Osprey Island—which is to say: for Eden, in this world—Margery the hen was about the closest thing she had to a friend. Margery was the sort of friend Eden respected. She made her needs known when she had them, and otherwise she minded her business. Eden thought—in new ways every day, it seemed—how much there was that people could learn from chickens. At the school— Eden knew through Reesa, who'd heard it from her kids—at the school they called her the Bird Lady. No doubt they meant to mock her, to poke fun at a strange old lady, as kids were wont to do. But the name, and the notion, had simply tickled Eden. She could imagine a lot of worse things.

So in late May that year Eden had gone to fetch George Quincy's Cherry Egger cock, Franklin, and for a week or so she'd let Franklin and Lorraine do their thing, vent to vent, as it were. When Lorna used to help Eden with the chickens, she'd told Lance about the mating process and he'd been amazed: "A cock's got a *vent*? You're telling me a *cock's* got no *cock*?!" He'd say to Lorna, or to Eden when he saw her: "How's the cockless cock?" "You've got so much to learn," Eden'd say back to him. "You've got a hell of a lot to learn, Mister Lance."

And you could learn a lot from chickens, though a rooster was dif- ferent from a man in some ways. It took seven days, sometimes more, for the rooster's sperm to get where it needed to go. Then it got stored in its own sperm nest inside the hen for another couple weeks, just waiting there, patiently. A hen was born with her whole lifetime of yolks stored up in her ovaries. And those yolks, in a healthy girl, passed down pretty regularly, every day, every other day. The sperm cells just sat there, waiting for that daily yolk to pass by on its way to becoming an egg and getting laid. The sperm jumped aboard as the yolk traveled by, and there: a fertilized egg. An egg with the potential for chickenhood.

Each day that spring when she collected the eggs from the coop, Eden let Lorraine's eggs be. When she'd laid about ten or so, she stopped, and began to set. Franklin was sent home to George, his work at Eden's done.

On the day Lorraine had started to set, Eden calculated three weeks down the road and put the hatching date around Fourth of July weekend. Lorraine seemed well for a broody hen, feathers all puffed, her *buk buk buk* low and constant and contented. Such drive and devotion—these things impressed and inspired Eden. There were few people in the world Eden respected the way she respected some of those hens.

That morning Eden set out some feed and then sneaked into the coop to collect eggs while the hens bustled about their meal. She hadn't had the time to go pick up her weekly cache of oyster shells from Abel Delamico, so she gave the girls some extra kale and collards and promised herself to stop by Abel's fish market that day. The oyster shells were for calcium, and you needed to make sure the hens got enough so they didn't resort to eating their own eggs to get it. And then you also had to make sure you ground up the oyster shell finely enough and mixed it well into the feed so that the birds never knew they were eating shell, because that could make them think that eating shell was an acceptable practice and lead them to eat their own eggs, which is exactly what you were trying to avoid in the first place. You worried all the time about the quality of the eggs your hens were producing, and then the minute an egg got laid you had to worry about getting it out from under the bird before she broke it somehow and got tempted to have a taste. Or before she started going broody and got herself set on laying a whole clutch for hatching. Because a hen didn't go broody when it was convenient for *you*. A hen went broody whenever she damn pleased. But if she went broody over a nestful of unhatchable, unfertilized eggs, then you were going to be in for a time of it, trying to break her brood. You'd have to get her out of the coop, away from any eggs—because she'd take someone else's to set on if she was really fixed on brooding—and keep her in a hanging cage with cold air blowing on her rear end to get her out of the hatching mood entirely. An untimely brood was no fun for anyone.

Some folks said that chickens were about the easiest critters in the world to raise, but that, Eden thought, was only if you were keeping the specially bred broody-free birds, or if you kept hens and cocks and were happy enough to let them play and lay and hatch as they pleased. Eden's coop was a tightly run house, and such order did not happen on its own.

Eden was changing the water beside Lorraine's nest when she heard the door of Roddy's shack close. She hustled back outside.

"Roddy!" she called.

He lifted a hand. "Hey, Ma."

She shrugged the sweat and stray hair off her face with a shoulder, her henhouse-dirty hand up in the air. "You heading to the Lodge?" she asked.

"Heading to the Lodge," he repeated, his voice strained with the tired patience grown men use to talk to their mothers.

"Could you check in at Lance's? When you go down? Check on Squee, make sure he's OK. I'm worrying . . ."

Roddy stopped on the path and turned toward the chicken coop. The controlled annoyance was gone from his voice, replaced by a directed urgency. "Lance came for him here last night?"

Eden nodded. "You were busy . . ." She gestured toward his shack.

"Ah, shit." Roddy rubbed one eye with the heel of his hand. He looked tired. "Yeah," he assured his mother. "I'll stop in."

The Islanders thought Eden strange, and Eden might concede the point. She might even admit a sort of pride in that classification. When Eden looked at Roddy, she saw that her son was also maybe what people would call strange. He'd been a particular child, and he'd become a particular man, and a peculiar man, and Eden liked that about him. It marked, she felt, a certain freedom in his spirit. It marked him as her son. Eden had missed Roddy terribly after he'd left Osprey, and though she regretted the circumstances under which he'd gone, she also felt pride. Roderick had forbidden her to speak of it at the time, which was fine, since there was no one on the island to whom she might speak of such a thing. No one with whom to share the joy and triumph she felt when her son had said no to that ugly war.

Fifteen

IF THE PRICE WERE TREACHERY

The osprey should, in all honesty, have been named in its genus, for King Nisus of Alcathous, whose daughter, Scylla, sacrifices him to his attacking enemy, Minos, whom Scylla loves. But Minos rebukes her, disgusted by her betrayal of her father, and he quits the land she offers him. Scylla, mad with despair, jumps into the ocean to follow Minos' retreating ship, and is followed by her father—now turned into an osprey—who plucks her from the water as such a bird of prey is wont to do. Regard:

> *Her father saw her as he hovered near*
> *(changed to an osprey now with tawny wings)*
> *And swooped to seize and tear her, as she clung,*
> *With his hooked beak.*

> —A.D. MELVILLE, trans., "Scylla and Minos,"
> Ovid's *Metamorphoses*

Would that the early ornithologists had more closely read their Ovid.
> —DR. EDGAR HAMILTON, PH.D.,
> "How Our Island Was (Mis)Named"

SUZY WORKED THROUGH THE MORNING at the Lodge darning blankets and bed linens on a relic of a sewing machine she'd unearthed in the maid's room and managed to render functional. When the Irish girls broke for lunch, Suzy went up the hill toward her parents' place. The sun was high overhead, beating down on the Chizek house. Suzy could hear the air conditioner as she approached, a window unit installed at her mother's demand. It blew exhaust against the scrappy rosebushes Nancy had planted there in an inadequate attempt at camouflage.

Nancy Chizek was a finicky woman, but not necessarily thorough. She liked the edges of her world tucked and trimmed, but was famous for cutting corners in ways that were at best unceremonious and at worst downright tacky. She had lobbied for the air conditioner with the insistence of, say, one in line for a heart transplant. Then, once the thing was in, the offense of its unsightliness became the bane of her existence—a topic she brought up not only to complain of her husband's stinginess, but because she found such a topic interesting and worthy of lengthy discussion. Finally she'd bought a few twiggy, thorny starter rose bushes at Kmart, planted them herself, and then neglected their care entirely. The rose "bushes" were two feet tall, the air conditioner at least four feet off the ground. What could anyone possibly do in such an impossible situation, Nancy implied, but throw up one's hands and wait for the bushes to grow?

Suzy didn't knock. She could see her mother through the picture window, sitting at the kitchen table, telephone crooked to her ear as she flipped through a catalog of what looked like swimming pool supplies. Nancy looked up as Suzy entered, lifted a hand and wiggled a few fingers absently as she turned back to the catalog. Suzy poked her head into the stairwell. "Dad?" she called.

"Excuse me for a moment. I'm so sorry," Nancy said into the phone. "Suzy, your father's in the shower," she called, though it seemed like the information was being relayed as much to whoever was on the other end of the phone line as to Suzy. "I'm sorry," Nancy said, back to the phone again, her apology so vehement it was as if she'd just forced that person to overhear something of an intimate and mortifying nature.

Suzy sat down on a chair near the door to wait. She shuffled through a pile of junk mail on the hall table, leafed through a flier of the IGA's price specials. In the mirror beside the door she caught a glimpse of herself, wearing an old gray T-shirt that had never been flattering, and her failure to recall which boyfriend it had once belonged to made her feel slutty and juvenile. Her hair, which she had only wet, not washed, in the shower that morning, had dried to reveal a lumpish wad of matted hair at the back of her head, a knot that had no doubt formed the previous evening, in bed with Roddy. From her parents' coatrack on the other side of the door she grabbed a hat— one of the ugly lavender ones from the laundry equipment company, which wasn't even ugly in a kitschy or cute way, it was just ugly—and put it on. She pulled her hair through the hole in back and tugged down the brim. God, to be incognito! To be someplace where nobody even knew her name! She looked like a suburban housewife ready to carpool the kids on over to goddamn Little League. She never felt so misplaced as when she was at home.

"What's wrong? What happened?" Her father descended the stairs two at a time, and she turned to see the panic crossing his face. She felt sorry for him for a moment, imagining how he must feel, the dread, all of the many things that could go so wrong when you ran a large operation with a big staff and more loose ends than seams. His face was rigid. His eyes said, *Oh god, what now?*

"Nothing," Suzy said quickly. "Everything's fine. I just wanted to talk to you."

Bud released his breath, and as his chest sank his expression went from fear to annoyance: he was peeved that she'd caused him this moment's anxiety, put out at the notion that she wanted something else from him now, as if he didn't have enough to do and enough to worry about. "What is it?" he said, and though he did not look at his watch, he may as well have.

"I don't mean to *trouble* you," Suzy began obsequiously, for nothing rankled Bud more, and that's what it was always about between the two of them: who could piss the other off most. On your marks, get set, go!

"I've got a busy afternoon," Bud warned.

"I was just wondering . . ." She spoke so smoothly as to nauseate herself. "I was wondering if there was anything I could do to help in the search for someone to replace Lorna as head housekeeper. I know you're probably doing everything you can, but if there's anything I could do to help I'd be more than happy . . ."

"Is it so hard," Bud spat, "to put a little bit of work into your family's business?" His voice was raised. "Is it so much to ask . . . ?" His daughter's audacity rendered him speechless. Her selfishness never ceased to amaze him. Unbelievable! She was lazy and opportunistic, and she could be downright nasty when she didn't get her way. If he steered clear of his daughter as a rule, it was because his anger toward her was of a variety he recognized to be violent. Too often, he felt himself just one step shy of slapping her insolent face, or shaking that haughty defiance right out of her. Bud held his hands at his sides with a force of will as he managed to reroute his violence to his mouth instead of his fists. "Are you not able," he bellowed, "to do a single goddamn day's work without your griping and bitching that everything's so goddamn unfair?! A woman is *dead* here . . ."

Nancy, from the kitchen, in a voice that almost topped Bud's in pitch and command, said dramatically into the telephone (but so loudly that it was impossible to think of the phone as anything but a stage prop), "Look, I'm just going to have to call you back later!" Whereupon she slammed down the receiver, stalked past Bud and Suzy, and climbed the stairs to her bedroom, one hand firmly gripping the banister, the other held across her eyes as though the migraine brewing therein might just kill her this time, as if that's what her family had been after all along.

They waited for her door to close before they resumed. Then they turned back on each other like cats in a tangle.

"Do you think"—Suzy's fury was slow and leveled—"do you think I don't *work*?" His oblivion was unfathomable to her. He imagined teaching to be a cushy sort of a pastime—like taking tickets at the movie theater, or babysitting a few afternoons a week—something that spoiled, lazy, loudmouthed girls like his daughter did so they didn't have to work real jobs. Like what? Like running a hotel that was only open two months a year? By the time Suzy spoke again, she was shrieking. "I work twelve-hour days, five days a week. On the weekends I grade papers, I plan lessons, I advise three different extra-curricular activities, I sell Oreos at intermission of the goddamn school play! Teachers get three months in the summer because we work so fucking hard the other nine months of the year, and I didn't come here during my vacation to scrub toilets for six bucks an hour!" Suzy's face was boiling red, and she was gesticulating wildly with her arms. "Did you ever have any intention of looking for someone to replace Lorna, or did you just figure it'd be easier if I did it this season and you'd deal with it in the fall when you had some more time on your hands?"

They stood, faced off, as she waited for an answer and he waited for the wrath to continue as it always did. He'd learned that some-times the only way was to ride it through, let her tire herself out, the way you'd contend with a child's tantrum.

They stood, glaring at each other, Suzy's breath heaving now, the only other sound the chink and buzz of the window-unit air condi-tioner. It whirred and clicked and spun, and then it double-clicked, spat a hiss, and wound itself down for a brief thermostatic hiatus. In the silence that followed, Bud finally said, "Are you finished?"

Suzy said nothing. There was nothing to say. She spun around, threw open the front door, and walked out.

RODDY HAD STOPPED AT the Squires' cottage around eight-thirty that morning, but there were no signs of waking life inside. At ten he knocked again. No answer. He tried the outer door, which was unlocked, but the screen was latched from the inside. Roddy could see in, through to Lance's bedroom, where Lance lay sprawled across the bed, fully clothed, dead asleep. Further inside, the door to Squee's room was also open, the boy a lump under a sheet, a blond mop of hair poking out at the top. Roddy stood for a moment, frozen, to make sure he could see Squee's body rising and falling with his breath.

When Roddy came by again at noon, Lance was standing at the kitchen sink, ashing his cigarette into the drain. Squee was at the table, a bowl of cereal before him, though he was clearly not eating. He held the spoon in the milk as if he were about to eat but couldn't remember the next step. His eyes were blank. He looked small, and anemic, and gray, and it made Roddy very afraid. But before he could say anything or even make a move toward the boy, Lance was laying into Roddy as if it were high school all over again.

"Ro-od-LESS!" Lance cheered. When they were kids, if Roddy so much as spoke to a girl, the ribbing from Lance and Chas and Jimmy Waters and all of them was relentless. It had been enough back then to pretty much keep Roddy from attempting to even make eye contact with anyone of the opposite sex. Lance stood beside the kitchen sink, cigarette in one hand, and lifted his arms and swiveled his hips in a burlesque move that was as embarrassing as it was awkward. "Woo-woo!" Lance hooted. "It's Roddy the Rodless Wonder Boy!"

Roddy shot him a look: *Not in front of Squee, at least not in front of Squee.* At the same moment he caught sight of one of the Irish girls coming out of the staff quarters. Without pausing to second-guess, he pushed back open the door through which he'd just entered and called out to her across the path. It was Peg, whom he recognized, though he didn't know her name. "Good morning!" he called. She looked up, then away, and continued toward the Lodge. "Miss!" Roddy shouted. "Um . . . Miss? Hello?" Peg stopped, looked around to locate the person being addressed, saw no one, then looked to the Squires' porch and saw Roddy. She lifted two fingers to her breastbone—*Me?*—and then looked around again, making sure she hadn't missed anyone lurking in the trees.

"Hi!" Roddy called again. "Hey, you're one of the housekeeping girls, right? Hey, could you . . . Suzy wanted Squee here to help with something down in the Lodge—you think you could bring him down there with you, make sure he finds Suzy? That'd be great . . ."

"Of course," Peg said, her brow knitted as though this new task might require a great intensity of focus. She waited, on edge, as if for the starter's gun.

"Squee," Roddy called gruffly. He didn't look at the boy, just flicked his head. "Get down there, help Suzy," he ordered, in a voice more Lance's than his own. With one hand he held the screen door open. Roddy didn't look at Lance, lest Lance take the opportunity to object. Instead, he squinted into the distance as though trying to make out something he couldn't quite see.

Squee let his spoon fall into his cereal bowl and, also without looking at his father, walked stiffly across the room, past Roddy and outside. On the path, Peg clapped her hands to her thighs as if calling a puppy to come. The boy held the banister as he descended the porch steps, and there was something wrong about his carriage: he was off-center, or lopsided, as if favoring one side of his body but not sure which. When he'd made it to Peg—who put her arm around his shoulder and walked beside him down toward the Lodge—Roddy let the screen door close. Slowly he turned to face Lance, who was nodding his head with a patronizing swagger. "You got talking to do, Rodless. How'd you get in with that, old boy? Who'd ever think you'd grow up such a big stud? Such a fucking ladies' man . . . Rod-LESS!" he cheered again.

Roddy took a big breath. "How's things going, Lance?"

Lance looked around himself as if to assess his own situation right then and there. He looked down at yesterday's clothes, unclean when he'd put them on. "Life's a fucking piece of shit," he said brightly, his smile pinched with sarcasm. "But who the hell cares about me? Who cares about me when our own little Rodless Dickless Rod is fucking the boss's daughter? She good, Dickless? You know, I know how good she is, Rodless. You know, I fucked little Miss Chizek back then, when all you could do was cream your bed over her at night. Remember how it was back then, Rodless? Remember how much you wanted that fucking . . . that . . . You know, I'd've given her to you, buddy, back then, you know?" Here Lance's eyes started to well with tears, and he lifted his cigarette to his lips and drew in long and hard. "I didn't need . . ." He choked, coughed, took another long drag. When he spoke again his voice was wet and ragged. "I didn't need that. I had Lorna. What'd I need with fucking Suzy Chizek? Suzy-fucking-Bud's-daughter Chizek. I didn't fucking need that shit." Lance ground his cigarette out into the stained porcelain sink. "Get the fuck out of here," Lance said, and turned on his heel, slamming the bathroom door behind him.

Roddy went to his truck, turned over the rumbling engine, and started out toward Sand Beach Road. Stalking across the north parking lot was a girl in a baseball cap and shorts, and it wasn't until he got a lot closer that he realized it was Suzy and pulled the truck up alongside her. She jumped as though she hadn't heard him approaching, then saw who it was and put her hand on the door to climb in. There was a moment, then, as they looked at each other and went from seeing nothing but the roiling inside themselves to catching on and realizing that something was not right with the other. A different sort of concern crossed each of their faces. Quickly, and at once, they said, "What's the matter?" then both laughed for a pained half second, which was all they had in them.

"Get in," Roddy said.

Suzy inhaled deeply. "I have to . . ."

"Just get in. You have lunch?"

She shook her head no. She got in.

"Mia's with the girls?"

She nodded.

"Squee too." Roddy pulled the truck out onto Sand Beach Road and headed north. They rode without speaking, each sorting their own thoughts all the way to the Luncheonette on Old Post Office Road. Suzy leaned to check her face in the rearview mirror but bumped the bill of her baseball cap on the way. She tore off the hat as if she'd just discovered the ugly thing to be the root of all that was wrong, and she shoved it behind the seat of the truck.

Sixteen

A LONG TIME HELPLESS IN THE NEST

This is a typical predator's foot, better for gripping than for walking.
—"Function Forms the Foot,"
Life Nature Library's *The Birds*

L ANCE WAS NOT A GOOD FATHER. He knew that. It didn't take a genius. He could see himself, sometimes—the way you catch a glimpse of something from the corner of your eye—as the kind of father Lorna wanted him to be: a father out of a pancake syrup commercial, or from those sepia stories old people told about their back-in-the-day Norman Rockwell childhoods. Lance occasionally caught a moment's understanding of fatherhood, but then it would slip from him and he'd be back to being Lance Squire, whose fatherly instinct was a sentimental hiccup.

Sometimes he wanted to kill the kid. The desire was almost physical, and Lance had to hold himself back some days from beating the living shit out of Squee just for looking like Lorna, reminding him of Lorna, being a pain in the ass, always in the way, always causing trouble, always making other people think Lance was some kind of villain Squee needed to run away from. Lance never knew what Squee was going to go and do, what stunt he might pull. The boy, in Lance's opinion, was damn spoiled. Lorna doted on him, did everything for him; Lance was surprised the kid could wipe his own ass. And that made him angry at Lorna: What had she thought she was doing? Had she thought about what would happen if she acted like the kid's servant and let him grow up thinking the world was his? Lance—in rare moments—tried to show his son what the world was really like, how you had to fight for the things that were due you and beat out the people who'd inevitably try to take away what you'd won for yourself.

The coffee urn in the Lodge kitchen was empty, Jock was nowhere to be found, and it was Tito's favorite thing in the world to pretend he didn't speak enough English to understand what Lance wanted when he pointed at the urn, made the international symbol of drinking from a teacup, and shouted, "Coffee! Is there any coffee? Make. The. Coffee." Tito just smiled, shook his head, waved a hand by his ears to indicate either incomprehension or deafness, and continued to chop his garlic, swaying slightly, as though the music inside his head was so lovely he couldn't bear to tear himself away.

Lance slammed through the swinging doors into the dining room toward the bar to pour himself a Coke from the fountain. At a table near the windows a group of the Irish girls were gathered, some sitting, some presiding, spreading peanut butter and jelly on napkin-white bread they pulled from a bright plastic sleeve. Brigid was there, looking spacey and sullen and, Lance thought, sexy as shit. And there amid the twittering, officious, bored, giggling, hyperactive girls were Squee and Mia, seated at the table, getting fussed over and catered to as though they were some Egyptian king and queen, child rulers of a great dynasty.

Lance approached the table. Movement among the girls tapered, then stopped as they noticed him and turned to look. Brigid half raised a hand in greeting and Lance nodded in her direction, then made motion with two fingers at his son, like a coach calling his player off the field: *Come with me.* "Grab a sandwich and let's go," he said, and started to turn from the table again until it dawned on him that Squee wasn't moving, wasn't jumping to follow his command, instead was just sitting there like a fucking retard. Like a little fag, Lance feared, all happy to be a little girly-girl with all the girlies, trotting around like a prissy chambermaid. Lance stopped mid-pivot, turned back to Squee, and said, loudly this time, "Get your fucking ass out of that chair and get back to the house now before I make you do it."

There was a heavy pause, as though everything—the future—was about to be decided. And then Squee slid off his chair and walked toward Lance with the look of a cartoon character who's been hypnotized and brainwashed by aliens. Lance let Squee pass before he stepped up to the table himself, the girls parting as he approached. He took two peanut butter and jelly sandwiches from what they'd prepared, then turned and followed his son.

About one second after the back kitchen door slammed shut, Mia burst into tears. And about one second after that, Brigid stood up and hurried away, leaving the others to stare after her and then exchange among themselves the looks of maternal suspicion and judgment they practiced like disciples of a biddy schoolmarm.

Brigid went through the kitchen, ignoring Tito's eyes on her, then stopped by the door and watched through the screen as father and son went up the hill and into their cottage. She opened the walk-in, grabbed a package of Oreos from one shelf and a six-pack of cola from another. She carried these with her into the pantry, where she took a large bag of potato chips not marked for individual sale, before she started back to the screen door, shooting Tito a look just daring him to say a single word.

She knocked at the door of the Squire cottage with her elbow, her hands full. She could not have been more than two minutes behind them, but when Lance opened the door it seemed that something had already happened. Squee was at the table in the exact spot he'd occupied when Roddy was there half an hour earlier. There was a bowl on the table in front of him. In the bowl were two peanut butter and jelly sandwiches. The table was covered with milk and bloated Cheerios, which looked like piles of cat vomit. A trail of milk led to a spoon that lay where it had landed on the opposite edge of the table. Squee's shirtfront was spattered, and droplets fell down his face as though he were crying milk tears. He did not even move to wipe his face with his hand.

Lance held the door as if he couldn't decide whether to invite Brigid in or slam it in her face. He looked at her a good long moment before he said, with both pride and righteousness, "We don't need your charity here." It was something he'd likely heard on television.

Brigid took her own long moment before responding. She fixed Lance with a stare that was impassive and feisty at the same time. And then she plowed right past him and into the room, depositing the chips and cookies on the table. "If the charities are doling out food of this sort," she said, ripping cans from their plastic tether and placing them one by one into the empty fridge, "it's hardly a bloody wonder your country's full of fatties with rotted teeth."

Lance, still standing at the open door, relaxed his posture and now stood with his weight bearing down on the knob, watching her. "I like you," he said. "I always knew I liked you right off."

Brigid glanced around the room. "Do you have a fag?" she asked. "A *cigarette*?"

He jerked his head toward a pack and lighter on the windowsill. She retrieved them, then gestured out the door he still held ajar. "Shall we?" she said, and he gallantly motioned her through ahead of him.

On the porch, they sat in chairs and smoked in silence. It was too sunny out, and the smoke seemed to bellow from their mouths in an affront to the light, as though they were asserting themselves in opposition to it.

Lance rubbed his eye with the heel of the hand in which he held his cigarette, and for a moment the smoke seemed to pour from the top of his head. He squinted as if trying to make out something far off on the horizon. They finished their cigarettes, then lit up again. After a while, Lance said, "She was so pretty . . ."

Brigid waited, quiet.

"Beautiful," he said. "Tiny—a tiny, tiny little thing. But built too. Perfect . . . first time I remember seeing her was on the bleachers at some game. I was fifteen years old, and I took one look at that girl and I knew I was gonna spend . . ." He let it go. He couldn't say the words. He saw Lorna, and he knew. There wasn't much more to it than that.

After a time Brigid said, "May I ask a question, then?"

Lance didn't speak, but gestured grandly in front of him as though to indicate a stage that was all hers.

"You'll not yell at me, will you?"

"Not you, angel. Why would I do a thing like that to you?"

"You do it to the others," she offered.

"You're not them."

Brigid held on to her words for another moment. "Sitting here, you know, having a chat, you—you come across as rather an understandable sort of a man." She paused. "It's not my place to speak. Only it seems as though life might be a terrible lot easier, you see?" She spoke all these words to her hand and the cigarette it held. "You know, if you were kind like this, with the others . . ." When she finished and heard no response from Lance, no sudden movement to force her attention to him, she finally turned to look and see what she'd done.

Tears he was trying very hard to hold back were pooling out of his eyes despite him, and he was bearing them stoically. When he could speak he managed to say, "That's just what Lorna'd ask me . . ." And then he couldn't say any more. Lance's arms were laid across the armrests of the peeling whitewashed Adirondack-style chair in which he sat, and Brigid instinctively, and compassionately, reached out a hand and laid it across his forearm. He stiffened, shut his eyes. It made Brigid feel strange, and a bit frightened. She thought, *This is a man whom no one touches.*

THE REST OF THE IRISH GIRLS were still down in the dining room playing cards amid their PB&J detritus when Suzy returned from lunch. They'd managed (actually, Tito's butterscotch pudding had managed) to get Mia to stop crying, but the second she laid eyes on her mother coming through the sliding glass door Mia burst into tears, bounded from her chair, sending her rummy hand scattering, and rushed at Suzy, who squatted and caught her just as Mia let out a terrible sob.

"Baby . . . baby," Suzy cooed. "Shhhhhh, shhhhhh . . . What's the matter, Mia? Sweetie? What?" She stroked Mia's hair, looking over the girl's head to the Irish girls, asking with her eyes, *What's up with her? What'd I miss?*

But Mia wasn't talking, wasn't doing anything except burrowing into Suzy as if looking for someplace to hide. Suzy stood, scooping the girl up with her, and Mia wrapped her legs around her mother's waist instinctually, arms around her neck. For Suzy, a child's miniature crisis was more than welcome right then—a scrape, a lost game, a perceived injustice—something to supplant, or at least distract her from, all the larger crises at hand. It made Suzy feel strong: here was something she could make better again.

Suzy said, for the Irish girls as much as for Mia, "Why don't you and I take this upstairs, ma'am?" She sent a knowing look to the girls over there at their card game table, a look to apologize for Mia—*I know, I'm sorry, I know she can be a pain.* To say, *Thanks, be back soon*—but her look wasn't met with anything akin. The girls were worried, their brows furrowed. It was then Suzy realized that Squee wasn't at the table and that this was no kissable, soothable, manageable problem. She hugged Mia to her, spoke softly into her hair. "Where's Squee, baby? Did he have lunch with you?" At which Mia only began to sob more ferociously. "OK," Suzy breathed, "OK." Her pulse began to race. "OK, baby, OK, let's just go up to our room and calm down a little. It's going to be all right." Like a mantra: "Everything's going to be all right."

In the room, Suzy set Mia down on the end of one of the beds and knelt before her on the floor. She tried for patience—she'd dealt enough with crying children to know that her own anxiety wasn't going to get her anywhere. She tried to slow herself down.

"What's going on, babe?" She rubbed Mia's arms at her sides as if to warm her, though the sun shone in brightly through the window shades and Suzy was sweating with fear. "Can you try to tell me what's going on, Mia-belle? Maybe I can help if you tell me what's wrong."

Mia wiped her upper lip with the back of her hand and tried to sniffle through her clogged nose, but couldn't and choked, coughing instead. Suzy reached for a tissue on the bed stand. "Here, baby." She held the tissue around Mia's nostrils. "Blow. Give a good blow—good!" Mia honked into the tissue. Suzy refolded it and let her blow again, then wiped Mia off and tossed the tissue toward a wastebasket, which she missed by a hair.

Mia straightened and breathed in and opened her mouth to speak, but in the time it took for the words to get from her brain to her lips, the realization of their meaning came slamming back at her, so that as she said, "I hate Squee's dad," her face was already contorting, the tears beginning anew, flooding out as if they had never paused at all.

Another tissue. More blowing. "Did something happen, Mi? Why do you hate Lance? Did he yell at you? Did he do something that was mean? Did he do something mean to you?" And suddenly she was struck with what felt like a clear and full revelation of the extent to which Lance Squire was capable of doing *something mean*. Lorna had kept him in check to some degree—but Lorna was gone.

When she spoke it was far too angrily, and though she was clearly castigating herself, not her daughter, it might have appeared otherwise. She grabbed Mia's shoulders with enough force to scare the girl out of her crying. "Did Lance Squire do anything bad to you, Mia? You have to tell me *right now,* Mia: you *have* to tell me if Lance Squire ever did anything bad to you!" She couldn't believe the words coming out of her mouth. This was not what her life was supposed to be! She'd gotten away! Suzy Chizek had left Osprey Island! What the hell was she doing in an upstairs room at the Osprey Lodge, yelling into the face of her sweetest, only, baby daughter? "Mia, you have to answer me *right now*—did Lance Squire make you do something you didn't want to do?" She was pleading, her hands pulling at Mia's small arms, kneading, as if she could wring out the truth and the evil all at once.

And then, in the midst of—or maybe in reaction to—Suzy's sudden outburst of desperate and incredulous fear, Mia miraculously regained self-control. In a voice so adult and with such calm presence of mind it was eerie and horrible, she said: "No, Mom, it was nothing like that at all. It's just he's so mean to Squee. That's what's upsetting me. He's so mean to Squee, and Squee is my best friend. I'm scared . . . I want to go home."

Suzy sat there a moment, still, holding Mia's arms and staring at her daughter as though she'd just been the vehicle of an otherworldly transmission, a voice speaking through this girl from someplace beyond. Suzy's eyes were grave, and she was nodding her head. "OK," she said to Mia slowly. "OK."

Suzy carried Mia back downstairs and left her in the care of the Irish girls again. Then she went to find Reesa in the salon, which looked, as she entered, as though it had been ransacked. Reesa sat in the middle of the linoleum floor, surrounded by ten thousand bottles, tubes, and aerosol cans.

"Jesus," Suzy said.

Reesa tilted her face toward the door. "And I've got a shipment coming in today!" She looked around, trying to figure out where she might possibly store anything else. "I have to keep reminding myself how much spray those ladies like, and what a pain in the ass it is to deal with orders coming in midsummer. I'm planning ahead. Tell me it's a good thing." She looked to Suzy, then registered the concern on her face. "What?" Reesa glanced around her again. "It's not *so* bad . . . Really, you'd be amazed how fast it goes. Suzy! What? What's going on?" Reesa was getting it now: something was wrong. She started to her feet.

"No." Suzy shook her head, waved Reesa back down. "No, no, you're busy. I just . . . I need to get Mia . . . and Squee . . . You're waiting for a shipment?"

"Yeah, why? Suze, what's going on?" Reesa had gotten up anyway and was coming toward Suzy, wiping her hands on her jeans as she walked.

Suzy ran a hand through her hair, felt the scrap of cloth that was holding it back. "No, I just . . . you don't know what time, do you? When they're coming? I need to get the kids out of here, Reese. I need to go deal with things. Lance is . . . I don't know what he is. He's been at Squee, yelling, whatever, I don't even know . . . Mia's a wreck. I just want to get them away from him, just out of here for the afternoon. Just anywhere. I'm probably being totally melodramatic. Mia freaked me out though." Suzy gestured vaguely with a hand in the direction of their room upstairs. "I don't know what to do, but while I figure it out I don't want my kid in his line of fire."

Reesa put a hand on Suzy's arm to still her: *Hang on a minute, don't move.* She went toward the back of the shop. "Janna? Jan . . . you there?"

A head poked out from the storage closet. "Yes, ma'am," Janna chirped.

"Why don't you and that boyfriend of yours go to the beach this afternoon?"

"Um . . ." Janna regarded her quizzically, as if Reesa might be going a little off in the head. "Um, because I'm working . . . ? Is this a trick question?"

Reesa spoke slowly, letting out each word as she struck together a plan in her mind. "Why . . . don't . . . you and Mister California"— Reesa had become markedly skeptical about Gavin since hearing of his dalliances with Brigid—"take the afternoon, and take Squee and Mia to the beach? Not Sand . . . take them over across the island . . . Wickham, or Scallopshell . . . Why don't you guys do that?" She peered at Janna, waiting for an answer.

"You providing the vehicle, boss lady?"

"Ah, shit, that's right . . . yeah, no, take the truck. That's fine . . . I don't need it . . . Do I? No, that's fine." Reesa leaned toward the counter, pawed around for her keys. "Here . . . OK, so Mia's . . . ? Suze? Where?" Suzy pointed toward the dining room. "And Squee?"

Suzy gave a panicky shrug: Where *was* he? She didn't know.

"We'll find him," Janna assured them.

"He might be up with Lance?" Suzy suggested.

"OK." Janna took the keys.

"In which case, it'll be a good thing it's you, not me," Suzy said.

Reesa nodded ruefully. "Oh, he likes Janna, all right."

Janna started toward the door. "When'd you want 'em home, Suzy?"

"You keep them away as long as you can." Suzy dug in her pocket, thrust some bills at Janna. "Go for clam rolls for dinner . . . something . . . whatever . . . You want to go off-island to a movie, great. Keep Squee out of here as long as you can."

Janna paused by the door. She looked back at them with the first signs of her own worry. "Is everything *OK*?"

"Yes," said Reesa.

"No," said Suzy, at the exact same time.

Janna looked warily at them both. "Gotcha." And then she turned and fled before Reesa could have a change of heart.

"What the fuck am I going to do?" Suzy said aloud.

"What're you thinking about doing?"

Suzy waited, then said it, as if it had only just come to mind. "Leaving?"

Now was when Reesa had to pretend that Suzy didn't say that very thing every summer she came back to Osprey. Patiently, she asked, "Would it solve anything?"

Suzy thought. "I've never felt scared before. I've been pissed as shit—I've been livid!—but I don't think I've ever been scared. It's always been about me, not about Mia. Not about safety."

"What're you scared of, you think?"

Suzy mumbled, "I don't know." Then she said: "My dad's not even looking for someone to replace Lorna. He thought I'd just step right in, take over, spend the summer cleaning toilets."

Reesa only nodded sympathetically. There was little for her to actually say. Suzy had never been willing to be a part of her family's business, which was her right, surely, except that you also got the sense she was expecting to inherit the place someday but had no intention to lift a hand at the Lodge until that day came, when she'd probably put it up for sale.

Suzy said, "Mia wants to leave."

"She does?"

"She's scared."

"Of?"

"*Lance,* I think. That's what she says. I think I'd go, too . . . I think if it were just me and Mia I'd go. But now with Lorna . . . Mia's afraid for Squee, I think. I think I am too. I don't know how I'm going to do him any good."

"You do," Reesa said. "Like now . . . getting him out."

"It's a Band-Aid."

"They can be useful," Reesa said.

"I think I've been Band-Aiding myself," Suzy admitted.

Reesa smiled. "That's what I've heard."

"Jesus! Really? Christ, you can't have a conversation with someone around here without . . ."

Reesa was laughing, but not unkindly.

"I want to leave," Suzy said. "Just leave: get Mia out of here, leave my father in the lurch—which he totally deserves—but . . . leave this thing with Roddy . . ."

"Is it a thing?" Reesa asked. "Or a Band-Aid?"

There was an awkward pause. Then Suzy looked right at Reesa as though she were surfacing into another conversation entirely. "You ever worry that you don't know *what's* right for your kids? Like you try to do right by them, but what if you don't even know what right is?"

JANNA TRUDGED a sniffling Mia up the hill, prepared to drop her in Gavin's care at the staff barracks while she went and wrested Squee away from Lance, but as the Squires' cottage came into view she could see Lance on the front porch with one of the Irish girls, and Janna shifted direction and walked toward them, waving as she approached. No one waved back. Lance's head was down, and as they got closer he lifted his eyes, caught sight of Janna and Mia, and started fumbling fast to light a cigarette, turning his face away as though they'd come in on a strong wind. Janna smiled at Brigid. Brigid made no reciprocal gesture. She appeared to be at once ministering to and covering for Lance. From a good twenty feet away Janna made her voice offhandedly casual. "Squee want to come to the beach?"

Lance, still turned away, waved a hand and jerked his head toward the cottage door—*Go ask him yourself.* Mia stayed where she was, unwilling to come any closer. Janna went up the steps and leaned in the door: "Hey, Squee, get your suit! We're going to the beach!" She paused for a response. Her eyes were adjusting to the inside light, and for a minute all she could see were splotches and shadows. Then she made out Squee, still sitting, stonelike, at his chair. "Come on! Move it, grab your suit!" She watched as he slowly collected himself and got up from the table to follow her orders. On the porch Lance started to speak. He was looking straight out at Mia. From where she now stood on the porch, Janna could see that Lance had been crying.

"You know what pisses me off the most?" Lance said to Mia, his voice ugly and threatening. Mia said nothing, just stood there, frozen. "They think I'm stupid. *Send Janna,*" he cooed in a singsong mimicry. "*He liiikes Janna. Send Janna over to get the little fucker . . .*"

Mia just took it in, rooted to the ground in her fear. Janna went inside to hurry Squee. Brigid reached her hand out and pressed it to

Lance's upper arm in consolation. He turned at her touch, put his elbows on his knees, and bent over them, shaking his head at the floorboards as if they'd let him down once again. And just when it looked as if he was giving up, he raised his head to Mia again and spat as he spoke. "Your mother is a back-stabbing cunt." He stood, quickly—Brigid jerked back in alarm—and slammed inside.

PEG SPENT THE ENTIRE AFTERNOON worrying herself nearly sick over the fate of the little Squire boy. Someone else might have excused herself from the maid's room, gone down to the office, looked up Roddy's home telephone number, and called him the minute Lance had ordered Squee away from the lunch table. But it was important to Peg to be dutiful, obedient, and—perhaps above all—blameless in all that she undertook, and thus she agonized through her chores until the five o'clock whistle blew down at the ferry docks, whereupon she dashed with breathless determination to the Lodge office and found Cybelle Schwartz behind the desk, reading a dog-eared, three-year-old issue of *Cosmopolitan*.

"May I . . ." Peg began, "please, can I ring someone?"

Cybelle eyed her suspiciously.

"I've . . . I've got to—you—I've got to make a call . . . on the telephone!"

"Staff's supposed to use the pay phone downstairs."

"Please!" Peg cried. "It's desperately important!"

"Is it long distance? I can't let you call long distance."

"No—it's right here! Do you . . . can you get the number, for the man, the one who fixes things . . . Roddy?"

Cybelle was nodding, haughty and self-important. "That's Roddy Jacobs. He doesn't have a phone himself, but you can sometimes get him here." She dialed the number at Eden's and passed the receiver to Peg.

Someone answered, and Peg asked for Roddy. He wasn't in—an obstacle Peg hadn't anticipated. She paused for such a long time that Eden asked, "Hello? Can I help you with something?"

"Oh," wailed Peg. She looked to Cybelle nervously, unsure of how she might proceed. "I don't know . . . I . . . I'm working here at the Lodge and I've . . . I've got to talk with Mr. . . . with Roddy." She said his name as if it were a foreign word. "I'm terribly, I'm afraid . . . with Squee . . . I'm just entirely . . ."

"*Squee?*" Eden said sharply. "What happened to Squee?"

"What?" said Peg. "No, I don't . . . I've just . . ." And then she burst into tears.

Cybelle, embarrassed, disappeared into the back room.

"Please, sweetheart," Eden said on the line, "please calm down. Did something happen to Squee? I'm Roddy's mother," she explained to the sobbing girl. "Can you tell me what happened, please?"

Peg's tears abated slightly. "Do you . . . ? You know the Squire . . . Squee? You know Squee?"

"What happened?" Eden's voice was rip-cord tense. "I'm his god-mother," she said, and though it wasn't true, she couldn't find words that were, some way to explain her relationship to the child. "*Please,*" Eden said shrilly. "Please, is he all right?"

Peg took a gulp of air, and when she let it out inside another sob, all she could think to say was "It's really that I don't *know* . . ."

Eden broke in. "You're at the Lodge? Why don't I come there? I'm coming down there."

Peg's next sob conveyed acquiescence.

"Go down to the Sand Beach Road entrance," Eden instructed. "I'll be there in five minutes."

Roddy, who'd also finished up work at the Lodge at five, pulled into the driveway at home just as Eden was pulling out. She saw him and bristled: What in god's name was Roddy doing home when something was wrong with Squee down at the Lodge? Then she felt relief: if

Roddy was home, it could be nothing too bad down there. And then the relief turned to fear: Roddy was home to tell her about whatever terrible thing had happened down at the Lodge. They stopped their vehicles in the driveway and spoke through the windows. In the confusion it took some moments before they were able to make themselves clear.

"I was just there," Roddy said. "Nothing's wrong down at the Lodge. Not more than usual. Now . . ."

"She wanted to talk to *you*," Eden said.

"Well, what?" Roddy was tired, and unprepared for this welcome home. "*What?* You want me to come down with you?" It was not what he wanted at all.

"She's waiting by the road. Just come with me."

Roddy did as his mother instructed.

Eden wasn't sure exactly what would happen when they reached the girl at the Lodge, but when they pulled up beside her on Sand Beach Road, Peg tugged open the back door of the Caddy and climbed in gratefully. She was no longer crying, but her pale skin was splotchy red, her eyelashes slick and wet. "I'm so thankful to you," she said as she pulled the door shut behind her and slid across the seat, "just for getting out of there for a bit, you know? Just to be away from it all?" So Eden pulled a wide, unruly U-turn and drove straight back the way she'd come, as if it were what she'd planned all along.

Peg sat in the very center of Eden's couch, perching so precisely in the exact middle of the middle cushion, you might have suspected her of some obsessive tendencies. Eden gave the girl a cup of water and sat opposite her. Roddy hovered, filling the doorway, ready to make a hasty escape should the need arise.

"I've wanted to know," Peg said, "if there'd be someone we might talk with about the legal issues involved here, you know? I don't know about, like, American law . . . but I'd thought if we might talk with a professional . . ." There was something proprietary and hoarding about her concern for Squee's welfare, as though she were fighting for his custody. When she described what she'd witnessed that day, and in the course of her brief tenure at the Lodge, she seemed to cast blame for Squee's circumstance not only on Osprey Island as a whole, but on America at large. Nothing so ugly and unfortunate, she seemed to imply, would have come to pass on Irish soil. Peg appeared at once to trust Roddy and Eden while reserving an incredulity that anyone— even if only through *in*action—had allowed a man like Lance Squire to have his way about the island. Peg wanted to see something *happen,* and was loathe to understand why she—an outsider and virtual stranger—was the one making this call to arms.

Roddy heard her out and held his tongue, not out of respect but for fear he might open his mouth and say something befitting a crooked southern sheriff: *Well, missy, that's just not the way things work around these parts* . . . Except the girl was right. Lance was a car without breaks, plowing down everything in his path, and he'd probably keep going until he hit something big enough to stop him.

Seventeen

AS THEY FLEE YOU'D THINK
THEY FLOAT ON WINGS

He that had been present would have deemed
Their bodies to have hovered up with feathers. As they seemed,
So hovered they with wings indeed. Of whom the one away
To woodward flies, the other still about the house doth stay.

—ARTHUR GOLDING, trans.,
"Procne's Revenge," Ovid's *Metamorphoses*

SUZY WAS SITTING ON THE END of her bed when Mia returned from the beach early that evening. Their travel bags were out, unzipped and open-mouthed as though waiting to be fed. Dresser drawers had been pulled out, but were still full, and clothes from the closet sprawled across the bed as if they'd paused there to rest before their internment. Suzy sat immobilized, head in her hands, trying to see every potential decision through to its ultimate outcome. It was impossible; there were too many variables. But thinking kept her from moving, and not moving kept her from deciding. She'd been as she was for most of the afternoon: getting up to collect her soap and shampoo from the shower, then leaving them in the sink and returning to the bed, rising to sort Mia's laundry but folding only one small T-shirt, which lay in the middle of the floor as if to mark the spot. The rest she left in a wrinkling lump. She felt so incapable of decision she found it hard to understand how she'd managed to leave Osprey Island in the first place. How had she ever just picked everything up and gotten on the ferry? She needed one more push from Mia, one more sob, one more plea. She needed Mia to come in the door and rush at her with relief to see the packing begun, thankful to be reaching the start of the end.

There was shuffling outside, a bump against the door as Mia shifted the contents of her hand to reach for the knob. Suzy felt such gratitude, anticipating the necessity that would emanate from Mia's very body and provide Suzy a purpose and a direction. But as the door swung open and Mia pushed in from the hallway, the imperative she was to instigate first dwindled and then vanished altogether like the evaporation of a dream. Mia was barefoot, wearing an enormous Stanford T-shirt, the hem of which hit her about mid-calf, the collar slouched, coquettish, over one shoulder. Her arms were loaded down with a hodgepodge of sand-laden accoutrements that seemed to drop away from her as she moved, falling to the carpet like a flower girl's petals. She was sunny across her cheeks and nose—sunnier than Suzy would have allowed—but she looked beautiful, freckled, as if she'd been dipped in sunset and rolled in stars. She drifted into the room, dropped the remainder of her burdens in a sandy heap at her mother's feet, and flopped herself down onto the bed as though exhausted.

"Did you know that in Russia they killed the whole family of the czar, who's like the king, except for his one daughter who had to lie under all her dead brothers and sisters until everybody was gone and she could get out and escape and nobody knew where she was because they never found her body because she escaped and then people, ladies, all came and said they were her so they could be the queen and they were all lying except the one who was really her but they didn't have fingerprints back then so they had to tell by your ear who you were because every person has different ears than everybody else . . . And in the band the Beatles they got tired of being so famous and one of the men in the band wanted to take a vacation but he couldn't so they had to pretend he was dead just so he could go on vacation and everybody thought he was really dead because if you listen to a song backwards it says I buried Paul, and in one album the car has the license plate number of the day that they said he died and also the cover of a different record was supposed to have all of them with aprons like a butcher and knives and meat like at the butcher shop and also broken up baby dolls but then they said they couldn't have that but they had already made them and the people were lazy so they just put the new covers over the old ones instead of making them all new so if you have one that has the new cover over the old, if you put it in steam and take it off then it would be worth a lot a lot of money . . ."

Mia paused then, seemed to breathe in for the first time since she'd entered the room, and actually took notice of her mother, registered her as a separate being who might also, perhaps, have something on her mind. Suzy's eyes on Mia were fixed and grave, and Mia's face in sudden response went tight with concern. With a great emphatic gush she said, "Mommy?"

Suzy felt unable to speak. She just stared at her daughter, the words she'd been preparing, perhaps even unconsciously, all afternoon, were stuck in her throat: sweet coos of milky sympathy, whispered assurances of a future frothy with ease.

Mia was confused. She watched as Suzy stood up from the bed with awkward decisiveness and blurted: "OK, get packed. We're leaving. Hup to."

Mia lay there, unsure whether this was a joke. Her face tried to smile but couldn't because her eyes were so tied up in trying to understand what was happening before her.

Suzy regarded her daughter. "I'm glad you had a good time at the beach, baby. But that doesn't change anything. Not really."

"But . . . but I don't want to leave anymore . . . I changed my mind," she cried, the tears of frustration on their way.

"Well," Suzy said, "so have I. I've been thinking all afternoon, and I feel like it's not safe to stay here, and I'm not letting you stay somewhere that isn't safe."

Mia wailed: "But it *is* safe! It *is*!" She was panicking now, that profound desperation of being misunderstood.

"Mia," Suzy said in a studied and patronizing calm to which Mia was entirely unaccustomed. "There are some times when you're a parent when you have to make a decision that a kid maybe doesn't understand. But it's my job to take care of you, and there are going to be times when I have to do what I think is right, and now is one of those times, and you can hate me if you want to, but I'm not doing this to make you mad. I'm doing this because I feel like it's the best option we have right now." She was softened somewhat by her own speech, and she broke in the end and became, for a moment, the mother Mia thought she knew. "You've got to trust me, babe, OK? I'm sorry, but you've got to trust me."

Mia stood up from the bed, her body and her expression rigid with indignation. She was livid, and incredulous too, unable to believe this was really happening. She faced her mother down with as much rage as Suzy had ever seen in the child, and said with a vehemence she could only have inherited from the woman she was saying it to: "I don't care. I'm staying here."

"No, actually," Suzy countered, "actually, you're not."

"I am. You can go. I'm staying."

"No, Mia, you're coming with me."

And they went at it like that for some time, until Mia locked herself in the bathroom, shouting, "I hate you! I *hate* you!" at the top of her lungs, and Suzy stormed from the room.

She went downstairs, found a housekeeper to post outside the room upstairs to watch Mia, and then went straight for the office and grabbed the keys to a Lodge truck. In the parking lot she tried the keys in three vehicles before she found the right one, cursing herself, the trucks, her father, her daughter, Osprey Island, and everything that had ever conspired to get her born there in the first place. When the engine of the old tan Ford finally turned over, Suzy sank down in the seat, put her head back, and squeezed her eyes shut.

She swung out of the parking lot onto Sand Beach Road and sped up the hill. It felt good to drive, to move that fast, the whipping of wind, the adrenaline of speed. She wanted to stay with that speed, just to drive away, far. And what struck her was the dreadful familiarity of that sensation. It was high school. It was dying for flight, anything just to drive and keep driving. The preposterous, insidious envy she felt for people who lived in open spaces, who could put their car on I-80 in Pennsylvania or Illinois and keep driving until they hit the Pacific. God! The freedom in that! You dreamed of flight on Osprey Island. You dreamed of getting in your father's Chrysler and gunning for the docks. Dreamed of how it would feel when the wheels lifted off the cobbled planks and took air.

It explained everything. The high school kids who just drove and drove around and around and around that little island, so fast they squealed the curves, grazing the guardrails. They'd swipe the fence on Sand Beach Road and leave their mark in the whitewash, streaking Daddy's fender. It made the blaming easy. Citizens in their homes heard the skid: tires screaming on asphalt. They called the police, called the sheriff at home in his bed, said *Sheriff, it's the kids again out joyriding* . . . and Davey Mitchell and Sheriff Harty roused themselves from sleep to get out and hunt the hooligans down and haul them in, maybe even keep them overnight in the island jail, which was fine; it was better, really, because for those kids anything was better than sitting still. Anything was better than driving your car up onto that ferry and knowing Chip or Matty or whoever was on duty that night would have a call in to your folks, who'd be down there hauling your ass back to bed before you could even smoke a godforsaken cigarette in peace. It wasn't worth pulling your car onto the damn ferry, since you knew they were going to make you back it right off again.

Suzy pealed off the asphalt and onto the dirt road that bordered the old golf course. The truck slid in the sand, kicking up a spray of pebbles in its wake. She steered into the skid and barreled on up the hill. Rounding the rise, she could see both Roddy's truck and Eden's car in the driveway, and Suzy parked beside them, jumped out, and went down the ravine toward Roddy's shack. She knocked, poked her head in, then turned, let the door fall shut, and went back up toward Eden's. Halfway up the path, near the chicken coop, she saw the back door open onto Eden's porch, and Roddy stepped outside. He raised a hand in tired greeting. *Such a sweet man,* Suzy thought, and the sight of him there in all his exhaustion was such a comfort. She couldn't think of the last time a man had inspired comfort in her; she wasn't sure it was something she'd ever felt. The thought made her desperately sad. If she could have done anything in the world right then— the kind of thing Mia asked constantly: *If you could be anybody in the world who would it be? If you could have any candy in the whole world, which kind would you get?*—if she could do anything right then, she thought, she'd have loaded herself and Roddy and Mia and Squee into Roddy's truck, all their bags piled under tarps in back and held down with bailer's twine. They'd drive to New York, enroll Squee at Mia's school, find Roddy work easily doing construction, contracting . . . Families had been built on a hell of a lot less than that.

Roddy pulled off his hat, ran a hand over his head, back and forth, rubbing the hair one way and the other so it stuck up like he'd slept on it wrong. She climbed the porch steps and he began to speak, updating her on the latest developments as though he were the one with something to tell. "We've got one of your housekeeping girls inside." He flicked his head toward the door, replaced his hat and secured it down as if preparing to go out into a storm. "Peg?" he said. "Peg, right?" He rolled his eyes slightly. "She's *worried* . . ." He said it half-mockingly, then seemed to retract the judgment as it came out of his mouth and just shook his head, saying, "Worried about Squee. About what Lance might do to him."

It was all the validation and prompting Suzy needed. "He's *dangerous,*" she said. "Mia's been hysterical all day—he *is* dangerous." She felt the power in that reiteration; it became truer each time she said it. She felt a blooming sense of freedom, the freedom to say anything, because she was out of there! She was already gone, she was on that ferry, and nothing mattered anymore. She wasn't going to get up tomorrow and do her father's bidding another day. She wasn't going to put her kid through this any longer, no matter how that kid felt about it after a day at the beach and three scoops of pistachio ice cream.

"Lance *is* dangerous," she said again. She fought the urge just to keep saying it, over and over and over again. "Of all people, I should know how dangerous Lance Squire really is."

"What?" Roddy was confused. "What do you . . . ?" And then he commanded himself to stop—all thought, all action, everything—until he understood what she was saying. She could see him shutting down, the way you'd close the doors and batten down the windows in the threat of an oncoming twister. Only it ceased to look like steeliness. It was a slackening, if anything—like the way Squee looked when Lance came at him.

Suzy choked. Then she began suddenly, almost violently, to cry. She sucked in breath and held her hair in her hand, the arm blocking half her face to cover at least a fraction of her shame. Her words came in sputters. "You can ask your mother," she choked out. "She knows it all." And then she didn't know how to go on, for she was saying something she had never said in her life, and though it had always been true, she had never felt its truth the way she felt it right then. "I lost my virginity down in that ravine"—she threw a hand out behind her—"when I was sixteen years old."

"To Lance?" Roddy said. "I knew you . . . I didn't know it was—"

"Everybody and their fucking grandmother knew I slept with him. He basically raped me—Lance, there, in that ravine—when I was sixteen years old. Ask your mother," she sobbed, "just ask your mother. She probably remembers more than I do. Ask Eden . . . *That's* how I *know*. That's how I know what Lance is capable of." She paused then, drew in her breath, and looked up at Roddy for the first time since she'd begun. "I have to leave," she said. "I feel like I'm losing my mind. I can't stay here. I can't. I have to leave."

She started to say "Come with me" but he stopped her.

"I can't . . . ," he said.

"You *could* . . . ," she said. She didn't know if it was true, or if she wanted it, but she said it anyway.

He said, "My mother . . . Squee . . ."

And she just sobbed harder until finally he had to take her in his arms. It was easier to hold her and feel her sadness than it was to stand by and feel his own. So he held on to her, relieved that he had something to hold on to, at the same time realizing that the real relief would be in letting her go.

BRIGID WAS IN THE ROOM when Peg returned from Eden's. She was lying on her bed, on her back, in gym shorts and a skimpy tank. It was hard for Peg to know what to say to her. It was hard for Brigid to know what to say to Peg. Peg was well enough aware that Brigid hadn't come back to work with the rest of the girls after lunch; she'd run off after Lance Squire and never returned to her duties. The way Peg thought of it, she didn't see Brigid as having run after *Squee*—didn't even consider that Brigid might be concerned about the boy at all.

Brigid, for her part, had still been sitting on the Squires' porch with Lance when the other girls had gotten off work, and had seen Peg climb into a car and get whisked away down Sand Beach Road. She hadn't come to dinner. No one knew where she'd gone, not even Jeremy, who'd passed the meal in a state of demonstrable concern.

"Where've *you* been at?" Brigid said, looking off toward the window as if she was merely asking out of politeness and couldn't have cared less where Peg had spent the last few hours.

"Pardon?" Peg said.

Brigid turned back into the room. "People wondered where you'd gone," she said.

Peg paused. "The girls were likewise wondering where *you'd* knocked off to this afternoon."

Brigid's face went deadpan with annoyance as she tried to stop her eyes from rolling. "I was in plain sight of the lot of you on the Squires' porch all afternoon. You couldn't've wondered all that much, now could you?"

Peg couldn't help herself. "How's the boy?" she said, her tone a mixture of accusation and longing.

"Squee? He's just fine," Brigid said quickly. "They took him to the beach, with Mia."

"*Who* took him to the beach?"

Brigid paused, waiting for the acid to drain back from her lips before she spoke. She forced a terrible smile: "Gavin and his new little hoor."

"Well, if you're getting off with *Lance Squire,* what precisely did you expect?"

Brigid sat up. "You've bloody got to be kidding."

"What?"

"You think I've passed over *Gavin* in favor of *Lance Squire?*" Brigid took it for granted that no one in her right mind would ever pass over Gavin.

"So you *haven't,* then?" Peg said casually.

Brigid flopped back down onto the bed and turned to the window.

"Oh, I see, now," Peg said snidely.

Brigid lay fuming in her bed by the window, words flashing through her brain, retorts and explanations so loud in her skull it seemed Peg should have been able to hear them. She tried to speak, but whatever came to her tongue felt inadequate, and she swallowed a number of beginnings before she managed to sit up and say: "The man's wife has just passed on. Am I the only one around in this bloody place who thinks he deserves a bit of sympathy? You lot treat him as though he'd killed her himself!"

That struck Peg unexpectedly, for it was true: that was precisely the way she thought of him. "Oh, don't be thick," she snapped. "I've simply a bit more concern for the welfare of the child who's been left in his care and'll likely be scarred for life, or worse, if no one steps in and does a bloody thing about it—"

"Jesus Christ!" Brigid cried. "Who do think you are, then?" She was stammering for the next line when Peg cut her off.

"I'm someone who bloody cares what'll happen to that child!"

Brigid's astonishment stopped her from replying. She just sat there blinking at this girl who was her roommate. "My god," was all she could manage. "Oh my fucking god."

Peg was riled, every ill feeling she'd ever entertained toward Brigid rising to the surface. "You pass your time licking up to this man and that without opening your eyes and seeing what's in front of your bloody face! I don't see how you can so much as sit and *talk* with the man when you've seen the way he treats his son—the way he treats bloody everyone!—acting as though it's altogether just grand!"

Brigid shook her head back and forth, slowly, in utter disbelief. "Heaven forbid," she said, "that a man who's just lost his wife doesn't act like a bloody saint every fucking minute of the day! God forbid you cut the man just the tiniest bit of slack when he's been through the worst thing you'll ever imagine!" She stood up, the words jamming in her throat. She held up her hands: there was nothing more she could even think to say to someone so ignorant.

"You must be *blind*!" Peg hissed, but Brigid waved her hands by her ears to say she'd hear no more.

"You're bleedin' unbelievable," Brigid finally managed to say. She stared at Peg another moment as she tried to figure out what she might do with herself at that point. Then, suddenly, she snatched the covers from her bed and grabbed up her pillow with the other hand. "Absolutely unbelievable!" And she slammed out of the room.

"Where do you think you're going?" Peg cried. And then she heard the outside door slam at the end of the hall, and she was quiet, listening. All she could hear were the crickets.

Brigid hadn't a clue where she was going except that she was going *away* from that self-righteous, arrogant, preachy little priss she'd been unlucky enough to get lodged with. It was dark out, and the first thing Brigid saw were the lights of the Squire cottage across the way. People were still out on the porch of the Lodge, but Brigid didn't want to see any of them. She walked across the path and up the steps. Through the window she could see Lance sitting in his easy chair, a beer in hand. Squee was on the couch, his legs crossed under him, playing with an action figure of some sort. They were watching TV. Like any normal, regular, American family, Brigid thought—even a normal, regular American family who've recently lost one of their own!—peacefully watching the television in their own bloody living room! She hated Peg with all the ire in her. She knocked on the door, heard Lance call, "C'min," and opened the door.

"Hi," said Squee, looking up briefly from his play.

"Hey there," Lance said, waving her inside.

"Could I knock about with you lot a bit this evening?" Brigid said bitterly. "My roommate's a bloody mulchie wanker!"

Lance's face broke into a wide, winning grin. "I don't know what the fuck that means, but our casa is your casa." With his old magnanimous flair Lance swept an arm broadly across the room. "Beer's in the fridge."

She got herself a can, and as she shuffled toward the couch to curl up beside Squee with her blanket and pillow, Brigid could honestly say that she felt welcome and grateful and at home for the first time since she'd arrived on Osprey Island. And as they watched mindless American blather, Brigid settled into an oblivion of comfort for which she was enormously thankful.

Eighteen

WWCD?

One July day in 1957, when Great Island should have been a scene of activity with young birds at the flying stage, I scanned the marsh through my telescope. I saw the usual number of adults about—but where were the young?

The nesting season obviously had been a failure. The next year confirmed my suspicions. Although young ospreys ordinarily pip the shell in about 5 weeks, many adults sat on unhatched eggs for 60 to 70 days. Other eggs mysteriously disappeared. One bird brought a rubber ball to the nest and faithfully sat on it for six weeks!

—ROGER TORY PETERSON, "The Endangered Osprey"

WHEN EDEN RETURNED HOME after dropping Peg back at the Lodge, she went straight down to the henhouse. The lamp was on at Roddy's place and Suzy's truck was gone. Eden went first to Lorraine's coop to check on her. They weren't far from her hatching date now, and Lorraine was viciously defensive about her clutch. Only when Lorraine was off the nest could Eden get in there to make sure she had enough nesting material, stick in a few sprigs of wormwood to deter insects and pests. Eden poked her head into the coop for one, and before her eyes could even adjust, Lorraine was letting out a terrible *crrrrrrawk crrrrrrrrrrrawk,* loud and screeching. As far back as she and Eden went, if anyone tried to mess with those eggs, Lorraine'd peck their hands into bloody stumps before she'd let them have at her unhatched babies.

In the main coop old Margery lumbered off her roost the minute Eden entered and wobbled over to say hello. She was like a dog. Eden sank down into an old half-broken chair she'd set by the door, and lifted Margery up onto her lap. Eden stroked the hen's feathers.

Once upon a time Eden had tried to teach Lorna how to care for the chickens, and the girl had been happy enough to cuddle the feather-puff babies but hadn't really taken to it beyond that. Seemed you couldn't teach a woman to mother any more than you could make a hen go broody. Lorna'd been willing enough to go walking with Eden, to help out with the osprey nesting platforms. The thing Lorna lacked, Eden thought, was initiative. Then she thought about why it was that people were always trying to figure out what it was that Lorna was lacking. Maybe they felt if they could isolate what made Lorna who she was they could more easily assure themselves that they weren't like her, couldn't be like her, that they were immune. It was that easy. There. Done. Eden—a veritable Napoleon of initiative— could look at Lorna and say, *There, that's it, that's what she's missing. That's what she's missing and that's what I've got in spades! Therefore I am different from Lorna. Therefore I am safe.*

It was all so flawed. So inherently and fundamentally and self-servingly flawed. And it helped them all through another day of their problems and kids and strife and grief. It was hard to imagine what the Islanders were going to do without Lorna. Who was going to step in to come up short in every comparison and make them all feel relatively better about their own pathetic lives? It was Osprey's system of moral certitude. Sure, you could ask, What Would Jesus Do? But that was often a tough question to answer, because Jesus' life, well, it was pretty different from their own. But at any time you could ask yourself, What Would Lorna Do? and it was pretty much certain that if you could manage to accomplish the exact opposite of whatever that was, you'd probably be just fine.

Now, What Would *Chickens* Do? *That* was a question that got you somewhere. Because what *they*'d do was actually about what *you* did. If you did what you were supposed to, the chickens followed in turn. You took care of them, gave them everything they needed: food, shelter, vitamins, place to run around, games to play—a head of lettuce in a netted bag on a string, say: tether-lettuce! They loved it!—mates to mate with, a job to do, eggs to lay, babies to raise . . . The occasional egg-eater notwithstanding, if you treated a chicken right, it treated you right in return. And to Eden's way of thinking about things, that was exactly as it should be, and there was no reason for such a philosophy to stop with chickens. It hurt Eden's heart to think of the havoc people wreaked through their own offhandedness, their own laxity, their own systems of ignorance and denial and fear. There were ways to live in the world that kept the world spinning! Why couldn't people see that? And if they saw it—and this was Eden's greatest heartsickness—if they saw it, why couldn't they live it? Why wasn't it cut and dried? If something was wrong with the chickens, you went in and figured out what was causing the trouble—Why were they eating their eggs? Why were they plucking out their vent feathers?—and you corrected the problem! Why—and this was maybe all that Eden had ever really wanted to know—why couldn't we be more like the birds?

"Ma?" Roddy was calling from outside the coop. Margery hopped off Eden's lap and flapped back to her roost. Eden pushed herself up from the chair and went outside.

Roddy looked anxious, in a sad way—a way that made Eden want to take her son in her arms—but when he spoke, his voice was flattened out. He kept his eyes down. "They're leaving," he said, "Suzy and Mia. She's going back to New York."

Eden waited, silent. Roddy was packing the ground with the heel of his boot. He said, "Everything I hear makes me more scared for Squee, about what Lance's going to do." He looked up at his mother. "Suzy said I should ask you about something, and I'm afraid you're not going to give me a straight answer, and I need you to give me a straight answer on this. Suzy said you could probably tell me better than she could what happened to her . . . in high school? Out back here . . . down the ravine? With Lance?" Roddy paused to let his mother answer, but he was preparing the further assault of his interrogation. He wasn't going to let her squirm away.

"She told you that?" Eden was saying, nodding her head in consideration as she spoke, as though this information meant something particular to her. "Suzy told you that," she said again, not a question but confirmation of the facts as they stood.

Roddy nodded. "She said you'd tell me." He looked at the ground. "She's *afraid* of him, Ma."

"Well, Christ!" Eden swore. "You're talking about something that happened twenty years ago, and suddenly she's so terribly afraid!" Then something struck her. This "fear" they were talking about, this fear Suzy was calling her reason to flee—who knew what was really driving that girl? Suzy could well be leaving to get away from *Roddy* for all Eden knew, and that thought roused in her a sudden and vicious anger toward Suzy—for being a coward and a conniver, and mostly for not loving Eden's son the way he deserved to be loved. "I'll tell you," she said to Roddy, "I'll tell you, but I don't know it'll shed any light on anything at all."

They sat across from each other at the picnic table, mother and son, and she talked. It had been some sort of a party, maybe, Eden dimly recalled. There'd been people over, friends, kids from the school. Suzy had come with Chas, but he'd been unable to find her when he was ready to drive home and figured she'd left earlier, walked home. He took off alone. It was Eden who found her, just past midnight, soon after Chas had gone. She was behind the old woodshed, holding her knees to her chest, crying.

"I got it out of her, what had happened, to some degree. Enough to understand it hadn't been something she'd particularly wanted to do . . ."

"So he did rape her?" Roddy asked cautiously.

Eden sighed. "Sure what I'd've called it. Then *and* now. Now maybe people'd agree with me. *Then?* Then she was more a girl who got herself in a bad situation. Nineteen sixty-eight, on this island? They'd for certain blame that one on her."

"She got pregnant?" he asked skeptically. "You said Lance was . . . that he couldn't, you know . . . so she *didn't* get pregnant, right?"

Eden shook her head sadly. "But I didn't know that—about Lance—for a good 'nother year later from Lorna." She spoke hesitantly, measuring the words, still trying not to let go of more than she absolutely had to.

"What?" Roddy's thoughts lurched to words and then broke uncertainly. "What, did every pregnant girl on this island get routed through you? I don't . . ."

"I don't think Suzy was ever pregnant then. Though we took precautions just in case—"

"Wait," Roddy commanded. The even-tempered keel of her voice angered him, made him feel accused, irrational. He was struggling to understand, and every word out of his mother's mouth confused him further. "Wait," he said again, "that's not the point. What do you mean, *precautions*? How'd they wind up with you?" All the words were wrong, his thoughts too incomplete for articulation. He was fighting himself.

Eden watched him, her eyes steady. She took a breath. She said, "Things are different now from how they used to be."

Roddy waited, his leg jackhammering beneath the table.

"We're talking about nineteen sixty-eight, 'sixty-nine. We're talking about a very different world here, OK? And then with the chances a girl had to take—" She broke off.

"What? You doing abortions out back to every knocked-up girl on—?"

"No," Eden snapped. "Not like that. Not like you mean." She paused a moment, collecting her thoughts, focusing her argument. "There are herbal methods of—"

"Oh Christ, Ma—"

"Wait!" Eden snapped. "You just listen now. Listen to what I'm telling you."

Roddy closed his eyes and bowed his head. He clasped his hands together between his knees.

Eden began again, slowly. "There are certain herbs that have been used for centuries for certain curative effects." Her voice was controlled and cautionary. "Certain herbs that have certain effects on different systems in the body. There are particular herbs with beneficial effects on the female reproductive organs. So much we take in in this world is poison to us. Certain herbs help the body to expel and rejuvenate."

Roddy listened.

"Certain herbs—pennyroyal, for instance, black cohosh—these certain herbs—herbs I take regularly, mind you—they help a woman my age with the troubles of being a woman my age. Many other uses at other times of life, different preparations and doses.

"Now, some of these have been used to stimulate an abortion—stimulate the body to abort. And wait, now, before you say anything: listen to me. These can be dangerous, dangerous things unless you know what you're doing. And these are procedures that you've *got* to do early on—I'm talking about the first day a girl's late on her period—once you're six days late it's too dangerous. OK? You see what I'm talking about? You see how careful you have to be?"

Roddy nodded dully. It made sense. Someone on-island had to have been helping those girls; it figured it'd be Eden.

"But back then," Eden was saying, "an herbal abortion was the safest way there was. It might still be." She should have been a politician: such conviction. Except that her conviction was never about anything that anyone else on Osprey supported.

"You said Suzy wasn't pregnant," Roddy said, his tone more accusatory than he intended. "I thought she wasn't—because of Lance . . ."

Now it was Eden's impatience that showed. "Well, wouldn't it be nice if we all toiled with the power of hindsight! What I knew *then* was that Suzy Chizek was sixteen years old and might have been on a nine-month course from virginity to motherhood because of a boy who had about as much right to be a father then as he does now!"

"She was lucky. Suzy. What I could get from her then, she knew at least that she was due on her period soon, and that, that was just lucky. God, she was scared. And I tried explaining what it was I knew we could do. I don't honestly remember what I gave her. There's lots of things to take into account—a person's health, everything. Honestly. I don't remember. But we did it. Started her on infusions—nothing easy for a high school girl to manage, but she did it, went through with the herbs, and a few days later she was bleeding normal, and that was that." Eden stopped.

"And *that was that*? No wonder you're such a friggin' outcast on this island! Did Dad know? Did *everybody* know? What, so when Lorna got pregnant you did the same thing then too?"

"No!" Eden snapped. "No. And don't you dare blow this into something it was not. I helped people who needed help at a time when their government would have rather seen those girls die than let them—"

"Please, not the protest rally—"

"I helped individuals in individual circumstances that they needed help getting out of."

"Yeah? So why'd Lorna need out of her situation?"

"I did not help Lorna then. Not like that," Eden said, and there were years of bitterness in her voice. "I did not help Lorna. And she turned around and she threw it in my face. It was after Lorna I stopped everything. Nineteen sixty-nine. After that, the girls who came, I gave them the name of someone off-island."

"Why wouldn't you help her? Why was it any different? You'd help Suzy but not Lorna—how's that fair?"

"How it's *fair*," Eden shrilled, "is that Suzy was a sixteen-year-old virgin who got raped out back of my house. And Lorna was a calculating young woman who got herself knocked up on purpose so she could marry Lance Squire and get the hell out of Art and Penny's house. And then once she'd gotten what she wanted she decided she didn't want it. Because it wasn't *Lance's* baby. And she got mad at him for something, and told him that. Just to hurt him, I'm sure. Told him that she'd been trying to get herself pregnant by him as long as they'd been having sex and it just plain didn't work, and she had to see was it him or her or what? So she did what she had to do. And she's saying to him, hadn't she gotten it so they could get married? And didn't they have a good deal there now at the Lodge, with a place to live and a job that took no work and how she'd done it all for him and he wasn't even grateful, and she didn't want a baby, she just wanted him, and to marry him and to be with him, and she'd done everything it took to make that so, and look how he showed his gratitude . . ."

"Whose baby was it, then?" Roddy asked.

Eden stopped and just stared at him as if she couldn't rationally comprehend what he was asking. Was he a moron? Had he not heard a damn word she'd said? The look on her face was of utter disbelief. "Bud," she said. "Bud."

Roddy's face bulged like he was going to vomit into his hands. *"Bud* got *Lorna pregnant?"* He spoke as if to lay those words out in plain sight and see if they evaporated like figments or had the weight to sit and submit to scrutiny.

"I'd say she got her*self* pregnant, *by Bud,"* Eden countered. "I'd say Lorna Vaughn got that man through the worst spring of his goddamn life. Chas was dead, killed over there . . ." She paused, as if mere mention of *that war* rendered her exhausted beyond speech. "That news," she said, "it came pretty damn close to killing Bud and Nancy themselves. On Nancy you could see it—I mean, she very near lost her mind. But with Bud it was all on the inside. And maybe that's no excuse—I'd never heard him do anything like it before and I've never heard about anything since . . ."

"Did he . . . ?" Roddy cut in, then stopped, sat on his hands and shook his head to stop himself from speaking.

"The thing is," Eden said, as though in reply to the question he hadn't asked, "it was Lorna who went to him. I'm not excusing. She was seventeen; he was a grown man. I'm just saying. Here's a man whose son is dead. Again, I'm not excusing, but to lose a child . . ."

And Roddy knew that for Eden such a loss did not excuse, but it did perhaps explain something.

"Here was a man out of his mind with grief. Not right, not seeing the world through right eyes. And here was this beautiful girl. You remember how Lorna was then? Just a sprite, you know, a little spirit. Oh she was so pretty."

Roddy nodded silently. He watched Eden's eyes well up for the first time since the fire. And he watched as she swallowed, ordered the tears back down their ducts. "She just showed up one day—and I know this from after. She only told me later, years—I didn't know at the time. It was only after when she came to me. Otherwise maybe I'd have been able to stop—oh, I don't know. Anything's easy to say now, I guess . . ."

"She went to him." Eden picked up her pace. "Showed up one day that spring after Chas died, this girl Bud'd known since she was in diapers showing up one day asking, *Mister Chizek, could I have a ride out to Scallopshell Beach? I'm sure it's where I lost my necklace in the parking lot last night* . . . or some such thing . . ."

Roddy breathed in audibly. He squinted, as though in pain.

"I'm sure Bud knew the whole time it wasn't right. But he'd been angling toward something. Something bad and wrong. Like he could get back at the universe that killed his son. Something like that, you know?

"Lorna's a smart girl. You look at what she did. She had a plan how she was going to get out of her folks' house, and if it was going to take her being pregnant to do it . . . And she'd been trying with Lance—not that Lance knew . . ." Eden scowled. "Not that the idiot took any protection against knocking her up! Look what she did: she didn't go to some high school boy—someone who wouldn't be able to keep his trap shut about it. No: she found someone who *couldn't* tell. Bud was married, had children—OK, a child, then—he was grieving. She got him at his weakest."

"That sounds a hell of a lot like an excuse to me," Roddy said, and his voice was not without disdain.

"I'm not saying he was innocent," Eden said quickly, "just that she was smart. I'm saying she knew what she was doing. Bud had money . . . But when it turned into *Bud, I'm pregnant,* it wasn't money for an abortion she wanted—which is what he thought, of course—it was just his word that he'd never try to make a claim on that baby."

"But that was . . . that wasn't Squee . . ."

"Way before," Eden said. "It must have been spring of her junior year. She knew she was pregnant early as a girl can know. She'd been waiting on it for months. And don't think Penny Vaughn didn't have her daughter into Doc Zobeck for a test the first morning she heard that girl retching in the toilet. They had her married off to Lance Squire before she was eight, ten weeks gone. It was a few weeks more before she came to me asking could she have some of the special tea— but it was too late for that. I wouldn't do it past three weeks. Well, *now.* Back then I did. Six weeks at the latest, even then. Never any guarantee it's going to work, and if it doesn't you pretty much don't have a choice but for a surgical abortion, what with how likely it is you'll have birth defects from trying to do it with the herbs. It was after the wedding that Lorna came to me. She needed the pregnancy to get herself that far. She came to me when she didn't want to go any farther."

"And you said no . . ." Roddy prompted.

She was nodding. "And I said no. And we talked about it," Eden spoke bitterly; she still castigated herself over the events that had followed. "And then Lorna—and I do blame myself for this, I do, because I had it there, in the house, I shouldn't have, I was too easy about it . . . Lorna let herself in one day when your father and I were out, helped herself to what she needed, and did it on her own. That was the last. I got rid of everything. That was it."

"So she did it herself?"

"Except it didn't work," Eden said. "And god knows what she'd done, how much she took of what . . . But the risks of birth defects— it's not even *risks,* it's *guarantees.* I'd told her all that. Before, I mean.

And then she came to me hysterical. Confessed what she'd done. Begging me for help: *What do I do? What can I do?*" Eden paused. She stared down at her hands on the picnic table. "And I did feel responsible. I was angrier than I think I'd ever been at a living person in my life—I swear to you I could have strangled her, I could have—but it felt like my fault, or responsibility, at least. I got her to a doctor on the mainland. Someone to do it surgically." She paused again. "We didn't speak for years, me and Lorna. Embarrassment. Anger. We didn't speak until she got herself pregnant again—with Squee—and she came asking for my help. She said she knew I knew what was right, and all she wanted was to do right by this baby. This miracle baby that she swore up and down was Lance's, which I believed for all of five minutes. About as long as Lance believed it, I'd guess. But she wanted to do things right, take care of that baby. And *that's* when Lorna and I got close, then, when she was carrying Squee. Until he was a year or so and she was back to drinking, and everything else, and avoiding me like the plague since I was the only one who'd say right out, *Lorna, what the hell are you doing to yourself?*"

Roddy sat at the picnic table a long time, even after his mother had gone up to the house to finally start dinner. He held his head in his hands as if everything inside might come cracking out if he let it go. This was everything he'd tried to steer his life away from. In high school geometry they taught about how parallel lines never intersected, and he'd tried to run his life on that principle: everything on its own separate track. But Osprey Island had too many tracks and not enough acreage to spare each its private orbit.

Nineteen

THE SHORE RECEDES,
AND I TOO ON THE SHORE

Much harm has been done by guessing at a bird's motives, and assuming always that he is in mischief. I have rejected all conjectures of the sort, and accepted only what has been thoroughly proved, and reported by trustworthy witnesses.

—OLIVE THORNE MILLER, *The Second Book of Birds*

BUD CHIZEK WAS AWAKENED the next morning by a phone call from Chip Gruder down at the ferry. "Don't suppose you got any idea why one of your trucks is sitting in my No Parking five-a.m.-to-midnight zone, mainland side?" Chip said.

"Mainland?" Bud repeated groggily.

"Yes, sir." Chip's inquisition voice was practiced; the man had three sons of his own, and he'd seen it all before. "We in for another summer of your staffers running wild, Bud?"

Bud was in no mood for a coy ferryman, especially not before he'd had his morning coffee. He told Chip, "I'll handle it." They'd had some problems in the past with this sort of thing. Lodge waiters getting drunk, driving over to the mainland for a movie, or getting a motel room, or getting in a fight, winding up in jail. Once, a Lodge worker had just disappeared altogether, took off, hopped a bus or a train from Menhadenport, had his roommate mail his clothes after him.

"You want I'll call Lovetsky's, have her towed back over to you?"

Bud growled, "I'll have a man on the next boat," and slammed down the phone.

He tried Cybelle down at the front desk but got no answer and slammed the receiver down again, cursing the girl, until he put on his glasses and saw that the bureau clock said five-thirty-five. Chip Gruder hadn't wasted any time calling.

In the double bed beside him, Nancy lay on her back, a silk embroidered sleep mask over her eyes, pretending to be dead to the world, as wakefulness could have gotten her name added to the roster of people Bud might send to fetch a truck in Menhadenport. Bud wrestled himself out from under the bed sheets and went hunting for a phone directory. In a cloth-lined basket by the downstairs phone he found an Osprey telephone book—one hundred pages, if that, three by five, spiral-bound, the cover an airbrushed photo of an osprey silhouetted in its nest against an orange and purple sunset, the words *Osprey Island 1988* sprawling across the darkened beach as though painted in fire. He looked up Jacobs. If there was anyone you didn't have to worry about waking up at some ungodly hour of the morning it was Eden Jacobs, who, people were known to say, probably woke up at the first crack of light or before, since it was suspected she took her beloved chickens to bed with her. Bud dialed.

Roddy hadn't slept much, and his state of animation was robotic at best. He drove by the Lodge first to get the extra set of keys, then went around to the ferry and parked his truck. The morning was bright, and he scrounged behind the seat of the truck for a hat. There was only the ugly purple one from the laundry company that Suzy'd left there, but it probably looked better than his hair did, so he pulled it on and walked toward the docks. Though the sun promised a warm day, it was windy that morning, the flag whipping against its pole with tireless ferocity. The sound of the halyard smacking up against the mast was a sound that brought Roddy back to a number of different places in his life. Anywhere there was a flagpole there was that sound, rope against metal, clanging in the wind. It was, Roddy thought, both comforting and maddening, if such a thing was possible.

The ferry line at that hour was full of Islanders who worked early morning mainland jobs and drove down every day before five-thirty when the boats started running to be the first ones across. There were two boats on that morning, and Roddy watched them pass each other in the bay. The crossing was hardly more than a mile, took seven minutes, maybe nine in bad weather, poor visibility, ice.

The Osprey Island ferry landing was one slip, with two breaker walls of tall wooden pylons stretching out from the dock like open arms. The pylons were near-rotted, of a wood washed gray with decades of seagull droppings. No two posts were the same height or thickness, but each one had a seagull perched atop like a sentry. Roddy watched as the boat approached, the gulls eyeing it as if they were playing a game of chicken, just daring that tremendous hunk of steel to come within a breath of their roosts before they took off in a cacophonous swarm of flapping screams and cries. The ferry was a behemoth of a raft, a floating platform—like an ice rink, almost—with a watchtower sticking up from the top for the ferryman to see out while he steered. The ferries (there were three, though no more than two ever ran, one or the other perpetually in need of repair) were painted white, buffered around the sides with old truck tires strapped on to protect the ship—and cushion its landings—as she lumbered into the shore, barreling against the pylon walls, which swayed and creaked under the pressure but always managed to bounce the boat to the opposite wall like a pinball, back and forth as she shimmied her way into the slip and the ferrymen secured her to the dock.

Chip Gruder was captaining that morning, and a younger guy whom Roddy didn't know personally, named Derrick Darlington, was working the dock, directing cars. He swung open a wide chain-link gate and stepped out of the line of traffic as he motioned the first car off the boat, up the ramp, and onto dry land. It was a full ferry, twelve cars or so, engines turning over, drivers refastening seat belts, passengers preparing to disembark. Roddy stood by the ticket shack as the cars filed off and Derrick turned to the line of cars behind him, started motioning them onto the boat. Matty Lux was at the bow, guiding drivers into place, getting them squeezed in tight; it was a puzzle, packing on as many cars as the ferry could hold. Roddy waited until all the vehicles were on before he boarded with a few other foot passengers—two guys with lunch pails and a man in a business suit—who'd come up behind him, as well as two teenage girls who emerged from the ticket shack in waitress uniforms, clearly heading over to work the breakfast shift at Baldy's in Menhadenport. Derrick Darlington stopped each of the pedestrians, exchanged brief words, and punched tickets for them from the thick rolled pad in his gloved hands. When Roddy got to him, Derrick said, "One way, round trip?"

"One way, on *foot*."

Derrick lifted his eyes from the ticket book. "You picking up the Lodge truck?"

Roddy nodded.

Derrick flexed the hole-puncher in his grip as if it was cramping his hand. "Trouble with the staff again?" He spoke like a jaded disciplinarian, though he could not have been more than nineteen himself and had the remnants of a nasty-looking black eye on his suntanned face.

Roddy shrugged.

"You know who did it?" the kid said. "Who left the truck?"

Roddy just stood there looking at him. "Yeah," he said curtly. And then he clamped his jaw shut and stepped onto the boat. His fare would go on the Lodge account.

The water was choppy, waves reflecting sunlight like undulating glass, and the ferry rocked and sloshed in the slip, bucking up against the pylons, which creaked and groaned in response. These were, for Roddy Jacobs, the most familiar sights and sounds in the world. Just the smells of this place—the fishy seaweed rot, the salt-drenched, sun-baked wood, gasoline, engine exhaust—all whipped by the wind and sprayed from the water in a fine mist as the ferry pulled away from the dock. Roddy leaned against the railing and turned his face to the sky, eyes closed against the sun. He heard the honking call of the ferry whistle, the churn of the rudders beneath him, the push of water through the gunwales, the clanking of chains on the gate, and the constant arrhythmic clang of rope against metal as halyard smacked flagpole atop the captain's tower.

If there were other places like this in the world, Roddy Jacobs hadn't found them. And he'd traveled plenty. Two decades, and travel was mostly what he'd done. He'd been up and down the West Coast, the East Coast, through Canada, and down to Mexico and below. He'd even ridden ferries—every ferry he could find—all over Puget Sound and the San Juan Islands, across Lake Michigan and Lake Champlain and through the locks of Sault Sainte Marie. He'd been to Cape Cod, and Martha's Vineyard, Nantucket and St. Simon's. Block Island, Shelter Island, Staten Island, Fire Island. And all of them were nice—he was sure that the people who'd grown up in Vineyard Haven and Vinalhaven cherished their ferries the way he cherished Osprey's and thought their island the *most* beautiful, *most* breathtaking, *most* comforting place in the world. He was glad for those people who had their places. Because he had his. Roddy Jacobs had longed for his home every day he'd spent elsewhere. It was only on returning that he fully realized—a gulp of ocean air pounding into his lungs as though he hadn't really breathed for twenty years—how much will it had taken to keep himself away.

He knew very well who'd left the truck illegally parked in Menhadenport, though he was finding it hard to get his mind to focus on what that really meant. Bud hadn't even known which truck it was, told Roddy to take all the spare keys, but Roddy'd gone to the vehicle shed and grabbed only the set for the tan Ford, though he suspected he'd find the truck unlocked, keys on the floor just beneath the seat. He didn't expect there'd be a note—she couldn't know who'd be the first to see it—and, after all, she'd already come to say good-bye. And then, after good-bye, he imagined she'd gone back to the Lodge. She'd have thrown everything into their luggage. Probably even stripped the beds to make less work for the Irish girls. She'd have coaxed Mia out of the bathroom with promises she probably never planned to make good on. Or Mia would have come out on her own, teary-eyed and sleepy and just wanting her mother, all that anger replaced by the simple need to be held in her mother's arms. And to that end, Suzy would have obliged, hauling down all the bags by herself, then going back upstairs to lift Mia to her chest and carry her, floppy-limbed and docile, to the waiting truck.

It would have been late, Roddy imagined. But how late? Before midnight, all those waiters and housekeepers still lounging on the deck? Would they have seen her? Wondered what was going on? Or had it been very late, the Lodge silent but for Suzy's patter up and down the central stairs? Had they missed the last ferry, twelve a.m., and slept in the truck on the Osprey side, right by where his own truck was parked now, Mia breathing softly on the seat, Suzy dozing off, then waking every few minutes to a rumble in the running engine or a car on Ferry Road? Had anyone come by—police, security, the usual nosy Islander—to see why on earth someone—*My goodness! Not just* someone! *Suzy Chizek!*—was sleeping in a beat-up truck in the Osprey Island Ferry lot? Or had they slept there peacefully until the horn awakened them? Or maybe Suzy set an alarm, making sure they were on the first ferry across, in time to catch the six o'clock train for New York? No, he realized, they had to have gone over the night before; the guys on the morning boat didn't know who'd left the truck; they hadn't seen her go over. That she'd left it in a No Parking zone was nothing but a final *fuck you* to her father. Even through his confusion, Roddy was able to see that Suzy Chizek was the kind of person who really did need to have the final *fuck you*. He had at least that much objectivity left.

What was he supposed to have done? Begged her to stay? Agreed to go with her? Watched her sail off toward the other shore, then realized—*I cannot let you go!*—and dived into the water after the ferry, trying to grab on to something that was already half gone? That wasn't Roddy. Truth be told, it would have been just like Roddy to waffle and hedge, agonize over the decision, entertain every option: stay, leave, stay, leave . . . And then he'd finally say, *Yes! I'll come with you! I'm coming!* They'd board the boat together for their final crossing. And then, about halfway across the bay he'd realize, *I can't do this.* A moment later he'd be leaping from the back of the ferry, going down in the foam and waves, choking, sputtering, and then finding his breath as the boat moved on, left him treading water, exhausted, in the middle of the bay, with a lot to explain to a whole lot of people on both shores.

Stuck between the steering wheel and dashboard she'd left a note on a folded flier from the Harbor Department Store, Menhadenport. The outside was not addressed. Roddy unfolded the paper. As he read the note, and read it over again, and again, conflicting emotions vied inside him. He didn't know whether he felt more heartbroken or disappointed.

Dad—Please try to forgive me. I'm sorry. Suzy

Suzy Chizek couldn't let a burning bridge burn.

It was seven before Roddy got back to the Lodge, parked the truck, and went up the hill to find Bud to ask for a lift down to the ferry to retrieve his own truck. He found the Chizeks eating breakfast at their kitchen table. If they had any inkling of what their daughter had just done to them they didn't betray it; they looked just as discontented as usual.

Nancy was already standing as he came in the door. "Coffee, Roddy? I'm sure you haven't eaten. You want some pancakes?"

Roddy looked to Bud. "I could use a ride down to pick up my truck at the ferry."

Bud nodded squarely at the table, mouth full, jaw working. When he finished chewing he said, "Sure, sure, have a bite first," and pointed his chin toward an empty chair.

"Thank you," Roddy told Nancy. He took a seat, removed his cap, hung it on the back of the chair, and smoothed his hair down with his hands. Nancy brought him a Pyrex mug of coffee, weak but hot.

Bud wiped his mouth with his napkin. "Lance?" he said.

Roddy waited a moment for more, but nothing came. "Lance?" He shook his head, not understanding.

Bud looked back, confused by Roddy's confusion. "Was it Lance that left the truck in Menhadenport?" He said it the way they all did, fast, and dulled: m'NAYdnpore.

"No, sir," said Roddy. Nancy passed him a plate of pancakes and bacon, which made him feel even stranger. It didn't seem likely he'd get to eat a bite of it. It was hard to imagine that once the news had been sprung Bud was going to stay at the table sipping coffee. Or that he'd leave Roddy there to finish breakfast.

"Syrup's on the table," Nancy told him.

"Thank you." He reached for the bottle.

Bud watched impatiently. "You planning on telling me anytime this morning who *did*?"

Roddy set the syrup back down without using it. If it crossed his mind just then to say, *You planning on telling me about how you got a seventeen-year-old girl pregnant? You plan on telling that to your wife here?* he managed not to. For all he knew, Nancy might be well aware of it all. He looked to her apologetically as he reached into his back pocket for the note. He passed it to Bud. "This was in the truck."

Bud eyed Roddy suspiciously, took the note without lifting his gaze from the man across the kitchen table. Then he looked down at the paper. There wasn't much to read. He stared at it longer than necessary, then lifted it in his hand and slammed it down as he stood. "Jesus!" he cried, and stormed away from the table.

The contents of the breakfast table jumped, and so did Roddy and Nancy. Then the front door slammed, and the bang set them in motion again like a starter's gun. Nancy moved to the table, a dishrag in one hand, her eyes questioning Roddy, and picked up the note. What Roddy really wanted to do was pour some syrup on his pancakes, eat breakfast, and get to work. What he most wanted to do at that moment was to act as if nothing had happened. But before he could think even a step beyond that, Nancy had finished the note and was shaking it in her hand, saying, "Did you *know* about this?" She looked at the pancakes she'd given Roddy as if she meant to take them back. "Do you have something to do with this?" she asked, then, at a loss, repeated herself. "Does this have something to do with you? Did you two have a fight or something?"

"*What?*" Roddy couldn't help but feel like he kept missing something.

Nancy jumped on him: "You can't tell me you think we don't know what's . . . going on between the two of you." She gestured back and forth with her dish towel, as though pointing between Roddy and an invisible Suzy she'd decided to seat beside him. "Christ Almighty, you're smarter than that!" Nancy spat out her words, and the effort turned her ugly, made her mouth large and gummy. She looked, Roddy realized, like her son. She looked—he could see the resemblance so clearly now—like Chas. Her mouth open in shock, she just kept looking at him, expecting something.

Finally he said, "She came by my mother's last night to say good-bye." And maybe during that moment's admission Nancy could see for herself—maybe it was written right there on his face?—the magnitude of the loss that *he* was suffering in the wake of Suzy's departure. Something in her shifted, as if she'd lost her train of thought and instead of searching just decided to shake it off and move along. There was a moment more of silence while they got their bearings and reclaimed their places in the world, and then Nancy took off her apron and went toward the staircase. Halfway to the bedroom, where she would take to her bed for the day like an invalid, she paused on the step and turned back to Roddy. She said, "Don't let your breakfast get cold." He took it as a blessing, for which he was thankful, and he poured the syrup and began to eat, realizing something as he chewed. Suzy'd left a note for her father, and she'd come by Eden's place to say good-bye to Roddy before she left. Her mother hadn't gotten anything at all.

Twenty

GRIEF-SPURRED, SWIFT-SWOOPING

"Bird" in Greek and Latin also means "omen."

—DR. EDGAR HAMILTON, PH.D.,
"How Our Island Was (Mis)Named"

BRIGID WOKE EARLY THAT MORNING on the Squire cottage sofa to the smell of frying bacon wafting up the hill from the Lodge kitchen. The doors to both Lance's and Squee's bedrooms were closed, and Brigid could remember drifting to sleep on the couch with Squee curled beside her. She remembered vaguely the television station signing off and Lance coming by to lift Squee from her arms and carry him to bed, and how she'd been touched, even through the wash of sleep, by a tenderness in Lance, and wished she could have invited them all in—Peg and Jeremy and the lot of them—to bear witness. Lance put Squee into bed, closed the boy's door, and came back toward Brigid on the couch. She'd been quite awake by then. She felt a rush of fear and caught her breath, the act of which took that fear and transformed it, took her quickened heartbeat and moved the pulse of blood down between her legs in an arousal that in turn both scared and excited her. She lay on the couch beneath her own dorm blanket, eyes closed as if in sleep, and waited for what Lance would do. A waft of sweat and cigarettes traveled with him, emanating from his clothes when he got near, and he stopped by her head and bent down toward her, and then she could only smell the sweet yeast of beer clouding hot and dense out of his mouth as he put his lips, hot and cracked, to the bare skin of her forehead and said, "G'night, angel," before he stood again, walked to the bathroom, and pissed for what seemed a very long time. And then he'd flushed the toilet, flipped off the light, gone into his own room, and shut the door. And the next thing Brigid knew it was morning and there was bacon on the griddle down at the Lodge.

She was hungry. Wrapped in the blanket, pillow in hand, Brigid hurried back to the staff building. She walked into the room without knocking—it was her room too, wasn't it?—and found Peg and Jeremy asleep in Peg's bed. Even in sleep, Jeremy seemed to be trying to envelop Peg's body like a human cocoon. He stirred as Brigid entered and struggled to focus. He lifted his head, a nod of greeting or acknowledgment. Brigid flashed a split-second mockery of a smile and proceeded to change her clothes without giving a bloody fuck whether he watched or not. She found some flip-flops under her bed, took a sweatshirt from the hook on the back of the door.

In the dining room she sat alone at a table near the windows. The other girls weren't yet up—which was fine with Brigid, as she'd decided that they were, to a one, boring and insipid—and she'd certainly no intention of sitting at the long east wall table with the lot of Neanderthal construction workers who looked about ready to whip out their waggling cocks whenever she passed by. *Hello,* she had a mind to tell them, did not mean *oh please let me blow you.* She thought she'd rather sit about with Jock, the cook, who liked to tell them all to suck his fat French dick but at the end of the day was really quite a sweet man, who'd been a young widower and raised, on his own, two teenage girls, whose photographs hung in plastic-wrapped frames by Jock's workstation in the kitchen. Once Brigid had inquired about his "girlfriends up there," and Jock had wiped his hands on his apron, motioned Brigid over, and told her all about Margeaux and Jeanine, both married now, one in Cleveland, the other in France, with a grandchild on the way. "The first," he beamed, thumping his chest.

When she finished eating, Brigid picked a cheap paperback from a shelf of guests' discards in the office and went out onto the deck to smoke. The novel turned out to be in Italian, so she just smoked and watched the birds instead. There looked to be ospreys in two of the nests she could see from the Lodge, busy with their breakfast as well, taking off from the nest and looping out over the water, just swooping and gliding, hardly any motion to their wings at all. Even after two cups of Jock's industrial coffee, the broken night of sleep on the Squires' couch caught up with her, and Brigid began to doze off in the deck chair, Italian novel open face-down on her lap, half-smoked cigarette falling limply from her fingers and onto the deck, where it went out, unnoticed and meaningless.

When she woke again, the girls were all inside, eating around a circular center table with the waiters. The construction workers had gone up the hill, and soon the boys went to join them, leaving the girls to clean up the mess of the meal while they waited for Suzy to come down and give them the day's directions.

At eight-fifteen when Suzy still hadn't shown, Peg was dispatched to go knock on her door upstairs, and returned reporting no answer. She sat back down, and someone dealt her in to a hand of rummy.

At eight-thirty Reesa Delamico came in, and when someone asked if she knew where Suzy might be, she got a funny, mischievous look on her face and went into the office to make a phone call. She got Eden, who said that no, the driveway was empty and as far as she knew she was home alone. Reesa reentered the dining room, frowning, shaking her head with a shrug, saying, "I'm sure she's on her way," but she didn't look sure at all as she left them to their vigil and went about her own business in the salon. Cybelle Schwartz and Janna Winger got to the Lodge a few minutes behind Reesa, but neither of them had any idea where Suzy Chizek might be. Peg—as she was wont—began to worry.

At eight-forty-five Bud Chizek came down the hill, through the back kitchen door, and into the dining room on his way to the salon to see if Reesa was in yet, when he came upon the table of card-playing Irish girls. He stopped in his tracks, as though he'd happened on some infestation of vermin he'd forgotten to exterminate. Bud stood there in the middle of the dining room, trying to say something, with a look on his face that was—a number of the girls would later note—just this side of sheer hatred. He stammered, then finally spat out: "Take the day off—all of you!" He scowled, as if his words alone should have succeeded in removing them from his sight instantaneously. "Just get out of here!" he cried, and then he stormed toward the salon, leaving the girls with a distinct sense that when he reemerged they'd better have been long gone.

They conferred quickly among themselves. A moment later Peg stepped from the group and came tentatively through a sliding door and onto the deck toward Brigid, who stared her down as she approached. Peg said, "You heard that, did you? Bud's told us to knock off work for the day . . . We thought we'd go to a different beach, if you'd like to come . . . ?"

It was a peace offering in which Brigid had little interest. "No thanks," she said coolly, and picked up the novel on her lap as though eager to get back to reading.

But Peg didn't leave. She just kept standing there, with something else she wanted to say but didn't know how. Brigid slapped the book back down: "*What?*"

Peg looked as if she were swallowing a lemon. "I suppose," she began, "that I'm the last person you'd want to do a favor for . . ."

Brigid lifted the corners of her mouth into a mean smile that conceded the point.

"It's not for me," Peg qualified, then inhaled deeply and let the breath out in a slow wash as if to steady herself. "We'd like to bring Squee—have him come to the beach with us today—and if *you* might ask his father for us, ask if the boy might come along. It would seem . . ." Oh, she was trying so desperately not to spoil it! "We thought, as you're . . . perhaps he'd be more inclined to agree if it was you who asked, don't you think?"

If what Brigid really wanted to say was *You pathetic whining coward,* she managed to merely nod definitively in Peg's direction and spit out a curt "Fine," as she flipped the book back over and attempted to feign great absorption.

Peg still wouldn't leave. "We'll be ready to go just as soon as we've changed . . ."

"Bleedin' Christ!" Brigid slapped the book down on the table beside her, got quickly to her feet, and stalked off. And Peg watched after her, unsure as to whether she'd succeeded in getting what she wanted or if she'd simply managed to drive Brigid away.

REESA, JANNA, AND CYBELLE were sitting around the salon drinking coffee from Styrofoam cups when Bud came up to the glass door that divided the dining room from the beauty parlor and stood outside, miming a knock. Reesa waved him in, but already she could see something was wrong. The pieces started to assemble in her mind: Suzy missing in action, Bud looking mad . . . She didn't know what it added up to, but she couldn't imagine any way that it might be good.

Bud pushed through the door. He was a man who dispensed with niceties like *Good morning,* as if it was generally acknowledged that it was his wife who took care of such civilities in their family. "Reesa, I need to talk to you alone" was all he said. He did not acknowledge Janna and Cybelle except to make clear his wish for their absence.

Reesa, equanimous to a fault, reached for her purse and pulled out a few dollars. "Why don't you guys go pick up some doughnuts from the IGA. We've got plenty of work here today . . . we'll need them." She tossed Janna her keys. "North lot."

Reesa stood. "What's wrong?" she said, before the door had even finished closing.

Bud looked down at his shoes with mild surprise, as if he couldn't remember how they'd gotten on his feet. "Well, Suzy's run off again," he began.

"She's gone?" Reesa broke in. Then more softly she said, "She did it."

Bud nodded suspiciously. "Last night, maybe this morning. Left a truck in Menhadenport. Room's cleaned out." He gestured to where the proof lay.

Reesa waited for more.

"Look," Bud said, "here's what I came down to ask: I need a head of housekeeping. I need someone who knows this place. Someone who can put all those girls to work . . . I don't know what the hell's going on with her, but you know Suzy . . ." His words were frothing with bitterness. "I got to assume she's not coming back."

Reesa sat there a moment, not realizing that Bud had already gotten out what he'd apparently come to say. Then she understood. "Are you asking *me?*"

"There's you . . . There's my *wife*," he said, as though the absurdity of such a thought was patently indisputable. "I don't know who the hell else knows this place well enough not to just make more trouble instead of cleaning it up . . ."

"Bud"—Reesa was trying to keep her voice calm—"I've got a business to run here."

"Not if *I* don't have a business to run, you don't."

Reesa breathed in sharply. "It's not coming to that."

"Well, it just might!"

"A hotel does not go under because it's missing a head housekeeper!"

"Yeah?" Bud said. "Exactly what do you know about what keeps a hotel from going under? What exactly do you know about running a hotel?" He was getting angrier, and it was Reesa's bad luck to be the one still left on the island to take it. "Why don't *you* take over running the damn hotel then?" he spat. "You take the hotel, and *I'll* be the goddamn chambermaid! Or we'll just let the whole place fall to shit and you can cut hair in your goddamn kitchen all year round!"

And with that he turned and stormed back out into the conspicuously empty dining room.

LANCE WAS ON THE PORCH SMOKING when Brigid came fuming up the hill. He started to smile, but his expression shifted as hers came into view. "Oh boy," he said, "that's one pissed-off girl coming up the way." The words took on an inadvertent singsong. "That's one pissed-off girl, I'd say . . . What's pissing off the pissed-off girl?" He looked almost happy, prattling on. "Come tell me who went and pissed off the pissed-off girl . . ."

He'd actually almost managed to make Brigid crack a smile. "Well," she said, "we've been given the day off for god knows what reason, and the *girls*"—she sneered—"are heading to the beach and they'd like to bring your son along, only they've commissioned me to ask your permission, as they're rather afraid you'll eat them if they get a bit too close." She stood squarely on the ground before him and waited for a response.

"Eat *their* nasty shit?" Lance puckered up his face in distaste. "No fucking way I'd eat their nasty asses!" They both laughed. Then Lance said, "You going with the *girlies*, Pissed-Off Girl?"

"Are you joking? I'd rather be working."

Lance smiled broadly. Then he got an idea. "You been over to Dredgers' Cove yet?"

Brigid shook her head. She'd not even heard of it.

"Tell you what," Lance said. "I say we give them the damn kid, and you and me take a cooler of beer and some fishing rods and we go over to the prettiest cove on this island and get the fuck out of this place for a little while. What d'you say, gorgeous?"

And if there was a part of Brigid that said, *Don't do it*, there was a bigger part, a stronger part, a part that was more important to her that said, *Don't be like them, don't be like Fiona, don't be like the people you don't want to be,* and so whatever fear or dread or caution or suspicion she might have felt got covered in a sleepy, grateful, relief-filled smile as Brigid said, "Mr. Squire, that'd be *lovely.*"

Dredgers' Cove was on the far eastern side of the island, an old clam-digging site that had been incorporated into the Manhanset Nature Preserve. It was accessible only via an abandoned logging road, which was now prohibited to cars by a heavy padlocked chain stretched between two thick oaks. Lance yanked up the emergency brake, hopped from the truck and strode ahead. At the tree he stopped, took a ring of keys from his belt, undid the lock, and loosened the chain. It clunked to the ground, and Lance stepped back to the truck, drove over the chain, and then went back to pull it taut again and resecure the lock.

"What do they do—just pass round keys to the lot of you who live here?"

Lance grinned. He hadn't been so animated since the fire. "Nobody *gives out* anything around here, baby. You want something, you *find* a way to get it."

"You've a lot of friends, then," Brigid ventured.

Lance thought about that. "Nope. But I know lots of folks."

The road was pitted and bumpy, unmaintained and almost never used. Lance went along at a good clip for such conditions, and Brigid wished she hadn't opened a beer from the case, since she'd have been far abler to enjoy the ride if not for trying to keep herself from getting drenched. She had a go at drinking off a good portion to get the liquid level down, but the truck hit a rut mid-gulp and sloshed half the can onto her face and neck. Lance glanced over and laughed largely. "Ha-ha!" he whooped. "Starting off the day *right*!" The truck rumbled along, pitching and bucking, Brigid wiping her face on the sleeve of her T-shirt, still attempting to hold the beer can steady. Finally Lance reached over, grabbed the can, and pitched it from the truck, and Brigid watched it arc through the air behind them, giving off a fountain spray of foam before it landed in the woods beside the road. They barreled on. "That's why you get a case," Lance declared. "That's why you get a *cheap-ass* case! Afford to give one to the raccoons."

They'd stopped for the beer at the IGA in town, had both gotten out of the truck and gone into the store, ordered sandwiches from the deli, pulled chips from the rack, and Brigid picked up a bottle of suntan lotion in the health and beauty aisle. Lance had grandly insisted on paying for it all himself. He was in full social mode, chatting up the cashier, who happened to be the mother of a school buddy of his. It was possible that he didn't even notice how the people in the store looked at him and at each other as he passed. He was flying, and they were so far below him—specks, dots of fish in the ocean. The cashier looked at Brigid as though she'd have liked to take her into the back room and give her a good talking to, and Brigid felt almost surprised when Lance paid and picked up the beer and they left through a door that slid open and parted before them. The clerks looked on as though Brigid and Lance were shoplifters about to be stopped at the exit. But the door just slid magically open and they walked from the bleak fluorescence back into the bawdy sunshine, leaving nothing more than a wake of gossip.

They parked the truck in a pine clearing where the ground beneath them was rusty with fallen needles, the air infused with a rich, heady evergreen. When a breeze swept in from Dredgers' Cove—the water was right there, just through the branches—the pine scent swirled with the briny smell of the sea. Lance carried the beer, Brigid the sack of food. Lance had forgotten the fishing poles. Brigid followed him down a narrow path toward the beach. It was strange, that line where the forest turned to seashore, as though someone had trucked a load of sand into the woods and thrown up a trompe l'oeil mural of the ocean horizon.

It was eleven or so, the sun high and hot. Brigid, at Lance's suggestion, set the food down in the pine-shade.

"Should've bought ice . . ." Lance started to say, as he set the beer by the food, but they wouldn't have had any use for ice, as he'd also neglected to bring a cooler.

Brigid walked toward the water. She took the towel from her beach bag and laid it out on the sand. Lance didn't appear to have brought anything with him. He was wearing jeans and a T-shirt, work boots, as though it had never dawned on him to wear something different to the beach. He hung back on the periphery of the woods, inspecting things, checking out the place, jumping onto a great chunk of driftwood, kicking a horseshoe crab over onto its back to expose the brown skeletal legs, its underbelly. Another swift soccer kick, a crunching crack, and the shell launched into the air. Lance lost interest then and wandered, picking up bits of sea glass, then tossing them back down, or skipping them out into the bay. He seemed agitated, or nervous, and it made Brigid feel the same. He didn't even have a towel to sit on, and Brigid wondered how long he'd actually planned on staying. They had food to last them the afternoon, and beer for a lot longer than that, but Brigid feared that maybe she'd misunderstood his intentions for the day. Back at the Lodge, she was the sharp-talker, fearless and crude, the only one who could deal with Lance Squire. But out here she felt like Peg—tentative and vulnerable, and pathetic—and it made her loathe herself a bit. She got up and went for a beer.

She downed half the can as she returned to her towel, then nestled it into the sand where it wouldn't spill. She lay back, face to the sun, to let on like she couldn't have cared less what Lance was doing, because *that's* what made her feel she had power: not caring. And not thirty seconds later, there he was beside her, plunking himself down, the heels of his boots digging into the sand, arms draped casually over his knees, as if he had all the time in the world to just stare out at that horizon.

All across the beach, mixed among the shells and pebbles and seaweed, there were spent shotgun shells—red or green, big as a man's thumb, with rusted metal rims—and Lance plucked one up, shook the sand from inside, and then put it to his lips like a reed. "You can whistle 'em," he said, "like a bottle," and he blew into it: a hollow, deep, mournful call, like the island ferry's.

She sat up, reached over, and took the cap from his hand. It was all about proprietorship, she reminded herself. About deciding what was yours and claiming it for yourself. She blew into the gun cap; it left a salty taste on her lips, and she reached for her drink. Such a gorgeous day, she was off from work, there was more than enough beer, and they could stay as long as she liked. And if she decided she wanted to return to the Lodge, then they'd return. It was precisely *why* the rest of them were such namby-pambies. They didn't know what they wanted—and if they did, then they'd have to scour up the courage to ask for it. It helped Brigid a good deal in times of stress to isolate the exact ways in which she was far more capable a human being than most. Certainly poor Lance was about as far down the ladder as people came in terms of having control over their lives. Which was probably why he liked spending time with her: she offered him a glimpse of what it was to take charge. It was probably, Brigid thought, why he'd got on with Suzy back when they were young; Brigid definitely saw Suzy as sort of a kindred spirit. She and Suzy were both—in Brigid's mind—soaring examples of strong, independent women who didn't stand for the crap that men dished out. Some people might have even agreed with her—*no sir, those ladies don't stand for one ounce of bullshit*—but there were other folks who'd say that Brigid and Suzy were *girls who wouldn't know from bullshit if you stuck their pretty noses in it*. And still others might contend that some people's lives were so steeped in bullshit they didn't even know it stank.

Lance stood. "You want another?"

Brigid shook her can. "Yessir," she said, and drank the last gulp down.

She watched him walking back with two new cans, and then he stopped ten feet away and lobbed one at her. It sailed past—actually, she pulled her hands away instinctually, as she always did in games in which one was meant to catch things—and skidded into the sand.

"Oopsie," Lance said. "Oopsie daisy . . ."

Brigid cocked her head. "Bastard."

He held his own beer to his heart, drooped his eyes and mouth in puppy-dog innocence. "Me?"

Brigid rolled her eyes. This was how she liked things. With him fetching, eager to please. And herself: sarcastic, mocking, entirely in control. She flipped over and stretched to retrieve the wayward beer without having to stand. It was a sexy maneuver for a girl in short shorts, and she was well aware of it. She reached the beer with her fingertips, managed to roll it toward her and grab hold. Then she sat up and began turning to Lance, who'd sat himself down beside her again. She had one hand around the beer and one on the flip top, and when she cracked it she caught Lance dead on in the spray. He jerked back, sloshing some of his own beer onto himself as well. "Whoa-ho!" he cried, his shirt and face splattered, wet with dots of foam. "So she's playing dirty now, is she?" he jeered, half mocking, half sinister. He lifted his chin toward her: "Got yourself there too, darlin'."

Brigid set her beer in the sand. "But I," she began, "have dressed for our outing appropriately," and she pulled off her beer-splotched T-shirt, then wriggled out of her shorts. She stood, reclaimed her beer can, spun on her heel in the sand, and stalked down the shore and into the surf wearing a striped bikini, about which even Lance was sharp enough to call after her: "There's nothing in the world *appropriate* about what you got on, angel." She laughed without looking at him, and raised her can in the air to toast her agreement, calling "Cheers!"

Brigid kicked around the shallows for a time, can raised above her head as she improvised a one-handed backstroke. On shore, Lance polished off his own beer and fetched another from the pine-tree stash. When Brigid came dripping back up the beach toward her towel, he was sitting on it, eating generic-brand sour cream and onion chips. He offered her the bag. Shaking a spray from her hair, she declined, indicating her desire, rather, for the towel, and when he understood what it was she wanted he clambered to his feet—no easy task with both hands full, and on a surface of sand—and then he set down his burdens and tried to pick up the towel for her. He seemed to want to wrap her in it, the way a parent might greet a child emerging from a bath, but the towel was covered in sand, and as he raised it a breeze caught and lifted it like a sail, whipping Brigid with a small sandstorm. She looked down at herself, dredged like a cutlet ready for frying, and let out a burst of laughter. "Thank you very much," she said, snatched the towel, and left him chuckling as she went back down to the water to rinse off.

She dropped the towel near the shore, walked out waist deep, held her nose, and dunked under, arching her neck as she rose so the hair slicked back over her head. When she reclaimed the towel from its slump on the beach, she lifted it exaggeratedly in a display for Lance: *Correct beach-towel procedure, sir, please watch as I demonstrate.* She shook the sand away from her body, then wrapped herself dramatically, a game show hostess modeling the prize mink. Lance just stood there watching her from a distance, laughing, and it felt grand—it *was* grand, Brigid told herself—to bring laughter to a man who'd been through so much. He truly seemed to be enjoying himself. Whether Brigid was enjoying herself was another matter entirely, which—some people might have been inclined to point out—was something you'd expect might concern a *strong, independent* woman like Brigid, a woman *who didn't stand for any bullshit.* A claim—the same folks might say—which was in itself a crock of bullshit big enough to sink an island.

The beers were growing warmer by the can, but they'd drunk enough that they didn't much care. It was cheap, shitty beer—*piss-water,* Brigid teased, saying her friends in Dublin would be horrified—and it went down just like water, pretty much. They ate their sandwiches, and Brigid went in the water again, not because she felt like a swim but because she had to pee. Lance had already gotten up a few times to piss in the woods, and it seemed that every time he got up he sought out a closer tree, so the last time Brigid could literally hear his urine streaming and hitting the ground. She paddled a bit, floated around while she emptied her bladder, then splashed about to dispel the impression that she might've only gone in the water to pee. The bay felt grand anyway, refreshing, though it made her feel drunker than she'd thought she was, the way you might stand up from your table in a bar not feeling scuttered at all, but when you go to use the toilet, the bathroom starts to spin. When Brigid came out of the bay—water sweeping off her body, evaporating almost instantly under the intensity of the early-afternoon sun—she was overcome with tiredness: the night before, and the beers, and the heat all catching up with her at once in that kind of postlunch, postexercise exhaustion that might have felt rather glorious if she hadn't been drunk, except she was.

Lance was squinting, laughing at her as she came up the beach, and as she flopped down onto her towel—facedown, her limbs sprawling out from her, useless as jellyfish—he said, "Siesta time, señorita?" all the while chuckling, mocking her for such alcohol intolerance. All Brigid could get out in response, her mouth already mashed sideways into the ground, was a muffed "Mmmmnn." She would be asleep in seconds, one side of her face dangerously exposed to the sun, the other cheek growing warm with drool bleeding slowly from her open mouth as she slept.

The sun crept across the sky toward the west, and by early midafternoon shade had begun to overtake Dredgers' Cove, spreading from the tree line out as the sun moved behind the pine woods. Brigid was still asleep as their spot on the beach lost its sun, first dappled by the leaves, then shaded altogether, and in her sleep she was growing chilly. The first thing she would remember feeling—remember being conscious of at all—was warmth, and she was grateful for it, as though someone had noticed her there, shivering in that tiny striped bikini, and thought to drape something over her—a jacket, or some clothes that were lying about. But there was weight to the covering, a warm, heavy pressing-in that came up beside her, curling around, cupping, and she curled into it, letting the warmth come over her like a dream, a good dream, an erotic dream where everything is warm and wet, everything coming together as though under warm bath water.

But then, wrongly, the weight was *on* her, not around her, heavy on top of her, and it was *too* heavy, like a carpet unrolled over her back flattening her into the sand with not enough room for her lungs to inflate inside.

And then she was awake, and he was moving on top of her and though she *felt* cold, her sunburned skin was noticeably warm under his hand, which was cool as it came under the fabric at the bottom of her suit, tracing the crack of her ass down like he was going to push his cool hand in and warm it up inside of her. She knew what was happening; her head was still swirly from beer and sun, but she knew what was happening, had enough sense about her to think it wasn't the smartest thing in the world, but it wasn't the worst thing anyone had ever done, and Brigid wasn't averse, necessarily, to doing things that were a bit bad. No one was cheating on anyone, and his wife *had died,* and didn't people seek human contact in times of grief to try to get through their pain and claim a life for themselves in the face of death? Isn't that what people did?

She could have paused things, she thought, maybe just for that moment, to focus and get her bearings, but she was groggy, and it felt so nice, anticipating the coolness of his finger sliding its way up inside of her, pushing up and making her aware of herself inside, the way you could only be aware of inside when something came from outside and touched the inside and made you realize what was there and how empty it had been, how much you wanted something there, pushing through, feeling out the dimensions and making a space from a void, creating the space as it was entered, as though the walls appeared only as he made them with his touch. She breathed in, ready to feel the coolness of his hand, her inside warmth taking it over and transforming it, making it warm within her. He shifted awkwardly, and fell more on top of her, a greater crush of weight that pushed the breath back out of her and jerked her one notch further into wakefulness, aware suddenly of the sand pasted with spit to the side of her cheek, and the angle of one arm pinned underneath her, asleep, stiff, and painfully inert beneath her body. And as she became aware of these discomforts, on top of her back he shifted heavily again, one hand pressed into the sand beside her as though he might do a push up from where he was propped. But then, at once, the full weight of his body seemed to come crushing down on her from behind, and in the same motion he caught her from below and with one thrust had shoved the whole of himself, erect, inside her.

The shock she felt first was the shock of what was *not* happening—the shock that what was inside her was not the slim pencil-cool of his finger, as though that was something she'd been anticipating for hours or days, and not just seconds, fragments of seconds. It hit her like disappointment first—the largeness, the hotness of it—and then she felt the dig of the zipper on his jeans into her ass, and the sand from his jeans grinding into her skin. She tried to say something but couldn't, like in a dream when you scream and nothing comes from your mouth, the horror of that, her mouth crammed down into the sandy towel, lips scraping grit as she tried to move but couldn't shape a word with all the weight from above. And though she *could* breathe, somehow, through her nose, she panicked, her body seizing up in terror like one drowning, and she thrashed, trying to lift her head and open her mouth to the air.

He should have rolled off her then. He should have rolled off when she jerked like that, realized from that spasm that something was wrong—she couldn't *breathe*!—rolled off her and checked to make sure she was OK: *Honey, what's the matter, oh, jeez, sorry, was I crushing you there?* In fact, if she'd heard his voice, alone, with no accompanying movement, she'd have actually thought he meant to soothe her, because that's what it sounded like when he whispered, "Shhhh, shh, shh, shh, shh, shh," blowing those shushes into her ear like reassurance. But as he shushed, his breath hot, she felt his hand clamp down on the back of her neck, hard, like he meant to hold her there, his fingers around the side of her neck pressing in too deeply. It panicked her further, the desperation of being unable to breathe, her face pushed into a towel, her throat constricted under the pressure of his grip, and she thrashed harder, and he held her harder, his grip tightening as he braced himself, kicking a foot deeper into the sand for purchase, all the while cooing "Shhh, shh, shh, shh, shh," in her ear, the sound changing into something lordly and dominant, a farmer trying to calm a struggling chicken as he holds its neck steady against the chopping block.

Brigid squirmed under the weight of his body, tried to wrench her head around with such force—such impeded force—that she bit down fiercely on her own tongue and that absolute, terrible, thudding pierce of pain replaced everything else the way a scream shuts down a roomful of conversation, the pain in her mouth filling with hot blood, stopping everything else in her body. When she stopped kicking he let up the pressure on her neck, and she found she could turn her head into a pocket of air, and the pocket of air calmed her enough that she could breathe and feel the blood drain from her mouth, hot into the sand under her face. The blood-pulse in her tongue seemed to match the one inside her, hot throbbing mixed with gritting sand, sand in her mouth, sand inside, rubbing as he thrust, grating against her, and it seemed that she just lived inside that pain, the rhythm and tear of it, until somewhere something changed and he arched his back up as he came, and then fell again into her, gratefully this time. He lifted his hand from her neck and moved it through her hair, combing and rubbing and kissing the side of her face and her neck as he rubbed, still kissing, nuzzling, cooing, "Angel, angel, angel," as he pulled himself out of her and rolled away, onto his back, breathing hard. She lay on her stomach, almost as she'd fallen asleep, almost nothing changed— just the towel wrenched away, one arm dead beneath her, her tongue swelling in her mouth, her crotch grated raw, and her bathing suit bottom hitched to one side and wedged up in the crack of her ass. She couldn't move her arm to pull it down. She couldn't move at all. She lay there, and she breathed.

After a time Lance sat up. He tucked himself in and closed his pants, and then he leaned over to her, and pressed his face into the flesh of her exposed buttocks and breathed in deep before he tucked a finger inside the elastic and pulled it out for her, settling it around the curve of the cheek as though with that act, that gesture, he could make it fine. Snapping the elastic back into place, he pushed himself to his feet. She could hear him walking back toward the trees, then the sound of a flip top cracking. She could hear him return, flop down into the sand again beside her, and then she felt him place a beer, the can warm, on her back, try to balance it there on her as if he was playing a game. When he took his hand away the beer stayed upright for a second as she breathed, then toppled and fell, rolled off into the sand.

There was still sun on the water, and Lance unlaced his boots, strode down to the shore, pulled his shirt over his head, slipped off his jeans, and went naked into the salty sea at Dredgers' Cove.

Brigid heard the splash and summoned the strength she had to pull on her shorts and shirt, slip into her beach shoes, and gather her things. She would have been thankful to dive into that water. It would have made the ride back easier somehow if they'd *both* been clean. But to follow him, naked, into the water was not an option, so neither was cleaning herself. She stood and walked into the woods, past the food and the beer to the truck, and she climbed in the passenger side and slammed the door and waited.

Lance dove shallowly, then twisted around under water and came back to where he'd begun. With both hands he rubbed his face with water and then stood and marched back onto the beach. He shook himself off like a dog, paused to judge the results, then shook again before shimmying back into his clothes.

And then he was there, opening the driver's side door, pushing in the rest of the beer and the bag of food and climbing in behind them. Brigid was grateful for those packages on the seat between them; they were something in the way—not much, but something. He hoisted his hips up from the seat to reach in his pocket for the keys while Brigid watched him, aware of every move he made as though she had to keep track of it all from now on. She watched him as if it was the only thing that mattered: to account for every single thing Lance Squire did from the moment he got into the truck. This focused her second to second, gave her a purpose then, second to second to second. It took a great deal of focus, this accounting, to notice every detail, every twitch and glance, and Brigid was able to lose her sense of herself. In her awareness of him she was able to forget a bit of who she was, what she might look like, how she was sitting, what sort of expression she wore. As she watched, she lost her self. She made herself invisible; she watched him like prey.

He put the keys in the ignition, turned the engine over, put the truck in reverse, and began a five-point turn to get them headed back in the other direction down the logging road. A few minutes along, when he'd gotten the feel of the ruts and bumps again, he looked to her, then back at the road, and said, "You pissed at me now, Pissed-Off Girl?"

Brigid said nothing. She watched. She did not know how he might read her expression. She did not know what her expression was.

"Hey," he said, like a plea for clemency, "you don't have to worry: nobody ever gets pregnant off me." He laughed a little, smiled over at her winningly.

Brigid turned away, realized she was mashed up against the passenger door, putting as much space between herself and Lance as the truck allowed. She leaned her head out the window and let the wind rush by, blowing back her hair, the air heavier with pine the deeper inland they traveled. She would go back and take a shower—a very hot shower—and she'd sober up, and sleep. She concentrated on the shower without imagining it too fully, because imagining the water scalding on her body made her want it so badly she thought she might cry out.

When Lance stopped for cigarettes at the gas station and paused outside the truck to lean back in the window and smile at her and ask, offhandedly, "You need anything, darlin'?" and she shook her head no and watched him turn and enter the store, heard the *ding-ding* of the door, saw it fan slowly closed behind him, she was cognizant enough to marvel at the macabre absurdity of the moment. She thought: *I've lost my mind.* She thought about simply saying to him, when he got back to the truck and offered her a smoke, which she might accept—she thought she might let him light it for her, inhale, then simply say: *Is it my imagination, or did you just hold me by the neck and fuck me?* But when he did get back with his pack of Merits and offer one to her, leaning across the packages on the seat to light it, she said nothing. If someone asked, later, she'd have said she was in shock. For it was shocking, she'd explain, to understand—to truly understand for the first time in your life—that what has happened to you is really only what you *think* has happened. There was a truth: she and Lance Squire had had sex on the beach at Dredgers' Cove. Beyond that, how was she supposed to account for anything? If two people looked at each other, who was to say which one was the watcher?

Twenty-one

THAT FLESH OF HIS OWN FLESH

As in the life experience of man, so in the life of birds, some of the many accidents which befall the birds may easily be averted by man, by means of a little forethought.

—B. S. BOWDISH, "Bird Tragedies: Even Birds' Lives
Are Not Exempt from the Tragic Element"

L ANCE PARKED IN THE NORTH LOT, and he and Brigid walked together up the path, then parted between their respective residences. He waved, turning back to her as they separated, calling, "I'll put these beers in the fridge—come by later if you get thirsty."

Brigid went to the room in the barracks that she and Peg shared. The building was mercifully empty, the other girls not yet back from their day at the beach, the boys still down the hill working on the new laundry. Brigid dropped her bag, took a couple of towels from her hook behind the door, and went to the shower room, toward the water she could finally allow herself the desperation of wanting.

While Brigid was in the shower—sitting on the floor of the stall, just letting the water spray over her, hot as it could go, because it seemed right to feel the burn of her burned skin, as if she'd been pricked by a million needles and the water flowed not just over but *into* her, the scald of it turning her inside out with pain so insistent and encompassing she could lose herself in it—Peg and the girls returned.

Six housekeepers, plus Squee, had crammed into Jeremy's car, which they'd borrowed for the trip to the beach. Peg—in what had to be the most undeniably unconscionable thing she'd ever done—drove. Even Jeremy, who was superhumanly tolerant of Peg's monstrous sense of propriety, ribbed Peg, in his own inimitable fashion: "The day you get arrested on Osprey Island for driving without a valid international license is the day I'll . . . I don't even know what." On the way back from the beach, it was Peg's idea to drop Squee off at the Jacobses' place, to keep him away from Lance as long as they could, and she'd been pretty sure she could find her way to Eden and Roddy's, and back to the Lodge from there. She was good with directions, she told the others. She had an uncanny memory, an instinctual knack.

Brigid heard a few girls come in to use the toilets; she had the water so hot that when they flushed and all the cold disappeared for a minute there was barely a difference. She dried herself inside the stall behind the mildewed vinyl curtain and wrapped her hair in one towel, the other around her body, for the walk across the hall to their room, which she sincerely hoped was empty. There were few people she'd have liked to see less, just then, than Peg.

But, of course, there she was—seated at the desk, penning her eighty-seven thousandth *Hi! How are you? I'm fine* postcard of the summer. She turned at the sound of the door shuffling open like the lid of a cardboard box, saw Brigid enter, started in horror, looked again more closely, and let out a scream—short and sharp, worthy, perhaps, of an aging Agatha Christie heroine, but a bona fide scream all the same.

"*Christ,* it's only me," Brigid said. She shot Peg a look of deadly annoyance and turned toward her shelves for something to wear.

Peg was practically on top of her in seconds. "My god—oh, god, Brigid, what's he done? Oh, Jesus god!"

"What is your problem?" Brigid shrilled. She shoved past Peg to the closet, where she didn't need anything. The room was so tight there wasn't anywhere to go, and Peg kept coming at her, her hands outstretched as if she were ready to grab Brigid by the throat and throttle her.

"Have you lost your mind?" Brigid screeched. "Stay the fuck away from me!"

Peg stopped, stood trembling, her voice a quiver; "My god, Brigid, your *face* . . ."

Brigid paused then, for the first time since she'd entered the room. She looked down at the thready fuchsia of her old bath towel, her too-pink legs sticking out from beneath—sunburned, and reddened too from the heat of the shower. There was no mirror in their shoe-box room. She tried to look at her shoulders. She'd been out in the sun a good long while and never had put on any of the sunblock she'd bought. It would be just like Peg to fly into fits over a sunburn. Brigid fixed her roommate with the most patronizing look she had and spoke in a voice so saccharine and mean she surprised even herself: "It's called a *sunburn.*" *Sunburn:* as though it were a new vocabulary word on educational television. "It's caused by the *sun* . . . ?" *Sun. Is that a word you understand, you stupid, annoying little tool? Sun? Sunburn?* "Most victims survive them." And then she turned from Peg and opened the closet door.

"No!" cried Peg—and Brigid thought for a second that Peg was telling her, *No, under penalty of death, please god I beg you don't open that closet!* "No . . . your neck . . . your *throat* . . ." and Peg dissolved again.

Brigid stood before the open closet door, wrapped in her sister's hand-me-down beach towel, her back to her roommate and their tacky hole of a room, and it was, in that moment, as though she were naked, completely, in the open and exposed, a wash of shame like urine running down her legs in public, and there was nowhere to run. All she could do in the panic-rush of her brain was scream at the top of her voice, the pitch cracking and breaking as it rose: *"Get out of here! Get away from me! Get out! Get out now!"* The sound of Brigid's voice was terrible, and Peg was terrified, and she ran.

Brigid thought of her own throat. It might have been someone else's throat, for she could not feel its attachment to her body, could not even lift her hand to touch it, as if doing so would bring it to life on her body, the way everything turns to color as Dorothy cracks open the farmhouse door in Oz. She sank down, the towel slipping from her body as she bent into the closet, rummaging, riffling, tearing open the travel bags that lined the floor. There was a makeup case somewhere filled with stuff she hadn't even thought to use since she'd arrived on the island; not even through the courting of Gavin had it seemed a place where one would brush on a little gloss. She felt the case there, under her hand, a nylon zippered sack crammed and stretched full of bottles and tubes the authorities had searched at customs not two weeks before, as if they might have been sticks of dynamite. She tore it open, dumped its contents on the unfinished wooden floor. There was a compact, square and brown, which she grabbed and flipped open. The towel was falling from her head, and she pulled it off, loose from her hair, and let it drop to the floor beside her. The compact's mirror was dusted with powder, and she rubbed it clean with her thumb, held it up, tried to angle it right, to see her throat, pulled it away, rubbed the mirror with the towel that was pooled in her lap, then tried again. The mirror was so small it was hard to see much, but she could see enough to know.

She flicked her hair out of the way of her view, and it was the brush of her own fingers across the skin of her neck that did indeed bring the pain to life, animating it as if by a magic so strong and swift it choked her, as if his hand was there again, fingers curled around her neck, pressing purple welts into her throat like a handprint in ink against the white-pink of her flesh. She coughed and the pain spread inward, as if she'd been bruised from the inside as well—the raw, swollen pain of strep throat she'd had as a child, right there on her skin. Where had she been not to notice the pain now clamping down on her airway as if to gag her? She sat in the mouth of the closet, naked but for the towel now fallen to her hips and in her lap, choking as though her throat were swelling shut by the second.

. . .

Peg didn't pause to think. She ran from their room in the staff's barrack quarters and across the path toward the Squires' cabin. She did
not knock at the door or stop in the doorway but flew straight into
the living room of Lance Squire's home, where he sat drinking down
the final can of that case of beer. Peg flew at him, then stopped, yards
from Lance's chair, shouting, hollering as loud as her voice would
take her, "You *bast*ard! You *bast*ard! What did you do to her? You
answer me! So help me . . . tell me what you did to her, you . . ." and
it was only when Lance stood—stumbling backwards as he did so
but then holding steady, standing tall. Only then did Peg seem to realize where she was and what she was doing: swearing in the booze-
stinking face of a man she feared perhaps more than she'd ever feared
a living, breathing person. Lance steadied himself and Peg backed
away; for every step she took from him he took another toward her,
sneering as though it were a game. The front screen door had closed
itself, and now Lance backed Peg up to it. The smell of him nearly
made her retch, that sick stink of alcohol blowing out of him in gusts.
Peg had not in her life known this desire—a want that felt so much
like need—to hurt someone the way she wanted to hurt this man, to
beat him bloody with her fists and make him crawl away in shame.
She suspected that to slink away was something Lance Squire would
never do; he seemed, to Peg, incapable—*inhuman,* she realized, that's
what he was, and she cried it then: "You're in*human*! You bastard!
You *in*human *bast*ard!"

Which is what she was screaming when Lance stepped back. He
took one step away, as if *he'd* become aware of a terrible smell, something coming from her that made him instinctually retreat. He dropped
his chin, narrowed his eyes to slits, glanced around the room as if to
check that there was no one to see when he pounded her one. Then he
fixed on her, this dishrag of a girl hollering at him as if that blue vein
was going to pop right out of the middle of her forehead. Lance said,
"Where's my son?"

Peg stopped yelling.

Lance said it again, every word a stress of its own. *"Where. Is. My. Son."* He reclaimed the offense, gave her a fraction of a second to answer, and then laced in: "You're the one who took him today, you little piece of shit. You tell me where my son is, and you tell me now!"

He was only a few paces back, but her movement was so unexpected he didn't even have a chance to reach out and grab her before she was gone. She spun, somehow her hand already on the screen door handle, and was out and down the steps and running for the barracks before it slammed again behind her. She ran for her room, then realized Jeremy's keys were still in the pocket of her shorts and switched course mid-sprint, veered down the hill toward the north parking lot, where she jumped into Jeremy's boat of a car and drove out of the Lodge and up the hill toward Eden Jacobs's house in a decidedly more reckless manner than she'd perhaps ever done anything in her eighteen precious, law-abiding years.

Lance saw her run for the parking lot. He heard a big old engine turn over and saw the car itself come over the rise on its way up Island Drive, and it didn't take much—even for Lance, even after consuming the majority of a case of beer and whatever else he'd put away while no one was there to see—to figure out where she was going. His own car keys were still on his belt. He tore out the door not five minutes behind her.

Peg burst into Eden's living room with all the gumption that a girl of her sort possessed, which is to say that she knocked hard and waited, her face contorted in anguish, for Eden to open the door. Eden and Squee appeared to be in the midst of a game of cards, which was spread out on the coffee table, and Eden had something cooking in the kitchen for dinner. Peg entered with urgency, urgency instantly drenched with pity: Why, she wanted to know, couldn't this child just be left alone to eat his dinner and play a bloody hand of rummy? And now that she was there, she didn't know what to say. Squee had to get out, they had to get him away, hide him, but she'd have to explain *why*, wouldn't she? What was the answer to that question—why? Squee had to get away because Lance was coming for him. Lance was coming for him, and he was shit-faced drunk, and he'd probably just beat up or raped or done something horrible to a nineteen-year-old girl who was stubborn and stupid enough to stand there in broad daylight and sneer as if it was *Peg* who'd done something wrong.

Eden stood waiting for Peg to form words. "Would you like to come in? Sit down?" she said finally, and that managed to jump-start Peg.

"We've got to get the boy away from here!" she cried, and Squee looked up at her from the couch. He'd been trying to pretend that this wasn't anything to do with him, this crazy girl bursting into Eden's living room, that she had to do with something else entirely. Eden turned to make sure Squee was still where she'd left him, then spun back to Peg, who was spewing out the words now as fast as she could think them. "Something's happened, and I don't know what, but something's happened to Brigid, my roommate, and now Lance wants Squee. He's probably followed me here . . ." She looked over her shoulder and out the living room window as though she might see him coming up the drive behind her. And then she looked again to the window, and there *was* a truck coming up the drive toward the house. Peg gasped, and then she hung there, waiting for Eden to make the next move, ready, it seemed, to run.

The truck approached, Peg's panic mounting, Squee's heart beginning to beat faster, the voice in Eden's head telling her to stay calm, watch, wait, see what unfolded. The truck came closer, low sun reflecting off its windows, blurring the color of its flanks. Eden had one foot in front of the other as though she was ready to pivot around, scoop Squee up from the couch, and run him out of there herself, out the back door and down to the ravine, where they'd hide him, swaddled among the rushes, while they went back to the house and waited for Lance, aiming shotguns out the windows like outlaw vigilantes defending their own.

The truck turned to park in the driveway and Eden sighed audibly, the breath rushing out of her lungs as if she'd been holding it longer than she'd realized. It was Roddy, home for the day. The five o'clock whistle had sounded some minutes before. It was only Roddy, and Eden let herself feel, for just a moment, the tremendous sense of relief: it was *Roddy*. She wasn't alone. Roddy was back. There were things in the world for which she was thankful. Her son had come home.

He was worried already, just seeing the strange car there in the driveway, and he came straight up the front walk to the door. Knocking but not waiting for a response, Roddy entered the house and pulled his hat from his head penitently. He held it before him in his hands. "What's going on?"

Peg looked to Eden, as though she, as the elder, were more qualified to address such a question. Eden said, "I can't say I'm sure, but"— she, in turn, looked to Peg for confirmation—"I think maybe you and Squee need to go out and get some dinner someplace . . . ?"

Peg nodded fervently. Squee was looking around at all of them, trying to keep up with a game whose rules he didn't quite understand. Roddy froze briefly, taking stock of the situation around him and formulating a plan. A second later he was moving toward Squee. He reached out his hand to help the kid up off the couch, then realized he had a hat in it. He gave the hat a shake, then, inspired, flapped it onto Squee's head. "Shakes or Morey's, Squee-man?"

Squee peered out from beneath the lavender brim of the hat. "Shakes!" Eden mouthed the same word—*Shakes*—at Roddy. She was nodding. Lot less of a chance of running into Lance at the ice cream parlor/snack shop than at the joint where the man's mother tended bar.

Squee hopped up from the couch with surprising energy. He glanced toward the kitchen, briefly wondering what would become of Eden's dinner (which surely involved some weird constellation of lentils and broccoli) from which he was pleased to escape. He stood before Roddy, who lifted the cap off Squee's head, adjusted the band as tight as it would go, and replaced it on the boy.

"Let's do it," said Roddy, and he scuttled the kid ahead of him and out the door. He turned back to Eden. "I'll call?" he said. "See when it looks OK to come back?"

Eden nodded. She waved him away, and then she and Peg watched from the living room window as Roddy and Squee climbed into the truck and began to back down the driveway. They were still watching seconds later when another truck came over the rise and sped up the driveway straight at Roddy and Squee.

Peg drew in a sharp breath, anticipating the impact—a sudden smash of glass and metal. Eden simply held hers. Roddy saw the other truck. He braked, then put his own truck in forward drive, ready to go over the lawn, around the side of Lance's truck, and down the hill. In her mind, Eden saw Roddy hesitating over whether it would be wrong to run tire tracks through his mother's lawn, and it wasn't until Peg looked at her that she realized it was her own voice saying, "Go! Just go!"

Roddy pulled out forward, steering his truck to the right, onto the far side of the lawn. Lance—coming up from behind him, his vehicle bucking as he took the ruts too quickly—saw Roddy turn off the driveway and onto the lawn, and he swerved his own truck right as well, as though his plan—if Lance was capable of having a plan—was to block Roddy's exit. Lance didn't know who was in that truck, besides Roddy. He couldn't see Squee in the passenger seat from that distance, four feet tall and hidden beneath the lavender hat.

Then came the crash that Peg had braced for, Roddy's brakes squealing as he slammed them, Lance's truck coming straight for Roddy's passenger side as though he'd never thought to brake at all. The trucks seemed to hit in the flash of an instant, just a slam: the front of Lance's truck into the side of Roddy's. And then everything went slow: the protracted skid of the trucks across the lawn, joined in a lopsided T, Lance's pushing Roddy's as if to nudge it along, impeded by the surface of the grass, which tore beneath them and slowed them down as though the ground itself was offering what help it could by way of traction.

When the trucks stopped altogether, Eden and Peg were running from the house and across the lawn. There was a moment of nothing, no movement from the vehicles whatsoever, just the two women running, their steps nearly silent, across the grass toward the collision. Then, first, the door of Lance's truck flew open and Lance stepped out, tall, and seemed to hover on his feet for a moment, his face wrenched with fury, before he pitched and stumbled sideways, his expression shifting from anger to confusion as his feet slipped from under him and he buckled to the ground.

Lance was struggling to stand when Roddy's door eased open. Roddy stepped out, then leaned back in to pull Squee across the seat toward him. Getting a purchase, he gingerly lifted the boy from the driver's side of the truck. Squee was balled up into himself, his right arm under his left like a broken wing he was protecting from the wind. Roddy held the boy to him and started toward Eden. He said nothing, just moved, because moving the boy to safety seemed the only imperative. Eden went toward them, but Peg was rooted where she stood. Roddy and Eden came at each other, their focus direct and intent and singular, as if Roddy were going to hand Squee off to her, the next sprinter in this terrible relay. But then Peg screamed and Roddy and Eden broke the lock of their eyes and looked up. From a few feet away Lance was lunging at them. He looked unsteady, drunk and furious, yet he flew toward them with as single a purpose as Eden and Roddy had in rushing to each other. Lance yelled, spitting as he growled, "Stay the fuck away from my son!" and he grabbed for Squee as though a boy were something you could steal like the ball in a game of Keep Away. Roddy was just lifting Squee away from his own body, preparing to pass him off to Eden, when Lance dove and caught them all just off-balance enough that when Lance grabbed he managed to catch what was closest to him: Squee's upper right arm. As Lance grabbed, Roddy lost his grip and his balance at the same time and went stumbling backwards as Squee was wrenched away.

Squee screamed. Lance had grabbed his arm, wrenched it hard without any purchase or balance of his own, so in snatching Squee he sent them both down, Lance with a look of surprise turning to annoyance at what he saw as a great injustice keeping him from remaining upright as he tried to go about the business he'd come for. Squee fell between Lance and Roddy with a cry of awful pain, and on the ground he curled tighter into a ball, holding his right arm desperately to him, rocking and crying into the grass.

Lance and Roddy both struggled to their feet and lunged for the boy. Roddy tried to throw his own body over Squee's to protect him; Lance went at his son with arms outstretched, ready for a tug-of-war. Lance reached the boy first, grabbed hold of the collar of Squee's T-shirt, and pulled. The boy screamed. Lance grabbed again, this time with both hands, trying to take Squee by the shoulders and stand him up. He was pulling at him, hollering inches from Squee's head, "Get up! Get up and get in the truck! Get the fuck up!" and Squee wailed, just trying to curl in and protect the arm that his father kept ripping away from him, and he wailed louder as if trying to out-scream the pain.

Roddy, unable to throw himself on top of Squee without hurting him even more, instead came around and tried to tackle Lance from behind, tried to pin Lance's arms behind him and stop him from reaching for Squee. But as Roddy pounced, Lance flung him off and sent Roddy sprawling and stumbling backwards, his legs buckling under him as he landed, ten feet back from where Lance and Squee struggled in the grass of his mother's lawn.

Eden, in the midst of it, watched in terror for a moment, then turned and ran for the house, grabbing Peg from where she stood and pulling her as she ran. She pushed the girl up the steps and into the house, then shoved her toward the kitchen door, pointed at the telephone on the wall: "Call the police!" she shouted. Peg looked at her blankly, uncomprehending. Eden's voice was cold and hard. "Call nine-one-one," she said. "Call the police." Then it clicked and Peg understood. She reached for the phone.

Eden dashed for the living room. She rummaged frantically in the organ bench through old musical scores and polishing rags, came up with a key and set across the room. Her late husband's gun case stood by the entrance to the hall, virtually untouched since his death that spring. She fumbled with the key in its cheap tin lock, flimsy as the clasp on a child's diary. Her hands slipped and the key fell to the carpet. She bent to find it in the shag, then stopped and spun around, her eyes on a bookend, a marble pedestal topped with one bronzed baby shoe. Roddy's. She picked it up and hurled it through the glass door of the gun case, drawing her hands back over her face as it struck. Then she peeked out, saw the bookend on the ground, the shattered glass, more glass still falling around it, and she stuck her hand out, grabbed the barrel of a shotgun and yanked it out. It was heavier than she'd expected, and she faltered under its weight. Her arm slipped, slicing into broken glass, but she hardly noticed, just reestablished her grip farther down the long shaft and hefted it to her chest. She was running back out the door then, both hands on the gun, lifting to aim it as she ran.

Outside, Lance had left Squee writhing in the grass while he went after Roddy, who'd come at him again from behind. Lance threw him off, then staggered to where Roddy'd fallen and kicked him, hard, in the stomach and the ribs. Roddy curled into himself, fetal, like Squee across the yard. He tried to catch Lance's leg, but Lance kept kicking, sent a hard-toed boot flying into Roddy's back someplace that shot a blinding pain through him, and his back spasmed, and then he blacked out.

He came to seconds later on the ground, and lifted his head to see Lance dragging Squee by the arm across the lawn toward his truck. Squee was limp, blacked out too, just a body being dragged across the ground. Roddy struggled to stand. Lance fell against the truck, lost his grip on Squee, then got himself turned around and pulled the dead weight of the boy up against him and flung him into the cab. He pushed Squee's legs inside, then wedged himself into the driver's seat, pausing to look for his keys. He found them right there in the ignition, and fumbled to start the engine. The truck had stalled where it hit Roddy's so the key was still in the on position and wouldn't turn.

Lance was confused, tried again, then wrested the key out of the ignition and started from scratch.

When the front door of Eden's house shut behind her she was already halfway across the lawn, coming at Lance with the shotgun raised to fire. Lance was so absorbed in trying to get the keys into the starter and turn over the engine that he didn't even see her coming, hadn't remembered Eden at all until the shotgun butted through the open truck window and into his shoulder. He lifted his head from the ignition, shoving the gun aside as he rose. Eden tightened her grip on the stock, her finger ready on the trigger, and replaced the gun at Lance's chest. He was surprised, almost tickled, to see her there—Eden Jacobs, the lady who'd fed him cheese and crackers after school—with a shotgun aimed at his breastbone.

Eden saw Squee slumped beside his father and nearly dropped the gun. She didn't want Lance—she wanted the child. She wanted the child out of the way of harm. Now that she had Lance stopped against the nose of her dead husband's shotgun, she wasn't sure she knew what to do. Should she say something? Threaten him? Or just stand there with her finger on the trigger and wait for the mercy of sirens to round the crest of Island Drive? She moved her eyes from Lance to Squee inside the truck, his arm twisted, she now saw, at an angle that made Eden cry out. And as she did, Lance started to speak, and she turned back to him and saw his dirty, drunken, stinking face curl into a smile, his watery eyes lit with what Eden could only think to call merriment. He laughed then, a choke of a laugh, false and patronizing. He laughed and said, "Why don't you shoot me, Eden? Why don't you just kill me?" The stale beer stench of him was enough to make Eden draw her face away instinctually, and Lance laughed at that too, made as if he was going to inhale and blow a whole gust of his foul breath right at her, but then he faked, reached up, brushed aside her gun, and leaned back down to resume his fumbling with the keys in the ignition.

Eden stood there, her shotgun now pointed into the seat-back cushion. She had a shotgun in her hands and felt more impotent than she'd ever felt in her life. She had no words to use. She stood dumbly as Lance fiddled under the dashboard, his total concentration on the gadgetry. He was so blind drunk he couldn't even line up the key in its slot, but he fought on stubbornly, a child trying to force the round peg into the square hole. And then it worked: as if by accident the key slipped into the ignition. Lance sat up, gratified. He grinned at Eden. And as he turned the key he laughed and said, "You think I don't want you to shoot me?" His words were slurred. He said, "What the fuck do I care?" and then the engine turned over and Lance's sick smile broadened, and Eden thought of this piss-drunk bastard driving that boy down the hill on a goddamn dirt road, and she could already see the truck, its front end bashed in, flipped and smoking on the burnt-out turf of the abandoned golf course, Squee's body thrown limp against the ceiling, and that was all it took for Eden to lift the gun again and jab it at the side of Lance's smiling face.

The truck stalled. Lance doubled over onto Squee, his hand flying up to his face to cup it where the gun had slashed. When he rose again, the shock on his face was mixed with pride, as though he were somehow responsible for the nerve of this old lady. The angle had been awkward, the swipe relatively ineffective, like a pool shot slipped at the last second, the cue just glancing the ball and nudging it aside. Lance lifted his head as if to congratulate Eden on a brave try there, only to find that in the seconds he'd been down she'd managed to turn the gun around. She had one hand on the barrel, the other on the stock, and as Lance opened his mouth to speak, she steadied herself, and with the kind of force she'd only ever used to bring an ax down across the neck of a chicken, Eden Jacobs slammed the butt of that shotgun into Lance Squire's forehead.

Twenty-two

NIGHT IS THE SUREST NURSE
OF TROUBLED SOULS

Carl Jenkins, 67, of Strawberry Lane reported a speeding car on South Ferry Road. Police responded to the call and were unable to locate the alleged vehicle . . . Firefighters responded to an anonymous call reporting the smell of smoke in the vicinity of Wickham Beach; a homeowner was found burning leaves with a valid burn permit . . . Police jump-started a car on the Osprey Island Ferry line . . . A Scallopshell Beach resident reported a deer in the woods, but was uncertain as to whether the deer was sleeping or dead. Police were unable to locate the alleged animal.

—from the police blotter, *Island Times*, 1988

L ANCE FELL OVER SQUEE on the truck seat; neither of them moved or made a sound. Yards off, Roddy gave up the struggle to stand and just lay there breathing at the sky. Peg peered out from behind the door of the house, which she had employed as a full-body shield. Beside Lance's truck, Eden had gotten the shotgun turned back around so that it was once again aimed at Lance's chest. She had no idea whether or not the gun was loaded—had always been somewhat afraid to check, envisioning the headline: "WIDOW DIES AT OWN HAND—LATE HUSBAND'S HUNTING RIFLE TO BLAME." At the very least she could see herself in the *Island Times* weekly police blotter: "*Eden Jacobs, 56, summoned police to her home on Island Drive after a shotgun accidentally misfired, causing damage to her living room wall and sofa. Mrs. Jacobs claimed to have been attempting to unload the gun, which belonged to her late husband, Roderick, when it went off."* She'd always made Roderick promise to keep them empty in the gun case, but she knew he lied to her and kept a few loaded for raccoons on the property, a deer down by the ravine, the occasional stray pheasant in the driveway. In either case, loaded or not, she felt safer standing there with the more dangerous part of the gun pointed away. She had no idea how hard she'd hit Lance in the forehead. As she waited those painfully long minutes for the sirens to come up the hill, she feared that she had killed him—envisioned a trickle of blood right now running out from his ear and onto his son beneath him. Such things happened. Agatha Christie killed people off with candlestick and statuette blows to the head all the time.

Eden realized then that she didn't much care if Lance Squire was lying dead in the truck in front of her. Which is what she contemplated during those eternal minutes as she stood there and watched Lance breathe: *If he were to stop, what would I feel then?* She'd have rather seen Lance Squire die by his own hand, drive his old truck as fast as it would go and plunge it off the cliffs at the far end of Sand Beach Road. He'd been driving in circles so long that when finally the ground lapsed and the wheels hit air, you could only imagine he'd feel some gratification at the sheer difference of it. Time would stretch then too, and when the steel nose of that truck hit the water off of Sand Beach Cove like it was slamming a wall of solid stone, and then crumpled, sinking, time would stretch out so thin that it snapped— *pop!*—one last breath before the truck just disappeared, one sigh of relief for Lance Squire—maybe the first true breath of respite of his short, sad life before he exited the world. An exhalation that would free him, divest him, allow him one flash of unencumbered existence. One pure sigh with which to end his life as he slid beneath the surface of the water and was gone.

· · ·

They cuffed him for the trip off-island to the hospital, though he didn't come to until the ferry was halfway across the bay. The ambulances turned off their sirens for the ride; no sense polluting everyone's ears when—at least for that stretch of the trip—they could go only as fast as they could go. The sirens resumed their blare at the Menhadenport shore: two ambulances crying for the hospital in Fishersburg. They'd put Roddy in with Lance; Squee rode in the other with Eden.

And back on Osprey, Peg was left to drive herself back to the Lodge in Jeremy's car and spend the rest of the night—and the rest of the summer, and probably the rest of her dun-colored life—telling of what had happened up on that hill during her stay on Osprey Island.

WHEN THE MORNING SUN ROSE on Osprey Island it was almost as if nothing had happened there at all. The air was sea-cool and the island had that scrubbed-clean feel, as though everything had been washed in salt spray and scoured with sand. Stones and pebbles along the shoreline glimmered, drying in the early sun, the sand beneath them still cold from the night before. Scrolls of dark seaweed lay unraveled across the beach like tremendous clumps of ruined cassette tape scattered with shards of clamshell, some chalky and white as bone, some tide-polished and glistening like teeth. Smaller shells rested like eggs in seaweed nests, with tiny inhabitants curled and protected inside. On Sand Beach Road, an osprey patrolled the shore, riding the wind back and forth like a bored kid riding his bicycle up and down the street, just waiting for something to happen.

AN EYRIE OF OSPREY

What is a bird family? In life, a bird family is exactly like a human family. It consists of father, mother, and children. But in the books a family means quite another thing.

—OLIVE THORNE MILLER, *The Second Book of Birds*

IT WAS NOT A GOOD SEASON for the Lodge at Osprey Island. A fire was one thing; a fire, and a death, and a family rift, and a restraining order were quite another. Not to mention rumors of a rape too, but the girl wouldn't press charges or even admit she'd been harmed in any way. It was her roommate who'd started the rumors, and she'd fled home to Ireland, too shaken by the whole incident to remain at the Lodge. The alleged rapist—a longtime staffer and head of maintenance at the Lodge—got taken in on a drunk and disorderly. When further charges were filed against him—trespassing, reckless endangerment, child abuse, assault—there was no one willing to put up bail, so he sat in jail on the mainland. They couldn't be sure how long he'd stay away, but that didn't keep people from speculating. Some said he'd never return to Osprey Island, that they'd never hear from him again. *Nope,* said others, they'd hear about him, all right, when he got himself killed in a bar fight or died midwinter on a subway grating in some large eastern city, all the liquor in his veins not enough to keep him from freezing to death. A few Islanders who'd been around a long while were on hand during such speculation to

remind folks that the man in question had never spent a night—
let alone lived—anywhere but Osprey Island in his entire life, and it
didn't take a great mind to guess that regardless of what he'd done,
the minute he could he'd come straight back to Osprey Island, where
his mother'd probably take pity and let him live in a trailer out back
of her own house, and it would be there that he'd die, by his own
hand if the alcohol didn't take him first, or by the hand of whomever
he managed to piss off badly enough. There might not have been a lot
of people on Osprey Island that summer, compared to usual, but there
was more than enough talk.

The Lodge lost plenty of guests—not a lot to recommend it that
year. They lost staff too: a few waiters who wanted out of the whole
deal, out of that place and away from everything that had happened
there. Plus two other Irish housekeepers who felt frightened and
uncomfortable and just wanted to go home. Service in the dining
room was inconsistent and rampant with neglect. Housekeeping was
shoddy at best; at worst it was nonexistent. The swimming pool was
leafy, the tennis courts weedy, the lawns overgrown with dandelions.
The laundry machines ran smoother than ever—when you could find
someone to operate them—and the food was the same as it had
always been—it was, some said, maybe even a bit better, as the chef
had fewer people to cook for and could afford to take time with his
preparation and presentation. There were certainly fewer complaints
that summer about hotel staff out drinking on the porch late at night.

When they opened officially for Fourth of July weekend, the Lodge
still hadn't found a head housekeeper. The new head of maintenance—
who started the season with three broken ribs, two black eyes, and a
heart that would take a lot longer to heal than the rest of his injuries
combined—had for his right-hand man an eight-year-old child with a
badly broken arm and a dislocated shoulder, not to mention a dead
mother, an absent father, and so persistent a habit of running away
from his custodial grandparents that they gave up and allowed the
boy to take up unofficial, temporarily permanent residence with an
eccentric widow who raised chickens and her quiet draft-dodger son

who lived in a shed out back of the main house, for it was where the boy seemed to want to be.

And if the rumors and tales of the bad luck that had befallen the Osprey Lodge weren't enough, two weeks of near-nonstop rain in August did such an effective job of emptying rooms that even the ever-diminishing crew of chambermaids could manage to get all the beds made each morning. By Labor Day, Bud and Nancy Chizek were ready, after thirty-nine seasons as proprietors of the Lodge at Osprey Island, to call it quits. They closed down the hotel for the last time, put the entire property on the market, and went south, first to North Carolina, people heard, then Georgia, then finally Florida. They had no family left on Osprey and they'd never had many friends, so there was no one to keep in touch with, really, no way for anyone to keep tabs.

The Lodge sold and got refurbished, and reopened for business the next summer. The new proprietors were capable and sure-handed, though it was hard going for the first few years. People'd heard enough of what had taken place that they didn't have such a pretty image of Osprey Island as a vacation spot anymore, and it took a while for the sense they had to fade, and change, be replaced by something once again quaint, and rustic, and charming. A nice postcard. *A great place to bring the family.*

It's funny, what people think. How real their ideas may seem, how proven and justifiable and true. But take reality. Take this: an image, a scene from right then, Fourth of July, 1988. A postcard, if you will. The New Hampshire Red hen has hatched her clutch of seven chicks, and they're yellow and new and velvety as pussywillow nubs. It's evening, then night, and the sky is dark, but with stars. The chicken coop is quiet. On the back porch of a clapboard house atop a steep hill overlooking a ravine, three people sit, intermittently looking up—over the hillside trees and above the beach that stretches far below them—to watch the sapphire sky. The woman sorts seed packets on a squat stump fashioned into a table by her late husband—stupid, but good with a wood saw. The man, bruised up like a scrap-fighter, sits awkwardly, accommodating his injuries, sipping at a can of beer. The boy, one arm bandaged and hung in a sling, is cross-legged on the floor, playing solitaire with his one useful hand, the visor of a lavender baseball cap pulled low over his eyes.

The woman glances up. There is a flash in the dark sky. "Oh!" she says, "Here they go!" and as the first pink and orange and yellow chrysanthemums explode, the boy lays down his cards. With his good hand he takes off his cap, then resettles it backward on his head, so he can see.

ACKNOWLEDGMENTS

Many thanks to Eric Simonoff (for his faith, patience, and support), Jenny Minton (whose insight, guidance, and pep talks were invaluable), Jordan Pavlin (who swooped in, took me under her wing, and did an amazing job), Myra Nissen (my favorite mother/editor/research assistant/publicist in the world), Lee Klein (for raising the bar and cracking the whip), Judy Mitchell (for all her invaluable help, especially The Great Wisconsin Eyes-Like-Papercuts Poll), Peter Orner (to whom I gratefully dedicate the prologue), Lisa Jervis (who is still willing to ask, "What is this story about?" ten years after the workshop that brought us together), Erin Ergenbright (for being there and reading this all the way along), Katie Hubert (for being brilliant!), Allison Amend (for trading monsters with me and for the Pixie Pit Scrabble that sustained us both during trying times), Malena Watrous (for listening to my point-of-view rants over Sunday breakfasts at Lou Henri), Dave Daley (for his support, and for putting "Morey's Dinghy" in the *Hartford Courant*), the PWW (Curtis Sittenfeld, Jeremy Mullem, Jeremy Kryt, Trish Walsh, Lewis Robinson and Bridget Garrity), Lucy Roche (for island research and lore), Josh Emmons (for listening to me rant), Sarah Townsend (for listening to me rant and making the best tuna sandwiches on the entire planet), Laurel Snyder (for listening to me rant and ranting back), everyone who got caught in the radii of my ranting, Michelle Forman (for coping with the highway superintendents while I sang Joan Armatrading, prime-rib blood trickling down my arm), Jennie Allen-Cheng (for long-ago baby-sitting lectures on Russian history and Beatles lore), Erik Maziarz and Robert Marshall (for their generous help with the details of fires and fire investigation), Roger Tory Peterson (for his very helpful and inspiring 1969 *National Geographic* article "The Endangered Osprey") and John Rutter (for his kind and patient assistance in securing permissions to said article), Michael Foley (for his thoughtful insights regarding issues of draft resistance), Jeff Skinner (future book designer!), Sandy Dyas (who came to my rescue once again), and, last, but hardly least, Gabriel Haman and Mary Schowey (the *real* Chicken Ladies).

A NOTE ABOUT THE AUTHOR

Thisbe Nissen is a graduate of Oberlin College and the Iowa Writers' Workshop. She has received fellowships from the James Michener Foundation and the Bread Loaf Writers' Conference, and she was the winner of the 1999 John Simmons Short Fiction Award from the University of Iowa Press. She has taught at the University of Iowa, the Iowa Young Writers' Studio, and the Port Townsend Writers' Conference, and she was the 2003 Zale Writer-in-Residence at Tulane University. A native New Yorker, Thisbe now lives in Iowa.

A NOTE ON THE TYPE

The text of this book was set in Sabon, a typeface designed by Jan Tschichold (1902–1974), the well-known German typographer. Based loosely on the original designs by Claude Garamond (c. 1480–1561), Sabon was designed in 1966 in Frankfurt. It was named for the famous Lyons punch cutter Jacques Sabon, who is thought to have brought some of Garamond's matrices to Frankfurt.

Composed by Creative Graphics,
Allentown, Pennsylvania

Printed and bound by Berryville Graphics,
Berryville, Virginia

Designed by M. Kristen Bearse